WILD AS HER

Content Warning

This book includes "on-page" adult content and language unsuitable for minors.

To my readers:
If you're here for the banter, the kissing, the small-town gossip,
and the hero who would burn down the world for her...
You're my people. Never leave.

Chapter 1
Cami

Wild As Her by Corey Kent

"Cami, is that you?" A voice calls out before I can step through the doors of the Bridger Falls National Bank. I glance over nervously and spot Maggie, our town's fairy godmother, beaming over at me.

"Oh. Hey, Maggie. How are you?"

"Well, well, Sugar. Where are you going all dressed up?" she asks, not answering my question.

"I have a meeting with Sterling," I tell her with my best smile. While I know she's supportive, I also know that word will travel that I was all dressed up at the bank for a meeting with the bank manager. She means well. But small towns are small towns. Everybody talks.

"Knock 'em dead!" She waves encouragingly and heads into Boots & Bangs, the beauty shop next door.

I take a deep breath and adjust my black blazer, smoothing down the tailored red dress beneath it that makes me feel professional. My black power heels click against the polished floor, each step confident and fueled with determination. The air smells like stale coffee and fake promises, but I'm here to save my family's ranch. Am I overdressed for a meeting at our small-town bank? Probably. Do I care? No. My ranch is at stake here.

My sleek, shiny black hair is swept into a professional chignon, and the bold red lipstick I've chosen matches my dress perfectly. The look I'm going for is professional-business-boss-lady-rancher. But really, on the inside? Yeah, I'm just a mess. I want this more than anything in the world. And I'm scared to death that they won't help me. This bank holds the keys to my future. They can choose to open the door for me or slam it shut in my face. And lately, there's been a lot of doors being slammed. I'm here to fight for the future of my family's ranch and work as hard as I can to make that happen.

I picked this ensemble so that I would look every bit the part of a businesswoman, a strong woman rancher, and a force to be reckoned with. That's my hope anyway.

In my trusty, soft, black leather satchel gifted to me from one of my favorite professors after I got my master's degree, I carry a folder with a meticulously crafted business plan, my desperate attempt to woo the bank.

The ranch will become more than just a small family-run ranch. It's going to be a gathering place. A cozy bed and breakfast with charm, trail rides with views that leave you breathless, a summer camp for kids, and a micro bakery-farmstand combo that people will drive hours to visit. It's going to be the heartbeat of Bridger Falls.

I've poured so much time and energy into this plan. It's been a nonstop dream – sometimes a fever dream – for me to put this together. This is something I eat, sleep, dream, and put into action every day with all that I do. I want nothing more than to make this come true for Wilder Ranch. And while I know that they're big dreams, I'm chasing them with everything I've got.

I think about my grandfather Wilder and wonder if he'd be proud of how hard I'm fighting for the family ranch. I remember the promise that I made to my grandpa when he was sitting in his rocking chair on the back porch of our family's home. He was near the end when he made me promise to keep the ranch in the family and do everything I can to fight for it. He and I were always very close, and my love for the ranch runs as deep as his. We were kindred spirits. I think he realized at the time that it wasn't safe with my parents, and while he hoped my mom would do right by the ranch, she didn't.

So yeah, on the outside, I probably look put together, but on the inside, my stomach churns with nerves. I won't let it show. I learned a long time ago that showing weakness does me no good. It only gives ammunition to the people who want to take me down. And no one is taking me down.

Sterling Atwood, a man in his late fifties, greets me as if he's in a hurry and ushers me into his office. His eyes don't meet mine. Instead, they rake over me like he's sizing me up, all while pretending to be a gentleman as he gestures for me to go first. I bite down the cringe clawing up my spine, fully aware he's watching every step I take as we head down the hallway toward the conference room off his office.

Any other day, I'd whirl around, call him out, and make damn sure he knew exactly how obvious he was being. But not today. I need him on my side, and biting my tongue feels like swallowing glass. Still, I keep walking, fists clenched, resisting the urge to spin on my heel and shoot him a glare that would melt the smug look right off his face.

His walls are lined with degrees, awards, and certificates that don't impress me one bit, but I pretend that they do. He gives me time to look over his accolades, and I don't miss the dick measuring contest he presents me with, making sure that I see how important he wants me to believe he is. To Atwood, I'm just a nobody here in this town. At best, someone who runs a mobile coffee trailer. He doesn't see me as the businesswoman that I am. I give him his moment, but I'm here to present my plan to him. I'm too educated for his bullshit. And my respect for him has diminished at his nonchalance towards my situation. In fact, it just pisses me off. But again, I'm not letting it show.

I smile at him and calmly lay the two folders in front of us, my bright red polished nails tapping lightly on the desk as I enthusiastically explain my plan. I tell him every step it'll to take to turn the ranch around and into the epic vision I've laid forth. My voice is strong and confident, and as I speak, I watch the boredom sweep across his face. That's when I realize that he has no intention of giving me a chance here. None. This was all for nothing. So much for the small-town bank slogan of helping out the locals. It's all a lie. He never intended to help me. I finish speaking and sit back in my chair, folding my hands in my lap.

Sterling leans back and sighs. "Miss Kendrick," he says dryly as if he's searching for the words to say.

"Just give it to me straight," I say, crossing my legs, nerves threatening to take over, but I shove them deep down and stay focused.

"That's... one impressive plan. And I'm curious as to who came up with this plan for you—."

"I did," I interrupt. "I wrote the plan."

The insinuation burns. Like I'm just some clueless woman who needed a man to swoop in brand draw a roadmap for me. But I don't take the bait. I shove the fury down deep, keep my chin high, and stay locked in, cool, steady, unreadable.

His eyes widen as he nods, surprised. A sliver of hope fills me that he could still actually help me. I worked so hard on that plan. Hours and hours went into it, and I left no stone unturned for my family's ranch, taking it from red all the way to black. I *know* my plan will work.

He continues and explains it to me in the same tone he'd use if I were a child. "We've given your mother every grace period possible for the ranch. I'm sorry, but there can be no more extensions. We're all out of time here." He slides a thick folder across his desk, and the pages that slip out are highlighted in bright red with PAST DUE stamped across the pages.

"If we could just..." I stammer, desperately grasping at straws.

Sterling interrupts me with a deep sigh like I'm exhausting him. "Miss Kendrick, your ranch sold off the livestock and equipment and even attempted to lease out your land. I see that you even held a little fundraiser. You've made attempts, but... it's simply not enough to make up the past due amount, catch up on the taxes, and sustain the ranch moving forward. I am truly sorry, but we must move forward with our buyer."

My heart drops and shatters on the floor into a million pieces, but I give no outward sign of emotion. "Mr. Atwood, this ranch has been in my family for generations. I just need a little more time, please. I really need your help with this. I can fix this. Really, I can."

He shakes his head and stands, guiding me to the door. "I'm sorry, but we have run out of time."

"Who is the buyer?" I ask frantically, searching his face as it hits me that this might really be it. It's over. He knows the fate of my ranch and what will become of it.

"I'm sorry, but I'm not at liberty to share the details at this time," he replies firmly.

I clear my throat, hold my head high, and try not to cry as I turn and walk out, not bothering to say anything more. He was never going to hear me out or give my plan a chance.

I have to figure something out. Because no one is coming to save me. I won't just give up my family's ranch. I'm going to figure this out. Just like I always do.

How? No clue. Maybe there's a Hail Mary pass out there somewhere. I rack my brain, trying to think quickly of another idea to present to him. There has to be something.

Teresa, my mom, already moved to town, leaving me to deal with the fallout. Her grand plan was to just give the ranch to the bank after she sold off whatever she could. Ollie, my brother, I love him, but he's out, too. For them, the ranch holds weighted memories that haunt them. For me, it holds a possibility for future memories. Good memories. And ones with my grandparents I refuse to give up.

I can't blame Ollie. He helped out as much as he could. He's a full-time firefighter here in Bridger Falls, and even he couldn't fix what he didn't break. I get it. It's not their dream. It's mine.

My mom is a full-time nurse at Bridger Falls Memorial Hospital and has been all my life. I'm still so angry at her about all of this. She could have told me that the ranch was circling the drain before it was too late, but she didn't. She continued to take the money that I gave her to help the ranch, never paying any bills like she said she would. When she ran out of time, she just packed up her stuff, leaving me to deal with the fallout.

This was her parent's ranch. She was raised here. After my grandparents passed away, my dad turned our world upside down in that house. He did his best to strip away every good memory he could of the ranch and our childhood. Broke everything he could, including us. Then, he did the best thing he could have ever done: he left. But really, it's only a matter of time before he's back again. And my mom will give him chance after chance, despite the chaos he's caused.

I glance back to Satan in a suit aka Atwood who smiles at me as if he won, raising his hand and waving at me. I walk out of the bank with my head held high. Screw that guy. Good luck getting your coffee somewhere else, pal. *Asshole.*

I'm not ready to go home, so I head to my coffee trailer, an old Airstream I gutted and turned into Steamy Sips. A local artist painted the name in big, swooping letters with my logo on the side, and every time I see it, I feel a flicker of pride. It might not be much, but it's mine. I source my beans from a roaster a few towns over, and if you ask anyone in Bridger Falls, they'll tell you, I serve the best damn coffee around.

I park my beat-up red truck behind it, unlock the door, and slip inside. The second it closes behind me, I lose it. Full-blown, ugly cry. I wish it helped. It doesn't.

Once I've cried myself out, I rage-clean the already spotless trailer, wiping down counters that don't need wiping, restocking cups that don't need restocking. Anything to feel like I'm doing *something.*

Because if I stop moving, if I let myself sit still, I'll unravel. And I don't have time to fall apart. Not when the ranch is slipping through my fingers.

Not when everything I've ever loved is on the line.

Chapter 2
Cami

Better Man by Little Big Town

After I pull myself together, I head to the Black Dog Saloon, the local watering hole with good food, drinks, and people. I take a deep breath, sighing as I lean back in my seat and struggle to find the energy to get out of the truck after all my crying.

When I finally make it in, I slide onto my favorite stool at the end of the bar.

Cash, the bartender, slides a soda in front of me. "Rough day?"

"You could say that," I say as I nod in gratitude at the drink.

"Well, I hope your day gets better, Cami. I sure hate to see you down." Cash smiles and heads off to help another customer.

Cash and his wife Codi are amazing people and have become great friends of mine. And that new little baby boy of theirs is just the sweetest.

I stare into my glass, watching the carbonation when Jack

Jessop slides onto the stool beside me. His familiar scent of pine and leather envelops me. I close my eyes. He smells so damn good. Why does he smell so good?

And of course, this day ends with the cherry on the top with Jack here. It seems he's always around these days. He's best friends with my brother, so that doesn't help. And his ranch is next to mine, and he always seems to find a way to join me on my morning rides with my horse. So, I guess it's fitting he's here in my space. It's not just that he's always there, it's that he constantly teases and taunts me that irks me. He loves to get under my skin. And sometimes he does that by simply existing. He looks and smells amazing, and boy does he know it. His arrogance drives me crazy.

"Cami," he says softly as he looks over at me and gives me a smile. "I like your dress."

"Thanks, I dressed up to look like you," I affirm, not bothering to look back at him.

"What's that supposed to mean?" he tilts his head, amused.

"A walking red flag," I say as I finally gather the courage to glance at him. I'm in no mood for Jack Jessop and his antics today. Or any other day. I have bigger problems on my plate.

He throws his head back and laughs. It's a deep, gravelly sound. Hearty and real, like he threw his whole body into the joy of it. As my mortal enemy, I find it super annoying. But as a woman with needs, it's captivating. "Jesus, Cami."

The humor fades as I stare back down at my drink, defeat pouring through me. I say quietly, "What do you want, Jack?"

Jack says nothing back, and I have no idea what he's thinking because I'm afraid I'll start to cry if I look at him. And I will *not* be crying in front of him.

I sip my drink and wonder what Jack's angle is here. Did he come to gloat? I'm sure word is getting around that my family's ranch is officially done.

Only when I finally look over, there's no humor in his expression. Instead, he looks at me with an unreadable expression. One that frustrates me because, normally, I can read Jack like a book.

He says softly, "I don't want anything. We're just two old friends having a drink..."

"Funny, because we're not friends, and I'm not old," I say, too tired to fight him tonight. "Bet you'll be happy to have new neighbors," I mutter.

I can feel his gaze on me when he says, "What?"

I can't stop at this point. I'm so mad about everything that has happened today.

"The bank will probably sell Wilder Ranch to some big-deal developer. Maybe you'll get your very own Costco next door. Just imagine all the people lining up for free samples while you're out branding your cattle. Or better yet, a hippie-dippie patchouli farm. I bet they'll host full moon drum circles right up against your fence line. They'll just love your methane-producing herd ruining their sacred air. Maybe they'll even stage little protests with cardboard signs and everything right outside those ridiculous Jessop iron gates. Which, by the way, look like the entrance to a villain's ranch in a bad western."

Jack stares at me and blinks. Then, he slowly drags a hand down his face and mutters, "I swear, talking to you is like arguing with a raccoon hopped up on caffeine."

I smirk. "That's rude to raccoons."

Jack reaches over and places his hand under my stool and drags me closer to him. I glare at him but have no energy to protest the closeness. And it's also rude how well he can read me and know that I probably needed to be close to someone right now.

And it's honestly unfair how good he looks. He's a grumpy

cowboy snack. His blond hair, tousled like he just ran a hand through it after taking off his hat, catches the light, a little messy, a little perfect. His jaw is wide and strong, the kind that looks like it's clenched more often than not, and right now, it ticks like he's holding back words or something else entirely. He usually keeps his beard neatly trimmed, but it looks like he needs a shave.

His sharp, mossy green eyes are the kind that don't just look at you. They look through you. Like he already knows what you're about to say and is halfway to calling you on it. There's a weight to him, a presence, like he was born in boots and battle-scarred denim, carved straight out of the land he works. Not loud. Not showy. But when Jack walks into a room or steps into your space, everything else just fades out.

But I know that Jack has a heart he keeps under lock and key and a soft spot he'd rather die than admit to having. I've seen it. It's rare, but I've seen it.

And right now, that whole six-foot-something frame of his is way too close, casting shadows over me, making me feel things I don't want to admit to when it comes to Jack. I need us to get back to our status quo. I can't handle him being nice to me. It's not normal. I like it better when we argue back and forth. It's what we do. This version of Jack makes me nervous.

"Cami..." His voice is low, rough, and dangerously steady. His eyes don't leave mine, not for a second. And when I don't immediately back down, he leans in closer. He's so close I can practically taste the cedar and soap on his skin and the lingering hint of hay and sweat.

"Maybe it won't come to that," he murmurs, reaching up, slow and deliberate, brushing a loose piece of hair behind my ear. His knuckles graze my cheek, and it feels like being touched by a live wire. "Maybe it'll all work out. Maybe I could help you..."

My brain short-circuits. I forget how words work. Why is he being nice to me?

"Help me?" I manage the pitch way too high. "I don't—no, I don't need—your... help."

God. Smooth.

Jack leans in, his mouth a breath from mine, and he's so smug about it. "You sure?"

My spine stiffens, and I lean back. "You're not worthy enough to be my knight in shining armor," I snap, praying he can't see the blush blooming up my neck. I hate when he makes me the butt of his jokes. I'm just an amusing game to him. A way to entertain himself by purposely making me stumble when he flirts with me.

"Give me time," he says, grinning. "I'm just getting started. I'll show you that you need me."

I stand abruptly, the stool scraping sharply against the floor, and heads turn our way. "Don't, Jack. Just don't. You can't help me. In fact, I would rather burn it all to the ground than you help me."

He stares at me for a beat and then offers a short nod, his face grim.

As I head for the door, a cowboy with the emotional range of a beer can steps right into my path. Tall. Grimy. Drunk. Clearly unfamiliar with the concept of self-preservation. I don't recognize him, and he's not from around here.

He grins at his buddy like I'm something to poke at. "She looks mean," he drawls.

My eyes snap up, razor sharp. "That's because I am. Move."

He hesitates, like his one remaining brain cell is debating whether to test me. Then I see Jack go still, silent, and give this guy a look that could salt the earth.

That's all it takes.

The cowboy mumbles something under his breath and steps

aside. I push open the door into the cool night air, my spine still tight with irritation.

I've had enough bullshit today.

* * *

My black heels sink into the grass and gravel as I make my way to the barn. I kick them off and pull on my worn boots I left inside the door, tossing my blazer onto the dirty barn floor without a second thought. Nothing matters anymore. Now it's time to figure this shit out. The gloves are coming off, so to speak. Only for me it's expensive shoes and clothes. It's time to fight dirty. Figure out a plan. And the best way I know to do that is to go for a ride and clear my head with my favorite boy.

I saddle up Mouse, my horse that has been my best friend for six years now. The only male I can count on these days to not let me down.

My Mouse.

Love, my trusty blue heeler cattle dog, watches from the barn door, tipping her head. Her warm brown eyes are alert, and she's always ready to follow me wherever I go.

I didn't name her that. I picked her up at a shelter a few years ago, and the name just stuck. Someone left her and her puppies tied to a dumpster in the next town over. Her puppies all got adopted, and she was set to be put down that Friday at four because nobody wanted her. I found her at the shelter at three.

I brought her home, and it turns out that the name Love suits her just fine. I've never met a more loyal and loving dog. I've been told our personalities match. I don't mind. Love is loyal, full of heart, and mean as hell when she needs to be. I've seen her go toe-to-toe with a black bear. It was not something I'd ever like to witness again, but she chased the bear off to protect

Mouse and me. I love that dog so much. Her and Mouse are all I have at the ranch now.

I hike up my dress since no one is around and swing onto my well-worn saddle. This dress will be ruined, but I'm beyond caring. This whole day is ruined. This dress is just a reminder of what I lost today. Maybe I'll even burn it later.

The sun dipping below the mountains casts shadows over the land, but the calmness doesn't do shit to loosen the pain coursing through my chest. My world is falling apart. And this time, I'm afraid that no amount of determination or hard work can fix this. The ranch is slipping away for good, and I'm supposed to just stand back and watch it all fade away one moment at a time.

Hot tears flow steadily as I ride, not bothering to wipe them away. They just streak down my face and neck. My arms are cold, but I don't care.

Out here in this pasture is the one place where I can feel everything. Always have. My safe place. I think about what things will be like a month from now and wonder where I will go. What will become of the ranch?

Moving back to town and renting a place isn't an option. I just can't. Living in town isn't for me. Our small ranch is about thirty minutes outside of town, and I love the quiet. That white picket fence life was never for me. I was always made to be wild and free.

This place is my anchor. My future family's legacy. It's not the biggest ranch in Wyoming, but it's home. I ride through the back pasture, and no matter how far I go, I can't chase away the ache that fills me.

I bring Mouse to a stop, the wind tugging at my hair that's starting to fall out of the pins. I rip out the pins and fluff it out. I dismount and walk for a while, stroking Mouse's neck. "Good boy. That's my boy."

I reach down and bury myself in Love's fur, grounding myself in her warmth. "They can't take this from us," I whisper, my voice hoarse. "I'm going to find a different way to keep us here."

Mouse whinnies, and I lean forward, pressing my forehead to him. Tears flow faster, and my body shakes with sobs as I wrap my arms around his neck and cry. He stands there and rests his head on my shoulder.

I cling to this moment. The only moment of the day that feels real. The only moment I want to carry from today.

When I finally head back to the barn, the weight of the world feels a little lighter. But reality smacked me across the face today. As I put Mouse to bed for the night, my determination is back. I might be losing everything that matters to me, but I won't be going down without a fight.

Chapter 3
Jack

The Cowboy in Me by Tim McGraw

A rifle cracks through the air, sharp, sudden, and way too close.

Pesto jolts beneath me, muscles twitching, eyes wide. I tighten the reins, steadying him with one hand. "Easy, boy. Easy."

But my gut's already twisting.

I swing him toward the tree line, the border between Jessop land and Wilder Ranch, and we bolt.

The wind cuts past my ears as we tear across the pasture, hooves pounding the dirt like thunder. My heart feels like it's beating just as loud.

Then another shot. Closer this time. I grit my teeth and push Pesto harder, every instinct in me locked on one thing: get there fast.

Because nothing good ever follows gunfire on ranch land. And if anything's happened to her...

God help whoever's responsible.

Fuck.

I run through potential threats as I race across the field. A pack of coyotes, a wolf, or maybe a wild bull. Those are the best-case scenarios. The worst-case scenario is that Cami has completely gone and lost it and is ready to shoot me for all the hell I've given her over the years. And to be fair, she's given it right back.

But I'll never stop worrying about Cami Kendrick. Hearing shots come from her property, I'll be damned if I let that go.

I come up over the hill, and there she is, and my heart clenches.

Cami stands in the pasture, her wild dark hair flowing down around her shoulders. She's wearing tan overalls with the butt of her rifle locked into the crook of her shoulder as she yells at someone on the ground. It looks like a human and not an animal.

Holy shit. My heart races a mile a minute as we barrel towards her.

"Cami!" I bellow, my voice barreling over the field.

Her head whips around, rifle still perfectly trained at the person on the ground. I flinch and reach for my shotgun holstered next to my saddle out of habit, but my hand freezes.

"Get out of here, Jessop!" she snaps, her voice angry. "I've got it under control."

The bastard lunges for her.

I'm off Pesto and between them before the man on the ground can touch her. Adrenaline roars in my ears as I slam him down, boot planted hard against his chest.

He snarls up at me, drunk, sloppy, stupid.

I lean in, jaw tight. "Big mistake."

Real big.

Because he just made it personal, lunging for her like that, never mind what he's doing here in the first place.

The man sneers and falls back to the ground, muttering something about a "crazy bitch." My boot digs into him just a little harder at that comment. I recognize him as Granger, the neighbor to the north of Cami's property. Sun-leathered skin from years in the Wyoming sun, but not in a rugged cowboy way, more like rotten beef jerky left on the dash. Greasy hair that he keeps shoved under a filthy ball cap. He's got yellow teeth and a voice like gravel soaked in bourbon. A mean old son of a bitch my father was friends with. "What are you doing here, Granger? You're on the wrong side of the fence."

Granger spits in the dirt, lip curled like a rabid coyote. "This ain't that bitch's property no more. It's the bank's."

Before I can speak, Cami points the rifle directly at him and squares her shoulders. "You're trespassing."

Her voice cuts through the air. Steady. Cold. Dangerous.

Jesus.

I keep my boot locked on Granger's chest, but my eyes flick to her.

Hell, I really believe she'll shoot this man.

"Cami," I say carefully, "You need to call Sheriff Matthews."

"No, I don't," she snaps. "That's just witnesses. And evidence."

She leans down and pokes Granger with the barrel. "I prefer to make this motherfucker fertilizer on the back pasture."

Granger's sneer drops straight off his face. The color drains out of him, and for a split second, I swear he's about to piss himself. I think he just realized he's in deep shit here.

And damn if I don't feel a little proud. Right now, she's the most terrifying woman in Wyoming.

"Get out of here," I grunt, as I kick him hard with my boot.

He scrambles to the property line and bolts over the fence, cursing as he goes. Cami fires another warning shot into the air, making him stumble as he runs. He turns and calls her every name in the book.

"Was that extra shot necessary?" I ask as I place my hands on my hips and give her a look. "You scared the shit out of me, Wilder."

"Very necessary," she huffs.

But I don't miss the look in her eyes when I call her the childhood nickname she's always loved.

"Why the hell are you here, Jessop?" Her eyes narrow, and I know she's about to give me hell.

But I can't focus on the words coming because I'm too stuck on how damn good she looks. White tank top clinging to her, overalls half-snapped and tucked into her boots like she threw them on in a hurry. She probably charged out here, ready to go to war. And I hate that she had to.

The thought of her chasing off a trespasser by herself out here, armed or not, makes something hard and cold settle in my chest. I'll deal with that part later. Right now, I'm just trying to breathe around the sight of her, adrenaline still buzzing through me, hands itching to keep her close.

She clicks the safety on her rifle and props it casually against her hip, probably still coming down from an adrenaline rush as well. "Get out of here," she says, now softer. "And mind your own damn business. I can take care of myself."

And somehow, I've never wanted to kiss her more.

Or throw her over my shoulder and lock every gate on this ranch.

Because my business? *Is her*.

She stands glaring at me like she owns the world.

And she does own my world. Always has and always will. The crazy part is that she doesn't even know it. *Yet*.

"You okay?" I ask, lowering my voice and ignoring her attitude.

"I'm fine," she huffs, her chest still shaking.

"Next time, try not to shoot anyone before breakfast," I tease as I watch her stalk back toward her barn. "At least try to make it to lunch."

She says nothing but glares at me over her shoulder, breathing heavily. Damn it, I want to take her into my arms and hold her.

"What was Granger doing here?" I ask as I follow her, pulling Pesto with me, trying to get a handle on my own heart rate. It's finally beating at a normal rate again now that I know she's finally safe.

"He was poking around my barn, probably looking for shit to steal," she calls over her shoulder.

Fucking Granger. I'll be paying him a visit later.

"Don't even think about telling Ollie about this," she says as she glares at me. But the glare doesn't reach her eyes. Her warm brown eyes are still full of fear. And that asshole Granger put that fear in her by creeping around on her property. Yeah, he'll pay for that, too. And I *will* be taking her brother with me when I pay that fucker a visit. Someone has to look out for her, and we aren't letting anyone mess with her.

"Where's Love?" I ask, glancing around and realizing her Blue Heeler isn't here. I love that dog, and she loves me, much to Cami's dismay. Sometimes, when I'm out working in our connecting pastures, she comes and finds me.

"I locked her in the barn when I took off after Granger. He had a hunting knife in his pocket he thought he'd introduce me to, and I don't trust her not to bite him, and then he'd hurt her."

I stare at her, mouth dropped, then shake my head in anger and say, "I meant what I said earlier. We need to call the sheriff."

She snorts. "Why? It'll take him at least half an hour to get out here. I'll deal with these fuckers myself."

I practically choke on air. "*These* fuckers? How long has this been going on, Cami?" I ask angrily. "This has happened before?"

Oh, hell no.

She shrugs, "A few times. They think they can pick this ranch clean as if I'm not still here. Love chases them off, and I have to get after them. I don't want them hurting her."

Damn. I don't like this at all.

"You need someone staying out here with you. Let me help you."

She looks at me. "We're not friends, Jessop. I've got it covered."

"We'll see about that," I mutter, turning and getting back on my horse before she can say anything. She yells something behind me, but I don't listen as I ride the fence line home in case someone else wants to mess with Wilder Ranch.

Nobody is messing with Cami. Not on my watch.

Cami is my kryptonite. The only woman I've ever truly loved.

Too bad she's too damn stubborn to realize it.

* * *

"What happened in the east pasture this morning?" Hank, my head ranch wrangler for the Jessop Ranch, asks. Hank's in his sixties and probably should have retired a long time ago, but he loves cowboying. He's the epitome of a Wyoming cowboy. He's got white hair, tanned skin, and a kind smile. This ranch has gone through a lot of changes, but Hank will never be one that we lose. He'll always have a home here. We're his family, and he's been here from day one. He's always been one to keep his head down and work hard. He didn't see eye-to-eye with our dad, but he was good to all of us kids. He's like a grandfather to us.

He joins me as we watch a few horses work in the pen. "I saw you take off like a bat out of hell."

"Old man Granger was over on the Wilder side, causing trouble."

He turns and looks at me, surprised. "And he's still alive? Got both his balls and everything?"

"For now. Unless he gets another idea to try to come on her land again. She shot at him. Twice."

Hank shakes his head. "Glad she has you, boss. I don't like how the vultures are swarming on the Wilder Ranch. It's a shame, and Cami doesn't deserve that," he grumbles.

"No, she doesn't. And you make sure every hand here on Jessop ranch knows that we protect the Wilder Ranch and their land," I say as I push off the fence and stride toward the barn.

"You got it, boss," he calls. Hank is probably one of the few wranglers that I can trust at this point. He's older, and I grew up with him here. But he's not like the other wranglers that were tight with my father and his shady ways.

I'm wound a little too tight, so I head to town for some supper. When I drive out through the ridiculous iron arches of the Jessop ranch, laughter fills my chest. Cami was right. It does look like a villain's entrance or whatever she called it. It's ostentatious and ridiculous, and I make a mental note to add it to my list to get it removed. The ranch still feels like my father's place, and I'm not used to it being mine. When I look over at the ranch, I see how much work I need to do to make it clean again. Because the business practices that my father had on this ranch are not how I want things to run. And my brothers and sister all agree. That's the one thing we're all in agreement on. Our father's path was trash.

When I see the future of this ranch, I do not share the philosophies that generations before me had. I can't get behind the bully tactics, stealing, gambling, and hidden agendas from my father's era. I've got different plans, and I'm meeting resistance everywhere I turn on the ranch. Old ways are not the way we're going to do things moving forward.

The Black Dog is unusually quiet for a Thursday night. The low hum of conversation and the sound of clinking silverware fade into the country music playing on the jukebox.

The owners, Walker and Violet, are a couple of musicians. I've known Walker since I was a kid, and he's a great guy. He and his daughter Mack have always been there for me. They even flew out for my Navy graduation years back. Walker is the closest thing I have to a father figure, but I think he's only about eight years older than me, so maybe more like an older brother. But he's a solid man. He chose a good woman with Violet. Her aunt Maggie owns the Dogwood Inn.

Violet wipes down the counter and watches me. Finally, she stands before me and leans her elbows on the bar. "You doing okay, Jack?"

"I'm fine," I say as I tip back my whiskey glass, which she just set down.

"You don't look fine," she says with a raised eyebrow.

"Well, I've got a lot on my mind," I admit.

"You mean you have her on your mind?" she says, her voice low.

I didn't have to ask who she meant, she knows Cami and I have a connection. She has a knack for calling me out on things, even when I don't feel like talking about them. Sometimes I text her when I have something on my mind. And sometimes, she bakes me muffins and cookies with Mack. She's been good to me and my sister, who used to work at the bar as a bartender after high school and has filled in recently when Walker and Violet needed help.

I sigh, looking over the bar. "Can't help it. She gets under my skin."

I feel my phone vibrate in my pocket, and I reach down to check it. Think of the devil, it's my sister, Jenna. I silence the call and make a mental note to call her later. I see that I've several missed calls from her. Shit. I'm really dropping the ball on everything these days.

Violet laughs. "When are you and Cami going to admit that you're hopelessly in love with each other? It's honestly so romantic. I could write a dozen songs about your epic love story," she teases.

I grin at that. Violet and Walker have been working on starting their own music label and recording studio here in Bridger Falls, and they've played some of their songs here at The Black Dog, and they're really good. Walker used to be a country music legend, and now he's a songwriter and owner of The Black Dog. He's a pretty big deal, but in Bridger Falls, he's a great guy and friend. Everyone treats him normal here. Because to us, he's just Walker.

I know where I stand with Cami. Always have. But I don't know where she stands with me, and that's the thing that scares me the most. I'm pretty sure Cami hates the sight of me most days. But then there's times when she thinks I'm not paying attention, and I could swear she's looking at me with something other than loathing. Sometimes it'll be at the Black Dog when we're all in a big group hanging out and I will catch her smiling if I say something. Of course, she'll pretend it doesn't happen or she'll look away if I meet her eyes. It also could be wishful thinking on my part.

I shoot her a look, but she doesn't back down. Not her style.

Instead, she grabs a rag and begins to shine the bar, waiting for me to spill my guts like she knows I will.

"It's...complicated." I admit.

"Tell me something I don't know. You're both complicated." Her tone softens, her eyes meet mine, and she nods, willing me to continue.

"You know why Cami is the way she is, right? Her dad is a mean son of a bitch and has been in and out of her life since she was a little kid. I don't know anyone meaner than him other than my own father. Everyone gave up on Wilder Ranch, even though it's been in her family for generations. They left Cami standing on her own, fighting for what's left of her family's ranch."

"Why do you think she pushes everyone away?" she asks as she leans against the bar, listening.

"She grew up thinking she had to handle everything because everyone around her lets her down. She doesn't push me away; she just doesn't know how to let me show her that I'm not giving up," I say quietly.

Violet's gaze softens, and she nods. "You'd stay."

"I'll always stay. I'm not going anywhere," I admit, my voice hoarse. "She drives me fucking insane. I can never win with her. We're like fire and gasoline."

"Every time you show up for her, Jack, it means something. Every time you fight for her, even when she doesn't ask you to, she sees it. Every time. Trust me. She feels it," she says with a knowing glint in her eyes.

"She's not the princess that needs saving. She's the warrior that needs a safe place to rest in between all of her battles," I say quietly. "She doesn't want me to fight for her."

She nods. "You need to be her home. Not her hero."

I glance down at my glass, the weight lifting off my chest.

"Think she'll ever let me in? Because I gotta be honest. I feel like I'm fighting a losing battle every day."

Violet's grin turns up as she grabs a bottle from the shelf. "If anyone is meant to break down Cami's walls, it's you. Just keep fighting for her, even when she doesn't seem to need it. That's when she needs it the most."

She pats my arm as she moves down the bar to help another customer, leaving me with my thoughts. I don't feel so lost for the first time in a long time. Maybe there's hope for me and Cami. It's not gonna be easy, but I have to keep fighting. She's worth it.

I eat my supper and wind down some more at the bar, but my mind continues to drift back to Cami. No matter how much I bury myself in work, the bar, or planning out my future, she's in it. She's never far from my mind.

Cami would burn the world down for the people she loves. I've never seen a heart bigger than hers. She's one of a kind. She was never meant to fit into a box. She's too powerful, wild, and unruly. The devil works hard, but Cami works harder. If you're lucky to have someone like her in your life, then you're lucky as hell.

On my way home, I pull in by the Bridger Falls Firehouse. I walk up to the open bay, and Ollie's there working on a piece of equipment. "Hey, Ol," I say as I give him a clap on the back and sit on a stool next to him.

"What are you doing here, Jack?" he asks with a grin as he sets down his tools.

"I just had supper at The Black Dog and needed a word before I head home," I say grimly, unsure how to broach this with him. He's not gonna fuckin' like it any more than I do.

Ollie's a good guy, but he got the brunt of it growing up when it came to his father abusing and mistreating the family. A lot of times, he had to shield Cami and her mom. No one blamed him when he left the ranch for good and moved to town. He still helps Cami whenever she needs him, but he wants little to do with the ranch anymore, and I can't say I blame him.

"Granger was on the property messing with Cami this morning. He had a knife. She shot at him."

He turns and looks at me. "What the hell? Why am I just now hearing this?"

I nod. "Yeah, well, you know your sister. She doesn't want anyone knowing. I'm going to stay at Wilder Ranch tonight. She says it's happened more than once. People have been poking around the property. I don't like it, man. She's not safe."

"I'm on shift tonight, but I can take my turn. But you know she won't like us babysitting her, right?" he says as he snaps the toolbox shut. "And especially not you. Hell, I'm not sure she won't try to shoot at *you*."

"No shit. There's no telling what your sister would do to me," I mutter, remembering how close we were at the bar and then how she seemed to want me gone off her property.

Ollie laughs and nods his head, agreeing.

"Plan on staying in the barn loft," I say. "I'll leave before she gets up."

"She's got that Heeler. She's a mean little shit, might chase people off," he muses.

"She's a good dog. But it's not enough. We need to keep an eye out."

"You gonna let me fuck up Granger with you?" he asks with a smirk.

"Absofuckinglutely."

* * *

Just after midnight, I ride out to the Wilder Ranch, take Pesto into the barn, put him in with Mouse, and get him turned down

27

for the night. Those two are happy to be side by side, based on their happy snorts. Cami and I may fight like cats and dogs, but I'll be damned if our horses aren't friends. It always bothers her, and she lets me know it.

Her truck is parked in the driveway, and I see a faint light coming through her kitchen window.

Love, her Heeler starts to growl and stops when she realizes it's me. I lean down to give her scratches and whisper. "Hey, girl. You been keeping watch over your momma?"

I head up to the loft, shake my sleeping bag out, and settle in. I sigh with relief and drift off when I feel Love snuggle in beside me, resting her head on my arm. So much for watching out for her momma. I guess we'll keep watch together tonight. She'll let me know if she hears anything.

Chapter 4
Cami

Fall In Love by Bailey Zimmerman

The cool and crisp mountain air swirls through the valley as I get ready to head out for my morning ride to watch the sunrise over the mountain range. I live for these rides with Mouse and try to take them as often as I can because I don't know how many of these I'll have left when the ranch is gone. It's the best time of day to clear my head and take in the fresh mountain air. I pack a thermos of coffee, apple treats for my favorite boy, and meat bites for my favorite girl.

I make my way to the barn and throw open the door, wondering where Love is. And then I freeze. Something feels off. Like someone has been here. Or is still here. I swing my shotgun up to my thigh and cock it, holding it to my shoulder. I clear the barn, one stall at a time, until I get to the last two stalls and tilt my head when I realize that it's Pesto, not Mouse. Then I look over and see Mouse looking happy as if he's proud that his buddy is here.

"What are you doing here, Pesto?" I coo as I reach over and stroke his head.

I turn and look around through the barn, so confused. Why is Jack's horse in my barn? I look up when I see movement, and it's Love's sleepy head popping up over the loft. *What the hell?*

I wondered where she went last night. Usually, she comes inside, but last night, she refused, and I figured that after everything that went down, she was keeping a closer watch on things.

"What are you doing up there?" I whisper as she makes her way down the side steps and wags her whole body, happy to see me. I reach down and give her a scratch and then slowly make my way up the loft stairs, shotgun ready for whatever I'm about to find up there.

I lower the shotgun with an irritated sigh when I spot the oversized sleeping bag. The messy, too-perfect-for-his-own-good blond hair peeks out from under it. And then I see the boots sticking out.

He's sprawled out like he's in a damn Marlboro ad, flannel shirt half open, long legs tangled in the sleeping bag, his stubble catching the early light like he rolled straight out of a romance novel and into my barn.

His chest rises and falls in a slow, steady rhythm, and his snores are just soft enough to be annoying. Peaceful. Relaxed. Smug.

I narrow my eyes and nudge his side with the toe of my boot. "Up, cowboy."

His sharp green eyes fly open, disoriented, and he bolts upright with a rustle of nylon. "Shit. I overslept."

His voice is gravely, and I hate how my stomach flips like he didn't just spend the night uninvited not far from my own bed.

I cross my arms and pretend to be annoyed. "What the hell are you doing here, Jessop?"

I try to make it sound sharp. But it comes out breathless.

Because, of course, he looks stupidly good just waking up, with his hair all tousled and his voice still wrapped in sleep.

Focus, Cami. Focus.

He blinks up at me, lips twitching like he knows exactly what he's doing to me.

"Watching out for you," he mumbles and stretches. "I smell coffee. Please tell me I can have some."

"Not doing a good job of it if you're sleeping." I scoff. "I can look out for myself. And why do you have my dog?"

I turn and glance down at my traitor dog, and her head tilts as she looks up at me.

"I love that dog," he says with a grin as he reaches over and scratches her ears, and she leans into him, closing her eyes and enjoying the affection.

"Get your own dog." I glare, doing my best to narrow my eyes and pretend I'm not staring at his body.

He does nothing but give me a sexy, lazy grin in return as he stretches, and his shirt rides up, exposing his abs that also should be illegal. Dickhead.

He picks up his sleeping bag, throws it over one of the rafters, and heads past me, down the stairs.

"Take your sleeping bag, Jessop. You're not staying in my barn," I huff as I follow him down the stairs.

"Come on, Cami. We're going for our ride."

"No, we're not. You're going home. I'm going for *my* ride."

"Hurry up, Wilder! You'll miss the sunrise," he says cheerfully as he ignores me as usual and heads over to Pesto, murmuring something to him.

Damn him. And I hate that I love the nickname he calls me. *Wilder*. It was my grandpa's last name, and I miss him terribly. He knows I hate the name Kendrick, so Wilder has always been an endearment. Or it was. But not anymore. I'm trying not to love it.

* * *

I lean forward, petting Mouse, and watch the sunrise, my favorite part of the day. The Wyoming sunrise doesn't just rise, it *owns* the sky. The horizon glows with a soft, golden blush that spills across the wide-open plains. Then, in an instant, the sun punches through the sky like a flame cracking open the dark and igniting everything in sight. The shades of rose gold, amber, and orange will stop you in your tracks. There's nothing like it.

I slide out my coffee thermos and pop off the lid, taking a sip, savoring the bitter but crisp coffee with a hint of cinnamon mixed with fresh milk from our dairy farmer up the road. My gaze sweeps over the land that I've called home my entire life. The rolling hills, endless sky, and it's all still mine... for now.

A hand reaches over, and I roll my eyes as I pass the thermos over to him. He takes a few sips, putting his lips right to where mine were before handing it back. He gives me a grin that makes me shake my head.

I give an exaggerated eyeroll just to make sure he knows he's ridiculous and impossible.

But inside, my heart flutters and I feel something else entirely. I refuse to let Jack see how much he affects me.

Mouse flicks his ears and reminds me he hasn't had his treat yet. I reach into my bag and pull one out, him leaning to take it. "Good boy," I murmur as I hand one to Jack to give to Pesto.

We move along the perimeter of the ranch, just like we always ride. Lost in my thoughts, Jack interrupts them with, "Got any sharp objects or firearms on you other than that shotgun?"

I sigh and say with exasperation, "Leave it to you to ruin my morning ride, Jessop."

"That's not an answer to my question," he quips as Pesto falls in stride with Mouse.

I sigh, shooting him a sidelong glance. "Wouldn't you like to know?"

"I would. Because you riding out here with no protection isn't safe," he says sternly.

I roll my eyes at him. "Did you not see me handle myself yesterday? I think I handled that just fine."

He just gives me a look.

"What?" I glare.

"You can't just shoot at people, Wilder," he says softly, looking worried. "They might shoot back."

"That's what happens to trespassers, Jessop. Take note," I warn as I scan the horizon. "And I missed on purpose. Next time, I won't."

"Well, I hope there isn't a next time," he says.

We ride in silence for a while, the horses falling in step together. I couldn't tell you how many morning rides we had when we were kids. And since he's been back, most mornings, I run into him out here. It's kind of something we've been doing off and on for months now. None of us really say anything or call it what it is. It just sort of happens.

Jack looks over at me, the sun reflecting his green eyes. "Don't you think it's interesting that our horses get along so well?"

I grip my reins. "Not really. You're an asshole and Pesto is not. You're the enemy."

"That's not true," he says, his voice softer. "We're not enemies."

I glance over at him and say, "All I know is that I can't trust anyone. You made me believe that I could trust you once and look where that got me. I don't know what's true anymore."

He opens his mouth to respond, but I don't wait to hear it. I click my tongue and guide Mouse back to the ranch, Love trotting faithfully beside us. As I ride away, I see her pause for a moment and glance back at Jack with longing. "Come on, Love," I call firmly.

Of course, we give each other shit, but it's nice to know he's around. But I'll be damned if I tell him that.

* * *

There's no time to wallow. I have responsibilities and shit to take care of. I make my way back to the house, shower, and quickly get ready for the day.

Sliding on my jeans and stepping into my boots, I pull my hair back into a quick braid before grabbing my keys off the counter. I've got to get to town and give the people what they want: delicious baked goods and coffee.

My coffee trailer, Steamy Sips, has been a lifeline for me for the past few years. It started out as a way to bring in some extra income to help out with the ranch, marrying my love of coffee with business.

At first, I took my trailer to festivals, fairs, food truck events, concerts, and anywhere else that would have me. Now, I rent a space in a parking lot and keep it there for the locals. Bridger Falls is a small town, but they love their coffee just as much as I do. I pride myself in giving them the best they've ever had. I've even been baking for the past year, and while I've gotten better, I'll admit I wasn't very good at it at first, but now I've got sourdough bagels and scones down. I'm proud of my latest pumpkin scone that I can't seem to keep in stock. It doesn't even matter if it's autumn or not, they're best sellers.

I grab my baked goods, which I stayed up late into the night baking last night, and load up. The drive is long, but it's something that relaxes me. The views are stunning, and I take this time to reflect and think about how I can figure out a way to keep the ranch.

As I drive through town, the streets are already bustling with trucks and cars. Word has spread that a film crew is setting up in town, but I'm not sure what they're doing here yet. Everyone has been tight-lipped about it. I'm hoping I'll get it out of someone today who is willing to trade secrets for treats.

I park in my usual spot behind my trailer and get everything unloaded. There's already half a dozen trucks parked, waiting for me to open up in twenty minutes. I get my fresh coffee going and stock the bakery case.

While the heat warms up the trailer, it doesn't take long for the line to grown even longer. Locals chat and speculate about the film crew on the picnic tables I have set up out front. I pour drip coffees, make lattes, and hand out pastries. The usuals have their small talk, and it's a welcome distraction from the stress I've been carrying from the ranch.

I work quickly, filling orders and handing out coffees to regulars, and I can anticipate what they need before they even need it. A familiar figure steps up to the counter. His dark brown cowboy hat and sunglasses don't hide who he is or what effect he has on me. The lazy smile he gives me shoots straight to my core, and my traitorous body responds, and I hate that, too.

"Mornin', Wilder," he says innocently with a slow grin. "Did you miss me?"

"No. I've already had enough of you for one day." I groan and look up at the ceiling, pretending to be bored. "What do you want, Jessop?"

"Coffee. You know how I like it. Black, just like your soul."

I glare at him and try to deny the thrill that sears through my body when he's in my space. "I see you're still following me, Jessop. You know, that's called stalking."

"Just here for coffee, Wilder." He leans back and gives me a grin.

"Pumpkin spice latte, coming right up," I say sweetly, with a deliberate lack of enthusiasm and disregard to his order. I slide the cup of black coffee I already poured across the counter, my fingers brushing his for the briefest moment. A current passes through me, and I ignore it and look away.

"Thanks," he says, his voice softening. "By the way, you've got quite the line forming."

"No shit. Now, move so I can do my job," I say dryly. But secretly, I don't want him to go and I'm glad that he's here.

He taps his card on the reader and stuffs cash in my tip jar. He steps to the side and chats with a few locals, sipping his coffee. His presence here is oddly comforting. Every so often, his gaze lands on me, sending a shock through my body.

It's lunchtime, and I'm exhausted and sold out of every single bakery item. And no one is offering any information on the film crew. Apparently, nobody can be bought with a coffee or a scone. Oh, well. I sink into the stool behind the counter and exhale a deep breath. Jack is still out there, only now he's perched on the tailgate of a local's truck chatting.

I watch him, thankful that he can't see me. He is the most exasperating person I've ever met.

He does seem different now. But being different doesn't take away all the hurt he caused me years ago.

Shaking my head, I turn back to the counter and focus on cleaning up. I don't have time for distractions. I'm about to lose everything.

* * *

I brew some nighttime tea and glance around at my kitchen, a mess with baking supplies. I'm baking my treats for tomorrow, but what I really want to do is crawl under my cozy blanket on the couch and take a nap. I know I won't stop until I have everything baked, cooled, and the kitchen spotless again, so I get to work, and time passes before I remember I still have other things to take care of around the ranch.

I sigh when I remember that I still need to go out and knock out the chores.

I hear a noise, and when I open the back door, I find Love. However, there's also a shadow of a figure sitting on one of my chairs. Panic settles deep inside as I reach for my knife, which is on a magnet next to my stove, while flipping on the light.

"Ollie! You scared the shit out of me!" I hold my hand to my chest, and he sits up in his chair.

"You can put the knife down," he says, as he eyes me like I'm a crazy person.

"You know you can just come in the front door like a normal person. Not creep around on the back porch," I scoff, still trying to bring my breathing down.

"I was watching the sunset with your dog," he says as he affectionately pets Love.

"I see that," I say as I reach into my apron pocket and turn off my phone alarm for the oven timer.

"Smells good in there. Whatcha got?" he asks with a grin.

"Come have your pick," I say as I hold the door open.

He shuffles in, not having to be told twice, opens the fridge, pulls out a beer, twists it open, and takes a long swig.

"I thought you were on duty?" I ask as I pull the pan out of the oven, slide the next one in, and set my alarm.

"I was, but we have a new guy doing some training, so I got off tonight at the last minute," he says as he surveys my baked treats and chooses a blueberry crumble muffin.

"Did you eat dinner?" I ask as I realize I haven't even stopped myself to eat tonight. Something I usually forget to do. Sometimes I get in the zone baking and then want to eat everything like a little gremlin.

"Not since lunch. I'm starving," he admits as he reaches for a second muffin.

I pull out a pot, fill it with water, and set it on the stove. "I'll make us some pasta," I say.

"Sounds good."

"You never answered my question. What are you doing here?" I ask as I reach for one of my home-canned jars of pasta sauce that I made last winter from my garden.

"You know why I'm here," he says dryly as he gives me a look full of concern.

"Jessop is such a snitch," I add as I pull down a box of pasta from the cabinet.

"Granger is mean, Cami. I still can't believe that you shot at him. You don't think he won't come back here and bring some of his other mean friends?" he asks as he sets his beer down and hands me a wooden spoon from the crock on the counter.

"I can handle myself. Love will warn me if someone is here. I have protection," I tell him, trying to not only convince him but myself, too.

"Oh, right. Like she let you know that I was on your back porch for fifteen minutes before you noticed me?" he deadpans.

He's not wrong. I know that I'm in over my head right now. The truth is, I haven't been sleeping. Every little sound keeps me up, and I hate it. I hate the fear that I have in this place. The nightmares have been even worse. Last week, when I finally fell asleep, I had a nightmare that someone set my house on fire while I was in it. I woke up and had to go out to the barn and sleep in the stall with Mouse. Finding Jack out there was a relief, but I can't tell either of them that.

Ollie's face softens, he sees through my bullshit. "Cami."

"I'm fine," I say softly, turning to the stove, trying to be busy so he won't see me upset.

"Come here," he orders.

I turn and sigh, heading toward him as he wraps his arms around me in a big hug. "Was that so hard?"

"Yeah," I sniff.

"It's hard being a badass, isn't it?" he teases as he pulls back and stares at me.

I give him a light shove and turn back to the stove to check the boiling water.

"I take it it's your turn to sleep over and babysit me?" I ask as I glance over at him.

"You would be correct," he grins as he reaches for a Monster Cookie.

Bummer. I kind of liked finding Jack in the barn.

"I'm cooking dinner, don't spoil your appetite," I tease.

"I'm so hungry that I could eat a horse," he admits.

"Then you're definitely not sleeping in the barn with Mouse," I tease as I dump in the pasta.

"Hell no, I'm not sleeping in the barn. I'm not an animal. I still have a room here," he says as he gives me a look.

"Yeah, but no bed. Mom sold it," I remind him as he rolls his eyes. We're both over our mom's crap.

"I heard Jack sleeps in the barn," he smirks as he grabs the Parmesan cheese. "Why doesn't he just stay in the house with you?"

I glare at him. "Because he's not invited. And he stole my dog, too. He's a jerk."

I turn, and he's smiling at me as he says, "Oh, yeah?"

I groan. "Not you, too. Why does everyone give me shit when it comes to Jack?"

"You know why, Cami," he says with a grin.

I do know why. But I'm an expert at pretending that I don't.

Chapter 5
Jack

Wait In The Truck by Hardy, Lainey Wilson

"You got it?" I ask Ollie as I pick him up on the edge of the property in one of the old farm trucks that barely runs.

"Oh, yeah," Ollie grins. "She's a ripe one, too." He picks up a cage with a thick tarp bungee corded over it and places it in the back of the truck, then slides in next to me. He reaches into his pocket and pulls out a paper bag.

"What's that?" I nod to the bag.

"Cami's pumpkin scones. I know they're your favorite," he says as he hands me the bag.

I won't admit to him that I go to the coffee truck most days and get her scones or send Tessa when she goes to town for supplies to get more. I love everything Cami makes. "Thanks, man."

We eat as we drive to the edge of our properties, and I try not to think about how her scones even taste like home.

"You think he'll learn his lesson?" Ollie asks as we pull in and park on the edge of Granger's property.

"He'd better. He really won't like the next one," I say as I get out, step into coveralls, and zip them up.

"Is that a beekeeper costume?" Ollie teases, side-eying me as he laughs.

"Yep, I'm not smelling like that thing," I say as I slide on the hood. I grab the top of the cage and carry it. I can feel it wiggling around in the cage.

"I hate to be the one to tell you, buddy, but that beekeeper costume isn't going to keep the stank off you if she sprays," he says as he follows me.

Whatever, at least it's something.

We work under the light of the moon, turning off our flashlights and headlights. We quietly walk to the driveway where Granger's souped-up, obnoxious, older-model white pickup is parked.

Ollie grins as he opens the driver's side door and ducks his head in. "He even left the keys in it."

"Idiot," I mutter.

Ollie picks up the keys and tosses them about twenty feet off into the brush.

Good luck finding those, buddy.

I unlatch the cage and put it up to the truck, and the skunk rushes into the cab. I shut the door. It's really mad and starts spraying all over the inside.

We both gag and cough. Ugh. It's so strong even with the door shut.

"Shit, that stinks," Ollie mutters, covering his mouth with his shirt. If we can smell it outside the truck, I can only imagine what it smells like inside.

"Yeah, it does," I say as I let the skunk finish before we open the door and let her run free again.

We just needed her for her lovely scent in there for Granger. That'll teach that stupid bastard to mess with Cami or Wilder Ranch. My blood still boils that he pulled a knife on her. He should be glad he's getting a skunk and not my fists.

When we return to my truck, we throw the empty cage in the back and take off, not wasting time. Ollie laughs. "He's gonna be so pissed. That truck was his pride and joy."

"Good," I say with a grunt. Nothing worse than a thief. He has no respect for anyone.

I drop Ollie off at his property line and call out, "Thanks for your help today, man."

"No problem. You still need help with branding coming up?" he asks as he leans against the truck.

"If you have time, I'd appreciate any help you can give. I know you're busy, though," I say, running my hand over my jaw.

"Just say the word, and I'll be there. I can see if Cami wants to help, too."

I shake my head. "She has enough going on. Don't bother her."

"Probably for the best, anyway. You two would probably end up branding each other or worse."

He grins as he claps the cab of the truck, and I take off for the ranch. I need to get ready for the meetings I have today. It turns out that running a ranch is a lot of meetings on top of the usual ranch work. Not glamorous, by any means.

When I get home, I look around and realize how much I hate staying in my father's house. It doesn't feel like a home, and everywhere I look, I see and feel his presence here. If I could move somewhere else, I would. It's just not practical right now when I've got so much work to do.

I grab my steaming mug of coffee and carry it to my father's old office, my new office that I share with my brother, Weston. He's been up in Montana for a few weeks at his house, but he comes back to work on weekends a few times a month. We've been working together to try to make sense of everything and get the ranch operating more smoothly.

About a year ago, the FBI raided our ranch, arresting my father. To say it was embarrassing is an understatement. My father has been an absolute menace to society all our lives. He manipulated, conned, stole, and did whatever he could to climb to the top and bring this ranch with him. He didn't care who he stepped on to do it. He's the worst of the worst and the reason why I left after high school and joined the Navy.

I specifically joined the Navy because I knew I'd be working with water, and bodies of water are furthest away from Wyoming, so that seemed like a good fit. I wanted to get as far away from here as possible. It worked, and I was gone for ten years. When I had enough of military life and my contract was up, I came back a few years ago and became a horse trainer at a ranch about an hour from here. I kept in touch with my brothers and sister. It was over a year and a half before I ran into my dad at a horse sale before he was arrested, and he figured out that I was out of the Navy. And hell, he was spitting mad that I hadn't come home to work horses on his ranch.

I didn't come back until after my dad was arrested. My two brothers have done their best to keep him at a distance as well. My sister Jenna moved out to LA not long after high school. She's been working in reality television. I don't understand exactly what she's doing, but she seems happy, so that's all that matters. She's always loved it, and I'm glad she's happy.

She's back now, working part-time in town at The Black Dog and working remotely on a project. She comes and goes. None of us like staying here at the ranch. Too many memories, and not good ones. Since I've been back, I haven't slept well until the night I was at the Wilder Ranch. That was the first night of peaceful sleep I've had in, I couldn't tell you how long.

I pore over the reports that Weston emailed me. Surprisingly, after the FBI shut us down, they were willing to help us get back what we needed to keep the ranch going with promises of cooperating with them, of course. It came with a price, as it usually does.

But it hasn't been easy to run a business in a town that doesn't trust the Jessop name. My dad did too much damage here. And now we have to try and build a better reputation. It feels impossible most days. Grudges seem to run deep around Bridger Falls.

Luckily for us, none of us give a shit about our father. Him being in prison is the best gift he could have ever given any of us. Weston worked to get everything pulled out of his reach and safely into ours. So, between Weston, Jenna, Tucker, and myself, we've all pooled together to pull the ranch back to better than where it was – at least when it comes to the legal side of things.

We've had our struggles. Weston wants little to do with the day-to-day operations. He's an attorney up in Montana, and he loves paperwork and financial crap. Which is fine with me. Tucker doesn't mind ranch work, but he's the youngest and not ready to run anything yet. He works as a wrangler and runs cattle most days. But if he's being honest, he loves the rodeo circuit, and that's where his heart is. I know he'd get back to it if he could.

I do horse training and keep up with the day-to-day stuff that the wranglers don't keep up with. Which is a lot, because they're lazy and still have a strong allegiance to my father. They don't seem to like listening to what I have to say. But that's about to change.

Tessa is the longest employee at the ranch, along with Hank. Those two carry the brunt of the work on daily operations with me. And both are like family.

Jenna can ride and do everything a wrangler can, but she refuses. Our dad worked her as hard as an adult ranch hand when she was a teenager, and she still resents it. She put in full-time hours along with school, and it didn't leave much time for her to be a kid. The ranch is a source of pain for her, and she can't even bring herself to sleep at the lodge here at the ranch most nights. I learned from Walker that she stays at the bar some nights and sleeps in his office. I'm doing my best as the oldest brother to pull this place together and salvage what I can for all of us. I want to make this place safe, so everyone feels comfortable here.

My phone buzzes, and I look down to see it's Weston. I put him on speaker when I answer.

"What's up?" I ask as I sip my coffee, which has now run cold. Just great. I make a face because no matter how hard I try to make it taste like Cami's, it never does. What is her secret?

"I met with our father yesterday," he says, as if he's telling me that he stepped in a pile of shit.

"How was that?" I ask, pretending to care as I shuffle some papers around the desk.

"Oh, the same old usual shit. Just another day. Still trying to control us from prison. Failing miserably," he adds. "I had to get him to sign a few papers. Luckily, he did it."

"Good," I muse. "You staying at the ranch this week?"

"Nah, I have work up here in Bozeman. Jenna talk to you, yet?" he asks, and something in his voice catches my attention.

"No. Why, what's up?" I ask as I pinch the bridge of my nose, not sure if I even want to know.

"Have you seen the film crews in town?" he asks.

"Yeah, what are they doing here?" I ask as I lean back in my chair. "No one is talking."

"Well, apparently, our sister has set up our ranch for a reality TV show, and she's supposed to talk to you about it," he says. "But seeing as how she hasn't been able to get ahold of you, I'll take the liberty of filling you in."

"What do you mean a reality show for our ranch?" I reply, confused.

"I've gone over the contracts," he says, switching to attorney mode. "I'm going to level with you, Jack. The ranch isn't doing so hot. Our sales are down, nobody is booking us for horse training or boarding, and this is a great way to bring good attention to the ranch. Hopefully it will distract people from talking about the Jessop who destroyed everything and more about the Jessops who are rebuilding it for the good. The income from doing the show is solid. Enough to get us to a good place."

My brother is a hell of an attorney. Our father basically deemed me worthless when I joined the Navy and tried to use the rest of our siblings to offer some sort of usefulness to him and his agendas with the ranch. He sent Weston to Harvard and law school. He groomed him to be able to fight all the battles on the ranch. He just didn't expect Weston to be smarter than him and not want any part of his shady dealings.

"What kind of money are we talking about here?" I ask as I look over our profit-and-loss statements for the month, which are luckily in the black, but not by much. A lot of changes have been happening around here, and we've realized that if we don't make big, long-term changes, we could potentially lose it. It's going to take us all working together and working our asses off to make it happen. And if he's talking about big money, we could all definitely use that.

No one realized how hard it was going to be when he got arrested, and everyone came back to help out. Coming back here alone is hard mentally, let alone working it alongside the ghost of our father.

"Big money," he says. "Our sister is a damn genius."

"Okay, so what's the catch? They want to film our ranch for

a reality show?" I shrug. "How boring would that be? I guess we can get it looking nice for filming."

He laughs a little. "Well, Jack, that's where it gets interesting. *Really interesting.*"

"Just tell me," I sigh.

"You are going to be on a show where you find a wife."

I blink. "Come again?"

"Yeah, there's going to be a lot of women, and it's kind of like that show, The Bachelor. Only a rancher. And that's you, you're the lucky rancher. They haven't set a title for it yet, but it's something along the lines of *The Rancher Finds a Wife.*"

"What the hell?" I ask, pinching the bridge of my nose, wondering if he's fucking with me. "Why not you and Tucker? Tucker would eat this up."

And he would, too. He's a little ladies man pro bull rider. Hell, women flock to him as it is.

"Well, they're going to use the part of dad's story how he was the villain and we're the kids taking it over, and since you're the oldest and in charge and share his name, you're the man for the job."

Absolutely not. This is horrible. I don't care how much money we're getting. There has to be another way. "What if…"

"There's no other way. We have no other money. You used your inheritance from mom's estate, remember? We could have used that, but its gone now. This is it," he says firmly.

"How can she sign me up for a show without my permission? Don't they need a producer to get people to sign something? Is this even legal?" I complain.

I hear Weston's keys on his keyboard. "Yeah. They do. Only our sister *is* one of the producers."

"Are you being serious right now?" I ask. "A wife? I don't want a wife."

"Dead serious. And you'd better find her and talk to her.

She said she's left you a few voicemails, emails, and repeatedly tried getting ahold of you. You have been MIA. Where have you been, anyway?"

Shit. I do vaguely remember her saying that we needed to talk. Several times. I've been so busy with the ranch and then everything that happened with Cami and Granger. I forgot to call her back. I put Weston on speaker and scroll through my emails, and there are several from Jenna detailing this whole plan.

Double shit.

"I've been busy running the ranch. I don't have time for this. I have a ranch to run, not some stupid reality show," I hedge.

What I want to say is that I'm in love with Cami. I don't want some random wife. I want *her*.

"*We* all have a ranch to run," he reminds me.

"Tucker knows about this?" I ask as I stretch and stretch my neck.

"Yeah, he's good with it. You know how Tucker is. Pretty much goes with whatever we want," he says. "Plus, it didn't hurt that he was at The Black Dog the other night with Jenna when she had a meeting and saw pictures of the contestants. He said in his words that they were 'all babes.'"

"Jesus," I groan.

"Yeah, Jesus isn't coming to save the ranch, Jack. We need cash, and Jenna just saved our ass," Weston says matter-of-fact.

"What happens if I say no?" I ask.

"You could. But, she's worked really hard on this. She's some sort of producer on it. This can help her career out a lot, too. So, we're not just saving our asses, but hers as well."

"By pimping out her brother?" I say dryly. "This is weird."

"You don't have to do it, but I mean, why wouldn't you? There's a lot of money at stake here that can really help the ranch. You'd be crazy not to just do it."

"And I'd be crazy *to* go along with it," I add.

"Look, I'm going to tell you what she explained to me. Most of the reality shows are staged. They're not real. You don't *really* have to marry someone. Unless you want to," he adds.

This sounds...awful. Like it's going to be a lot of show-boating and fake nonsense that I want nothing to do with.

I groan. "I'll think about it."

"Speaking of money, the Wilder Ranch sale is almost final," he tells me as I hear him shuffling papers on the other end of the line.

"Good. And you set up the trust?"

"I did. As much as our family battled with theirs, there was some weird clause on their ranch with the bank that they couldn't sell to anyone without offering it to us first. Apparently, it was some sort of gambling debt that Clay Kendrick had with our dad. Weird as hell. I had never seen anything like that before, but apparently, it was legit, so I could bypass all the other offers. And there were others, Jack. *So* many developers wanted to get their hands on that ranch. Our father was an asshole, but apparently, he did one thing right with protecting the boundaries of our ranch. He at least ensured they couldn't build a mall or something next door."

Relief fills me as I realize Cami and Ollie's family ranch will be safe. "How much did this set me back?"

"It's not pretty. It wiped out your entire inheritance from mom's estate. Since you're thirty now, you can access your portion, but Jenna and I have a few years to go, yet. Another reason why we need to do the show and get the money. I know you have this crazy, weird attachment to Cami and Ollie, but spending your inheritance on a woman who seems like she hates your guts doesn't seem smart."

"It is the right thing to do," I say gruffly. "But it's for sure a done deal?"

"Yes. You said you wanted to keep it to yourself for right now. right?"

"That's right," I say adamantly.

"I'll finish up the details and get everything over to you."

"Weston?" I ask, my voice lowering. "Thanks."

"Anytime, brother. Things are different now for all of us. He can't touch us. We're doing things our way. No more bullshit."

"No more bullshit," I add with relief.

Except this show? It feels like a lot of bullshit.

* * *

I glance at my watch and realize I missed my morning ride with Cami. "Shit," I mumble as I get up and head to the barn. I'll ride fences anyway just to keep an eye on things. Ollie's stayed the past few nights, and I've been busy at the ranch.

I make my way to Pesto's stall, and he's not in there. "Where's my horse?" I call out to the other wranglers.

Nothing. Crickets.

I look around at a few of the wranglers and notice that Jace, a wrangler who usually takes care of the horses, is missing. None of them meet my eyes and ignore me.

"Jace!"

"He's not here," one of the wrangler's named Anson calls.

"Where's my horse?" I demand, anger filling my chest. No one rides my horse but me.

"Jace has him out running fence."

"The fuck he does," I quip

as I take one of our spare horses and get him ready.

That fucker did this on purpose. He knows no one touches my horse. There are at least a dozen horses the wranglers ride, and they're all still here. He took mine on purpose, and I'm sick of the slacking off, shady crap, and taking my horse to goad me. Big mistake.

"Which way did he go?" I ask.

The wrangler shrugs and looks away, not wanting to tell me.

"You're fuckin' fired. Get the fuck off my ranch." I point to Anson.

He scoffs, and kicks up dirt with his boot.

I glance around at the other wranglers. "And if any of you want to remain working here, I suggest you start doing your actual jobs and remember who signs your fuckin' paychecks now."

Hank walks in the barn, looking around at the commotion. And if I had to guess by the look on his face, he looks relieved. I'm done with people walking all over this ranch. They want to be loyal to my father and his old ways, then they can go find a new ranch to work with or join my father in prison for all I care.

"Hank!" I call as he turns and looks at me. "Anson is out of here."

I head out and ride the pasture until I come over the hill and find Jace talking to someone on the fence line that borders our property to the north. When I get closer, I see that it's Granger he's talking to.

Anger sears through me at seeing him near my property and my horse.

I ride up, and Jace looks over at me and sneers, then looks back at Granger and says something.

"Why the fuck do you have my horse?" I ask when I get off and walk over to where Pesto is standing next to him. I snatch the reins out of his hand and walk Pesto over to the other horse and tie him to her.

"Now you can fuckin' walk. And you can head that way with your friend," I say as I point to Granger's property.

"You think you can get away with that stunt you pulled with

my truck?" Granger snarls as he spits and stands with his hands on his hips. He smells of skunk, and I hold back a smile.

"Granger, get the fuck away from my property." I turn, ignoring him, and point to Jace as I mount Pesto. "Don't step foot on my ranch. If I see either of you on my property again, you're a trespasser. And neither of you want to find out what I'll do to trespassers."

"And just what do you think you are going to do about it?" Jace scoffs.

I level my gaze at him and say calmly, "I'll remind you what my fuckin' last name is and where it came from."

Chapter 6
Cami

Weren't for the wind by Ella Langley

I'm sitting at the tiny table in my coffee trailer with my old-school calculator, running numbers. And these numbers are looking really good. The only problem is that I'm not sure if I'll have a ranch to actually do any of the plans that I'm working on.

I hear someone pull up, glance over, and see Jenna walking up to the window. She bypasses it and comes straight around the back to knock on the screen door.

"Hey, come on in," I call out to her.

"I think my brother is going to kill me," she says as she plops down into the seat across from me.

"Oh, yeah? Why's that?" I ask curiously.

"You promise you won't say anything? I mean, you have to really promise. Like pinky swear and all that shit," she says, looking stressed.

"You know I'd never betray you, Jenna."

She nods because we've grown up together as neighbors, and we've kept in touch on social media. She's one of the few people on this planet that I can truly trust. When you grow up in an unstable home, and other kids have too, you learn to build a community in other places, because your own family is shitty.

A look of sadness crosses her face, but then she nods. "I know. That's why I'm here."

I nod back. "So, what's up?"

"By now, you've probably seen all the film crews around town. They're here filming b-roll footage and planning out the show. And they're here for my brother," she says as she takes a deep breath.

I startle and blink. "Wait, what? Which brother?"

She leans forward, and her face lights up when she tells me. "It's a new reality TV show that I'm co-producing. We're calling it *The Rancher Finds A Wife*, and we're filming it here at the ranch. Jack is going to be the star."

My mouth opens and closes. This is not what I expected to hear. Wow. I shake myself back to what she's saying, and I have so many questions swarming around my brain right now. The biggest one is about Jack finding a wife.

"What do you mean, 'find a wife'?" I ask, trying to keep it cool. But the truth is, there's no coolness in me right now. Not even close. In fact, I'm the exact opposite of cool. I'm an inferno. I could explode at the thought of Jack getting married. And to who? What the actual hell is happening? I didn't want him to date anyone else, much less marry someone.

She crosses her legs and leans back, excited. "The women are going to date him, and it's kind of like The Bachelor. Wyoming ranch style. At the end of the show, the hope is that they find the love of their lives."

No.

Instead, I say, "Jenna, that is... wild," as I try not to give away that my heart is pounding so hard right now.

"I know, right? And the best part is that I get to help produce it!" she says excitedly. "This is my chance to break out as a producer."

"What does Jack think about this?" I ask. He didn't mention this at all. Not that we are big on sharing, but still. This is huge. He probably knows I'd give him shit about it.

"He doesn't know, yet," she mumbles. "He's been avoiding me."

"You're right, he's going to kill you." I shake my head and blow out my breath. "Where do you want to be buried?"

"Yeah," she breathes. "So, that's why I'm here. I'm hoping you can help me talk him into doing it."

I laugh, then when I look at her, I realize that she's serious. "Wait, what makes you think he'll listen to me?"

She looks at me and says, "He'll listen to you. I'm pretty sure you could talk him into anything. You guys are the weirdest best friends I've ever seen."

I shake my head. "I don't think you realize that your brother and I are not really even friends. We're more of the rival variety."

She snorts. "Right. Everyone knows that's bullshit. Whatever you have going on with each other is...weird."

I glance over, and Jack's dark blue truck pulls in and parks. "Well, Jenna, it's your lucky day."

"Why?" she asks as she turns to look behind her out the window.

We both go still as Jack kills the engine and stalks toward the trailer like he's about to arrest somebody, with that wide-shouldered, long-legged, cowboy-on-a-mission stride that makes my brain short-circuit.

I pop the service window open, trying to bite back my grin. "What can I get you, Jessop?"

His eyes flick to mine, sharp and stormy. "Where's Jenna?"

Yikes. Not here for scones and coffee.

"Right here!" Jenna chirps from behind me, voice a little too high. "Hi, Jack!"

He doesn't even blink. "Out here. Now." He says it calmly. Clipped. No room for negotiation. Just points to the spot in front of him like it's marked for judgment.

Jenna practically shrinks.

And me? I nearly drop the coffee I'm holding. Because bossy Jack? Yeah, that gets to me, too.

I cross my arms and lean against the trailer window, enjoying the show. Oh yeah. This is gonna be good.

I watch with fascination as she reluctantly exits the trailer. I want to watch what happens and pretend to be busy making coffee, even though there are no coffee orders.

I hear Jack say, "Why would you do this and not even ask me first? I had to hear it from Weston."

"I tried talking to you multiple times, Jack. I even resorted to email. You've been so preoccupied lately. I had to sign you up for it, guaranteeing your spot to the other producers. I did it for you, Jack. For all of us. This money could really change things for the ranch. We can make it ours and not our father's. We can do things the right way. The way mom would have wanted to do them. This is my way of contributing and helping get the ranch in a stable financial place."

"This is our lives, Jenna. Do you want us to put you on a show to find you a husband? How would you like that?" he asks as he crosses his arms.

His beefy arms, I might add. He looks pissed under his usual black cowboy hat, sunglasses, and faded navy t-shirt.

"Actually, hell yeah," she admits. "But it's TV. It's for entertainment. A lot of reality TV shows are scripted and for views. You can do this. I know you can. And then you can have money for—"

"That's enough," he snaps.

"Okay, I get it. I was just trying to help. I promise. I'd never put you, Weston, or Tucker in a bad position," she reassures him.

"A little heads up would have been nice. They're here in our town starting to film, and I'm just being made aware of it. It's my fucking ranch, too."

Now Jenna looks angry. "The ranch is all of ours. I have a part in this."

"Oh, yeah? Then fucking act like it, Jenna. You won't even come home to sleep. He's gone, you know. And he's never coming back."

"I know," she says quietly. "It's just hard. It's like his ghost is lurking there. And he's not even dead."

"He might as well be. All of us need to make decisions together," he says with emphasis on "together".

I can't see where he's looking because he's got sunglasses on, but then I realize he catches me staring, so I look down and pretend to wipe down the counters. I've been wiping them for five minutes now, and they're already spotless.

Jenna says something and then heads to her SUV, and I'm relieved that they're done fighting. I hate seeing them fight.

That's when I feel something behind me. I turn and startle when I see him leaning against the doorway, his arms folded across his chest. "Enjoying the show?"

I straighten my shoulders and smirk at him. "Maybe. Heard you're going to find a wife."

"That right?" he asks, not looking happy about this fact.

"God, I hope they're paying those women enough for this," I say, trying not to laugh. "I mean...I guess you've been through half the women in the state of Wyoming, so now they have to fly in a gaggle of women who are lucky enough *not* to know you."

Jack stares at me and shakes his head. "Haven't had you. Want to make the list?"

I stare at him and offer my best eyeroll. But butterflies fill my belly at the thought of being with Jack. Not telling him that though. "Not a chance, Jessop."

He changes the subject and asks, "Granger been around your place any?"

I shrug. "No, it's been pretty quiet. I think my shotgun scared him off."

His eyes are fixed on me, a smirk turning at his lips. "Yeah, that must be it."

He pulls his wallet out of his back pocket and fishes out a twenty. Prowling toward me, he takes up all the space in the trailer. He cages me to the counter, and I can feel my breath hitch and my heart skip a beat. I'm 5'7", and Jack is easily over 6 feet tall, and his height towers over me, giving him an advantage. I crane my neck to focus my eyes on him, unable to speak at how close his body is to mine. He never looks away, as if he's challenging me.

He's close enough that I can feel his heat, smell his body wash, and count all the various hues of green flecks in his eyes. The length of his eyelashes is brutally unfair. His neatly trimmed beard makes me wonder what it would feel like under my hands. His muscled forearms and biceps are on display, bulging under his t-shirt sleeves.

He presses even closer, the points of my nipples grazing his shirt ever so slightly, to the point where I have to bite back a whimper. "I sure hope my new wife bakes half as good as you."

He reaches behind me and sets down the money. He takes two scones and sets them on a napkin. Then, without a word, he scoops the bundle from the counter, turns, and leaves the trailer, pointing his truck back towards the ranch.

Did he just—did he just do that?

I stand here, still caged between the counter and the lingering scent of Jack Jessop, my brain absolutely short-circuiting.

Because what was that? What the hell just happened here?

It feels like someone just dumped a bucket of ice-cold water on me, bringing me back to reality, and back to ignoring my feelings for Jack. He's messing with me. Like he always is.

Also, is Jack going to find a wife? What the hell? I hate this.

I pull out my phone and start to text Violet, but then I remember what Jenna made me promise. I can't talk about this with Violet. Who can I talk to? This is worse than not knowing. Now I know and can't talk about it with anyone.

When I look at my phone again, I realize that I have a few missed calls from the bank. Glancing at the clock, I realize it's too late to call back now since they're closed.

Crap.

Maybe it's for the best. I don't think I can take any more news today. And I still have three weeks left before I need to leave the ranch. But I am curious to hear what they have to say. Maybe it was something good. But a feeling in my gut says it isn't.

I pack up the empty containers and the used coffee grounds for the garden compost. I load up my truck and head through town, deciding to stop in for a quick bite to eat at The Black Dog before I head home.

I see Ollie's truck out front and head inside, scanning the bar for him. He's playing pool with a couple of other guys in the corner, so I wave to him. He smiles and lifts a hand to wave back.

Walker and Violet stand behind the counter, lost in each other and in conversation.

I love how they are together. Walker dotes on Violet, and they're always holding hands, sneaking kisses when they think no one is watching. Violet loves him and his daughter Mack, and they've become a family. I want someone to want me like that. To do the daily mundane things. Ride horses, cook dinner together, work on projects at the ranch, go for long drives in the truck, and maybe have picnics. I want stolen kisses, hand-holding, and cuddles. They're goals.

"Hey, lovebirds," I call as I slide onto a stool.

"Hey, Cami," Walker says as he saunters over. He's eight years older than I am, and when he first moved to Bridger Falls, he was a young single dad. I was in high school, and he hired me to babysit for him. He's a super nice guy, and I adore his daughter Mack, who is now fifteen.

I glance up at the specials written in chalk on the menu board. Today's meal is meatloaf, mashed potatoes, and green beans. Yum. "I'll take the special if you've got any left."

"Sure thing," Walker says as he heads to the back.

Violet comes up and slides onto a stool next to me and whispers. "Please tell me you know about the reality show."

I stare at her with wide eyes and say, "I can't talk about it."

Violet scoffs, "I know you know. Jenna told me. I know she told you. I need to talk about this with someone."

"I need to talk about this with someone, too," I groan.

"Okay, let's ask Jenna," Violet grins as she stands and heads down the hallway. "She's in the back."

"How convenient," I mutter. I'm still trying to wrap my head around the bomb she dropped on me earlier and then left after arguing with Jack.

Violet comes back to the front. "She said it's fine. Only you and I can talk about it, though."

Gotta love the sanctity of small towns.

"Okay, so what have you heard?" I ask.

She fills me in, and it's basically what I know, minus Jack not knowing part, which I fill her in on.

"Are you upset about it?" she asks, looking concerned.

I sigh, "I don't know. Yeah? No? What right do I have to be upset?"

"Every right," Violet exclaims. "You and Jack are meant to be. You're end game. He can't find a wife!"

Jack and I are not endgame. I don't know what we are, but that's not it.

Walker walks up and sets down a plate in front of me, and I smile at him, "Thanks, Walker."

He looks between me and Violet and says, "What are you two talking about?"

Violet whispers loudly to him, "Jenna's show."

Walker groans, "I lost her as a bartender over this show. She was my best one other than Cash."

Violet swats at him with her hand playfully. "Excuse me! What about me?"

Walker grins at her. "You're not my bartender anymore. You're my fiancée."

I smile, watching them, then point my fork at her. "You two are adorable."

"I know," she breathes as she stares at Walker lovingly.

"I'm...gonna go," he says as he backs away slowly and disappears to the back.

Ollie saunters over. "Hey, sis." He takes my fork and takes a bite of my meatloaf.

"You know you could get your own, right?" I ask playfully. Although he knows I'd share anything with him.

"And where would the fun be in that?" he asks, handing me back the fork. He glances over at the door, and his face drops as he murmurs, "Mom just walked in, and she's headed our way."

I drop my fork onto my plate. "You can have the rest. I'm not hungry anymore." I start to stand and realize she's standing right next to me now.

"I'm glad you're both here. I have news. Big news," she says excitedly, out of breath. My mom had me and my brother very young, and she's only forty-eight. She wears her long brown hair in wavy curls and has her makeup done every time I see her. In fact, I have rarely ever seen her not dressed up and without make up. She's not a jeans, t-shirt, and boots kind of woman. She's always loved clothes, make up and shopping. It's just her thing. We've never had much in common.

I stand here and stare at her and wonder why I don't have a connection to this woman. She feels like any other person in the bar. Not my mother, someone who is supposed to be close to me. She's clueless when it comes to me and my life.

"What?" we both ask at the same time. Me, partly frozen in terror because usually when she would have big news like this, it was usually that my father was back in town and they'd be reconciling, which happened often. He'd come back and everything would be oddly calm for two to three weeks. Then he'd start to pick fights with everyone, empty out the bank accounts, steal her car, and leave. By the time I was in fifth grade, we were on our fifth car.

I brace myself for whatever's coming, and she says excitedly, "The bank sold the ranch. It's a done deal, and it's over. We can finally move on."

My heart shatters into pieces in my chest. My stomach plummets, the breath in my lungs evaporating. I feel like I've been taken out at the knees. "What?"

She happily nods, not even reading my emotions, and says, "Isn't this great?"

Ollie watches me closely and asks the questions he knows I want to know since I'm frozen in place.

"Who bought it?" Ollie asks carefully. But there's something off in his tone. Like he already knows who bought it, he's just confirming.

"There was some loophole the bank found. And they handled it. I don't know, it doesn't matter. We should celebrate," she says, not even considering how upset I am.

I swallow and fight, the tears threatening to unleash. This can't be over.

"Oh, and here's the paperwork," she says as she reaches into her purse and thrusts a folder into my arms. "Take care of this, will you, Cami?"

She turns, not even waiting for a response, and runs off to where a group of her friends are sitting. They all stand and hug her, congratulating her as if she has just won something.

Meanwhile, my heart aches in my chest. I look over at Ollie, and even he looks torn. And he hasn't been as emotionally attached to the ranch as I have. But he knows how much this meant to me.

He reaches over and places his arms around me. "I'm sorry."

"Why is she like this?" I ask, tears filling my eyes. "Heartless."

"She doesn't even care about us or our feelings." I hold up the folder. "It means nothing to her. This was my dream."

I reach into my pocket for some cash. I lay down enough plus a tip and swipe away the tears. I turn and can't look at anyone as I walk out to my truck and get in the front seat. I set the paperwork down. Ollie follows me and climbs in next to me.

"What are you doing, Ollie?" I swipe away the tears and reach for the glove box for some napkins.

"I don't think you should be driving like this," he says as he looks at me worriedly. "Let me drive you home."

"I'll be fine," I say calmly. "I'm giving myself a minute, then I just want to go home. I still have a lot of baking to do tonight."

Then it dawns on me that I won't even have a kitchen to bake in much longer. I don't know what I'm going to do or how I'm going to continue to keep Steamy Sips going if I don't have a place to bake. I shake my head and lean back in my seat.

"I'm going to follow you home," he says as he gets out of the truck. "I'll help you bake tonight. Do chores, whatever you need."

"Thanks, Ollie," I whisper, grateful to not be alone. I buckle in and start my truck. "See you at the house."

He nods and heads to his truck. Ollie's always been the best little brother I could have ever asked for. We're only a little over a year apart in age, so we've always been close. Even though he and Jack are best friends. They weren't always best friends, though.

When we were kids, our parents forbade us from being friends with the Jessops. But once we got older, there wasn't much our parents could do. Our grandparents always loved the Jessop kids. But my parents and grandparents always had issues with Jack Sr.

I get home and change into comfy clothes and head downstairs to bake. My heart isn't even in it. I feel numb.

Ollie dries his hands and says, "The chores are done. What can I help with? Are you hungry? You didn't eat your food."

"I can't eat," I mumble, blinking through hot tears on my face. "I still have to go through these papers and see what we're up against."

"Okay, let's get the baking started and then you can dig into that," he offers.

We work side-by-side quietly, and I tell Ollie about the cookbook I've pitched to an editor. I told him about the beautiful pictures of the garden and the homemade recipes I wanted to share with the world.

"It can't end here, Ollie. It can't. I'm not done yet. I have so many dreams," I say softly.

"It's not over. Whatever happens, those are your ideas. You can still do anything that you want to do."

"Why don't you care about the ranch?" I ask, emotions filling me.

He slides a pan into the oven and turns to me. "This place just isn't where my heart is. I know it's where yours is, and that's okay. But for me, this place holds memories that make me sad."

"I'm sorry, Ol."

"Yeah, me too," he says wistfully.

When Ollie heads out to check on Mouse, I look around at all my fresh herbs hanging from the window. I think of all the beautiful recipes I've created in this kitchen. And my dreams for the future of creating a bed and breakfast, writing a farm-to-table cookbook, and turning this place into a somewhere families could enjoy a vacation and have beautiful experiences are now just dreams.

Sitting down to flip through the file Mom gave me, nothing in these papers makes any sense to me. A trust bought the ranch. I google the name, but there's no information listed. It's completely private.

And I'm officially screwed.

Chapter 7
Jack

Ain't No Love in Oklahoma by Luke Combs

I saddle up and head out before any of the wranglers make it out to the barn. Which isn't saying much because they haven't been working that hard, anyway. Tucker and I have been picking up the slack, and let me tell you, things are going to be changing around here.

After I fired Jace and Anson, who both had misguided loyalty, there's been dissension in the ranks. Apparently, it's gotten so bad that Tessa, one of the seasoned wranglers, has asked me to meet with them. Tessa's been around since my mother died when I was ten. She's been like a mother to me and my brothers and sister. We love her and couldn't imagine this ranch without her. She has always said that she could never leave us kids or the ranch.

I ride the fence line and swear when I see a whole row down. I slid off my horse and inspect it. It was purposely cut.

"Damn it!" I say as I pull out my phone and call Tessa.

She answers, "Yeah, boss."

Boss. Shit, that's what she used to call my dad. And I hate that she just called me that. It's like I'm being compared to him, and I am nothing like him. Tessa is pretty much the only wrangler left that respects me, other than Hank. The rest have been acting out since my dad was arrested and I took over. Most of them aren't happy with the way things have been going. They used to get away with a whole lot more and do a whole lot less when he ran things. I'll be damned if my brothers and I work circles around lazy hands we're paying.

"Tessa, I've got a row of fence down along the east pasture. Purposely cut. I need you to get a team out here as soon as possible and get this patched up."

"You got it, boss," she says and disconnects.

Yeah, I'll be asking her to call me something else.

I'm so pissed at how much fencing we need to repair that I don't even see Cami until she's right up on me.

"Who pissed in your Cheerios?" she asks as she stops Mouse in front of Pesto.

I grunt. "My fence is cut all along here. And so far, I'm missing at least a dozen head of cattle."

She looks surprised and upset on my behalf. "Let's ride and see if we can find them."

I look over at her, surprised at her offer. I'm also surprised she's not screaming at me and trying to beat me up right now. She definitely doesn't know yet that I bought her ranch. I wanted it to be anonymous because I wanted to tell her myself when the time is right. If she'd already found out, she'd be giving me an earful. Waiting for the other her shoe to drop and for her to find out is excruciating. I have no idea how she's going to respond. There are so many layers to this onion, I don't even know where to start. I put everything I have on the line for her ranch, and I'd do it again if it meant keeping her safe.

Intrigued by her non-reaction, I just simply nod, and we ride along. Cami has a big heart for her neighbors and especially animals. I'm not surprised that she's offering to help. We don't say anything. I can tell she's upset, and I can't blame her. I want to tell her. But I don't know how she'll take it. I just want to help her. So, if she's going to play it like nothing's wrong, and we just ride in silence like we sometimes do, so be it.

That's one of the things I love about Cami. We don't have to say anything. Something about being around each other has always been calming. When we're talking, we're sparring. But sometimes we're just...together. And that's a peace no other person has ever given me.

I clear my throat. "Got any more of that coffee?"

She gives me the side eye and then hands me her thermos. Every morning, she brings her coffee out here in a thermos and drinks it while she rides. She reaches into her saddlebag and hands me an apple cookie for Pesto. He pokes his head back, knowing the drill, and I hand it to him.

"Spoiling them," I mutter as I pat Pesto. He's a good horse, and he knows it.

"Pesto deserves it for putting up with an ass like you riding him all day." She smirks as she pats Mouse, who huffs as if he wants to be praised as well.

"There she is," I mumble. I knew she'd give me grief today, so I just grin and shake my head. "You talking about my ass, Wilder?"

"Why are you so quiet today, Jessop?" she asks, ignoring my jab. Because this is how it is with Cami. We've always been so in tune with each other. Despite our differences, we have always had a palpable connection that neither of us can seem to get past, no matter how much we try not to like each other.

"Been dealing with a lot back at the ranch. Had to fire two wranglers yesterday," I drawl.

"Which ones?" she asks curiously.

"Anson and Jace."

She doesn't look surprised and nods. "Jace was always a hothead and a bully. And I know he and Granger are tight. I see them at The Black Dog together all the time. Wouldn't be surprised if that's who cut your fence and took your cattle."

"I need to hire new wranglers. Thinking of cleaning house and making a fresh start. I want things to run differently," I admit.

"I'm sure you'll find good wranglers," she says as she points at another fence down in the distance. A calf lingers on the other side of the fence, the mom nowhere in sight. My blood boils.

"Yeah," I grunt. "Hard to find good people who trust the Jessop name these days."

She just looks at me and doesn't say anything. We both know how it is to have a mean asshole of a father ruin our names and ranches. That much we have in common.

"Damn it," I say, getting angrier as I see more fence cut and cattle missing. I don't have time for extra work right now.

We come up on the calf, and Cami slides out of her saddle. She carefully slides over the fence and cautiously walks up to the calf. I hang back so we don't startle the calf into running. She gently ushers the calf back into the fence, props up a piece of wood, and blocks the opening.

"Well, look at you, Cami. Maybe I should hire you to help me get my ranch in shape. God knows you're mean enough to deal with assholes."

She gives me a look. "Not happening."

Actually, shit, that's not a bad idea. Cami could help me act as a liaison with the town. Get them to trust me if they see us working together.

"I have my hands full at the coffee trailer," she says as she looks over at me and realizes I'm serious. "I don't have time for another job. And I'd never work for you, Jessop."

"What if you moved Steamy Sips out to the Jessop Ranch? You could even use the kitchen to bake at the house while you work the trailer, so you're not burning the candle at both ends," I offer.

She stares at me suspiciously as if wondering how I know she bakes in the evening. But it's the only thing that makes sense, because she keeps up with a massive crowd and works her trailer in town during the day. "Why would I help you, Jessop?"

"Steamy Sips will draw a crowd out to the ranch and might make more of the town trust us when they see we're trying to do things the right way," I add, as I glance over at her to see what she's thinking. "It would help bring people out to shop, and we could really use the meat sales."

She stops and stares at me for a beat. "I'll think about it."

Really? Wow. Cami grew up working her own ranch. She knows what to do. She knows what not to do, that's for sure. And I can use people around me who will give it to me straight. I need loyal people who have my back. And while Cami and I have a different sort of relationship, I know deep down she would do anything for me, and she knows I would do the same for her. We just don't admit it.

"I'm not taking your shit, Jack," she says firmly, staring at me.

"What shit?" I scoff. I wait for the jab, but it doesn't come. She's serious.

"If I don't take shit from a thousand-pound animal with a mind of its own, you better believe I won't put up with your shit or any other person shit out at your ranch. No one," she swears as she shakes her head with finality.

I point at her, feeling excited that she is on the same page as me. "See? That's what I need. No bullshit."

Cami just watches me and raises her eyebrows as if to tell me to continue.

"I've got my hands full cleaning up the ranch. Figuring out where the snakes are and getting rid of them. Can't trust a snake. They only shed their skins and become bigger snakes. I don't do second chances, Cami," I tell her as I reach into my back pocket for my tools to tighten the fence and twist it.

Her eyes snap to mine when I add that last part, and she watches me curiously.

"Have you been to see your dad at all?" she asks quietly.

"No. I don't have anything to say to him," I mutter. But that's a lie. I do have a lot to say to him. I just don't want to see him.

She just gives me a look and stays silent.

"Have you heard from your dad lately?" I ask, putting the ball back in her court. I know fathers are a sore subject for both of us.

"Nope. He pops up when he needs money or a place to stay. Now that the ranch isn't an option for him anymore, he'll probably move on to siphon off someone else," she sighs.

We continue to ride and check the fence, and it feels good to be with her.

"I guess it's good that mine can't just pop up at any time. At least mine is right where he needs to be, behind bars," I say with disdain for the man who tormented me and my siblings for most of our lives.

"Stay out of trouble, asshole," she says as she takes off, Love reluctantly following her as she stops to gaze back at me and Pesto. I watch as she makes her way across the pasture.

And I wonder to myself how many times we went on rides in this exact same spot. I think the first time we met up out here we were twelve. We always had to meet in secret at our tree that we used to climb and hang out in because our parents didn't get along and didn't want us kids to be friends. One time, my father caught us out here riding our horses, and he beat me with a belt so badly that I couldn't hardly walk for two days. That's the kind of man my father is. A real winner.

Tessa always tried to cover for me and my siblings, and I'll be forever grateful for that. She always looked out for us kids. While she was semi-loyal to my father and probably knew of most of his dirty dealings, I never doubted her love and loyalty to us kids. Without her, I'm not sure any of us would have ever made it out and be who we are today.

I think of what Weston said about building our own homes and making this ranch clean and our own. I look around at the pasture and realize this is the spot where I'd build a home. I can see it now. A big home with a wrap-around front porch that faces the mountains. A barn off to the east. The ranch has never felt like a home to me. But right here in this spot, I can feel it. And it's on the Wilder side of the fence, so that's probably why.

I turn and make my way back to the ranch to get Pesto situated for the day. I have a feeling that Granger took my cattle. And I'll be handling that. A few of the wranglers are in the barn, but not one of them acknowledges me when I walk in, not one "good morning" or "hello."

And that speaks volumes to me. Yeah, I need to clean house.

I get to the lodge and smell food when I walk in. Jenna and Tessa are in the kitchen. Jenna looks tired, and she's cradling a mug of coffee in her hands, and looks up at me when I walk in.

"Good morning," she murmurs.

"Good morning," and I pause as I realize she must have stayed here. "Did you stay here?"

"Don't make it weird, Jack. And, yeah, I stayed here. Are you happy now?" she mutters.

I walk around the counter, pull Tessa in for a hug, and kiss her cheek. "Good morning," I say.

"Good morning, honey," she says. She's respectful to every-one, and I have always respected the hell out of her. She's the hardest worker on the ranch, and these wranglers should have taken notes on how Tessa shows up. That probably would have saved their jobs. But now it's too late.

"I made you a plate," she smiles as she hands me a plate with eggs, potatoes, and fruit.

"Thanks, Tessa," I say as I take the plate and slide onto the stool next to Jenna.

She takes a plate from Tessa and smiles. "Thanks. I'll move back in if Tessa cooks for us every day."

I grumble. "It's not Tessa's job to feed us."

"I wouldn't mind." Tessa grins. "Now tell me what's going on because it's feeling icy out in the bunkhouse."

I let out a breath and shake my head. "A lot of bullshit going on. I want everyone gone and to do a fresh hire. Tucker, you, and Hank are all still that have a job. People can reapply and be considered, but I doubt most of them stick around."

"Is this about Granger threatening Cami?" Tessa asks, looking mad.

Jenna's jaw drops, and she shakes her head. "I heard about that. I don't like her living alone."

"Ollie's been staying there, and I've stayed in her barn when he's on shift at the station. We've got eyes on her." I add as I take a forkful of food, and the flavors hit me. Damn, Tessa is good. I can't remember the last time I had a real meal in this kitchen.

"The ranch is going to be run my way. Above board and clean. We're not doing cons, stealing, lying, none of that," I instruct.

Tessa nods and smiles with approval. "I like it. It's about time. And I'm proud of you. You are not your daddy, Jack. You're a great rancher."

Knowing that I have her support fills me with relief. Jenna has been quiet, and she says, "You could never be him."

I nod and drop my next bomb: "I asked Cami to move her trailer out here to help keep an eye on things. I told her she could use the kitchen to bake. I think having her out here and drawing traffic from town will help us with our meat sales and get the town to build up trust with us."

Tessa laughs and smacks the counter with her hand. "Granger will be the least of your worries if you bring her out here."

Tessa has always been leery of anyone outside of the ranch. My father made a lot of enemies, and now no one is sure who we can trust. But I know she trusts Cami. She's always loved her and Ollie, too.

"I think it's a great idea," Jenna argues. "Weston and Tucker said sales are at an all-time low. The freezers are full of meat, and nothing is selling out there. This time of year, we should be doing way better."

"Nobody trusts us enough to buy from us," Tessa says as she wipes down the counter and frowns.

"Did you hear that someone bought Wilder Ranch?" Jenna asks as she looks at all of us.

"I bought it. And don't you dare tell her." I point to her. "It's in a trust. I don't want her to know until I know she won't kill me."

Jenna grins with approval. "So, you just plan to not tell her? How long do you think you'll get away with that?"

"I haven't thought that far. But I'll tell her soon." I shrug, looking at my plate.

Tessa looks at me with soft eyes. "You really bought Wilder Ranch?"

"I used my inheritance from my mom." I smile sadly. "I think she would have liked that."

Her face softens, and she cups my cheek. "She sure would have. She always loved the Wilder's. It was a shame when they passed," she says.

I feel the same. I always loved Cami and Ollie's grandparents.

My mom and Tessa had been close friends when she passed away. I've always thought her and Hank had a thing, but Tessa claims they're just friends. And maybe they are. But I've always been grateful that Tessa shares stories with all of us about our mom. I think she's stuck around to raise us when our mom couldn't.

The front door shuts, and Weston strolls in wearing his usual dark jeans and button-down shirt with a messenger bag over his shoulder. He always dresses the part as a lawyer. All of us are so different. Sometimes I'm amazed that we come from the same family. Tucker and I are cowboys and dress the part. Weston always dresses professionally. And Jenna is every bit the L.A. woman. When she moved back here after Dad got arrested, she brought seven large suitcases. They filled up the entire back of my truck and the back seat when I picked her up at the airport. I still give her shit for that. She claimed that was her packing for a trip, and she still had more clothes back in L.A. Good God.

"Good morning, sweetie," Tessa says as she gives him a hug.

"Good morning, Tessa. I see I'm late for the meeting," Weston says as he sets his bag down and surveys the room.

"Just having breakfast and shop talk," I muse.

"What do you think about our brother buying Wilder Ranch?" Jenna asks as she sips her coffee.

Weston says, "I think if it keeps developers away from our ranch and water sources, I'm a fan."

Tessa nods. "That is true. We have to protect that end of the ranch."

"Are you ready to find a wife?" Jenna asks as she refills her coffee cup.

I scoff. "I'm *not* finding a wife. You said the show is scripted and for views."

Jenna grins and reaches for another piece of toast. "You have to at least pretend. The women are great. I think you'll have fun."

I give her a look of disdain. "No. I won't."

I haven't been on a date in over a year. Much to Cami's dismay and her giving me crap about being with half of Wyoming, that's far from the truth. I haven't been with anyone in a very long time. In fact, since I came back to Bridger Falls, I haven't even looked at another woman besides Cami. It's hard to imagine being with anyone but her. Go figure. The one woman who doesn't want anything to do with me in that way, I can't stop thinking about and picturing a life with.

She's on my mind constantly. And I can't handle any more complications. But for the ranch and for Cami's ranch, I'll play a role.

"We'll see, grumpy bear," Jenna says with a smirk.

Weston slides onto his stool, opens his bag, pulls out a folder, and hands it to me.

"Thanks again for handling all of that," I say as I set the folder down next to me.

"Sure," Weston says. "Now, just let us know if we should be planning your funeral when Cami finds out."

"Cami is so going to kill you," Jenna says as she shakes her head.

I scoff. "When I explain everything, I'm sure she'll understand.""

Jenna looks at me like I'm in delulu land. "Right." She pours another cup of coffee and hands it to Weston.

"You'll see," I say, as I finish my food.

"Your funeral, buddy. I'm going to get ready. We're setting up and filming a few clips around town today. I emailed you the filming schedule. Make sure you all are ready and on the same page with all of it," she calls as she heads out.

"Speaking of filming. We have stagers coming in today to stage the lodge for the show. It's going to be busy here. Tucker's staying at the bunkhouse. He likes it better down there. Just a heads up," Weston tells me as he pulls up the schedule on his laptop.

I groan. This house is already the worst. Now we're going to have even more strangers traipsing through it. I hate this place.

"You're lucky the contestants are staying at the Dogwood in town. Maggie is glad to have the business, but if you want, I can have them all stay here," he says smugly.

"You could always stay at your other house," Tessa chirps.

"What other house?" I ask confused.

"The Wilder house," she says with a grin. "Although living with another woman might not help your chances of finding a wife on the show."

"I'm *not* finding a wife." I roll my eyes.

But staying at Cami's does sound more appealing than staying here and dealing with the crew filming here. And I can keep a closer eye on her since Granger and Jace have been up to bullshit with fence cutting and threats. Hell, even staying in her barn sounds better than staying here. I'm sure Ollie would appreciate it if I kept an eye on things.

I need to somehow convince Cami to let me stay there. I could stay in Ollie's old room. Maybe she wouldn't even realize I'm there.

I need to face her sooner or later and tell her what I've done.

Chapter 8
Cami

Strangers by Kameron Marlowe, Ella Langley

I get back from my morning ride and shower, rushing as usual because I need to get to the trailer. I gather up my stuff for town and grab the paperwork in the folder, determined to look all of it over and figure out all of this legal verbiage. I can figure this out, I tell myself. Last night, I got two pages in, and my eyes glazed over. I don't know any lawyers who can help me figure this out. And that offer to move the trailer out to the ranch is looking pretty good right about now. I would like to be able to bake at the Jessop Ranch. Watching Jack find a wife might be torture, though.

Since I have extra time, I head to the feed store to stock up on horse feed and dog food for Love. I'm in line when I notice Weston Jessop heading into Harvest & Honey. I haven't seen him for a while. We went to school together and he was always into sports and academics. We took a lot of AP classes together, and he was always nice.

He's also a lawyer. Maybe he could help me make sense of some of these papers.

I finish paying and stow all the bags in the back of my truck and throw my purse over my shoulder and head over to the deli. I head inside and scan the dining room until I see him at a booth by the window reading something on his phone.

I hesitantly walked up to his table, "Hi, Weston..."

"Cami," he asks, looking surprised to see me. "How are you?"

"It's been a while, but I was wondering if I could talk to you. About a legal matter," I add.

He motions for me to join him, "Sure. What's up?"

Weston is about a year younger than Jack, and they have a few similarities. Jack is more of a rugged and blue-collar cowboy, and Weston looks every bit like the lawyer that he is. Buttoned up, with a nice haircut and clean hands.

I bite my lip, nervously. I hate to bother him. But I'm lost here. I need help. I'm waving my white flag and hoping he'll help me.

"I need an attorney to explain some things to me," I admit.

"Okay..." he says, hesitantly.

"You see, the bank sold my ranch, and I have the paperwork here that my mom gave me, but I don't understand what's going to happen," I admit. "All this legal jargon I'm just not sure about."

He swallows. "Have you talked to Jack?"

I tilt my head. "Why would I talk to Jack?"

He shrugs. "I don't know. I just figured you were closer to him, and you'd ask him."

"Jack's not a lawyer," I add, confused.

Weston looks perplexed, and I realize that this is a mistake, and I shouldn't have bothered him.

"You know what, never mind. I'm so sorry for bothering you,

Weston. Coffee is on me," I add, looking down at his cup. I quickly lay down some money and slide out of the booth.

"Cami, wait..." Weston says, but it's too late. I'm already heading quickly towards the door.

"Have a good day," I call before I can embarrass myself anymore.

I shouldn't have bothered him. I walk down Main Street and stop when I see something familiar on display in a storefront. My grandpa's saddle sits in the window, for sale to anybody with enough cash to buy it. I peer into the window, and my heart breaks at the sight of the well-worn saddle that means more to me than anything. It's not just a saddle to me; it's a personal connection to my grandpa. I bite my lip to stop the sting of tears as I look at the price tag, and I sigh.

I understand why my mom sold everything she could. But I don't understand it at the same time. Why the saddle? Why doesn't she care about any of this? Why doesn't she care about me?

I head back to my truck and head to The Black Dog on my way home. I can grab some lunch before I head home to start baking for the night. And then I need to start packing and figure out where I'm going to go.

The door swings open to The Black Dog, and it's surprisingly busy after the lunch rush. I wave to Cash and take a seat in one of the back booths. I don't feel like chatting with anyone today. I just need a quiet moment to think about everything.

I stare down at my hands, processing everything. Today really sucks.

A figure slides onto the booth beside me, and my heart skips a beat when I look up and it's Jack. He's so close, our thighs are touching, and my heart does a stupid little flip.

I close my eyes for a brief moment as the sensations of him being close pass over me. The smell of him is familiar and comforting. The leather, cedar, a hint of hay hit one after another, and my chest tightens with a rush of something warm and dangerously familiar. I'll never admit that to him, but he feels familiar. Like a safe space.

Damn him.

I close my eyes for half a second, just long enough to get my reaction under control. Because even after the bickering and banter and emotional whiplash, Jack still feels like home.

Not that I'd ever admit that to him.

"Wilder," he drawls, voice low and lazy like he owns the air between us as he reaches over and takes a sip of my drink. Hell, I forgot Cash had set it down, I'd been so lost in my thoughts.

I close my eyes and grunt, "Jessop."

He's got that grin, the one that's equal parts charm and trouble, and leans an elbow on the table like he's settling in for a good time giving me shit. Something he seems to live to do.

"Care to have lunch with me?" he asks, all innocent.

I narrow my eyes. "What's the catch?"

He lifts both hands like he's unarmed. "No catch. Just two neighbors. Sharing a meal. Like civilized ranch folk."

I snort. "Right. Civilized."

He shrugs, still watching me like I'm the most entertaining thing in the building. "It's a free country, Wilder. I figure I'm allowed to sit where I want. And I want to sit by you."

I sip my drink, closing my eyes and picturing his lips on the same glass, and glance at him sideways. "Guess I can't stop you."

His smile widens, just a little. "Wouldn't want you to anyway."

And damn it, I hate how much I like this game.

Because somehow, every time he's near, I stop caring a little more every time who's winning. It's like a ride at the carnival that I don't ever want to stop.

Cash comes over, and Jack holds up two fingers for the special. We're both creatures of habit.

"So, given any thought about moving your trailer out to the ranch?" he asks with a grin.

"I've given your proposition some thought," I admit.

Something hits me in the back, and I look around to see Granger and Jace standing behind us across the bar, leaning against the pool table, glaring over at us. I look over at Jack, and he looks livid. I look down, and it was an empty plastic cup that one of them threw at me.

Jack tenses up beside me, and his fists clench. He slides out of the booth and looks ready to murder these guys. He's fired up. I slide out of the booth and put my hand on his arm, a beat of something passing between us because we don't usually touch each other. I shake my head lightly, eyes on Jack telling him not to kill them. His fury-filled eyes, clenched fists, and grinding jaw make me feel tingly. Like a good tingly.

My own anger is mounting. Guys like this, who think it's okay to assault and harass a woman, need to be humbled, preferably with an audience. "Aw, the poor little babies are throwing their pacifiers out of the stroller." I scoff and roll my eyes, demonstrating how juvenile I think their actions are. "Grow the fuck up, *boys*."

Cash strides over and says to them and gets in their faces. "You want to fight someone in this fucking bar, you can get the fuck out. There's no harassing anyone, let alone a woman. You do that, you better be prepared to take on all of us."

"Our business isn't with you, it's with those two assholes." Jace fumes as he glares at Jack Brand me.

"Which one of you fuckers are trying to sabotage me?" Granger barks.

Jack and I exchange a look, one where a silent conversation

passes between us, even though no words are shared. Yeah, these fuckers are going down.

"What are you talking about?" Jack asks.

I watch, waiting to hear what they have to say. Because I'm pretty sure Jack is going to destroy them after what they did to his fence and cattle.

"You put a fuckin' skunk in my truck!" Granger thunders.

Surprise fills me. "I absolutely did *not* put a skunk in your truck. That's nasty."

But damn, I wish I'd thought of that. I would have absolutely put a skunk in his truck if I even knew where to get one.

Jack is surprisingly silent beside me, but I don't miss the way his lip quirks slightly.

"No, but you'd send a glitter bomb to my house, you stupid bitch," Granger spits, he's so angry.

I hold back my laughter because Poppy and I did in fact send him a homemade glitter bomb.

I deny it, because duh. "First of all, I'm *not* stupid. And second, glitter bombs are amateur. Why would I even do that? Glitter and skunks are messy." I shrug and glance over at Jack.

"Glitter bombs are what bitches would send," Jace bites out.

"Well, I guess you'd know," I shrug.

Jack looks at them. "First of all, watch your fuckin' mouth when you talk to her."

"Or what?" Granger asks looking over at Jace who moves forward, leaning up against his pool stick.

Jace looks like he wants to make a move for me, but I know he won't with Jack and Cash here. Plus, I'd destroy him. He might start something, but I'd finish it.

Cash looks like he's about to start knocking their heads together and isn't having as much fun as Jack and I are, so I decide to lighten the mood a little. "You know what? I'm just going to say it. Sharks aren't eating enough people," I say with finality.

Out of the corner of my eye, I sense that they're going to make a move towards us. I feel Jack tense, and he glances at me with a silent warning, and I give him a nonverbal response as well. We can unpack later how we're able to communicate like this, but for now, it's handy.

Before they do, Jack has Granger in a chokehold with the pool stick practically wrapped around his neck, choking him out. "Listen to me very carefully. You put my fuckin' cattle back or you'll figure out why my last name is Jessop. You remember my father? Well, what I'm capable of doing to you is in another realm than what he had in him. You nod if you fuckin' get me."

Holy shit. Badass Jack is hot.

I glance at Jace who looks like he's about to raise his pool stick to hit Jack. Before he makes contact, I'm on his back, choking him with it. "I think the fuck not." I take a page out of Jack's playbook and squeeze with all my might. Jace is surprisingly sluggish and can barely fight back. What a pansy.

Cash watches this with fascination and surprise, looking like he's ready to jump in at any moment.

Jack releases and shoves Granger, who falls to his knees, clutching his neck, sputtering.

Jack says quietly, "If you so much as look at her, never mind throw something at her or step foot on her land, I will make your life a living fucking hell."

He grabs Jace. "Same goes for you, you piece of shit. Stay off Wilder and Jessop Ranch. Trespassers will be shot."

"Next time I won't miss," I smile as I wipe my hands on my jeans.

"You heard that! That was a threat!" Jace yells as he looks around the bar, and Walker and Cash are standing, hands on their hips, watching all of this with a look of anger on their faces towards Granger and Jace.

"I didn't hear shit," someone mutters loudly.

"You hear anything?" Cash asks Walker.

Walker shakes his head "I just came out here and you were breaking my pool sticks."

"I'll get you two more," I promise with an apologetic grin.

"I'll tell you what, if I ever thought you two were perfect for each other before, well, it's crystal clear now." Walker points to Jack and me and starts wiping down the bar. "Two peas in a pod."

"Definitely," Cash mutters. "Both of them are fuckin' nuts."

"Better pick up an air freshener from the general store!" I call out to Granger and Jace as they leave.

Granger and Jace take off, still yelling as they head to their trucks. I straightened up all the stools we knocked over and set the broken pool sticks next to the bar.

Jack apologizes to Walker, and he shrugs, "Never much liked those two anyway."

"Did you really put a skunk in his truck?" I whisper to Jack back at our table as Cash walks away after dropping off our food.

"Did you glitter bomb him?" Jack asks at the same time.

"Maybe," I carefully admit with a whisper as I take a sip of my drink.

Jack laughs. "I wish I'd have thought of that."

"Where'd you get a skunk?" I ask as I take a bite of the chicken pasta. I close my eyes and sigh. Damn it's so good. I look over and give Momma Mary, the cook, a thumbs up, and she waves from the big kitchen window that divides the kitchen and bar.

"Ask your brother," Jack shrugs as he drags his bread through the Alfredo sauce.

"Where the hell did Ollie get a skunk?" I wonder aloud, surprised.

"I have no clue," he says. "You were surprisingly badass there, Wilder. I'm surprised you didn't shoot him like you tried to last time."

"What? I would never shoot anyone," I say in mock horror. "I'm a delight, Jessop."

"You know what? You remind me of Christmas lights. Complicated and a mess. But once I figure you out, you're festive and actually quite pleasant," Jack jokes.

"Did you just compare me to Christmas lights? *And* call me pleasant?" I give him a look of disdain. "Are you feeling okay?"

"Yeah, they're eating together. No, yeah. Not killing each other at all," Walker says on the phone to someone.

We both shake our heads and look at him, and he mouths, "Violet," and points to the phone, grinning.

I turn back to Jack suspiciously. "Why are you being so nice to me? And why are you in such a good mood?"

Jack looks straight ahead, guiltily.

"What did you do?"

"I need a favor," he says, leaning forward earnestly.

I raise an eyebrow. "You need a favor from *me*? I'm not giving you a kidney, Jessop," I say, returning to my pasta. "You're going to have to just die."

"Can I crash at your house for a while?" he blurts, his eyes darting around.

"No, absolutely not. And you're not staying in my barn, either," I quip.

"Cami, please. I really need to stay with you. The lodge is full of all this filming bullshit. I can't stay there. Please. Ollie still has his room there. Can't I just stay there? You won't even know I'm there," he pleads.

Yeah, right. I wouldn't be able to concentrate if Jack were in my house. Much less down the hall from me at night. He'd probably put night crawlers in my bed like he did when we were kids. I shudder at the memory.

I can't help but replay our conversations that linger like ghosts from our past.

I don't love you, Cami. Get it through your head. You're Ollie's sister. I shouldn't have kissed you. That was a mistake.

He told me that years ago. A lot has changed since then. Jack left immediately after high school and joined the military. He didn't even show up for his high school graduation. He couldn't get out of here fast enough, something he doesn't talk about to this day. And a lot has changed for both of us since then. We're both completely different people now. He might be able to come back and pretend that nothing happened, like he didn't just break my teenage heart, but he did.

Back then, it was hard for both of us, growing up on neighboring ranches. After my grandparents passed away, my parents tried running the Wilder Ranch. Jack's father hated my family; our fathers were both mean and didn't make our lives easy at home. Jack's mother died when he was around ten, so he didn't even have a mom like Ollie and I did. At least we had her to act as a buffer with our dad. But then, later on, our mom's excuses just got even bigger for our dad.

I don't know if I can do it: let him live in the same house as me. I'm not a masochist.

I sigh when I look at him. "Not happening, Jessop. Plus, I'm not sure how much longer I'll have the ranch. Someone bought it. I have to find my own place to stay."

He stares at me for a beat, his mouth still. And damn if it's not a beautiful mouth.

"Cami, I'm going to tell you something and I need for you to not get mad. Okay?" he says, tilting his head to meet my eyes.

"Okay, you're starting to freak me out, Jessop. What?"

"I bought your ranch," he says quietly.

Yeah, right.

I throw my head back and laugh. "You're an asshole. And that's not even funny." I take a bite of pasta and chuckle again. Very funny.

I laugh some more and then freeze when I see the look on his face and realize that there's truth there. The sinking sensation in my gut turns my laughter to bitterness, disbelief, and hurt.

Tears fill my eyes, my body exhausted from tidal waves of emotion pulsing through it. "What? Why would you do that?" I whisper.

I stumble from my chair and turn to leave. I turn to him, tears brimming and threatening to pour over like a dam trying to hold back the floods. My stomach pinching, I look him in the eye, noting his tortured expression and gasp out, "I thought it was just a game. I didn't think you really hated me."

I turn and dart toward my truck, stumbling as I get in, locking the doors and digging for my keys, my hands trembling. I've got to get out of here. Right now.

I jab my key into the ignition and start the truck and take off, pausing at the stop sign to buckle.

He had no right. He took the one thing from me that matters.

Of course, he'd want to stay at the house. It's his house. He probably just wants me out so he can move in. It's his now anyway.

I scramble into my kitchen and to the kitchen table where I feverishly thumb through the papers. The ranch was bought by a trust, which I understood. The name of the new owner I hadn't noticed until now stares up at me from the page: J + C Trust.

This makes sense why Weston didn't want to tell me. He knew his brother did this. He's probably the one that helped him.

What does this even mean?

I drop my forehead into my hands. Why would he do this?

Chapter 9
Jack

Never Say Never by Cole Swindell and Lainey Wilson

It's summer, sticky and golden, and Cami's standing in front of me, all attitude and sunburned shoulders, her tank top soaked with sweat from riding horses.

We're sixteen and stupid with tension.

"You ever kissed anyone?" I ask, leaning against the trunk like I'm cooler than I feel. I've got sweat dripping down my back, and I can't look at her for too long or I'll combust.

She grins. "Have *you*?"

"Plenty," I lie.

She raises a brow. "Right. All those Bridger Falls girls lining up for Jack Jessop."

I grin. "Girls love a cowboy with grit."

She steps closer, dust kicking up between us. Her braid is messy, and I swear I'm about to die right here at the base of this tree.

"I dare you to kiss me," I say.

Her eyes flash with surprise at the challenge. "What do I get if I do?"

"I'll stop running my mouth." I swallow. "Maybe."

She looks at me like I'm a wild horse she's already figured out. "You're all talk."

But then before I know it, she grabs the collar of my T-shirt, yanks me down, and kisses me.

It's fast and clumsy, and I forget how to breathe.

And when she pulls back, she smirks. "Guess you're not the only one with grit."

She walks away like she didn't just change my whole damn life.

* * *

I wake up before the sun even thinks about rising. Body sore, my mind is a mess. I had nightmares again. Sometimes they stay gone, sometimes they're pretty bad. I've just come to terms that this is what I have to live with now: struggling to sleep after my time in the military. And last night I couldn't stop thinking about Cami. The only thing that seems to clear my mind are my rides with her.

And she would never go on a ride with me today. Not after last night. She'd probably shoot me and bury me in the pasture somewhere where no one would find me. I can't get the look that she gave me out of my mind. It gutted me. She thinks I hate her and that this is a game. It couldn't be further from the truth.

The lodge is quiet because nobody is up at this insane hour. The coffee machine wheezes like it's already over this day, and I'm halfway considering crawling back into bed.

But the second my boots hit the dirt outside, the memory of

her mouth on mine at sixteen, wild, unstoppable, burns hotter than the July sun.

Damn it, Cami.

I throw myself into work. Fence needs mending. Water lines need checking. Tucker's supposed to be on mineral check this week, but he's been busy with extra wrangler tasks since we're short-handed right now.

I'm mid-shovel, sweat dripping, when Weston strolls into the barn.

"You look like hell," he says.

"Thanks. I'll work on that."

He gives me a look. "You need sleep."

I continue to shovel, ignoring him.

He leans against the stall, crossing his arms. "You hear about that old Wilder saddle?"

My shovel stills. "What saddle?"

"Her granddad's. The one he always used. Saw it in town for sale. Maggie said something to Mack, and Mack said something to Jenna, and Jenna told me."

I wipe my arm across my face. "You get it?"

"Nope. Figured you'd want to."

My heart trips. "Where is it?"

"Tack shop on Main Street. Still open 'til six."

I nod, already reaching for my hat.

Weston squints at me. "You gonna tell her?"

"I did."

Weston whistles through his teeth. "How did that go over?"

"She's Wilder mad," I mutter. "Which means she's mad forever and also not talking to me." And beneath that mad lies a whole bunch of hurt. And that's what cuts into me.

He snorts. "God, you're in deep."

"Shut up," I grumble.

"Well, you've already pissed her off buying her ranch. Better just add a saddle to it," he chuckles.

He's not wrong, but I don't want her to be pissed at me. I just want her. Period.

* * *

The shop is quiet, and the bell above the door jingles low and slow when I push inside. The place smells like leather and liniment and is full of old stories.

There's one old guy behind the counter, flipping through a magazine like he's got all day, which judging by the pace here, he probably does.

"Help you?" he asks, not looking up.

"I'm here for a saddle," I say, adjusting my hat. "One that came in on consignment a while ago. From the Wilder estate."

That gets his attention.

"Ah," he says, setting his catalog down. "That fancy old one with the tooled leather and the silver horn?"

I nod. "That's the one."

"She's a beauty." He tilts his head. "You a collector?"

"No," I say. "It belonged to someone I care about."

He squints, studies me like he's trying to figure me out. I must pass his inspection, because he jerks a thumb toward the front window. "It's still here."

The saddle sits on a low rack in the front window on top of a faded Pendleton blanket. The second I see it, something twists in my chest. The leather's aged, cracked in places, scuffed along the cantle, but it's still beautiful. Still solid. Still *his*.

Still hers. It belongs to her. Not here.

I walk up slow and run my hand over the seat, fingers tracing the tooled pattern, worn smooth in the center from years of riding. My throat tightens at the memories.

I remember being twelve, maybe thirteen, standing in the Wilder barn while Cami's granddad, Buck Wilder, taught me how to oil a saddle properly. He didn't talk much, but when he did, you listened.

"You treat your tools right, they'll never let you down," he'd said, passing me a rag and an old tin of oil. "Same goes for women and horses. Show up. Be consistent. Be kind."

He didn't mean it to be profound, but I carried that line around like armor. Especially when I'd go home and find my old man three drinks in, barking orders and breaking things. I realized early on who had the wisdom and who didn't.

Buck Wilder never yelled. He never raised a hand. Just worked hard, laughed soft, and always made sure I got a piece of pie after supper if I was hanging around.

The first time my dad saw me hanging out at the Wilder Ranch, he nearly lost it. Called me names. Said I didn't need to be playing around on someone else's land like a damn charity case.

But Buck had just patted my shoulder and said, "The boy is welcome here anytime, Jessop."

That didn't go well. But I never forgot it.

"You want it or not?" the man asks, cutting into my memory.

I nod. "Yeah. I'll take it."

He rattles off a price. It's too high, and he knows it. I know it, too. But I don't care. I count out the bills and hand over the cash. He writes up a receipt.

When I lift the saddle, it's heavier than I remember. Or maybe I'm heavier with everything it carries. My fingers curl around the horn, and I swear I can still feel the ghosts of childhood rides and slow, sleepy trail rides at sunrise.

My sunrise rides didn't start with Cami. They started with her granddad. He was so damn special to me and meant so much. He believed in me and saw something that no one else saw. I still don't know what, but I know I'll work my ass off to live up to the man he thought I could be.

I walk it out to the truck, trying not to get too damn emotional about a piece of leather, but it's not just a saddle.

It's the saddle of a man who treated me good and reminded me that there was still good in the world.

It's the first time he let me ride with her, a few years after my mom died. I was twelve and broken and trying not to show it. He had just called me over and said, *"Come on. You can go."*

I set it gently in the bed of the truck, laying an old wool blanket underneath it so it doesn't slide. My hands linger on the horn as I let out a slow breath.

Chapter 10
Cami

Good Horses by Lainey Wilson, Miranda Lambert

The back door opens, and Ollie comes in. He takes one look at my red, puffy eyes and pulls out a chair and sits. I'm waiting for the kettle for tea.

"I take it you know," he says softly.

"You knew?" I glare at him.

He shook his head. "Actually, no. He knows I don't like talking about the ranch. I put two and two together."

I harrumph. "Some best friend."

Ollie takes down two mugs and pulls out two tea bags. "Is it that bad that he's helping us?"

"Us? There is no 'us', Ollie. There's only been me in this. You and Mom vacated long ago, leaving me to figure this out. And I didn't get it figured out, did I?" I laugh, but it comes out in a sob.

"I'm here for you, Cami. I'll always help you. But this place suffocates me. I can't live here, you know that."

I nod as the teapot whistles, and he takes it off and pours the water into our mugs. I watch him, and exhaustion fills me.

"What does he want with the ranch?" I ask, softening my voice.

He shrugs. "You two need to talk about it."

"And why does he want to stay here?" I question.

Ollie sighs. "Have you seen the bullshit that he's dealing with the reality TV show? It's like a full-on circus over there. He's also never felt safe at the lodge. I don't think he's sleeping. I think, somehow, staying here feels safe to him. He's dealing with the demons of his dad and doesn't want to stay there. None of them do." He shrugs as he looks over at me.

I think about what he's saying and soften. The lodge has always felt like Jack Sr's, and it doesn't feel like a home, more like a prison. Which is fitting for where his asshole father is now. But it doesn't feel right that his kids are still living in his mess. Ollie and I know all about that. Ironic that Jack would be the one to save us.

"Also, the fact that you're not safe here with Granger and Jace pulling the crap they've been pulling. Until we know that's over, we're taking turns here. And if you even think about arguing with me on this, Cami, just don't," he says as he dunks his tea bag and watches me, giving me his best stern little brother look.

I give him a look and add honey to my tea. He's not wrong, and I've been sleeping better since they've been here. But I'm not telling him that because I have my badass reputation to protect.

"All I'm saying is, maybe go easy on Jack. He's dealing with a lot right now. Even if you don't see it right now, he means well. He would never hurt us," Ollie says as he takes a sip of his tea.

"Are you staying here tonight?" I ask as I put the rest of my scones away and get everything ready for tomorrow.

"Nope, Jack is. So don't murder him when he comes in," Ollie says with a warning look.

"Whatever," I grumble. "I'm going to bed. See you tomorrow. Love you, Ol."

I grab my mug of tea and head upstairs to my room. When my mom moved out, I took over the primary bedroom and painted everything, making it my own. It was my grandparents' bedroom before my mom had it. I painted the walls a dark green and added an accent wallpaper wall with dark gray floral patterns and a few pops of color. I have cozy lamps and a new iron bed. It's the one place that is mine in the world, other than the trailer.

For now, I guess. Until I figure out what Jessop is doing with the ranch. Maybe he can take payments. Or rent. I still can't believe he did this.

I get ready for bed and drift off to sleep. I faintly hear soft footsteps later on the stairs. I hear the shower kick on and drift back to sleep, dreaming of Jack naked in the shower. And my dreams don't disappoint.

* * *

The next morning, I get ready and head out to the barn and startle when I see Pesto and Mouse saddled up and ready, Jack standing next to them with a smile as he tips his hat to me.

I stand and stare at him, as if we're in a standoff. I want to be angry at him. I thought about it all last night between the dreams and fitful spurts of sleep. It's impossible to stay mad at Jack. I don't understand him. But I know that Ollie is right. Jack would never hurt us, and he's trying to help in his own way. Now it's a mess, and I have to figure out what I'm going to do and where I'm going to go.

"You startled me, I forgot you were staying here. At your ranch," I add and narrow my eyes.

He tilts his head. "It's still your ranch, Cami. Now, please tell me you brought coffee for both of us."

I sigh and hand over the extra thermos I brought.

Jack grins, "Forgot I was staying here, huh?"

"Whatever," I mutter as I go to get on Mouse and freeze. "Where did you get this?" I breathe, running my hand over the leather saddle.

"You know where I got it. It belongs here with you," he says as he gets on his horse and tucks the thermos into his side pocket.

"Jack," I say, my lip trembling.

In a flash, he dismounts and closes the distance between us. He cradles my cheek in his big and rough palm. He swipes my tear away and says, "Don't read into it, Cami. I'm making some shit right between us. Just take it."

He looks at me like he's wounded and there's something deep there. Something deeper than I've seen before. *Love.*

And it freaks me out. Scares the hell out of me. Jack loving me makes me feel more naked and vulnerable than I've ever felt.

"Thank you," I murmur. Confusion fills me, a warmth I can't explain that feels like love and gratitude, yet my guard is still up when it comes to Jack. He's the one person who can hold my heart in his hands and crush it if he wants.

I nod, and swipe a tear from my other eye. "I have something in my eye," I turn and get on the horse, still amazed that he got my grandpa's saddle back.

He watches me for a second then gets back on his horse and we are off, Love trotting beside us as usual. She spots them before I do and runs to the cattle running in my back pasture.

"Did you bring cattle over to stay with you, too?" I ask, confused.

He shakes his head, "I'm guessing that's the cattle Granger returned. I need to check them all over. God only knows where they've been."

I nod and ride beside him, as we count the cattle and look them over.

"Give any more thought to moving out to the ranch with your trailer?" He asks as the sun rises over the range, the colors as beautiful as ever.

"I'm still thinking about it," I say reluctantly. "I have stipulations, though."

"Of course you do," he smirks. "What are you waiting for? Let's get you moved out there."

I roll my eyes and shake my head. He's so bossy.

We ride further until we come to our tree. The tree we used to climb as kids and attempted to make a playhouse in before my dad tore it down. I gaze at the tree and then I see it. The worn carving in the wide trunk. J + C in the base of it.

"The trust," I whisper. "How did you do this?"

"I used my inheritance from my mom. She would have liked this. She liked you, Cami. She loved your grandparents, too."

I suck in my breath at hearing this. I loved his mom, she was such a nice woman. I was young when she passed away, but everyone in town new her and loved her. She was the one good thing about Jessop ranch. It all went to hell after she died. She had life insurance that went into trusts for all the kids. Jenna told me that a long time ago. It was the one thing that their dad had no control over and couldn't use as leverage over them.

The fact that Jack used that to save our ranch makes me love him even more. And feel even more confused. I'm questioning so much right now. Even a ride with Mouse can't work out all these feelings like they usually can. There's a lot to unpack here.

He swallows and looks away. Then he says softly, "The ranch is yours, Cami. I couldn't let a developer take it from you."

"What are you going to do with it?" I ask softly as my fingers trace the carving on the saddle.

"What do you think I want?" he clips, a hurt look in his eyes. "You're a smart woman, Cami. I'll let you figure that out."

He turns and rides off back towards his side of the property. His other side, I guess.

And I'm left even more confused than ever.

But I know what I want him to want. Me.

* * *

I get to my coffee trailer and someone spray painted on the side: Dumb Bitch.

How original, I think, rolling my eyes as I get out of my truck. This is irritating as hell, and I'm so pissed at the harassment.

"Good morning," I say to dubious-looking customers and open the trailer. I glance around and nothing appears to be out of order inside the truck, at least. The outside is nothing a pressure washer can't take off.

"What happened?" Violet asks, looking worried as she walks up and examines the trailer with me.

"Not sure, but we're going to keep making coffee, and I'll figure it out later."

And when I say figure it out, I mean handle it.

I have a good idea who did this. And I have a plan to take care of it.

* * *

I washed all the paint off earlier, parked my truck a block away, and waited in my trailer in the dark for them to come back. And they didn't disappoint.

They pull in and park, right in front of the new trail cam facing the trailer Poppy and I set up earlier that afternoon. I watch as Granger and Jace get out of the truck, this time with bats in their hands. I listen as Granger grunts, "Gonna teach this dumb bitch a lesson."

Yeah, we'll see about that. As Granger raises his bat to smash one of my trailer windows, I push open the door and hose down his face with bear spray. He squeals and jumps, dropping the bat. Jace rears back in surprise in the dark, cowering.

That's when I turn and hit him square in the face with the spray as well. I'm not even sorry when it gets in his mouth. Actually? I'm thrilled. Serves them right. These windows on my trailer are vintage and hard to find, impossible to replace, and too pretty for idiots like Jace and Granger to go smashing.

"You stupid bitch!" Jace screams, clutching his face.

"Oh, I thought it was 'dumb bitch.' You want seconds?" I snap, holding the canister up again.

He jumps back like I just threatened him with a chainsaw, and honestly, it makes my night. Good. Serves him right for trying to destroy my business.

Granger takes off down the street like his pants are on fire, Jace stumbling after him, both using their shirts to wipe their eyes and gagging like I sprayed them with acid instead of glorified pepper mist. They left their truck behind. Idiots.

I roll my eyes, lock up the trailer, and stroll over like I've got all the time in the world. Even better? They left the keys in the ignition. I yank the keys out and tuck them into my back pocket. A little souvenir. Hope he has a spare.

Granger's truck still reeks of skunk, so strong I have to turn my head to keep from gagging.

"How anyone drives that thing without permanently losing brain cells is beyond me," I mutter. Glad to see that Granger is driving around in the consequences of his actions.

I lock up the trailer and head home to get a few hours of sleep, pleased with my results. I can't wait to show Poppy how that went down. The trail cam was her idea. She's not going to even believe it.

I might even take it to Sheriff Matthews. I haven't decided yet. I haven't found them to be much help. When people started stealing and poking around my ranch, he said there wasn't much he could do. The law hasn't been on my side, and I'm tired of asking for help and not getting it.

I pull into my driveway at the Wilder Ranch, and Jack is standing in front of the barn, waiting, his arms crossed. He's shirtless, in jeans, barefoot, and his hair is tousled. And damn if he doesn't look so sexy right now. I squint at him and realize he looks really mad right now. But that just so happens to be sexy, too.

"Good evening, Jack," I call cheerfully as I exit the truck, locking the door. Can never be too sure these days. Skunks appear out of thin air.

"Where have you been?" he asks, arms crossed, looking pissed.

"Jack, we are not at the point where we know each other's comings and goings." I yawn and stroll past him, and he reaches out and catches my arm, spinning me to face him.

He leans down and says in my ear in his sexy rough voice, "Where. Have. You. Been?"

The air whooshes out of my chest, and heat pools through my body at his touch.

"Okay, okay. Granger and Jace tried to break the windows out in my trailer, and I taught them a lesson."

He opens his mouth and then closes it. He stares at me for a moment, his expression unreadable. "And just how did you teach them a lesson?"

"Bear spray," I add cheerfully.

He looks up at the sky like he's looking for patience, and I'm not sure what's happening right now, but he's still holding my arm, and it feels hot under his touch. In fact, I wonder what it would feel like to have those hands all over my body and not just holding my arm firmly. My dreams were full of Jack last night and the night before, and having him under the same roof isn't helping.

"You're not my dad," I scoff. "You don't get to tell me what to do."

"You want a daddy?" he says, edging closer.

Oh, shit.

"Because I'll be whatever I need to be to keep you safe." His voice drops lower, his gaze darker.

Why are my panties so soaked? Holy shit, that was hot.

"Come on," he grunts as he guides me gently towards the house and up the porch stairs.

Angry Jack is sexy. That's what I'm taking from this evening. I like sexy angry Jack.

* * *

The next morning I come downstairs to Jack, bent down, messing with my coffee maker, trying to figure it out. He looks frustrated, and he glances over at me and says, "What's the secret, Cami? Just tell me. Why does it taste so good?"

I chuckle and move beside him, reaching into a jar I have tucked off to the side. I hold it up. "Cinnamon. Just a pinch."

He sighs with relief. "Whatever it is, I need it."

I suck in my breath when he says that and smile as I finish making the coffee.

"What are you smiling about?" he asks.

"Nothing. Just making coffee." I hum.

"You scared the shit out of me last night," he says softly.

"You don't have to worry about me," I say confidently. "I can take care of myself. Have been all my life."

"You *can* take care of yourself," Jack says, calm and maddeningly reasonable. "But that doesn't mean you have to."

I sigh and cross my arms. "Jack, those idiots carry bats. I carry bear spray and a meat tenderizer."

He blinks like I just spoke in tongues. "Wait, why a meat tenderizer?"

I reach into my tote bag and pull out the massive orange canister like it's a trophy. "Industrial strength. This baby's meant for grizzlies. Works just as well on dumbasses named Jace and Granger."

Jack stares at me as if he's visibly concerned for the population of Wyoming.

"The meat tenderizer is aluminum. Spiked. Lives under my truck seat. You never know when someone needs tenderizing."

His mouth opens. Closes. Then he drags his hand down his face. "You are... completely unhinged."

I grin. "No, I'm just a woman who refuses to be messed with and has excellent aim."

He's still staring at me like he's equal parts turned on and afraid. "You know, normal people carry pepper spray, right?"

"Pepper spray doesn't stop a bear or Granger. You see, Jack, Some people were put on this planet to evolve. And Granger is a reminder of what it looks like if you don't."

He laughs, deep and rough, and mutters under his breath, "God help me."

The coffee finishes brewing, and I top off our thermos.

"I don't know if I'm more scared *of* you or *for* you right now," he admits.

The back door opens, and my mom walks in uninvited, and she surveys the kitchen, taking in Jack standing next to me as we get our coffees ready.

And this is how I know it's not going to be a good morning.

"Well, aren't you two just cozy," she remarks as she glares at Jack and me.

I glare back at my mom. "You know, you should knock when you come over to someone's house. You know, a house you don't live in."

"Well, you don't live here, either," she says as she puts her hands on her hips and stares at me with a look of disappointment. Her usual look for me. I'm used to it by now. I could never do anything right in her eyes. My brother can do anything he wants, though. Me? I get a master's degree, work at the family's ranch while starting my own business, and yet she still finds things about me to pick apart. She's never supported me. And the fact that she's here uninvited starting shit this early in the morning is pissing me off. I haven't had enough sleep or coffee yet for this.

"What?" I clip as I glare at her in frustration.

"What is *he* doing here?" she huffs. "And why can't you just walk away from this place like we did? No, you have to stay here and be the savior. Save it," she mimics in her mean voice.

"Do you have a reason for coming here?" I ask, my voice rising.

Jack sets the coffee down and reaches for my arm. I glance down at it and back at her.

"Actually, yes," she sighs. "Do you know anything about two men who were pepper-sprayed last night? They came into the hospital claiming that you assaulted them. I swear, Cami..." She shakes her head and sighs again for good measure.

I snort with laughter, "Oh, really? That's what they said?"

"Really," she says dryly. "Why would you even do a thing like that?"

"You know, Mom, it's funny you'll take the word of two strangers over your own daughter."

Jack is tense next to me, but he says nothing, just watching all of this unfold. But somehow, oddly, I feel like he has my back. Weirdly, come to think of it, he's always had my back. But I've learned that people have your back until they don't. Then you're left all alone again. This is why I trust no one.

"I wish you'd let this all go. I don't even know what *you're* doing here," she says as she glares at Jack.

I can't wait for her to finally hear that he bought the ranch.

She continues, not even bothering to read the room. "You need to find a place in town, start over. Stop squatting here at the ranch. Sometimes things just come to an end, Cami. When are you going to let this go?"

I glare at her, thinking what a disappointment she would be to my grandpa. I think about the memories I made with him at the ranch before he died. I remember his promise on the back porch not to sell the ranch. He'd told me that my momma would try the first chance she got, and he was almost right. Only she ran it into the ground, then let the bank take it. She really screwed it up.

Jack clears his throat and glances at me and to the door. We have to get our sunrise ride in.

"You know what, Mom," I say, steering her out the door and onto the porch as Jack pulls the door behind him, locking it. "We have to go."

"I'm not done talking to you," she sputters.

"It's time you know the truth, Mom. Jack bought the ranch."

"What?" she roars at Jack.

Jack stares at her and says firmly, "I think you need to go, Teresa."

She puts a finger in my face. "Your grandpa is turning in his grave for letting a Jessop in this house."

"Oh, yeah? Well, Grandpa is the one who welcomed Jack to this ranch in the first place. He loved Jack. And you ruined that after he died by getting in stupid feuds with Jack Sr," I say angrily. "Why do you even care? You wanted to sell it, now it's sold. You don't get to come back here and act like you're the victim."

"If you want to keep that finger, get it out of her face," Jack clips, coming between my mom and me.

She stands back. "You are trash! Just like your daddy! And you..." She shakes her head in disgust and turns and walks to her car, not finishing that sentence.

"Mom," I yell towards her back. She turns, and I call out, "For the record, it was bear spray, not pepper spray, and they were vandalizing my business, not that you care!"

He puts an arm around my shoulders and steers me towards the barn. "Let's go."

One thing I've noticed about Jack is that he and I can spar. But if anyone gets near me, he goes practically feral. We may be enemies, but he protects me. So, what does that make us, exactly?

That's the million-dollar question, isn't it?

Chapter 11
Jack

Ode To Bourbon by Treaty Oak Revival

There are good mornings, and then there's "your sister just handed you legally binding documents to sign for a reality TV show you never wanted to be on" kind of mornings.

Guess which one I'm having?

I scowl at the stack of papers in my hands, flipping through them like there might be an escape clause hidden somewhere between "Rancher agrees to participate in all scheduled romantic activities" and "Rancher will not abandon the show under any circumstances."

"Jenna," I say slowly, like I'm explaining something to a very stubborn horse, "there's a clause in here that says I have to participate in group bonding with the contestants."

Jenna, completely unbothered, sips her coffee. "Yep. There's going to be a lot of that. Weston already looked everything over and signed his, too."

"There's also a clause that says I cannot be verbally aggressive toward contestants." I groan.

"Correct."

I narrow my eyes. "Define aggressive."

She tilts her head. "Calling someone a raging pain in your ass would probably count."

I let out a low groan, dropping my head back. "Then we have a problem, because I call Tucker that at least four times a day."

"Yeah, well, try flirting with the contestants instead."

I choke on air. "Try what?"

Jenna grins, too pleased with herself. "Flirting, Jack. You know, being nice? Smiling? Engaging in lighthearted banter instead of looking like you're planning the fastest way to escape?"

Tucker chooses this moment to wander into the barn, grinning like an idiot. "Is Jack getting a lesson on how to seduce a woman? Hold on, let me give him notes."

I glare. "Shouldn't you be working?"

Tucker shrugs. "Weston told me to help get the meat delivery ready, but he started doing it himself with his 'determined older brother' energy, and it was stressing me out. So, I came to watch your suffering instead."

Jenna flips through another page in the contract, ignoring both of us. "Oh, and before I forget, I ran into Cami this morning."

That gets my attention real quick. I try to keep my face neutral as I toss the contract on the table. "Oh, yeah?"

Jenna smirks. Like she knows something I don't. "I was picking up a coffee. Funny, she mentioned you've been staying at her place. She also doesn't seem to like the idea of you finding a wife."

Something tugs at my chest, something stupid and hopeful that I have no business feeling.

I fold my arms, trying to keep my voice casual. "Oh, yeah?"

Jenna leans against a stall door, watching me too closely. "Very interesting, the dynamic between you two. Don't let it get in the way of the show. We have a job to do here."

Tucker lets out a low whistle. "Ohhh, does someone have a little Cami problem?"

I shoot him a warning look. "Shut up."

Jenna laughs. "Oh, please. You think I don't notice the way you two look at each other? It's like watching two feral barn cats fight daily."

Tucker leans against the wall. "So, are we just gonna ignore the fact that Jack's been in love with Cami since we were kids?"

I grab a nearby rope and toss it at his head.

Tucker dodges, laughing. "Nice try, lover boy. How's life at your new ranch?"

"It's still Cami's ranch," I reply, not taking the bait.

Jenna shakes her head, clearly enjoying my misery. "Anyway, I also may have let the cat out of the bag about the show over at Steamy Sips this morning. Everyone in town knows now."

I freeze and close my eyes. "Great."

Jenna beams. "I told Maggie. Figured it was best to get people excited, make it a whole event."

I stare at her, saying nothing.

"Now everyone is invested. This is what we wanted. We wanted the town to trust us and hopefully forget our father. This is the perfect distraction," she says, looking excited.

"She's right," Tucker adds. "You should've seen the group of ranch wives down at the Harvest & Honey plotting ways to get their nieces and granddaughters on the show as extras. You're a hot commodity, Jack. Who knew?"

I groan, rubbing my temples. This is hell. This is actually hell. I live in hell.

"Look at it this way," Jenna says, grinning. "The whole town is rooting for us now, especially you."

I drag my hand down my face. "Fantastic. That's exactly what I wanted, to be the town's damn entertainment."

Tucker claps me on the back, grinning from ear to ear. "Come on, big bro. This is gonna be fun. There will be beautiful women, and you're making money for the ranch. Don't be such an ungrateful bastard."

I shoot him a withering glare. "You know what's fun? Running a ranch without a camera crew filming me trying to find a wife. I don't need a wife. I need to get this ranch up and going. Why couldn't we have just made a reality show about that?"

Jenna grins wider. "Too late now, Jack. The contracts are all signed. Plus, no one wants to see how a ranch actually works. They want to see the highlights and the drama. And there will be drama with you, I have no doubt."

I look around at my siblings, one too smug, one too entertained, and let out a long, slow breath.

I am so, so screwed.

* * *

"I don't know, man," Ollie says, scratching the back of his neck as we stand in front of Steamy Sips in the dead of night. "Moving my sister's coffee trailer while she's asleep feels like a dangerous game. She always wants to kill you. But I don't want to be on that list."

Walker smirks. "You're just scared of her. She won't want to kill me. I feed her dinner."

Ollie narrows his eyes. "You're damn right I'm scared of her.

Have you met my sister? That woman holds grudges like an Olympic sport. I heard about what she did to Granger and Jace."

Walker shrugs. "Those bastards had it coming."

"Exactly," I say as I tap the side of the trailer. "Which is why this is necessary. When she's out at the ranch with the trailer, she'll be safer. No one is going to fuck with her on the Jessop Ranch."

Ollie lets out a low whistle. "When are you going to admit you have a thing for her?"

I ignore him and start unlocking the hitch. "I am not admitting anything."

"She's going to kill you."

"Details," I say with a shrug. "She'll be grateful we moved it for her so she doesn't have to."

Walker chuckles. "Just so we're clear, when she sets you on fire in retaliation, I'm gonna say I told you so."

I wave a hand. "Shut up and help me."

Between the three of us, it doesn't take long to secure everything and hook up the trailer and drive it straight out to Jessop Ranch, parking it right in front of the barn like it was always meant to be there. We even set up her picnic tables.

To top it off, we left a wooden sign in town where the trailer was:

"Steamy Sips has been temporarily relocated to the Jessop Ranch and is open for business. — Management"

And then? We wait for her to kill us.

* * *

The next morning I hear her before I see her. I purposely left and went over to the Jessop Ranch before she got up. I skipped the ride and got started because I knew she'd be livid. Several regulars claim they texted her and said they were waiting at her trailer at the ranch, so she knew it was moved.

The distant roar of an engine and the fury in the way tires grind gravel have the early morning crowd of nosy townsfolk gathered like they've been waiting for this exact moment. And she is understandably mad. But hopefully, when she sees the supportive crowd that has gathered, she'll understand.

Maggie has already pulled up a lawn chair, and a lot of townsfolk have formed a line next to her trailer, waiting for her to get here and make coffee. Some have even brought her decorations and flowers. I love seeing the town like that she's here.

Cami's old red truck comes barreling down the ranch road, kicking up dust like she's about to run me over on principle.

She screeches to a halt, slams the door, and stomps up to where I'm waiting next to the trailer, turning to face me with fire in her eyes. "What. The. Hell?"

I cross my arms, casual as can be, and smile. "Morning, Wilder."

"Don't you give me that, Jessop." She waves wildly at her trailer. "Why is my coffee trailer parked here?"

I lift a brow and say, "Temporary relocation like we discussed."

Cami leans in and glares. "You stole my trailer. I never agreed to move it out here."

"You were thinking about it," I shrug.

Walker, who's leaning against a fence post, grins. "Relocated. Sounds more official."

"You—" Cami makes a strangled sound, pointing a finger at me like she's debating if murder is worth the legal hassle. "I cannot believe you did this."

"You're welcome," I say, smiling. "I just helped with your decision. Plus, look at all the people waiting for their coffee."

She throws her hands in the air. "Oh my God, I hate you."

"You really don't, though."

"I DO."

The growing crowd of customers chuckles, thoroughly enjoying the show.

"Cami, honey," Maggie calls from her lawn chair. "We're all really glad to see you out here at the Jessop Ranch."

"Traitors!" Cami huffs, glaring at the crowd.

Mrs. Fernandez shrugs and winks at Jack. "Fresh coffee and cinnamon rolls. What were we supposed to do? We go where the trailer goes."

Cami turns back to me, fuming. "Ballsy, even for you, Jessop."

I grin. "Nah, I think it's great."

Cami gasps and holds up a finger. "Oh, you absolute—"

Before she can finish, a rancher from town steps forward, asking for his coffee. Cami glances over and sees him carrying a bag of Jessop Ranch meat that he'd purchased and a pamphlet for Jessop Ranch hanging out of his front pocket, and she softens. She knows this is already helping the ranch, her trailer being out here. We've already made a ton of meat sales this morning while people waited for their coffee.

"So, Jack," he says, nodding toward Cami. "What's she gonna do when you find yourself a wife on that TV show?"

The air shifts with the unspoken words he's not saying.

My jaw locks so fast I almost hear it click. The easy grin I've been wearing? Gone.

Because suddenly, the thought of parading a bunch of women around this ranch, pretending like one of them could be my future, pretending like they could fit here—

That doesn't sit right at all.

Especially not when Cami's standing right there, arms crossed, hazel eyes sharp, waiting to see how I react.

I clear my throat, rolling my shoulders. "We'll cross that bridge when we get there."

"Uh-huh," the rancher says, amused. "Better hope your future wife likes coffee, 'cause looks like she's got competition."

The crowd erupts into laughter.

I grumble under my breath, shaking my head, but I can't stop my eyes from flicking back to Cami, who's suddenly looking anywhere but at me. But I don't miss the slight blush to her face.

Huh. Interesting.

Later on, Cami is busy as can be, and our meat sales skyrocket even more. We are completely sold out of all our meat from the freezers, and we have a ton of future orders. Tessa and Hank have hired a dozen new hands, and we're going to be busy getting everything ready. And this is just the benefit from her being here one day. Having people like Maggie and Cami endorse us and bring traffic out here has worked wonders.

I've even had inquiries about horse training, which is usually my thing. Weston handles the sales, Tucker handles the day-to-day ranch work, and I train and breed horses. If we keep this up, it just might work. I just have to get through this ridiculous reality show. I will admit that the show will bring many more eyes to the ranch and help us too. So, I'm doing it. But I hate every second of this. But having Cami here makes it ten times better.

By noon, things are slowing down at Steamy Sips, and Cami seems to be settling in nicely. Ollie and I set up planters full of flowers in front of her trailer and add half a dozen more tables and a tent under Cami's watchful eye, but I don't miss the approval in her eyes. Which is a good thing because it's been packed, and the tent was needed. Her coffee is just that good. People will go where she is.

Maggie, Mack, Poppy, and Violet all sit at the table and

wave when they see me heading that way. Weston and Tucker must have the same idea because they're leaned up against the trailer talking to everyone as well.

I walk up and hear Maggie say, "That much tension? I give it a month."

Weston chimes in, "A week. Max."

"Y'all are weak," Tucker drawls. "They'll be making out by Friday."

"What are you guys doing?" I ask, but I already have a feeling that I know.

"Oh, just speculating on you and Cami," Maggie says casually with a grin like it's public knowledge.

It's been hours, and Cami is still going like she's powered by spite and caffeine.

Which, to be fair, she probably is, but that doesn't stop me from watching her work.

She moves like she's been doing this her whole life, slinging coffee orders like a professional, laughing with customers, handling the morning rush like it's nothing, even though I know damn well she was probably up at some ungodly hour baking fresh pastries.

She should look exhausted and be worn out, running on fumes. But instead, she's glowing. This is Cami in her element.

Face flushed, hair coming loose from whatever half-assed bun she twisted it into, flour still dusting the edge of her apron. She moves fast, sure-footed, sharp as ever, serving up coffee and baked goods that are to die for.

She's the most exasperating woman I know. And the best woman I know. And somehow, she's also the most beautiful damn thing I've ever seen. This is exactly why I need to focus on literally anything else.

Unfortunately, I don't get that luxury because right then, Cami leans down through the window of her trailer, eyes glinting like she's up to something. Soft music plays in the background, something slow and twangy, a stark contrast to the murderous look on her face.

I cross my arms, watching her carefully. "Are you selling coffee or plotting my murder?"

Cami doesn't even hesitate. "Two things can be true, Jessop."

Tucker, sitting nearby with his coffee, grins like a damn idiot. "This is fun. Keep going."

I exhale, pinching the bridge of my nose and glare at him. "I should've left you at the feed store when I had the chance."

Tucker shrugs. "Yeah, but then you'd make me miss out on all this." He waves a hand between me and Cami like we're some kind of live-action soap opera he subscribed to for free.

Cami grins at Tucker, then turns back to me, resting her arms on the counter, and glares. "Stealing a trailer is a felony, by the way."

Then she looks at Tucker and over to me, "How's your very own bustling empire?"

I look around. Sure enough, people are everywhere. Weston and Jenna are chatting it up with locals, and it feels like we actually have a chance now.

Farmers, ranchers, tourists, and even a couple of old-timers who usually grumble about anything new in town. They're all here, sipping coffee, eating pastries, and talking.

The Jessop Ranch hasn't seen this many visitors in years. And damn it, she brought this here.

I roll my jaw, giving her a look. "I'll admit it's pretty amazing. Thank you."

Cami gasps, pressing a hand to her chest. "Oh my God. Did you just thank me?"

"I did," I admit with a grin. At this point, I don't even have any crap to give her. She's worked damn miracles just being here today for just one day. We've had so much positive interaction with the town today that this has been a godsend. I know a miracle when I see one.

She laughs, shaking her head before grabbing another cup to fill. The sound of her laugh settles somewhere deep in my chest.

Tucker leans back in his chair, grinning. "So, Cami, you gonna be here full-time now?"

She glances at me, her expression unreadable. "Still thinking about it."

But I know that look. She's staying.

Chapter 12
Cami

Pretty Little Poison by Warren Zeiders

When I see my mother's car pull up at Wilder Ranch again, I groan and roll my eyes, not sure what she could possibly want this time.

She steps out, looking around like the very land that her family has owned for generations that she stands on offends her, arms crossed over her scrub top, and sighs in great disappointment like she's about to deliver me another lecture.

"Oh, Cami," she says, her voice already sharp with disapproval as she slams the car door shut. "Ollie says I owe you an apology. I guess I should apologize."

I exhale, gripping the reins of my horse, Mouse in my hands and say dryly, "Nice apology, Mom."

I stopped trying to get her approval when I was in high school. And I definitely stopped taking her crap here recently.

She walks up, surveying the now mostly empty ranch, and then she gives me that look—then says, "You're really doing this?" she asks, gesturing vaguely. "Still playing pretend out here with the Jessops?"

I stiffen. "It's not pretend, Mom. This is our family's home."

She lets out a dramatic sigh, stepping closer. "Cami, honey. You're working yourself to death on a ranch we don't even own. Cut your losses. Get out of here. Do something real with your life. Your brother has a real job. I don't know why you don't at least try."

A real job. Wow. A low blow, even for her. As I watch her, she really believes this.

The words hit way too hard, although I've heard some version of them my entire life.

I turn to her, crossing my arms. "I am doing something with my life. And I do have a real job."

Mom lifts a skeptical brow. She's either heading to work or coming off a shift at the hospital, where she works as a nurse. When she left the ranch and moved to town last year and let the ranch go, we stopped talking as much. Not that we've ever been close, but lately it's been downright contentious. She doesn't even try to hide her disappointment.

I feel my frustration boil over. "You wouldn't know that, though, would you? Because you've never even come to get coffee from my trailer. Not once."

A beat of silence.

And then she shrugs and looks away like I don't matter. And that's it. I'm done. That hurts. I don't argue. I don't try to convince her that the business that I've built is amazing. I just let her stand there in her judgment while I turn on my heel, throw my leg over my horse, and ride off into the pasture.

I leave her standing there in the driveway in front of the barn, and I don't care. I know we haven't seen eye to eye for a long time. Probably most of my life. I've always been closer to my grandparents, and when we lost them, things got really bad between my mom and my dad. That's when he tried to take over the ranch, and he ran it into the ground. He was selling off the ranch's equipment, embezzling money, and draining the bank accounts.

But for me, it has always run deeper. I love this place deep in my soul, and it's the only place I've ever truly felt peace. While riding in these pastures, I keep up with my grandmother's garden behind our house. It's gotten smaller in recent years, but I still keep it going.

The sun is just starting to dip below the mountains, stretching golden light across the fields, casting long shadows over the land I know better than my own reflection.

I ride slowly, letting my horse take me wherever it feels right. The familiar rhythm of his hooves against the dry earth steadies me, grounds me.

To anyone else, Wilder Ranch is a mess. The fences need fixing. The barn leans slightly like it's trying to decide whether to hold strong or give in. *Same, barn. Same.*

The pastures could use attention, more time, and more care than I can give on my own.

But to me? This is home. I see what it was, what it is, and what it could be.

And my vision for this place is something I get so excited about every time I think about it. I can't help but feel giddy when I think about where I see this place five years from now. Now that the Jessops own the ranch, I'm not sure where everything stands. Maybe Jack will let me be a business partner or something like that.

When I think of the future here, I see kids riding horses and going on trail rides for the first time, their laughter spilling across the hills. I see families gathering for fall festivals, hayrides, and bonfires with steaming mugs of cider warming cold fingers. I see our community, the kind that doesn't give up on people just because they've had hard years. They've proven time and time again that they can be forgiving and supportive of our neighbors.

I see a future here. One that isn't finished yet. And maybe Jack Jessop was crazy to take on this mess. This land? This ranch? It's in my bones.

And I'll be damned if I let anyone, even my mother, convince me it isn't worth fighting for.

A sharp breeze sweeps across the fields, cooling the dried tears on my face, and that's when I hear the faint sound of hooves behind me. I don't turn around. I already know who it is.

Jack rides up beside me, silent as ever, his horse Pesto keeping an easy pace beside mine.

We don't say anything. We just ride.

The quiet between us feels less like distance, more like understanding. Like maybe he knows that I need a minute, that maybe for once, we don't have to fill the space with bickering or jabs or stubborn pride.

I sniff, wiping my sleeve across my face, embarrassed to have been caught crying.

Jack doesn't say a word about it. Just keeps riding. And for some ridiculous, infuriating reason, that makes my throat burn all over again.

I finally break the silence. "My mom thinks I should leave."

Jack doesn't react, doesn't even look at me, just scans the horizon as we ride. "Sounds like your mom has a lot of opinions."

I let out a sharp, humorless laugh. "That's an under-statement."

Another stretch of silence. And then, quietly, he asks, "Do you want to leave?"

I turn my head toward him, the words instantly, fiercely there before I can even think. "No."

Jack finally meets my gaze, his eyes steady, like he already knew the answer before he even asked. He gives a small nod, then looks back out over the land.

We keep riding.

For a while, there's nothing but the sound of hooves, the wind, and the occasional creak of leather as one of us shifts in the saddle.

Maybe it's the way the sunset hits his profile, or maybe it's the fact that he's here, riding beside me, but I suddenly feel like I need to lighten the mood before I start sobbing again.

I clear my throat, tilting my head at him. "I assume you're here to offer some grand, wise, life-changing advice?"

Jack snorts. "I was actually just here to make sure you weren't planning on burning the place down out of spite."

I huff a laugh, shaking my head. "Not today. Don't worry, your new ranch is safe."

"Well, that's a relief. Would've been a damn shame," he says, looking at me.

I glance over at him, squinting. "Careful, Jack. People might hear you and think you care."

Jack sighs, dramatic as hell. "Don't make it weird."

I grin, the tightness in my chest loosening just a little. "Too late."

Jack smirks, shaking his head. "See, this is why I usually just stick to pissing you off."

"Oh, trust me, Jessop, you're still pissing me off."

"Good," he says easily. "Wouldn't want you getting soft on me."

I roll my eyes, but things feel lighter now between us. The weight of the day, of everything, isn't gone.

But it's easier to carry with Jack riding beside me. But I'll be damned if I tell him that. I steal another glance at him, watching the way he looks out over the ranch, the way he rides like he belongs here, like maybe he always has.

And then, because I can't help myself, I smirk and say, "Hey, don't you have a wife to go find?"

Jack smirks, eyes glinting with something dangerous. "You keep talking like that, Cami, and people might start thinking you're jealous."

I grin. "What? Isn't there a whole group of women arriving soon to fight for the honor of becoming Mrs. Jack Jessop, Jr?"

Jack arches a brow. "That's cute. Keep talking, and I'll sign you up for the show."

My stomach does something stupid, a little jolt, a flicker of something annoyingly close to panic.

Because for half a second my brain supplies the image of me standing on that ridiculous show, wearing some frilly dress, lined up with a bunch of women while Jack, smug, infuriating, too-damn-good-looking Jack Jessop stands there judging us like some prize cattle auction.

Nope. Absolutely not. I force a casual shrug, even though my ears feel too hot, and I suddenly can't look directly at him. "Wow, Jessop. Didn't know you were so desperate to marry me."

Jack just smirks, slow and easy, like he knows exactly what he's doing, like he can see right through me, and that only makes me want to kick him off his horse. "You've always hated your last name. You can have mine."

So, I do what I do best. I double down. I tilt my head, all mock innocence. "Wait, does this mean I'd get to be your wife in the end?" I clutch my chest, gasping. "Jack, are you proposing?"

Jack groans, dragging a hand down his face. "I should've just let you cry in peace."

I grin, victorious, but deep down, my pulse is still kicking up dust.

I laugh, letting the sound fill the air between us, and for the first time all day, I feel like I might actually be okay.

* * *

After a long afternoon of baking, I've showered and taken a two-hour nap that still wasn't long enough to erase today's annoyance of my mother coming by and acting toxic, so I grab my phone and dial Violet.

She picks up before the first ring even finishes.

"Oh, thank God," she breathes. "I was just about to call you. Are we in damage control or denial?"

"I guess both. I need a girls' night," I say, my voice flat, exhausted, done.

I can practically hear the grin in her voice. "Oh, hell yes. I'll make it happen. I'll grab the girls, and we'll come over tonight."

* * *

It starts normal enough at the house. A few drinks, some light venting, a lot of eye-rolling about my mother's visit.

The thing is, my mom isn't a bad person. In fact, everyone loves her around here. We just have never been close. And she's been through a lot. I'll give her that. But she just doesn't support me like she does my brother, and I don't know why. I could sit here and say it's not fair, etc. But guess what? I've learned life isn't fair. And whenever I decided that I was going to roll with the punches, life got better. Not easier. But better.

But then, somewhere between shot number three and four, my carefully held-in feelings explode.

"She's never even tried my coffee!" I shout, slamming my glass down as Violet and Poppy gasp dramatically.

Poppy shakes her head, scandalized. "I mean, that is criminal."

Violet points a finger. "I bet she drinks hospital cafeteria coffee and that's what she deserves."

I groan, dropping my head onto the table. "I'm just. I'm so done."

Poppy slams her hands down. "Then we are officially doing the responsible thing."

Violet nods. "We're getting wasted."

Somewhere in the mix of bad ideas and questionable choices, we end up going out for a walk, and I spill all of my dreams of the ranch to them, and they wholeheartedly support me and are excited.

Violet says, "I'll share it everywhere when you're ready for me to."

Poppy pulls me in for a hug, "It's going to be amazing!"

Maggie had to head home because she had work in the morning and made us promise to behave. "Bye!" we call and wave.

We had no plans to behave. Because, in our collective drunken wisdom, we decide we're going to sneak up on Jack and find out what he really plans to do with Wilder Ranch.

Poppy stumbles up the driveway. "I'm going to confront him."

Violet grins. "Yeah and see what he plans to do. He can't just buy up your ranch and be your sexy boss."

I point a wobbly finger. "He moved my coffee trailer, too." Huh, I don't remember my house being so far from the driveway.

Poppy face plants in the grass.

Love runs over and licks her face, looking at all of us with concern and confusion. "Come here, baby," I murmur.

We stop dramatically, staring at the glowing lights of the house.

Violet narrows her eyes. "What's the game plan?"

Poppy hiccups. "Did we have one?"

I wave my hand. "We're about to make choices, and not necessarily good ones."

And then, before we can process what's happening, the front door swings open.

And Jack steps outside. Shirtless. Jeans slung low on his hips, crossing his arms over his chest. Looking entirely too damn good.

The three of us freeze.

Violet whispers, "Wow."

Poppy nods, still propped up on her elbows. "Yep. Wow."

I squint, swaying slightly. "Damn it."

Jack watches us with an amused expression. "What are you three doing?"

"Ooooh, he has a daddy voice," Poppy hiccups. We all break into laughter.

Violet nudges me. "You're the leader. Say something."

I blink up at Jack, too drunk to come up with a good excuse. So, I say the first thing that pops into my head. "Your abs are distracting."

Poppy chokes on her own spit and howls with laughter, smacking the ground.

Violet cackles and falls over next to Poppy.

Jack drags a hand over his jaw, exhaling slowly, his abs tightening with the movement. "Do you need a closer look, Cami?" But the way his eyes flick down to my lips says he might just want me to look closer.

This causes Poppy and Violet to continue with laughter.

And that's how we ended up in the kitchen, drinking water like it was a court-ordered punishment.

The kitchen is too bright, my head is too heavy, and the sound of a truck rumbles in the distance, signaling that my partners-in-crime are about to escape.

We watch out the window as Walker and Ollie climb out of Walker's truck, looking like they find this funny. They come in the house, looking around in amusement at the scene. Walker strolls over to Violet and pulls her in for a kiss and hug.

"Ladies," Walker drawls, grinning like the smug pain in the ass he is.

Ollie stands grinning with his hands in his pockets. "Need a ride, Poppy?"

Violet mutters something unintelligible as she smiles at him, only causing Walker to grin even more.

Poppy, still looking like she just survived a natural disaster ignores Ollie raises a hand. "Hey, Jack! I'm really sorry again about disturbing you and your abs!"

Jack lifts an amused brow.

Poppy grins sleepily, still wobbling on her feet. "Hey, at least I didn't weld your truck door shut."

Jack snorts, shaking his head. "Thanks for that." He grins, which tells me that this ridiculous man is actually enjoying this chaos.

Ollie holds Poppy's shoulder, steering her outside and toward the truck and grinning. "Let's get you home before you cause any more property damage."

Violet shakes her head. "You know, it's really unfair that Jack, Walker, and Ollie look this good while we look like feral raccoons right now."

Poppy sighs dramatically, a piece of grass falling from her hair. "Right?"

I huff out a laugh, trying not to acknowledge the fact that I'm still standing here, feeling entirely too aware of Jack shirtless.

Ollie has a quiet conversation with Jack, and they both look at me, and Jack waves him off. Ollie grins and heads to the truck. I'm too tired to do anything.

The truck rumbles away, kicking up dust, leaving the ranch quiet again.

And just like that, it's just me and Jack. Alone.

I brace myself, turning toward him, fully prepared for whatever smart-ass comment he's got lined up.

But Jack doesn't say anything. He just watches me, his green eyes steady, too knowing.

And suddenly, my entire body feels heavy.

I exhale, rubbing my face, blinking slowly against the wave of exhaustion that hits me all at once. "I should probably—"

Jack cuts me off by stepping forward and, before I can argue, scoops me up effortlessly into his arms.

I squeak, immediately trying to wiggle free. "Jack, put me down."

"Nope."

"I can walk!"

Jack grunts, entirely unbothered. "Yeah, sure. Baby, you couldn't even make it up the porch."

Baby. He called me baby. And...I like it.

I want to fight him, want to tell him that I am perfectly capable of functioning on my own, but my body has betrayed me. It's too much, the warmth of his chest, the steady rhythm of his breath, the way he carries me like I don't weigh a damn thing.

"Say it again..." I mumble.

"Say what?" he asks.

"Baby..."

Jack smells so good, and I'm so tired of fighting him.

By the time we get inside, my head already lolls against his shoulder. He nudges open my door with his foot, stepping into my room, and I barely process the fact that he's laying me down on the bed and tucking the blankets around me. He steps out and returns a few minutes later with a glass of water and a few Advil.

I mumble something incoherent, already half-asleep.

Jack huffs out a quiet laugh. "What was that, Wilder?"

I sigh, rolling over, burrowing into the covers. "You don't need to find a wife."

Silence. And then, a low, amused chuckle.

I feel him sweeping my hair back from my face, and I wonder if I'm dreaming of his touch and this sweet moment.

Jack mutters, mostly to himself. "Oh, baby, I know I don't."

And with one long, slow blink, I'm out like a light.

<h1 style="text-align:center">Chapter 13</h1>
<h1 style="text-align:center">Jack</h1>

Single Again by Josh Ross

I finish up in the horse paddock, breaking in a colt, already sweating under the morning sun and in desperate need of caffeine. The second I see her, something low in my gut twists, tight and hot. I figured she'd sleep in today after her shenanigans with Poppy and Violet last night.

Cami, all legs and attitude, storms past me, hair a little wilder than usual, my damn flannel hanging loose off her shoulders.

My flannel. The flannel I left on the back of a kitchen chair at her house.

She doesn't look embarrassed. Nope, she looks pissed. Go figure that Cami would be pissed at me for her being drunk and showing up late to her trailer.

Cami marches past me, completely ignoring me.

Walker and Ollie are grinning like idiots, already gearing up for the shit-talking that I will never live down. But it's all good fun. Ollie's not letting anyone say shit about his sister, and neither am I.

"I need coffee," I mutter as I get in line.

Ollie nods and gets in line behind me. "Bold move, really, Jack. God only knows what she'll do to yours."

Walker smirks. "What's the plan for today? Another episode of when Jack and Cami try to kill each other?"

I exhale sharply, leaning against the fence. "You two done?"

Ollie grins. "Not even close. How's it been staying with my sister at Wilder Ranch?"

I rub my jaw, staring after her, already exhausted. Ollie smirks at me.

Walker chuckles. "So, when's the housewarming party?"

I drag my hand down my face. "I hate you both."

Ollie grins. "Nah. You just hate that we're giving you shit."

Walker dodges easily, laughing. "Oh, come on, Jessop. It's a fair question!"

I turn back, muttering, "One of these days, I swear..."

Walker grins. "Or, better yet, the real question is how you're gonna explain to your future wife that another woman that you live with just showed up wearing your clothes?"

"I've always wanted a brother-in-law," Ollie grins.

I groan, already regretting every single decision that led to this moment. "Someone just shoot me now."

"What time are the contestants showing up today?" Walker asks, changing the subject as we wait in the long line for coffee.

"Sometime this morning," I say as I gaze out over the pasture, already dreading their arrival. I really don't want to do this, but they're all right. I need to do it for the ranch. And just like Cami said last night. I don't need to find a wife. I really don't.

I give up in the line and go around back and lean in the trailer doorway. "What do you have here? This smells good," I murmur as I take note of the containers of baked goods stacked on the counter that Mack carries in for her.

"All of the baked goods that I baked last night before I drank way too much," she glares and starts unpacking them as coffee brews.

"I'll take some if one of them has my name on it." I close my eyes and inhale the scent of fresh blueberry muffins. I bet she put the crumbly things on top, too. They're so good, that's my favorite part.

"Sure, the one that fell in the dirt," she says as she carries a stack and leaves me to follow her inside the trailer.

I roll my eyes and grin at her jabs.

"Mack, what are you doing here?" Cami calls as she starts making coffee.

"Well, someone had to run this operation. You were too busy doing god knows what, and my Dad brought me down here to get coffee and you were nowhere to be found." She shrugs as she pours foam onto a cold brew.

"Wow, you're doing a good job," Cami says with an approving smile. "Where did you learn to make coffee?"

Mack grins proudly. "YouTube."

"Where do you want these?" I ask as I hold up the containers.

Cami looks like she wants to say something smart ass but takes them from me, sets them down and opens the container. She grabs a napkin, pulls out a muffin with it, and hands it to me. As she steps close, the smell of her body wash, vanilla and coconut, mix with the scent of the baked goods, and I'm not sure which I want to taste more: her or the muffin.

Our fingers brush as I take the muffin, and a jolt of awareness fires through me from our small touch. Cami's gaze flies to mine, a look of confusion as if she feels it too.

I grin at her, and she turns away, not meeting my eyes.

Mack watches us for a beat, then casually says to Cami, "Also, you should totally hire me."

Cami pauses mid-step, turning back to her. "You really want a job?"

Mack shrugs. "I'm already running things. Might as well make it official."

This kid is hilarious.

Cami stares at her for a long second, debating whether or not she has the energy to argue.

Then she sighs, waving a hand. "Fine. You're hired."

Mack grins. "Knew you'd see how good I am."

I break off a piece of the muffin she gave me. It's fluffy, buttery, damn near perfect. She might be a menace, but she can bake pastries like nothing I've ever had before.

I take another sip of my coffee, amused as hell. Cami might think she's in control of her morning, but between Mack's schemes and the fact that she's still wearing my flannel, she's fighting a losing battle. I just want to know why she won't look me in the eye.

* * *

I've done a lot of stupid things in my life. But, letting Jenna talk me into this reality show? The worst mistake of them all. Because right now, there are three massive black SUVs rolling up the ranch road, a full film crew unloading cameras, and an actual lineup of women stepping out like they just wandered off the set of a Hallmark movie.

And me? I'm hiding in the barn like a damn fugitive.

I press my back against the stall, watching from the shadows, wondering if there's a way to tunnel underground and escape into the mountains.

But before I can even entertain that thought, I hear footsteps that are light and purposeful and way too smug for my liking.

I don't even have to look. I know who it is. I can always feel her when she's near me. Like it or not, we've always had that connection.

"Well, well, well," Cami drawls, stepping inside like she owns the place, hands on her hips, eyes full of mischief. "Big, tough Jack Jessop, hiding out in his own barn. This is better than I could've ever dreamed."

I glance over, scowling. "Shouldn't you be making coffee instead of stalking me?"

She grins, leaning against the stall like she's settling in for a good show. "Oh, I shut the trailer down early. We sold out of everything again, and I figured I couldn't miss watching you meet your potential wives."

"Wife," I exhale, rubbing my temples. "What kind of show do you think this is? And you're really enjoying this, aren't you?"

"I doubt one woman is going to be able to put up with you, let alone multiple," she says dryly.

"Are you judging me or taking notes? I know you want the title of Mrs. Jessop," I tease.

Cami tilts her head ignoring my teasing, pretending to think. "Oh, I'm enjoying this. Let me see, cameras everywhere, a bunch of women competing for your love, and you looking like you'd rather be trampled by a bull? Yeah, Jack. I'm having the time of my life."

I groan, pinching the bridge of my nose. "I hate you."

She gasps, pressing a hand to her chest. "You don't mean that."

I lift a brow. "I absolutely mean that."

Cami grins wider, eyes sparkling. "You know, I could go out there and tell them where you're hiding..."

I stiffen immediately. "You wouldn't."

She smirks. "Wouldn't I?"

I stare at her. She absolutely would.

Cami spins on her heel, heading toward the barn door. "Guess I'll just let Jenna know—"

I lunge forward, grabbing her by the waist and hauling her back, holding her tight against my chest, feeling her warmth. God, she feels good.

"Nope," I clip. The second my arms wrap around her waist, everything shifts. One moment, I'm desperate to keep her from ratting me out to a horde of reality TV contestants and cameras, and the next?

I'm just holding her. And I don't let go. And that's a problem. Because Cami feels way too damn good in my arms. She's warm, soft, and laughing like this is the best thing that's ever happened to her.

She wiggles against mine, just enough to make me painfully aware of every place her body touches mine. And damn it all, she smells like coffee and something sweet like vanilla, maybe.

I tell myself I should let go.

I should focus on the real issue here, which is escaping my own personal TV show nightmare. But my hands? They stay. Because for a few dangerous seconds, I don't care about the cameras. Or the contestants. Or the fact that my "future wife" is apparently waiting for me outside.

I care about how Cami fits against me, like she's always belonged here. So I do the only thing I can, I drop my forehead onto her shoulder, groaning like a man on the verge of losing his damn mind. "Kill me now."

Cami pats my arm, completely oblivious to the crisis happening in my chest.

"Nope, sorry," she says way too cheerfully. "You have so much suffering ahead of you to look forward to."

And that's when reality slams back into me. I'm not supposed to be thinking about Cami like this or touching her. I'm supposed to be out there, smiling for the cameras, entertaining the idea of finding a wife.

Not standing in a damn barn, holding the one woman who's been in my heart since I was too young to understand what that even meant.

I let go of her like she's burning me. She doesn't move. She stays like she's enjoying it, too. And as I force myself to walk away, to step into the circus waiting outside, I already know no one on this reality show is gonna hold a damn candle to Cami.

And that's the real problem. Cami gives me one last smirk, full of delight and devoid of sympathy.

And as I walk toward the cameras, ready to meet my doom, I hear her call out,

"Smile, cowboy! This is what dreams are made of!"

* * *

I'm currently debating if there's a way I can go back into the military. Maybe they'll take me back, or I can just disappear from the ranch, and no one would know. Weston can take my place on the show. Because I hate this with every fiber of my being.

Jenna, my traitor of a sister, stands in front of the contestants like she's about to deliver a pep rally speech.

"Alright, ladies!" she beams, megaphone in hand because, apparently, she enjoys my suffering as cameras are rolling. "Welcome to *The Rancher Finds a Wife*! Now, before we introduce our eligible bachelor—" she turns toward me and whisper glares—"Jack, do me a favor and try to look like you're excited about this."

I force a smile, and it probably looks like I just stepped on a nail.

Jenna sighs and whisper yells. "Okay, no more of that. Let's just meet the women before you scare them off."

She turns back to the contestants, who are all smiling, standing perfectly poised in their boots and dresses, looking like they belong on a damn magazine cover.

And I'll admit it, they're stunning. All of them are very beautiful women.

Savannah – Blonde, bright blue eyes, the kind of woman who could be a model. She flashes me a perfect, sweet smile and holds out her hand. "It's so nice to meet you, Jack. I've always wanted to experience real ranch life."

Elena – Curvy, dark-haired, and carrying herself with the confidence of a woman who gets what she wants. "Jack Jessop," she says, tilting her head, studying me like she's already figuring out how to win. "I've gotta say, you're even better looking in person."

Ruby – Fiery red hair, freckles, and a mischievous glint in her green eyes. She smirks, crossing her arms. "So, do we get to see you in action? Or is this whole thing just for show?"

I'm already so overwhelmed, and this just started. My cocky bastard brothers stand along the fence, looking like they are really enjoying this.

Hannah – Soft brown hair, big brown eyes, with a shy but sweet smile. "I, um, have never been on a ranch before," she admits, tucking a piece of hair behind her ear. "But I'm a fast learner."

Juliette – Legs for days, dark wavy hair, and the kind of confidence that could intimidate most men. She looks me up and down, slow and assessing. "You're cute," she says. "But can you dance?"

They're beautiful. They seem nice. But I'm not remotely interested.

I just keep thinking about the woman who was in my dreams last night, who is probably making fun of this exact moment.

I bet she's watching from somewhere and mocking my life choices.

And that's the problem. Because no matter how damn gorgeous these contestants are, none of them are Cami.

Jenna claps her hands together, yanking me out of my thoughts. "Jack, any first impressions?"

I blink, realizing all of them are staring at me, waiting for some kind of meaningful response. And I've got nothing.

I clear my throat, shifting my hat on my head. "Uh, well... you're all... very nice."

Jenna groans, rubbing her temples. "Good God, Jack. Try again."

The women laugh, clearly amused.

Savannah smiles at me sweetly. "He's just shy, isn't he?"

Ruby smirks. "Or terrified."

Juliette raises a brow. "Do you need a drink, cowboy?"

Jenna mutters, "I need a drink."

I exhale, glancing toward the barn, already wishing I was anywhere else.

Instead, my eyes land on the coffee trailer.

And damn it all, I know exactly who's inside, probably watching this train wreck unfold with way too much enjoyment.

Cami.

Jenna snaps her fingers in front of my face. "Jack. Focus. Women. Right in front of you. Pick one to talk to first."

I let out a low sigh, tipping my hat back.

"Well," I mutter, forcing myself to look back at the contestants, "I guess we should get this show started."

And deep down, I already know that no matter what happens, this is gonna be a damn disaster.

Chapter 14
Cami

Wondering Why by The Red Clay Strays

The delicious smell of fresh coffee and caramelized sugar fills the air, mixing with the morning breeze and the low hum of chatter around the coffee trailer. It's barely past eight, and Bridger Falls is already alive and kicking, mostly because *The Rancher Finds a Wife* production crew has turned our small town into their own personal circus.

People have turned up from miles around to watch the show's spectacle. My coffee trailer has been busy nonstop ever since, with a line formed clear down Jack's driveway. They set up a makeshift parking lot, and Tucker has a ranch hand driving everyone up in a side by side. I'm not complaining. This morning, Maggie reported that Bridger Falls is overflowing with people, and all the businesses are booming. There was standing room only at The Black Dog bar last night, and the town is loving all of this attention. I'd say the Jessop reputation is getting better. No one is even talking about Jack Jessop, Sr. anymore, and rightfully so. He doesn't deserve to be talked about how he's treated everyone. *Good riddance.*

And maybe because everyone wants to see what happens with Jack. And I can't blame them, because I do, too. In fact, this is all killing me. I can't stand to see the way they're all flirting with him. Deep down, I hate this.

I sip my iced coffee, extra strong, because I need it today, and casually adjust the hem of my denim jacket like I don't care about anything happening around me. Like I didn't spend the entire night tossing and turning, replaying *that* moment in the barn.

The one where Jack *held me.* The way his warm hands felt protective of me. The way he seemed to like it and not let go. I loved the way he felt, and I loved being that close to him. And I let him. I didn't fight him off or move away. I pretended it wasn't a big deal. But it was a *big* deal to me.

The one where for the briefest, most unhinged second that I thought *Jack and I could be something.*

Then, like an absolute idiot, I played it off like it was *nothing.* Gave him a wink, a smirk, the whole nine yards. And now I have to suffer the consequences, standing here like an unbothered queen while I watch a group of intelligent and intimidatingly beautiful and put-together women flock around the man who wrecked my entire nervous system less than twenty-four hours ago. Hell, it was the reason for me staying up all night baking ten times more than I usually do, thankfully, because everything is selling out quickly. Again. I need more help. And not just Mack's help if I'm going to make this work out here while they're filming.

I crunch a piece of ice angrily.

"Easy there, killer," Ollie mutters, stepping up beside me, coffee in hand. My brother looks half-amused, half-worried, which is the default setting for anyone who knows me well.

"Haven't seen you look this homicidal since Jack bought the ranch."

I narrow my eyes at him at the reminder. "I was *just* admiring the local wildlife."

"The wildlife?" He follows my gaze to the group of contestants, all standing near Jack, talking to him, making him laugh, and having fun. Next to them are a bunch of different animals he's introducing them to. I want to *not* like them. But every time one of them comes up to the trailer to get coffee, I realize I could be friends with these women. They're smart, funny, and kind. Damnit. I wanted to hate them, but I simply can't. I even made plans to eat dinner with a few of them later this week when they have a break from filming. They're actually so sweet.

Jack stands there, arms crossed, looking effortlessly rugged and infuriatingly good. He's got that *"I don't want to be here, but I look sexy anyway"* energy, which is apparently catnip for women on reality television shows.

Ollie snorts into his coffee. "Damn. That's a *lot* of hair-flipping for the cameras."

I exhale slowly, reminding myself that this was *not* a big deal. That Jack and I are *not* a thing. That this whole situation is fine, totally fine, because I don't care what he does or who he does it with.

Not at all. Nope.

"Why are you standing like that?" Ollie asks, side-eying me.

"Like what?" I glare.

"Like you're trying to hex them with your mind."

I take a sip of my drink. "If I were hexing them, they'd be running in the opposite direction of Jack."

"Fair point." Ollie pauses, his expression shifting to something *way too observant* for my liking. "This about you and Jack's non-interest in each other?"

I almost choke on my coffee. "What are you even talking about?"

He looks at me like I just asked if cows lay eggs.

I snort. "That is *not* what's happening."

"Right," he says, nodding. "Which is exactly why I heard Maggie telling Mrs. Fernandez over at Harvest & Honey that you two are giving off *big 'future Mr. and Mrs. Jessop' vibes and this show is a waste of time.*"

I nearly choke on my coffee. "What? No!"

Ollie grins. "Oh yeah. Whole town's got bets on when you two finally snap and get together. Maggie's money is on you breaking first."

I sputter. "That's ridiculous."

"Cami," he says like he's talking to a child, "we're just calling it like we see it."

I groan and press my cold coffee cup against my forehead. "I *hate* you."

"No, you don't."

"Fine. I *mildly* dislike you."

"Still not true."

I sighed, dragging a hand down my face. "It's fine, okay? I'm just here to help the Jessops and sell coffee. They're helping me, I'm helping them. It's that simple. That's it."

Ollie gives a slow nod, then tilts his head. "And yet, here you are, steaming like an overcooked pot roast while watching him flirt with other women."

"He's busy finding a wife." I bite my lip as one of the women reaches out and touches Jack's arm. He gives her a polite smile, all gentlemanly, and *ugh*, and my stomach twists in a way I absolutely refuse to acknowledge.

Ollie grins. "Mmhmm."

"Shut up."

"I didn't say anything."

"You *thought* something."

"That's true." He sips his coffee. "And it was *hilarious*."

I exhale hard and glance back at Jack. Our eyes meet for the briefest second before I look away like a coward. My braid slides over my shoulder as I turn, and I *swear* I feel his gaze follow the movement.

But I'm probably imagining it.

Or hoping for it. Or both. Damn it.

I shake it off, forcing a smirk. "Well, whatever. He's the one stuck on this dumb show, not me."

"Uh-huh. So that's why you keep checking to see if he's looking at you?"

"I am *not—*"

Before I can finish, Jack's voice cuts through the air. "Morning, Cami."

Oh hell.

I fix my face and turn slowly. "Morning, *Jack*."

A corner of his mouth twitches. "You're really enjoying this, aren't you?"

"Oh, immensely. How's reality TV treating you?"

He looks at me like he'd rather be anywhere else. "Like a slow, painful death."

I smirk. "That's too bad. It looks like you're having so much fun, I was thinking about signing up for my own show. Maybe I'll find a husband."

Jack's entire body stills for half a second. Just long enough for me to *see* the flicker of something behind his eyes. And maybe, *just maybe*, it's a little satisfying.

Then he recovers, tilting his head. "You think you'd last?"

I take a slow sip of my coffee, letting my smirk deepen. "Jack, I'd do great on a show. The real question is, do you think *you* will? Which one of these lucky ladies is a top contender so far?"

Ollie whistles low. "Damn. She's competitive with everything."

Jack huffs a quiet laugh and shakes his head. But his gaze lingers, flicking down to my braid, then back up to my face like he's trying to figure me out.

Good luck, Jessop. I'm locking these feelings up like Fort Knox.

I flash him one last smug smile and turn back to Ollie. "Anyway. *We* should get going. I need your help taking all these empty containers back to Wilder Ranch to bake some more since I've sold out of everything. Again."

Baking at the Jessop Ranch is good in theory, but I do not want to watch Jack flirt with other women. I can't do it.

Ollie blinks. "Uh. What?"

I step on his foot.

"Ow—right! Yeah, let's go." He clears his throat and follows as I turn to gather up everything to take to my truck.

I glance back and don't miss the smug look on Jack's face as he watches me and gives me a grin that I can't help but notice he didn't give to any of the contestants. There was nothing gentlemanly about the way he looked at me like he wanted to wrap my braid around his fist and bend me over this trailer if Ollie hadn't been here. Or maybe that was me dreaming.

It's late. *Way* late.

The kind of late where the rest of the world has gone quiet, where the only sounds are the low hum of my industrial mixer mixing up a batch of icing and the country music twanging from my speaker. I hadn't even noticed the sun going down, but now the only light in the kitchen comes from the overhead bulbs and the soft glow spilling from the oven window.

Outside, darkness stretches across the ranch like a thick, quiet blanket.

I have *no* idea what time it is, and honestly, I don't care.

I'm in my happy zone with flour on my face, cinnamon under my nails, every surface covered in trays of cookies, loaves of bread, and hand pies that smell like they should be *illegal*. I've packed my three tall cooling racks full of cooling pastries, lining them up like soldiers in a sugar-coated army. The air is thick with the smell of vanilla, caramelized sugar, and browned butter, and my body hums with the kind of tired satisfaction that only comes from hours of getting lost in something you love.

And maybe... just *maybe*... it's because keeping busy means not thinking about Jack.

I flip another tray onto the counter and start humming along to the song blasting through my speaker. It's a heartbreak ballad, ironic, really, but I don't care. I sing loudly, off-key, fully committing to my little kitchen concert.

Spinning around, I toss my braid over my shoulder and catch my reflection in the oven door.

I look *ridiculous*.

There's flour smudged across my cheek, my braid's coming undone, and my apron is covered in baking ingredients.

I shrug. Could be worse. Then I feel it. A shift in the air. A presence. The one that has always stopped me in my tracks when I've felt it. I freeze. Slowly, I turn, and there he is. Jack, leaning against the door frame, looking like he'd been there long enough to enjoy the show.

He's got a cookie in his hand, *one of my cookies*, and he's taking a slow, deliberate bite, chewing like he owns the place. My heart skips a beat when I see him, and heat rushes to my face, feeling oddly comforted by his presence.

I cross my arms. "Here for a property inspection?"

Jack smirks, slow and lazy, and my stomach does an unapproved somersault. "Nah. Just coming home."

I scoff. "Oh, so is this about rent? How official of you." I gesture to my kitchen, admittedly, a disaster zone of flour, sugar, and cooling racks. "Welcome to my humble bakery. You like what I've done with the place?"

Jack's gaze drifts across the chaos, then back to me. He pops the rest of the cookie into his mouth, chews, and swipes another one off a tray right in front of me.

I gape at him. "Excuse you."

He lifts a shoulder, biting into the second one like a damn thief. "I can be paid in cookies."

My eye twitches. "Oh, how *generous* of you. How much is rent?"

Jack hums like he's thinking real hard. "Actually... I think these might cover rent."

"Oh, well then," I snatch a tray of hand pies from the counter, holding it up. "What's this worth?"

Jack steps closer, his eyes *too* warm, *too* knowing, and I hate the way my stomach reacts like it's still stuck in the barn, still remembering the way he held me last night.

"I dunno," he murmurs, reaching out—

And swiping a bit of flour from my cheek.

His fingers linger for half a second, and my brain short-circuits.

I swallow, suddenly *too* aware of how close we are. Of how it's just me and him, standing in the middle of my wrecked kitchen, with nothing but a tray of cookies and some unresolved tension between us.

I clear my throat. "You *really* came in here just to steal my cookies?"

Jack's smirk deepens. "Not stealing."

"Oh, you're sampling?"

"More like," he leans in, voice lower, rougher, "hiding out from the craziness over at the ranch."

Damn him. Damn the way my pulse *jumps* at the way he looks at me.

I straighten, feigning nonchalance, even as my fingers tighten around the pie tin.

His gaze flicks over me, flour-streaked, messy, barefoot in my own damn kitchen—then back to my face. And he says, real slow, "Just making sure you're okay."

Oh.

I lick my lips. "That's... oddly nice of you."

Jack smirks, swiping *another* cookie. "Get used to it."

I snap out of whatever spells he cast and shove the pie into his hands. "Here. If you're gonna steal, you might as well take the good stuff."

Jack chuckles, shaking his head. He turns to leave but pauses at the door, glancing over his shoulder. His voice is soft, but firm. "You look happy."

And just like that, he's gone. Or so I think. A second later, I hear a different sound, one that has nothing to do with baking. The faint creak of a saddle. The soft snort of a horse.

I glance toward the front driveway, and sure enough, Mouse is standing there, saddled up like he's waiting for me, his reins looped over the hitching post, standing next to Jack's horse, Pesto, also saddled up.

Jack stands beside them, eating his pie and watching me like he knows I can't resist.

I cross my arms. "You saddled up my horse?"

He nods, utterly unconcerned. "Figured you could use a ride."

I arch a brow. "Bossy much?"

Jack shrugs. "You've been holed up in here for hours. Thought I'd pull you out before you start naming your pies."

I huff. "I *do not—*" I pause, then mutter, "Okay, maybe once."

Jack smirks. "Come on, Wilder. Get some fresh air. Clear your head."

I glance back at the kitchen. At the cooling racks, the mess, the last tray I just pulled from the oven.

Then back at Jack. Then at Mouse.

I sigh dramatically. "Well... I *did* just pull my last tray out of the oven."

Jack grins, and before I can second-guess myself, I untie my apron, wipe my hands on it and toss it onto the counter, and step out into the night air.

Jack swings into his saddle like he was *born* there, easy and smooth, and I roll my eyes at how unfairly attractive that is. I mount Mouse, settling into the saddle as he shifts beneath me.

He snorts happily as she stands next to Pesto.

Jack studies me in the moonlight, that same unreadable expression flickering across his face. "Ready?"

I nod. "Lead the way, Jessop."

And with that, we take off into the quiet night, leaving the warmth of the kitchen behind, the scent of cinnamon and sugar trailing in the cool evening air.

As we ride side by side under the moonlit sky, I tell myself this isn't *a thing*. It's just a ride. Fresh air. A break from the heat of my kitchen. That's all.

Except... it doesn't feel like just a ride.

The steady rhythm of Mouse's hooves echoes in the quiet, Jack and Pesto moving in sync beside us. The world is still, the air cool against my skin, and the only sound, aside from the occasional creak of leather and the soft rustling of grass is my own damn thoughts.

The way Jack saddled Mouse up without asking, like he just knew I needed this. Like he knew I wouldn't step away unless someone made me. Full of the way he looked at me back in the kitchen, soft, full of intent, like I was something worth watching.

Like he was memorizing me. And the worst part? I didn't hate it. I should, though. I should hate this.

I should still be furious that he bought my ranch, that he's everywhere I turn, that he came back to Bridger Falls looking too damn good for his own good and especially for mine.

But instead, I feel this. This warm, fluttery, nerve-wracking thing low in my stomach when he glances at me. This stupid little thrill when he rides just a bit closer, like he's making sure I don't fall behind.

This quiet, creeping realization that Jack has wedged himself under my skin in a way I never saw coming. And worse? I don't think I want him to leave.

I know one thing for sure. Things are heating up, and it's not just in my kitchen.

Chapter 15
Jack

Worst Way by Riley Green

There are few things I hate more than what I'm doing right now, standing around in a freshly pressed shirt while a producer named Kyle, who has never stepped foot on a ranch tries to fix my damn cowboy hat like it's a prop.

I swat his hands away. "Touch my hat again, and we're gonna have a problem, Kyle."

He scurries off, looking scared, and I sigh, turning to look at the lodge. The Jessop Lodge. My father's pride and joy. The place where he made deals, drank too much, and single-handedly destroyed our family's reputation. It's not a home, it's a prop. It has always been, even before this ridiculous reality show. And I suppose it works well as a prop for that purpose. But it's not a home that you come home to and relax. Wilder House is a place to go to relax.

Instead of working my ranch and knocking out my endless to do list, I'm standing here in the shadow of the past, pretending I give a damn about "finding love" on national television when all I really want to do is get my hands in the dirt, fix fences, and forget I share a name with my father, the criminal.

But then Cami stomps into my line of sight, and suddenly, my day gets a hell of a lot better.

She's wearing tight jeans, boots that have seen actual ranch work, and her hair's tied back in another complicated braid that makes me itch to pull it loose.

But that's the thing about Cami. She gets under my skin in ways I don't even have words to describe. I can be irritated with her, frustrated, pissed off even, but the second she's near, all of it turns into something else. Something that scares me, but I can't get enough of.

"What's wrong, Jessop? Too much TV romance?" She grins, leaning on the fence post beside me.

"You say that like you don't already know the answer," I grunt out, grumpy at the world.

"Oh, I do. But watching you suffer is my favorite pastime."

Of course, it is.

I roll my shoulders, forcing my attention back to the contestants gathered by the barn, each one of them dressed in brand new cowboy boots, stiff jeans, and hats that probably still have the price tags on them.

I rub my temples. "I can't believe this is my life. I have a ranch to run. I don't have time for this."

"Cheer up, cowboy," Cami says, nudging my arm. "Maybe you'll find true love today."

I scoff. "Pretty sure the closest I've come to love is my horse."

Cami smirks. "Well, I'd say that explains a lot."

Before I can fire back, my traitorous sister Jenna strides over with Kyle in tow, her eyes locked onto Cami with the kind of determination that makes me instantly suspicious. I know that look. She has something she's planning. And I probably won't like it.

"Cami," Jenna says sweetly. Too sweetly. "You know the ranch better than anyone. Want to help us out?"

Cami blinks and gives them a deer in the headlights look. "What?"

Kyle, the hat toucher chimes in. "We think having a real-life cowgirl assist in challenges and help Jack run things would really add authenticity."

Cami tilts her head, confused. "Are you saying this reality show about ranchers... lacks authenticity?"

Kyle clears his throat. "I mean..."

Jenna cuts in. "We'd write you in as a ranch hand or an assistant or something. It'd be good for TV. It'll be paid, of course."

And then the worst thing happens. Everyone turns to look at me. Like I'm the deciding factor. Like I have any kind of say in this madness.

Cami, smirking like she just won the lottery, raises a brow. "What do you think, Jessop? Want me hanging around while you woo the ladies?"

But I don't miss the look in her eyes. She doesn't like that last part of her sentence. I can tell. And watching her mouth twitch when she says it tells me that she probably won't like doing the show and she thinks I'll say no.

Oh, for the love of—

I open my mouth to argue. To say absolutely not, under no circumstances, over my dead body.

But my brain short-circuits because suddenly, all I can picture is Cami, always near, always close. Always watching while I pretend to find a wife. I wonder what happens when I don't find a wife in the end. Because I don't plan on finding a wife. Maybe Never. Unless it's to a certain braid-wearing rancher and talented baker. And since she's not interested in me the same way, I might never have a wife. I grew up in a family where my dad was a terrible husband and an even worse father. He and my mom fought like crazy up until she died of cancer. And during her cancer, he wasn't there for her. I remember me and my siblings taking care of her and watching her die. What kind of husband would I be with that as a role model? I'm scared as hell of turning out like him. I'm not taking that chance.

Worse, I look over and find Cami watching me. And by the look on her face, it feels like she has some idea of what I'm thinking right now and that freaks me out even more.

My silence drags on too long.

Jenna grins. "I'll take that as a yes."

Cami beams, clapping me on the shoulder. "Can't wait, partner."

And just like that, everything got even more complicated.

* * *

Tonight, The Black Dog is packed with the usual small-town mix of ranchers, locals, and people who pretend to know how to ride because they likely bought new boots online last week and decided to visit Bridger Falls. Also, all the tourists who came to get a glimpse of the reality show being filmed.

Apparently, Walker's been handing out flyers with directions on them to the Jessop ranch so they can get coffee and buy locally-raised meats. I mean, that part I'm not mad about. But this is crazy.

The locals keep me on my toes. The crowd that drinks cheap beer like its holy water and talks shit like it's their second job. I shouldn't be here.

I should be back at the ranch fixing fences, checking cattle, and doing something useful with my time. Instead, I'm here, trapped in the middle of this town-wide spectacle that is *The Rancher Finds a Wife*, listening to people place bets on whether I'll "make a fool" of myself on national television.

It's fine.

I've had people talk shit about me for years. It comes with the territory with the last name Jessop. It's why all of us left this ranch and town as soon as we could, and we didn't come back when my father was gone.

Most of the town saw our family as nothing but crooks, liars, and cheats, thanks to my father. The man who ran our family name into the ground so deep, I'm still trying to dig it out. But the show seems to be helping people forget that, so there's that.

I tell myself I don't care. I've told myself that for years.

And then Cami steps into the fire for me. I don't hear the start of it, but I catch the tail end.

Violet murmurs next to me, her beer halfway to her mouth. "Oh, hell."

I turn toward the bar just in time to see Cami squaring up against a couple of out-of-towners, her hands planted on her hips, her chin tilted high, her expression looking dangerous like I've only ever seen when she's about to win a fight. My stomach tightens.

One of the men, some slicked-back haired bastard with too much cologne and not enough common sense, chuckles, swirling his drink. "I'm just saying, the guy's old man was dirty as hell. Why the hell would anyone trust a Jessop?"

I don't recognize him; he must be from out of town. Why he thinks he knows my family is beyond me.

Cami doesn't even hesitate. "You want to run that by me again?"

My brows lift. Interesting.

The man shrugs. "Look, I don't know what this little *Rancher Finds a Wife* show is trying to prove, but it sure as hell ain't making any of the Jessops look any better." He laughs, nudging his buddy. "I mean, come on. You really think he's different than his crooked old man?"

I expect Cami to roll her eyes. To smirk, take a sip of her beer, and let it go. She doesn't. Instead, she steps closer. I know that stance. It's the same stance she had at seventeen, when she punched a guy for calling her trash because of her own father and the reputation he left his family with when he was acting similar to my father. We've always had that in common. The shitty father club.

It's also the same stance she had at sixteen, when she walked into that rodeo and took first place on a horse everyone said couldn't be ridden.

It's also the stance of a woman who could tear someone apart with nothing but words and a sharp enough glare.

And I'm rooted to the floor, breath locked in my chest, watching her do it. Because it's always magical and a sight to see. Never argue with a woman whose mom was her first bully. They will dissect you in ways you've never imagined. She's been defending herself from a grown woman since she was a child. No one stands a chance against her.

"I don't think he's different," she says, her voice steady, smooth, lethal. "I know he is."

Oh, shit. And here it is.

The man snorts, shaking his head. "That right? What are you, fucking him?"

Cami ignores the jab and leans in, slow and easy. "I know for a fact that if you have something to say about the Jessops, you'd better say it to their faces. Not sit here running your mouth like some coward too scared to say it to someone's face."

He laughs and spits when he says, "And apparently he needs some bitch to fight his battles for him. What do you like work for him or something?"

She looks at him and says, "Getting real tired of men resorting to calling women bitches when their brain can't supply them with anything slightly witty. Keep it up, buddy and you'll have a battle of your own."

His jaw tics. "That a threat, sweetheart?"

She gives a slow smile. God help me, she actually smiles.

"Oh, honey." She reaches for his glass, dumps his whiskey out onto his lap, and sets it back down like nothing happened. "It's a promise."

Silence.

Thick, heavy, buzzing silence.

And then Violet and Poppy start cackling.

Walker leans back against the bar, crossing his arms, shaking his head. "Damn."

The guy stares at her, open-mouthed, then turns to his friend, as if to say, *Can you believe this shit?*

The friend just mutters, "You had it coming, man."

The guy mutters something under his breath, throws some bills on the table, and stalks off, wiping at the front of his pants.

Cami, completely unbothered, goes right back to sipping her drink, like she didn't just set fire to the guy and run him off.

I don't move. I don't breathe. I just stare at her. The woman who is supposed to be my enemy. The woman who fights me at every turn and drives me insane defended me.

And she did that without knowing I was watching. She turns back to her drink, acting like she didn't just do the hottest thing I've ever seen in my life.

And suddenly, I have a serious fucking problem. Because I don't just *want* Cami. I need her. I move before I can talk myself out of it, cutting across the bar until I'm right behind her.

She senses me before she sees me, stiffening slightly before turning, raising a slow, teasing eyebrow. "Well, if it isn't Bridger Falls' most eligible bachelor," she drawls, taking a sip of her drink. "You here to sign autographs, or are you still pretending to be too cool for your adoring fans?"

I cross my arms, desperately trying to keep my shit together. "Didn't know I needed a bodyguard, Cami."

Realization flashes across her face that I heard, and she looks away for a moment.

"You don't," she says lightly. "I just really wanted to ruin that guy's night."

"Uh-huh."

She smirks.

I should leave it there. Shouldn't push. But I'm not built like that. Not when it comes to her. I step closer. Not touching, but close enough that I know she feels it.

Close enough that I can smell her: vanilla, whiskey, and something warm that's just... her.

"You always go around defending me?" I murmur.

She lifts her drink. "I defend all helpless creatures."

I chuckle, low and slow. "Helpless?"

She shrugs. "What else would you call a man stuck on a reality dating show he clearly doesn't want to be on?"

Touché.

"Look at you," I say, tilting my head. "Acting all unbothered right now."

She smirks again, but this time, it flickers, just for a second.

And that's when I know. She cares. Maybe she doesn't want to. Maybe she hates she does. But she does.

And I like that way too much.

I lean in, dropping my voice low. "Kinda sounds like you like me, Wilder."

She scoffs, flustered. "You wish, Jessop."

Oh, I do. I really, really do. And that's a whole other problem entirely.

She huffs, turning back to her drink. "You're lucky, you know."

I lift a brow. "How's that?"

She flicks a glance at me. "Because if anyone's gonna talk shit about you in this town, it's me. And I'm not sharing."

I lean against the bar beside her, close enough that our arms brush when she lifts her drink. She doesn't pull away. Neither do I.

"Come on," I murmur, voice low. "Admit it."

She takes a slow sip of her whiskey, her gaze locked on the mirror behind the bar like she doesn't even see me standing here. "Admit what?"

"That you like me."

She makes a noise that's somewhere between a scoff and an outright laugh. "I'd rather admit I enjoy stepping on a pile of Legos."

I grin, turning my body slightly toward hers. "And yet, here we are. You, ruining a perfectly good whiskey just to defend my honor."

She shrugs. "Maybe I just hate whiskey."

I lean in, just a little, staring down at her. "We both know that's not true."

Her breath catches, just for a second. It's so small, so quiet, I might've imagined it. But I didn't.

Because suddenly, the air between us isn't just charged, it's an electric storm.

I see it in the way her fingers tighten around her glass.

I've spent my whole life pushing this woman, waiting for the moment she'd push back. And now?

Now, I want to grab her by the hips, pull her against me, and make her forget every single reason she's ever had to hate me.

But we're in a bar. In public.

So instead of doing what I want, I do the next best thing. I crowd her just enough to make her notice. Just enough that when she finally looks up at me, her breath hitches again. "What do you want?" she says, exasperated.

You.

The word nearly slips out. Nearly.

Instead, I grin. "Just wanted to thank you."

"For what?"

"For letting everyone in this bar know that if anyone's gonna ruin my reputation, it's you."

She finally smiles, and damn, if it doesn't hit me square in the chest. She shakes her head, setting her drink down with a soft clink. "You're welcome."

I tilt my head, considering. "Or maybe you just like things difficult. Or you just like hearing yourself talk."

"Maybe. But you're still standing here, listening." She huffs, exasperated, but she still hasn't moved.

And neither have I.

Then, before I can talk myself out of it, I reach out, tucking a loose strand of hair behind her ear. Her hair falling down in waves like she finally let it out of that damn braid she was wearing.

She freezes. For a split second, everything stops. The bar noise fades. The people around us disappear.

It's just her. Just me. Just this moment that neither of us were ready for.

Her lips part slightly, her pulse flickering at her throat. I could kiss her. Right now. She knows it. I know it. But then—

"Hey, lovebirds!" Ollie yells from across the bar, ruining my life. "You gonna make out, or can I buy another beer without throwing up in my mouth?"

Cami jolts back like she just remembered where we are.

I turn slowly, glare set to lethal. "Knock it off, Ollie."

He grins. "Not a chance."

Cami shakes her head, clearly needing an escape. "I'm getting out of here before I commit a crime."

She moves toward the door, but at the last second, she brushes past me, her fingers trailing lightly against my arm.

It's barely anything. But it's everything. I watch her go, half-tempted to chase her, half-tempted to let her run.

Instead, I grab my beer and mutter under my breath, "Yeah. I'm really screwed."

Ollie pats my shoulder. "Glad you're finally catching up."

I throw a peanut at his head.

It doesn't help.

Because Cami just knocked my world sideways, and for the first time in my life, I don't want to fight her about it.

Chapter 16
Cami

Me on You by Muscadine Bloodline

Jack Jessop has officially become a bigger problem than he's ever been. We're supposed to be enemies. Rivals. And now? Now, I don't even know what we are. It's confusing me and making me feel things, giving me hope, and I can't be hopeful about Jack.

Standing in Steamy Sips, rolling out dough with a little too much aggression, I can still hear the way he said my name at the bar last night. Slow, like he was savoring it. Like he knew exactly what he was doing. He was fully aware of how everyone was watching us and how his voice was doing unspeakable things to my nervous system.

And I hated it. Except I didn't.

Because now I'm standing here, pounding cinnamon roll dough like it insulted me, replaying every second of that interaction on a mental loop. The tension? Wild. The way he looked at me? Infuriating. The way my traitorous body reacted to it? Betrayal.

"Are you trying to kill that dough? What did it do to you?" Violet smirks as she straightens a stack of napkins.

"No," I mutter, wiping my forehead with the back of my forearm. "It's stress relief."

"Right," Mack says, expertly rolling the bread out. "She's been beating up that dough for the past hour like that."

"Hey," I snap. "Snitches get stitches."

"Stress. Definitely not because Jack turned you into a puddle of goo in front of us."

I point my rolling pin at her. "Don't start with me, you two."

"Oh, but it's so easy," Violet grins. "We were there, Cami. He had you looking like you forgot how to function."

"Gross," Mack adds and makes a face. "My ears!"

"I function just fine," I argue, even though it's a blatant lie.

Maggie, of course, chooses that moment to give her expert life advice. "Well, I, for one, think you should've kissed him right there at the bar," she announces, plucking a cooling cookie off the tray like she's on quality control duty.

"Oh my God," I groan, pressing my palms into the counter. "I need new friends."

"Too late," Mack singsongs, tossing chocolate chips into the dough. I love her creativity. She mixes flavors and adds in things that are becoming a hit with the customers. I've loved having her help with the trailer so I can go back and forth to Jack's kitchen and knock out a good chunk of my baking while the trailer is open during the day. He was right, that was a perk to being out here at Jessop Ranch. And he has a double oven, so that's a win.

But these guys? They're insufferable. Every last one of them.

But the worst part? I signed the damn contract for *The*

Rancher Finds a Wife this morning. Jenna showed up with a pen and a hefty paycheck, and even though I have no business adding reality TV chaos to my already chaotic life, I signed. Because money is one thing I can use right now to keep my trailer going and do some updates on the ranch.

And now I get to watch contestants fawn over Jack like he's a prize pony at the rodeo.

I shouldn't care. But I still watched today, arms crossed, while some girl batted her eyelashes at him like he was about to propose right there on the spot.

And I hated it.

Maybe that's what Jack likes. Someone who fawns over him. Not someone like me who is at odds with him. And definitely not someone who can beat people up at the bar and chase off intruders.

The thought makes my stomach twist, and I shove it down with more cinnamon rolls. I have a chaotic life here, but I love it. Now that my world includes Jack, I'm unsure how to proceed. But he sure didn't seem like he wasn't interested in me last night at the bar. He seemed *very* interested.

Ollie shows up halfway through my existential crisis, eyeing the absolute mess we've made. "You running a bakery or a food fight?"

"Bit of both," Violet says, handing him a cookie.

He bites into it and nods approvingly but gives me a look of concern. "Cami, you're burning the candle at both ends."

"I'm fine," I say automatically.

"She's fine," Mack echoes. "Just baking away her feelings. Plus, she has me, now."

"Uh-huh," Ollie says, not convinced. "Well, since you're taking on *even more* with this ridiculous show, I've got someone you should talk to. Beau Callahan. New guy at the firehouse. Amazing baker. He makes all kinds of stuff for us on shift. His pretzels are insane. He's looking for part-time work when he's not on shift."

I perk up. "Send me his number. I could use more help. Mack has the truck just fine, but I could use an extra set of hands baking."

"Especially since you'll be so *busy* being Jack's assistant," Poppy teases, and the entire trailer erupts in laughter.

"Y'all suck," I say, tossing a piece of dough in her direction.

"You love us," Mack grins.

Maggie clears her throat. "Oh, speaking of the show, the contestants are all staying at the Dogwood, and let me tell you— those girls are really cool. But I don't see a single one of them sticking it out in Bridger Falls, let alone on a ranch with Jack."

I perk up at this, but before I can say anything, Ollie leans against the counter with a smirk. "Yeah, but they're all hot."

Poppy glares at him and smacks him upside the head with a kitchen towel.

"Hey!" Ollie rubs his head. "That hurt!"

"Good," Poppy says sweetly, turning back to the cinnamon rolls.

I narrow my eyes, watching them share a cinnamon roll without a second thought. It's subtle, the way they interact, but there's... something there. Something deeper than before. I say nothing, but I notice.

Mack pipes up. "By the way, I'm getting my license soon."

I blink at her. "God help us all."

"Shut up. It means I can help more, drive stuff out to the ranch, make supply trips. Be useful."

"You're very useful, Mack. Let me know if you need driving lessons. We can go out in my truck sometime," I offer.

"Thanks," she grins.

"Yes. You're already useful," Maggie says, giving her shoulder a squeeze. "Just don't crash into the flower beds."

"That was one time!" Mack rolls her eyes, then says, "I'm excited to help out more at the coffee trailer, Cami."

"Me, too, Mack. You're a natural," I say as I smile at her. It's crazy to look at Mack and remember that I used to babysit her when I was a teenager. In a way, I feel like we've grown up together. The only time I didn't see her was when I was away at school. I love that kid.

"So, any word on your dad?" Maggie asks Poppy.

Poppy sighs, setting down the spatula. "No. And honestly? I don't know if he's coming back this time."

Poppy has been running her father's auto body shop since he's been gone. She's also taking care of her little brother, Owen. Talk about burning the candle at both ends.

Violet gasps, "What do you mean?"

She shakes her head. "He's been kind of... off. Like he's unraveling or something."

A hush settles over the trailer for a beat. Ollie, standing closest to her, nudges her with his elbow. "Hey. You know I got you, right?"

She smiles at him, soft and appreciative. "Yeah, I know."

The moment lingers a little longer than it should. Interesting.

Maggie, of course, breaks it. "You know we all will help you with whatever you need."

Poppy gives a sad smile and nods. "Thanks."

Sensing she's ready for a subject change, I say, "Alright. Let's get these cookies packed up before everyone eats them all."

I look over at my brother and Poppy and think if those two were together, it wouldn't be the end of the world. They've always been good friends. I think that's what I would want in a partner. Someone to be close friends with and have fun with. Someone who gets me, and I get them. I want passion, sure. But I want a lifelong partner and friend. Something like my grandpa and grandma had. Now, that was a love that was timeless. They lived their life together every day here on this ranch and were so happy. That's what I dream of, being happy. Just simple things. Like riding horses, working together on the ranch, and being together. That's what I dream of.

Someone like Jack. *Jack.*

We all get to work, but my mind drifts. Sometimes, Violet and Poppy tease me about not having a boyfriend, and I laugh it off, but the truth? I don't even look. Because if I ever met someone I could actually make a life with, I'd have to let go of the idea of Jack.

* * *

The next morning, I spend a couple hours sitting in a chair at the Jessop Ranch lodge, getting my hair and makeup done by a woman who apparently moonlights as a magician. Because somehow, I go from ranch dirt and coffee stains to looking... well, *good.*

This is my life now. Pretending with Jack. I stare at my reflection in the mirror. My hair is styled in soft waves that frame my face, my eyes look bigger, brighter, and my lips, don't even get me started on my lips. The look plump and perfect. I've never done my make up this good. My skin is smooth, and somehow, I feel...pretty.

Jenna whistles as she comes into the room. "Cami, you look hotter than the contestants."

"Uh, no. That's not the look I'm going for," I interject quickly.

She smirks. "Tell that to your boobs."

I glance down. The form-fitting red top they gave me is hugging all the right places. And the bra? Let's say it's doing some impressive structural engineering work.

I groan. "Jenna—"

"Too late, cowgirl. You're a certified smoke show. Own it." She winks like she's not actively ruining my life and casually jerks her thumb toward the barn. "Now go bust my brother's balls."

"I need you to never say that sentence to me again," I mutter. "Ever. Under any circumstance. In any lifetime."

She just grins. "What? It's accurate."

"No. No, it's *disturbing*."

Jenna shrugs like she didn't just verbally maim me. "Tell Jack I said hi."

"I'm telling Jack you said balls," I mutter as I stagger dramatically out of the barn like I've been emotionally assaulted. "I hope he never recovers."

She yells after me, "Get in there and make bad choices!"

I flip her off without looking back.

Truly. This is the friend I was cursed with.

Now I get to go face her brother, who is hot, infuriating, and unfortunately in possession of the aforementioned anatomy I now cannot un-think.

The second I step outside, the talking stops. Everything goes eerily quiet. A slow whistle from somewhere outside breaks the silence.

My eyes immediately scan, and I find Jack, who leans against the wooden fence, staring at me like he has just found a hundred-dollar bill in the dirt. His gaze sweeps over me, taking his time, and then a slow, sexy smile spreads across his face.

My heart trips over itself, and my stomach does an unwelcome somersault. Oh, no. This is *bad*.

"Damn, Cami," someone mutters.

"She's so hot," someone else murmurs.

Jack tilts his head, his eyes locked on mine. "You wear that for me, Wilder?"

I roll my eyes, determined to ignore the way his voice sends heat up my neck. "Yeah, Jack. The whole outfit was designed to impress the guy I can't stand."

"Could've fooled me," he drawls, stepping a little closer. "You clean up real nice."

I cross my arms, ignoring how his gaze dips briefly before meeting mine again. "And you're still a pain in my ass."

"Ah," he nods, smirking. "You're just mad 'cause now I got something gorgeous to look at while I boss you around."

I scoff. "Boss *me* around? In what world?"

And did he just say "gorgeous"?

"In the world where you signed a contract to be my assistant," he leans in slightly, voice full of mischief. "And now, you work for me, darlin'."

My heart jumps slightly at how close he is to me.

Jack leans in close to me and whispers in my ear. "Although you're an absolute smoke show, I still prefer you in dusty boots, Wranglers, and that damn braid."

I open my mouth to argue but close it because I'm speechless and staring at him. Jenna claps her hands, interrupting us. "Alright, time to film. Try not to kill each other before we even begin."

Jack chuckles as I turn away, grumbling under my breath. This is going to be hell. And worse? Some tiny, traitorous part of me is going to love every second secretly.

When the contestants showed up, my presence did not phase most. But for Juliette, if looks could kill, I'd be six feet under the barn before noon. And the town of Bridger Falls? My presence thrilled them. The other four smile and wave and Savannah asks me if we're still on for dinner.

"Yeah, of course. Looking forward to it," I say. And I am. This morning Savannah and Elena came into the trailer and sat with me while I worked, and we chatted it up. I feel like they're not big fans of Juliette either. But I didn't ask. I'm too employed for that nonsense and any drama there.

I swear, half the town turned up this morning, lounging in lawn chairs like they're here for a fireworks show. Maggie even set up a little table with Old Man Wallace from the feed store, and they're collecting bets. I caught snippets of conversation as I stepped up next to Jack.

"Five bucks says the mean one tries to 'accidentally' trip Cami."

Someone else snorted. "Nah, they wouldn't do that to our Cami."

Oh, fantastic.

Jack leaned over, his voice low and full of amusement. "You ready for this, Wilder?"

I huffed. "Depends. Do I get hazard pay?"

His grin widened. "That depends. You planning to fight back?"

Before I could answer, Jenna called everyone together. "Alright, contestants! Today, you'll be working with Jack and *his assistant—*" She shot me a quick, knowing glance, like she was fully aware she'd just dropped a live grenade into this situation. "—to complete a set of ranch challenges."

Hannah, the perky brunette in an off-the-shoulder floral top and perfectly applied lipstick, smiled at me in a way that was teasing as if she was in on an inside joke. "So, Cami, how exactly did you become Jack's *assistant?*"

I open my mouth, but Jack answers first. "She's overqualified, really. Knows this ranch inside and out. No one better for the job."

Juliette's smile tightens. "Oh. *Interesting.*"

Jack, damn him, smirks. "She cleans up real nice, huh?"

All the contestants smiled, and some snorted, except Juliette. She glares at me.

"Not helping things here, Jack..." I mutter.

Juliette's nostrils flare slightly. "I mean, you don't seem *like* the ranching type. You're...the coffee girl."

I arch a brow. "Thanks, Juliette, I'm usually covered in horse hair and dirt, but now and then, I like to get cleaned up."

"Eww, horse's hair falls off? Like cat hair?? I might have an allergy," she complains to Jenna.

Listen, I'm a girl's girl. I don't engage in tearing down other women, so this is by far not what I was expecting.

Jack lets out a laugh, and I see the precise moment Juliette's jaw clenches.

Jenna, sensing the tension, claps her hands together. "Alright, first challenge! You're all going to learn how to saddle a horse. Jack and Cami will demonstrate."

I step up beside Jack, tightening a cinch on one of the horses. "Wanna lead the way, or should I?"

Jack barely hid his amusement. "Oh, I've got this."

Jenna says something to Savannah, and I watch Savannah morph into a whole new character which is fascinating. When she walks by me, she says quietly for only me to hear, "All for the show, Cami. Don't worry."

Wait, what? Are they like paid actors?

She batted her lashes. Jack, to his credit, at least looked over at me first, clearly waiting to see my reaction.

"Oh, don't look at me," I said dryly. "I'm just your *assistant*. You're the big, strong cowboy."

The crowd of townsfolk chuckle.

I stepped over, adjusting the saddle in two quick movements, and pat the horse's neck. "There you go. All set."

Juliette scowls. "I could've done that."

I flash her an encouraging smile. "Of course."

Next challenge: lassoing.

Juliette tosses the rope three feet in front of her and groans.

"Jack, this is *hard*. Maybe you could stand behind me and, like, guide me?"

Jack scratches the back of his neck, clearly torn between playing along for the sake of the show and not running for his truck. "Uh—"

"No worries, Juliette," I cut in. "I can show you."

Her face falls in disappointment as I step up, grabbed the lasso, and nailed the target on my first try.

The crowd cheers.

Jack, looking way too pleased, turned to her. "See? Now you try."

She scowls and tosses the rope again, missing by a mile.

Old Man Wallace laughs. "This is better than the rodeo."

Ruby who had been suspiciously quiet until now, went for a different approach. She leans into Jack, placing a delicate hand on his arm. "So, Jack," she practically purrs. "What kind of woman *do* you see yourself with?"

And just like that, the entire place goes dead silent.

My stomach does something completely stupid, and I hate myself for it.

Jack looks down at Ruby, then turns to look at me. His expression is unreadable, but his eyes linger just long enough that I know everyone caught it.

My stomach dips and I clench my thighs together at the heat in his eyes. Holy shit.

Someone in the crowd actually *gasps*.

Ruby watches us with fascination.

Jack, obviously enjoying this far too much, smirks. "Oh, you know. Someone who can keep up with me."

Ruby's mouth twitches.

I need to leave before I do something embarrassing.

Jenna, ever the professional, jumps in before a full-on brawl breaks out. "Alright, everyone! Let's wrap up for now! Jack,

Cami, great work. Contestants, maybe practice saddling before the next round."

The girls give me apologetic smiles as they walked off, but I barely notice.

Because Jack is still watching me.

And I realize this whole "pretending not to like him" thing is going to be a hell of a lot harder than I thought.

* * *

I walk to the coffee trailer to pack up, and Savannah and Elena wait for me and offer a wave and a smile.

"Hey, ladies," I call as I unlock the door and step in, surprised when they follow me. "Okay, come on in."

"Okay, here's the deal," Savannah says. "I'm married. I'm here as a paid actress to work this show. I don't want Jack. In fact, no offense, but none of us do. Well, except maybe Juliette. Apparently, she's not a paid actress, she's actually really into him."

I open my mouth and close it, unsure what to say to that. "Okay, wow. Thanks for letting me know."

Elena chuckles, "Cami, we like you. And Jack is so into you, it's not even funny. We just wanted you to know that this is a job for us. Promise. So, when you watch us film, that's all it is."

I sigh with surprise and relief. "Okay."

"Okay, now please for the love of God, can we get an iced coffee? I know you're closed, but I desperately need one. No one in town has coffee like yours." Savannah groans with a grin.

"Of course," I answer with a smile. "Have a seat. We still on for dinner at The Black Dog?"

"Hell yeah," Elena says. "Hannah wants to come too, but she'll be a little late. She has to FaceTime her kid."

I turn, confused. "She has a kid?"

"Yes, girl. We all have good reasons for being here. Hannah's a single mom going to law school. This show is paying off all her student loans and a down payment on a new house for her and her son. We all need this job."

Holy cow.

"Ruby is paying off her mother's staggering medical bills. She also has a good reason, too. She has a boyfriend back home in L.A," Elena adds.

"Wow, I didn't know. I'm glad you guys are here," I say softly.

I hand one of the coffees over and Savannah sighs. "Best part of this show is your coffee, Cami."

This show might be okay after all.

Chapter 17
Jack

Tennessee Whiskey by Chris Stapleton

I was up before the sun, got the cattle checked, fed the horses, and even managed to fix a busted latch on the east pasture gate. Now, I'm hiding out like a damn coward. The fact is that I can't sleep. She's on my mind, and I can't shake her out of it. I can't even busy myself with work. She's everywhere. She's parked her trailer at my ranch and her heart in mine.

She's been on my mind so much. The past keeps replaying in my dreams. I have dreamed twice now of the day I kissed her all those years ago and then turned her down. I'll never forget the look on her face when I broke her heart. It shattered me. But I had to do it. If I hadn't let her go, my father would have done some bad shit to the Wilder Ranch. I had to protect her and her family. There's no telling how far he would have gone. He didn't want any of us kids to have anything to do with the Wilder Ranch. I shattered her when I rejected her. She was so sweet and innocent back then, and we had that young love going on. I remember that kiss and how amazing she tasted. I still think about that kiss.

The inside of the Steamy Sips trailer is clean and smells like vanilla and coffee. Although, judging by the machine sitting smugly on the counter, I'll never be able to figure out how to actually *make* a cup without screwing the whole thing up. I scowl at the thing, deciding water is just fine, and take a sip from my bottle as I slide into the dinette booth at the back of the trailer.

The place is tidy, and Cami keeps everything neatly lined up, nothing out of place. No clutter, no mess, just efficiency. A stark contrast to the chaos that surrounds *The Rancher Finds a Wife,* which I'm figuring out is mostly staged arguments, too much perfume, and contestants pretending they knew what a hay bale was for. Nothing was what it was, and it was driving me crazy. I can't wait for this to all be over. This is just all weird.

I check my phone, mostly out of habit. I missed a few texts from my brothers, one from Weston that just said, *"Survive the day"*—real helpful—and one from Tucker that was just a picture of a goat tied to the back of the feed truck with no explanation. Typical.

I lean back and drummed my fingers against the table. That's when I noticed the folder tucked neatly into the corner on top of a stack of papers, just peeking out enough to catch my eye. **Wilder Ranch** was scrawled across in bold black letters.

I hesitate. Not because I have any moral issue with snooping —if Cami didn't want people looking at this, she wouldn't have left it sitting out—but because I know whatever is inside is probably something important to her. And what's important to her, is important to me. Still, curiosity got the best of me.

Flipping it open, I scan the pages inside, expecting, I don't know... maybe some angry notes about how she was being forced to work with *me?* Instead, I found *plans.* Big ones.

Fall festivals, bonfires, horseback riding lessons. A whole operation built around families coming to make memories at Wilder Ranch. A *summer camp...* I could practically hear kids laughing and running through the fields already.

I kept flipping, my excitement growing with everything I read.

She wants to turn Wilder House into a B&B and a farm-to-table restaurant. Inside, with reservations only? A place where guests could experience real ranch life, made-from-scratch food? Damn.

And the wild mustangs? She'd researched the leasing programs and figured out how to bring in state funding while giving those horses a place to roam safely. The plans looked profitable, which showed how she could finance them to get three phases of the new business up and running while taking on minimal debt. It was well thought out. The plan was *genius.*

I lean back, staring at the papers. This wasn't just some half-baked idea, she'd thought this through. She knew exactly what she wanted Wilder Ranch to be, and hell if it didn't make my chest ache a little. This is *Cami's* dream.

The sound of the trailer door swinging open made me snap the folder shut.

"Find something interesting, Jessop?"

I looked up to see Cami standing there, hands on her hips, eyebrow arched.

She didn't look mad, just *curious.* Like she's waiting to see what I'll say.

I clear my throat and smirk. "You always leave top-secret documents lying around for just anyone to find?"

"Only when I want to give people something to think about."

She drops her bag onto the counter and eyes me. "You look suspiciously guilty."

"Me? Nah." I lean forward, resting my forearms on the table. "Just impressed. This is some plan, Wilder."

She blinks, as if she wasn't expecting that. "You actually read it?"

"Every word." I grunt. "Didn't even need pictures."

"Wow," she says dryly. "Look at you. A real scholar."

I chuckle and tap the folder. "You serious about all this?"

Her expression shifts for a second. A little flicker of vulnerability before she masks it with sarcasm. "No, I just thought I'd spend months writing a business plan for fun."

"Could've fooled me," I say. "I mean, I never took you for a *visionary* type."

"Right, because I'm just some hot-headed ranch girl who's making this up as I go."

"That's *exactly* what you are," I tease, "but this? This is real, Cami. This is *good*."

She crosses her arms, studying me. "You actually *like* the plan?"

"Are you kidding?" I lean back in the booth. "It's *brilliant*. The restaurant alone? The summer camps? The family events? You've got a goldmine here. This is something Bridger Falls needs. Heck, wish I'd had this as a kid."

Her lips part slightly, like maybe she didn't expect me to say that. "We did have this as kids. We'd just be giving this to other kids to experience."

Then, of course, she ruins the moment by squinting at me. "Alright, what's the catch? You want a percentage? Gonna make me sign my life away in a contract?"

I snort. "I was actually thinking I want to *help* you."

Her arms drop to her sides, mouth falling open. "You? *Help me?*"

"Yeah." I rub the back of my neck. "Look, Wilder Ranch—"

"You own it, which means you could make my life miserable at any second."

"Or," I say, holding up a finger, ignoring her jabs, "I could help you make this happen. Nothing is stopping you. What I was *about* to say is that Wilder Ranch is safe. No one is taking it from you, which means no one is stopping you from making all of this happen."

She studies me, skeptical as ever.

Finally, she sighs and drops into the seat across from me. "You *really* think it's a good idea?"

"I *know* it is." I tap the folder. "And for what it's worth, I don't think I've ever seen you this passionate about anything. Well, except maybe hating me."

She lets out a laugh. "Yeah, well. You make it easy."

I smirk. "And yet, here we are. Would you stop being so mean to me?"

She shakes her head, amused. "No."

"If I was dying, would you give me a kidney?" I ask.

She gives me a look of confusion then says, "Maybe. If you died, I'd have no one to tease."

For a second, we just sit here. And damn it, I like this, sitting across from her, talking about something that matters.

Her head tilt and knowing look shatters that moment. "So, how long have you been hiding in here, exactly?"

I scoff. "I wasn't hiding, I was just—"

"You don't know how to work the coffee machine, do you?"

I squirm slightly. "I... might have some technical difficulties."

Cami's grin stretches wide, downright predatory. "Well, well, well. Big bad, Jack Jessop. Defeated by a coffee maker."

I scowl. "Don't make this a thing."

"Oh, it's a thing now." She stands up, grabs a mug, and starts working the machine with an ease that makes me resent her a little. "So, let me get this straight. You can mend a fence, break in a wild colt, and sweet-talk a whole town into trusting the Jessops again... but you can't make a cup of coffee?"

"Not can't," I correct. "Just... haven't tried. Yet."

She hands me a steaming mug, looking way too pleased with herself. "Well, today's your lucky day, Jessop. Welcome to the world of caffeine. Try not to embarrass yourself today with all of your ladies."

I take the mug, sipping carefully as she smirks.

Damn it. It's good.

"That's one helluva business plan. Where did you learn all of that?" Setting my mug down, I asked.

"I guess there are things you don't know about me, Jack," she says as she pours herself a cup of coffee.

"I can't wait to find out," I say over my mug.

I almost spill my coffee in surprise when the door to the trailer swings open like a damn police raid.

Jenna storms in, eyes sharp, clipboard in hand, wearing a headset, looking like she is about to ruin my entire day.

"There you are!" she announces, throwing her arms up dramatically like she'd just found a missing child. "I knew you were hiding."

Cami, still smirking at me from across the trailer, snorts. "Told you."

"Oh, he absolutely is," Jenna confirms, marching toward me with the energy of a woman who was about to make my life significantly harder. "You finished your ranch chores and then what? Scuttled off in here to avoid interacting with the contestants?"

I scoff. "I don't scuttle."

Jenna ignores me and drops into the seat next to Cami like she owns the place. Then, without a second's hesitation, she snatches a muffin off Cami's plate.

Cami gasps, full-on betrayal. "Hey!"

"Possession is nine-tenths of the law, sweetheart," Jenna says through a mouthful of stolen muffin, flipping open her clipboard. "Shouldn't be harboring fugitives in your trailer."

Cami smirks at me. "I did *not* hide him in here."

I just kept sipping my coffee, praying if I stayed quiet, maybe, Jenna would miraculously forget she was here to make me miserable.

No such luck.

"Alright, Jack," Jenna says, flipping a page and leveling me with a look. "Time to earn that reality TV paycheck. You've got a *date* lined up this evening, and I need you camera-ready."

I frown. "A *date?*"

"Yes, a date," she repeats, sighing like she's dealing with a particularly dense toddler. "That's kind of the entire premise of the show, Jack. You *do* remember signing the contract, right?"

Cami snickers, still working on her replacement muffin. "You should see his contract-reading skills. Top-tier."

I shoot her a glare. "You gonna help me out here or what?"

She shakes her head. "Not a chance."

Jenna flipped another page on her clipboard. "You're filming in an hour, so you should probably go clean up first."

I blinked. "I *am* clean."

Jenna and Cami exchanged a *look*.

Cami sighs dramatically, waving a hand in my general direction. "Jack, you smell like the inside of a horse trailer."

Jenna nods. "Aggressively barn-scented. The ladies want fresh and clean."

I scowl. "It's called *working*, ladies. Maybe try it sometime."

Jenna pats me on the arm. "Oh, sweetie, I work all day. Just not in *manure*."

Cami wrinkles her nose. "Seriously, Jessop. I'd *pay* to see the reactions if you showed up smelling like you do right now. Actually, you know what? You absolutely should show up like this for them."

Jenna shoots her a glare. "Not helping."

I set my coffee down with an exaggerated sigh. "Y'all are the worst."

"We know," they say in unison.

I looked to the ceiling, praying for strength. "What exactly am I supposed to do on this date?"

Jenna checks her notes. "It's a romantic picnic date with Juliette."

I groan. Juliette spent all yesterday looking at the ranch like it was some kind of biohazard site.

"Oh, this is gonna be fantastic," Cami says, grinning as she takes another bite of her muffin.

I shake my head at her. She's enjoying this way too much.

Jenna steals another muffin from the case and flips to the next page on her clipboard. "Alright, so, you've got that super romantic picnic planned for later, and then tomorrow, we've got the team challenge, where the girls compete and winner gets the date with you."

"Another date?" I groan.

Cami perks up. "Oh, I want to watch that."

Jenna smirks. "I figured you might."

I lean back in the booth, rubbing a hand over my face. "I don't have time for all this. I've got real work to do before filming again. Fencing needs repairing in the west pasture. Water troughs need cleaning. We're still down a couple hands, and—"

Jenna holds up a hand. "Sounds exhausting. Take a shower first."

I scowl. "No."

Jenna blinks. "What do you mean, no?"

"I've got work to do."

Cami sighs like I was the most ridiculous man alive. "Jack,

no offense, but if you show up smelling like you do right now, Juliette is gonna file a complaint with HR."

I frown. "Do we even have an HR?"

Jenna points to herself. "It's me. And I'm already preemptively filing a complaint."

Cami smirks. "See? Now go wash the barn off yourself before I have to Febreze you like a dog that rolled in something questionable."

I glare at her. "You would do that."

"Oh, one hundred percent." She confirms.

Jenna nods, sipping the to go coffee Cami hands her. "She's not bluffing. She keeps a can of 'Clean Linen' scented Febreze in her truck."

Cami grins. "You bet your ass I do."

I sigh and stand from the table with a grumble. "Y'all are unbearable."

Jenna patted my arm. "That's why you love us."

"Not sure I'd use that word," I mutter, grabbing my hat.

Cami smirks, holding up a muffin. "I'll save you one of these for when you've showered."

I point at her. "If I come back to find zero muffins, there will be consequences."

She bats her lashes. "Oh, I'm so scared."

Jenna claps her hands. "Okay, go shower, cowboy. You smell like livestock."

Grumbling under my breath, I grab my hat and head out.

Their laughter follows me all the way to the lodge.

This show is gonna be the death of me. And worse? Cami's loving every second of it.

And they're right, I do need a shower. Mostly a cold shower because when I'm around Cami, I am more and more attracted to her, and my body betrays me. Damn it.

Chapter 18
Cami

Scared to Start by Michael Marcagi

I should be doing something productive.

Like handling actual business for Steamy Sips or tackling the never-ending to-do list at the Wilder Ranch. But instead, I'm on my way to the Bridger Falls Fire Station with a box of muffins that Ollie did not request but will absolutely demolish. Jack's on his stupid picnic date, and I hate this.

When I step inside, the station is already bustling, the scent of smoke, sweat, and something delicious mixing in the air.

Ollie looks up from where he sprawls on the beat-up couch in the common room, eyes half-lidded and hair a mess as if he's been running his fingers through it.

I raise an eyebrow. "Whoa. Did you actually get run over by a firetruck, or are you just committing to looking like a PSA for exhaustion?"

Ollie groans, rubbing his face. "Long night. Then a long day. People keep lighting dumb things on fire."

I set the box of muffins on the table in front of him. "Did you try telling them not to?"

"Yeah, Cami, thanks for the brilliant idea. I'll just politely ask people to stop having emergencies," he says dryly, before eyeing the box. "What's this?"

"Muffins. I made extra."

"You made extra?" Ollie smirks, dragging the box toward him. "Or did you conveniently decide you 'accidentally' baked too much because you wanted to come see your favorite brother?"

"You're my *only* brother."

"Exactly," he says, already peeling open the lid. "And that makes me the favorite by default."

"Favorite pain in my ass, maybe."

He grins around a mouthful of muffin. "That's rude."

I lean against the counter, watching as he inhales two muffins in the time it took me to check my phone. "So, how's life? How's living above Poppy's shop?"

He grunts. "It's fine. I'm here a lot, so not really there all that much."

Then, he squints at me and says, "You look like you're suspiciously spending a lot of time at the Jessop Ranch."

I stiffen. "Excuse me?"

Ollie smirks. "I saw you the other day when I stopped by to see Jack. Looked like you were *real cozy* out there."

"It's called working, Ollie. I have to pay bills."

He snorts. "Yeah, that must be what it is, because I totally believe you're not emotionally invested in any of this."

I throw a napkin at his face. "Shut up and eat your muffin."

Ollie laughs, but before he can push me further, someone else strolls into the room, and wow, is he ridiculously good looking.

"Cami," Ollie says, jerking his thumb over his shoulder. "Meet Beau. He's the new guy."

I turn just as he steps toward us, towel slung over his shoulder.

He has dark, wavy hair, an easy grin, and the kind of broad shoulders that could probably bench press me and the box of muffins at the same time. He has eyes the color of chocolate and a warm smile.

I blink. Wow. This is not who I was expecting Beau to be.

He wipes his hands on the dish towel and reaches out. "Hey, you must be Ollie's sister."

I shake his hand, eyeing the tray of fresh biscuits, jam, and cinnamon rolls he just set on the table. "Uh, yeah. Cami."

"Beau Callahan. Resident firehouse cook, and apparently, part-time baker."

I nod, still taking in the spread of baked goods. "Wait, *you* made all this?"

He nods, smirking. "Yep. Grew up in a big family, cooking's just second nature at this point."

Ollie grins. "He feeds us like we're a bunch of starving orphans."

Beau shrugs. "I like feeding people. And y'all eat like you haven't seen food in weeks."

I cross my arms, staring at the biscuits. "You ever thought about baking for extra cash?"

Beau raises an eyebrow. "You offering?"

"I might be," I say, glancing at the golden, flaky perfect looking biscuits. "I could use some extra hands at Steamy Sips, especially with my *other* obligations right now."

Ollie waggles his eyebrows. "Damn, Cami. You didn't even consider asking me for part time work."

"Because you suck at baking," I shoot back.

Ollie shrugs. "Fair."

I turn back to Beau. "So, what do you think? You have your shifts here, but I could use someone part-time."

Beau grins. "I'm in."

Ollie gasps, dramatically clutching his chest. "That's it? That's all it takes?"

I grab a biscuit from the plate and take a bite. It's perfect, soft, buttery, and flaky. "I mean, can you bake like this?"

Ollie glares. "No."

"Then shut up."

Beau chuckles, folding his arms. "I like her."

Ollie rolls his eyes. "Yeah, yeah, she grows on you. Like a fungus."

I playfully kick him under the table.

We settle into the firehouse kitchen, eating biscuits and drinking coffee like we aren't in the middle of a workday. Beau asks all about Steamy Sips, and I explain how I'm working out at the ranch temporarily, hence why I'm practically hiring on the spot.

Ollie, meanwhile, continues giving me hell. "So, are you gonna bring some muffins to the *Jessop Ranch* next?"

I scowl at him. "Why would I do that?"

Ollie smirks. "Oh, I don't know, maybe because you're contractually obligated to be there? Or maybe because you're secretly obsessed with Jack?"

Beau looks between us, amused. "This sounds like a story."

"There is no story," I say quickly.

"There's *so much* story," Ollie corrects.

Beau grins. "Oh, I guess I gotta hear this."

I groan. "No, you don't."

Ollie leans back, folding his arms. "She's Jack Jessop's assistant now. But it's definitely *not* personal."

Beau raises an eyebrow. "Jessop Ranch Jack?"

"The very one." Ollie smirks. "And Cami is definitely not interested in him at all."

Beau glances at me. "You look real guilty for someone who's *not* interested."

I stand abruptly. "Okay, this was fun, but I have places to be."

Ollie chuckles. "Yeah, yeah. Go check on your live in not-boyfriend."

I flip him off and wave to Beau as I leave the firehouse.

But instead of heading home, I found myself driving toward Jessop Ranch.

For completely legitimate reasons.

* * *

I should have gone to bed, but I was feeling restless. That could be because I had ended up making a detour earlier to the Jessop Ranch to spy on Jack on his oh so romantic picnic date. Now, here I am, out in the pastures, the cool Wyoming night stretching out like a quiet, open promise. The stars above are sharp and bright, the kind you only get in a place like this, where the sky isn't smothered by city lights, just endless and wild, like the land itself.

Mouse, my stubborn little sweet boy, flicks his ears as I guide him on a peaceful walk through the open field behind Wilder House. I didn't even bother saddling him, just hopped on bareback, letting the rhythm of his steps settle something restless in my chest.

I *am not* thinking about Jack or how he spent all evening on a picnic date with another woman. Fake contestants or not, it still gets to me.

I am not thinking about how he laughed at something she said.

I'm not—

A horse's snort sounds from behind me in the dark.

I sigh. Of course.

"You stalking me, Jessop?" I call without turning.

Jack's voice, smooth and lazy, drifts through the night air. "I could ask you the same thing. You were mighty interested in my picnic earlier."

I scowl but still didn't turn around. "I don't know what you're talking about."

"Mm-hmm."

"I saw you, Wilder."

Mouse flicks his ears again, clearly picking up on my tension. I exhale, forcing myself to loosen my grip on him.

Jack and Pesto walk up beside us, Jack looking obnoxiously at ease.

He studies me, smirking like he knows exactly what is going on in my head.

"So," he says casually. "Why are you taking a lot of these late-night rides?"

I shoot back. "Some of us have reality TV commitments occupying our very busy schedules."

Jack chuckles. "Ah, so you're saying you're jealous of my very demanding filming requirements?"

I snort. "Oh yeah, so jealous. Must be exhausting getting fed cheese and crackers while sitting in the grass."

"Don't forget the wine," he says. "She picked it out herself. Said it had 'earthy undertones.'"

I gag dramatically. "You poor thing. Must've been *so* hard for you. You don't even like wine."

Jack grins, but his eyes flicker with something more like amusement and curiosity, like he's waiting to see if I'll admit the obvious.

Jack stretches, resting his forearms against his saddle horn. "You wanna know how it went?"

"Nope."

"She told me she's allergic to grass."

I blink. "You're lying."

Jack shakes his head, looking downright delighted. "Swear on Pesto's life. She said it's 'so rustic' out here, but she's 'just not used to all the elements.'"

I stare at him. "You mean... *the outdoors?*"

"Exactly."

A laugh bursts out of me before I can stop it. "Oh my God. Jessop, you're gonna end up marrying someone who breaks out in hives every time the wind blows."

Jack tilts his head. "Who said I was gonna marry anyone?"

I roll my eyes. "That's literally the point of the show."

He smirks. "I think the point is to entertain the masses."

I turn, riding Mouse a little ahead of him, my fingers lightly running over the horse's coarse mane. The breeze is cool against my face, but my skin is still warm from the ride.

Jack follows. "So, you're really not gonna ask how the date ended?"

I sigh dramatically. "Fine. How did it end?"

"She tried to get me to teach her how to 'do cowboy things.'"

I choke. "What the hell does *that* mean?"

He grins. "Your guess is as good as mine. I asked for clarification, and she said she wanted to 'lasso something.'"

"Oh, this just keeps getting better," I mutter. "Did she manage to lasso anything?"

"Almost," Jack says. "Would've been real impressive if she hadn't accidentally roped herself to a fence post."

I lose it. The kind of laugh that makes my stomach hurt and my shoulders shake as Mouse keeps moving forward, utterly unbothered by my outburst.

Jack just keeps looking at me, smirking. "Glad to see you're so supportive of my reality TV journey."

I wipe a tear from my eye, shaking my head. "I love that you're on this show."

"You hate that I'm dating other women," he corrects, his voice just a little too smug.

I shoot him a glare. "Don't flatter yourself, Jessop."

I wonder if Jack knows that most of the women aren't really here for the show. I don't want to say anything, and I definitely don't want him to think that I'm jealous.

His eyes gleam in the moonlight, but he doesn't push further. Just lets the silence settle around us. We ride in easy quiet, the distant sounds of the ranch on the wind, the rustling grass, the occasional snort of a horse wrapping around us like a familiar song.

We ride in silence for a while, the soft thud of hooves in the grass, and the night settling over us like a blanket. The stars are scattered thick above us, and it's so peaceful.

I'm just starting to feel... calm. Which is exactly when Jack opens his mouth. "I'm proud of you, you know that?"

My head snaps toward him. I blink. "What?"

He doesn't even flinch, just keeps riding steady, like he didn't just casually drop a bomb on my heart.

"The ranch," he says. "Your plans for it. All of it."

Something tightens in my chest—sharp and deep and stupidly unexpected. My fingers flex on the reins. He sees it. Not just the land. Not just the old Wilder legacy. He sees what I want to build. And somehow, that hits harder than anything else has all week.

I swallow around the lump in my throat. "Thanks."

Jack nods like it's no big deal. Like he didn't just undo me with five words and that stupid soft tone of his. "It's a good plan, Cami," he says. "Smart. Big-picture. You've got great dreams. I can't wait to see them come true."

I let out a breath and look up at the stars again because if I look at him too long, I might say something embarrassing. Like marry me. Or stop looking at me like that with your damn green eyes and your barn-built biceps.

A warmth spreads through my chest. Unwanted. Uninvited. Completely undeniable.

Because when Jack tells me he's proud of me? It hits different.

The silence falls again, but it's not heavy this time. It's full of unsaid things I'm not quite brave enough to name. Not yet. And the best part? Jack doesn't push.

He doesn't fill the quiet or prod me for a reaction. He just rides beside me, calm and steady, like he's content to be in my orbit for as long as I'll let him stay.

And maybe that's the thing that wrecks me most of all.

Chapter 19
Jack

Devil You Know by Tyler Braden

I pause halfway down the lodge hallway, carrying a broken latch I'm repairing and a bad attitude, and narrow my eyes when I hear Cami laugh at something. That laugh was a flirty one. The "I'm flirting or at least thinking about it" laugh.

I follow it and stop when I see some dude in my kitchen with Cami.

Flannel sleeves are rolled up, forearms dusted in flour, and his hair is pushed back like he is some celebrity chef. And Cami stands beside him, grinning at a bowl of dough.

"What's going on?" I say coolly.

Cami doesn't even flinch. She just turns with a spatula in one hand and one hip cocked like she'd been waiting for this moment. "Well, hey there, Jessop. Didn't see you sneak in while we were *baking*."

"Storm is coming. I was getting everything ready," I tell her as I watch them work side by side, hating every second of it.

She smirks, "Do you mean the weather or is that just your mood entering the chat?"

"Very funny, Wilder," I reply, glaring at the dude next to her.

Beau clapped flour off his hands and gave me a nod that was *just* polite enough to make me want to throw something. "Morning, I'm Beau."

He said it like he expected we were going to be *friends*.

"We're making cinnamon rolls," Cami announces proudly. "Beau is going to help me with the baking."

I nod at Beau because I'm not a total asshole.

"Why do you need more help?" I ask, keeping my voice neutral. "Thought you had Mack."

Cami rolls her eyes like I've missed something obvious. "Because Beau has *skills*, Jessop."

"Mack's great in the trailer, she helps prep dough, does the early shift, but she still has school. And I can't do it all alone anymore." Her eyes flash. "I need both of them. *Not* that it's any of your business."

I open my mouth, then close it.

Beau doesn't say a word. He just slides a pan out of the oven with the confidence of someone who's done this a hundred times. Like he belongs here.

The smell hits me like a punch to the chest with the warm sugar, butter, cinnamon. It floods the kitchen like a memory I didn't ask for. My mother used to bake cinnamon rolls in this same kitchen. Sunday mornings. Before things got complicated. Before everything cracked wide open.

I swallow hard and look away. It's stupid. It's *just* cinnamon rolls. But the longer I stand here watching Beau move around the kitchen like it's *his*, the tighter my chest gets. I know it's irrational. I know Cami can hire whoever the hell she wants. But something about him in this space with her, makes my skin itch.

She glances over at me like she's waiting for another smartass comment.

I stay quiet.

Because if I open my mouth right now, it won't be about Beau. It'll be about the fact that the kitchen smells like home. And this place hasn't smelled like home since my mother died. And now the only thing that feels even close to home for me is Cami. Wherever she is, that's where home is for me.

Cami looks over at me and when she catches my eyes, she softens, "What do you want, Jack?"

Because I'm feeling all the feels today, I tell her, "Didn't realize we were holding auditions for Husband Material in the kitchen today."

Cami smirks. "Oven's hot. Gotta strike while the dough is rising."

Beau looks confused and also like he'd prefer to be anywhere but in this kitchen right now. "Should I... go stir something?"

I mutter, "Yeah. Preferably away from her."

Cami licks frosting off her finger, slow, sinful, like she knows exactly what she's doing. Her eyes lock on mine, full of mischief and absolutely no shame.

Okay, so she wants to play dirty. She has no idea what she's about to unleash if she wants to take it to that level.

"Jealousy's not a good color on you," she says sweetly, her tone a little too smug for a woman committing dessert-based crimes.

My breath catches, and my heart does something violent in my chest. *Jesus. That mouth. That look.* The way her tongue sweeps over her fingertip, like it was the most natural thing in the world, I felt it all the way in my dick.

I shift my stance, trying to ignore the very real and obvious reaction in my pants. No such luck.

"You keep doing that," I say, my voice low and rough, "and I'm going to forget there's anyone else in this room."

Her eyes flare, just for a second. There's a flicker of surprise, heat, challenge.

"Oh?" she asks, cocking her head, finger still halfway to her lips again.

I step closer, my body practically buzzing with the need to touch her. "Yeah. And if you think I *seem* jealous now, wait until I show you what I *do* when something's mine."

The air between us snaps. She freezes, breath hitching, frosting completely forgotten.

Cami bites her lip, cheeks pink, eyes dancing as she smirks at me, saying nothing. She doesn't have to.

We lock eyes across the kitchen like two people about to either kiss or body slam each other. Honestly? Probably it could go either way. This is why she gets under my skin. She's my kryptonite.

"Fine," I say, stepping closer. "Bake with *him*. See if I care."

"Already am," she smiles up at me with murder in her eyes. "And guess what? He's *nice* to me."

"You don't think I'm *nice* to you?" I challenge.

"Oh no, *you* are. *So* nice." She rolls her eyes, and it makes me want to spank the sass right out of her.

"Good," I say, leaning in a little closer. "Glad we agree."

We stood there, toe-to-toe, eye-to-eye, and probably one cinnamon roll away from setting the whole place on fire with tension.

Beau clears his throat behind us. "Uh... should I give you two some space?"

"No," we snap in unison.

I stalk out of the kitchen, feeling murderous.

Ollie sits in the living room, coffee in hand, watching the whole disaster unfold like it's reality TV.

"I take it Beau showed up for baking duty?" he asks, grinning.

"Beau's making cinnamon rolls." I say dryly.

"And that's a problem because…?" Ollie shakes his head, confused.

"Because he has a smug little grin like he invented frosting. And she *laughed*, Ollie. She laughed like she likes him."

Ollie sips his coffee. "You're adorable when you're jealous."

"I'm not jealous. I'm just right."

He smirks. "So, what's your next move, loverboy? You gonna bake her a pie and share your feelings?"

I exhale, dragging a hand down my face. "I hate him."

"No, you don't."

"I hate that she's smiling at him like that."

"You love her," Ollie says bluntly.

"I'm *not* talking about that right now."

"Right. Because feelings are scary, and cinnamon rolls are the enemy."

I point at him. "Exactly."

Ollie grins like he's been waiting all morning for this exact breakdown. "C'mon. Let's go tear something up. Burn some energy before you explode with your emotions."

I sigh. "What're we tearing up?"

"Don't care. Fence post, old shed, rusty tractor, hell, I'll let you punch the hay bales if it keeps you from beating up innocent Beau." Ollie laughs.

It's the way she laughed with him. The way she looked up at him like he belonged there, elbow-deep in flour like he was some missing piece she hadn't realized she wanted until he showed up with a damn spatula and a smile.

And maybe I'm losing my mind. Hell, maybe I already have.

Because every time she smiles at someone else, it feels like getting kicked in the chest. And that scares the crap out of me.

I've spent years keeping my head down. Running from my problems, hiding from this ranch. And now I'm back, facing everything head-on, and it's a lot. And now she's here, loud, infuriating, messy-as-hell Cami, and she's set up camp in the middle of my life like it's hers to claim. The worst part? It is.

* * *

I'm on a barstool after a twelve-hour day of wrangling cows, fixing a busted gate, and pretending I don't care that the woman I'm not supposed to be in love with spent the afternoon baking with another man.

Then add in filming a staged date at a lake for that damn reality show with one contestant who referred to hay bales as "crunchy couches," and yeah, I earned this beer.

Ollie slid a fresh bottle in front of me with a knowing look. "You look like a man who got trampled by his big feelings today."

"It was a shit day," I mutter, peeling at the wrapper on my beer.

"Ah yes, the holy trifecta of emotional breakdowns."

We clink bottles and take a long drink. The Black Dog is busy tonight; low music, clinking glasses, that cozy hum of small-town people settling in. The kind of place where everyone knows everyone, and no one could mind their business if their life depended on it. Tonight, it's busier than usual, with more tourists coming through with the show filming. People stop by to see if they can glimpse any filming or find out any gossip.

Ollie gives me a side glance. "Avoiding my sister tonight?"

I hesitate and stare down at my beer. I don't like seeing her with Beau.

He smirks. "Ah. That's a no."

"Things were weird earlier."

He raises an eyebrow. "Weird like... romantic tension? Or weird like she almost set you on fire?"

"A little column A, little column B." I shrug.

Ollie takes a swig of his beer and laughs. "I heard that you called him 'Gluten Hercules.'"

"He flexed while kneading dough, Ollie. He *knew* what he was doing."

"So, how's it been going with you staying at Wilder Ranch in the barn?"

I groan. "I've been sleeping in your old room. On the *floor*. In a sleeping bag."

Ollie winces. "Ooof. Sure you don't want to stay at the barn? The hay bales up there are probably softer. Cami's less likely to kill you in the barn. The dog might even protect you."

"I'd rather take my chances and sleep on the floor. And the dog does sleep with me."

He barks out a laugh. "Well, now you're just punishing yourself. I can help you move a bed from the lodge over."

"That would be great," I add, dropping my voice. "I still don't trust Granger or Jace. They've been *too* quiet."

Ollie's grin fades slightly. "Yeah, I heard Jace picked up some job out in Casper. Ranch work or construction or something."

I raise an eyebrow and sigh with relief. "Good riddance."

"Still doesn't mean Granger's not planning something. You're right—they're too petty to just let it go."

I nod, but my attention shifts as a crowd comes through the front doors. And in walks chaos.

Cami, laughing at something Poppy says, hair in a messy braid that makes her look too damn cute for her own good. Jenna trailing behind, already scanning the bar and waving at someone. And Beau—towering, annoyingly tall, walks in behind them. And all the contestants came filing in behind them.

I immediately grumble and glare.

Ollie follows my line of sight and snorts into his beer. "Dude."

"What?" I exclaim.

"You're burning holes in him again with your laser eyeballs."

"I am not." I object.

"You're one eye-twitch away from a full-blown aneurysm," Ollie says with a grimace.

Cami looks over, spots me, and raises her eyebrows like *oh, you exist.*

I raised my beer and gave her a half-assed nod. *Smooth, Jessop. Real cool.*

"She's gonna figure it out eventually," Ollie says, watching me like I'm a live soap opera. "Everybody knows it but her, man."

"Shut it."

"You're head over boots in love," Ollie singsongs.

"*Shut it,*" I grit.

He leans over and whispers, "You're like a barn cat who hisses every time someone else pets her."

"You know I will punch you in the throat, Ollie."

"Wouldn't even blame you," he says cheerfully, tipping his beer back.

They come over to our side of the bar, pulling tables together. Jenna makes a beeline for some poor guy by the dartboard and gives him a hug, knowing him from somewhere. Poppy gives Ollie a mock salute and sits down across from him. Beau leans on a chair, all easy charm and polite nods.

And Cami?

She slides onto the stool next to me like we hadn't fought earlier. Like she hadn't nearly made me combust with our tension.

"Jessop," she says.

"Wilder."

She orders a hard cider, settles in beside me, and throws me a lazy glance. "You look like someone who's one beer away from making a scene."

"And you look like someone who *wants* to be the reason I do."

Her lips twitch. "What can I say? I'm a giver."

"Careful," I murmur, "I bite."

"Even better." She winks and clinks her glass against mine.

But before I could say something smart, Beau turns toward her with some joke about baking and offers her the last of his fries.

I hate him.

Cami laughs. Genuinely. And leans in, brushing his arm as she takes a fry.

I hate him *more.*

Ollie leans over. "You're doing the eye twitch again."

"I'm not," I protest.

"You are. It's like watching a sad country song in real life."

"I will bury you under the pool table," I tell him.

"You need to *say* something to her."

I glance over at Cami again. She's still smiling at someone next to her, but then her eyes slide to mine. Like she *feels* me watching. And she holds my gaze for one long, loaded second.

Maybe I don't have to say anything.

She hops off her stool and comes over. "Want to shoot a game of pool? Or are you going to sit here glaring until your beer cries?"

I shrug. "I'll play. But don't cry when I win."

"You haven't beat me at anything since we were fifteen, and I let you win at horseshoes because you looked like a sad cowboy whose horse ran away."

"I did lose my horse that week."

"I *know*. That's why I let you win," she says with annoyance.

She grabs a pool cue and walks toward the table like she didn't just rip open an old wound for sport. That's the thing with Cami. We have so much history. Some good, some bad, and some new. The new stuff is what's been hard to navigate.

I follow her. Of course I do.

We line up for the break. She leans over the table, and I definitely do not stare. I absolutely do not lose focus when she looks over her shoulder and smirks.

"Eyes up, Jessop."

"Not my fault your aim is shit."

She cracks the break, balls scattering like my rational thoughts.

We play. She trash-talks. I trash-talk back. Beau and the others cheer her on, which makes me extra obnoxious on purpose, which only makes her laugh more.

And by the end of the game, we're toe-to-toe again. Just like always. One breath away from too much.

She leans in, close enough for me to almost taste the cider on her breath.

"You still mad about earlier?" she whispers.

"Nope."

"Liar." Her eyes sparkle. "I like it when you're jealous. You get all grumpy and broody and say dumb things."

"I never say dumb things."

"Yeah," she whispers. "You do. But they're kind of my favorite."

And then she just... *walks away*. Left me there holding a cue and my pride in pieces.

Ollie passes by, slapping me on the back. "Head over heels," he says.

And you know what? I can't even deny it.

Chapter 20
Cami

Am I Okay? By Megan Moroney

The house is quiet by the time I pad out of the bathroom, still drying my hair with a towel and trying not to think about how weird things had gotten at the Black Dog.

We joked. We bantered. Jack *almost* smiled like he meant it. And then, of course, I went and said something flirty and stupid and walked away before I could face the consequences like a total coward.

It's fine. I'm fine. Everything is *totally normal.* I roll my eyes at my reflection in the mirror. "Yeah, keep telling yourself that."

After I brush my hair and wash off the bar air, I tug on my favorite sleep set—gray cotton shorts and a tank top that doesn't try to be sexy but absolutely is. Then I tiptoe down the stairs and out onto the back porch, careful about the creaky floorboards and waking Jack, who's probably brooding in his sleeping bag upstairs like a sad little cowboy.

Love lifts her head from the couch as soon as I step onto the porch.

"There you are, fuzzball," I whisper, crouching to scratch behind her ears. She huffs and flops into my lap as I drop onto the wicker couch and pull the faded blanket around us. "You missed all the drama at the bar."

She blinks up at me with her concerned warm brown eyes.

I sigh. "Fine. I'll fill you in. Jack was doing this broody stare thing every time Beau opened his mouth."

Love thumps her tail once, like she knows *exactly* who I'm talking about.

I look up at the stars, trying to ignore the warm flutter in my chest that always comes with thoughts of Jack. "It's getting worse, Love. Like, dangerous worse."

She tilts her head.

"I mean, did you *see* him in that henley last week? That thing clung to his arms like it was scared of being left behind."

Another tail thump.

"And tonight at the bar? When he leaned over to take that pool shot? I swear to God, I almost asked him to take me right there on the pool table. He's going to ruin me."

Love paws at me. I swear she's judging me harder than a therapist would.

I lean my head back against the cushion, staring out over the moonlit pasture. "The worst part is, he has no idea. Zero. He looks at me like I'm this walking, talking tornado and still *shows up* anyway. And I just—" I blow out a breath. "I'm falling for him so hard it's stupid."

Behind me, the floor creaks in the kitchen.

I tense. And then... footsteps. Slow. Bare. And then... "Someone used up all the hot water." Jack's voice. Low. Sleep-rough.

I turn my head and freeze. There he is. In the doorway.

Dripping. Glowing in the moonlight like some kind of vengeful ranch god. And wearing...Only. A. Towel. Just a towel.

My brain shuts down for a full three seconds.

His hair is wet and messy, curling slightly as water drips down his forehead. His chest is all shadows and sculpted heat, and the damn moon *reflects* off him like it has a personal grudge against my self-control.

"Oh," I squeak. "Hi."

His eyes narrow slightly. "Are you talking to the dog about me?"

"No."

Love barks.

"Love," I mutter.

Jack crosses his arms over his chest, which did *nothing* to help the situation. If anything, it made his biceps flex in a way that should've required a warning label.

I slap a hand over my face. "God. How long were you standing there?"

"Long enough to hear you compliment my henley."

"Well," I say weakly, "it's a nice shirt."

He steps forward, the porch board creaking under his foot. The towel shifts slightly, and I nearly choke on my own tongue.

"Cami."

"Nope." I huff.

"What?" he murmurs.

"Whatever you're about to say, I can't handle it while you're looking like that and dripping all over my emotional instability," I tell him, but I'm mortified he heard all of that. My cheeks feel hot, my palms grow sweaty, and my stomach is full of butterflies. I wish I could crawl under this blanket and take it back from him hearing that. And I know he won't let me run and hide. He's having this out now. Right now.

"You were also saying something about pool. And taking you

right there on the table?" He grins, and something about those words repeated back to me makes me squirm even more under the blanket.

"I didn't know you had a thing for wet cowboys."

"Jack, I am one weak moment away from making a really bad decision and blaming it on moonlight and your lack of clothing."

He smirks. "Noted."

Love chose that moment to hop off my lap and trot inside, abandoning me to the full wrath of my own thirst.

Jack raises an eyebrow. "You said you were falling for me."

"I also said you'd ruin my life," I say, pulling the blanket over my face. "Let's not forget that gem."

He takes another step closer. "Is that... a serious offer?"

I peek at him from under the blanket. "Do you *want* to ruin my life?"

He looks at me, something in his eyes, something soft and unguarded, that makes my heart stutter.

"I don't want to ruin your life, Cami," he says softly.

Oh.

He dropped down beside me, still holding the towel in place with one hand like we weren't in the middle of a scene straight out of my most unhinged fantasies. "I want to *be* in your life."

I stare at him. "You're not wearing pants."

He smirks. "That's what you took from that?"

I turn toward him, blanket still clutched to my chest like it might protect me from my own feelings. "I'm distracted. And you've been avoiding being near me. You barely look at me. Then you glare like I've betrayed you if I even *smile* at Beau. I have emotional whiplash, Jessop."

"I glare at everyone," he says casually. "It's part of my charm."

"I *thought* you were mad at me."

"I was mad at myself," he says. "For not saying something sooner."

"Well, now I've said something. Loudly. To the dog. While you were lurking half-naked like a ghost of shirtless cowboys past."

He chuckles again. "It was a really nice speech."

"Oh my God," I groan.

"And for the record," he adds, voice dropping just slightly, "I would have made you come so hard on that pool table. All you would have had to do was ask."

I forget how to breathe.

His eyes flick to my lips. And then...nothing. He stands.

"Goodnight, Cami."

I blink. "Wait, *what?* That's it?"

"I'm not going to kiss you while I'm in a towel. That feels like something out of a spicy romance novel."

"I *love* spicy romance novels!"

He grins, all smug and maddeningly confident. "Then you'll love what happens next."

He snaps off the towel and drops it on my chest. And with that, he turns and walks back inside. And the view does not disappoint.

I stare after him, heart hammering, face on fire, and brain completely offline.

Love trots back out, glances up at me, and drops her head back onto my lap with a sigh.

"Don't look at me like that," I mutter. "I blacked out. That wasn't my fault. And you ratted me out. Don't think I forgot that."

Upstairs, Jack's bedroom door creaks shut, and the thud hits me in my core.

I smell the damn soap on his towel.

I roll my eyes at the way my body reacts to that man. He's so infuriating... and so damn sexy.

"Goodnight, Love," I say to my Judas of a dog and make my way to my bedroom. Flopping down onto the bed, I turn my head and stare at the nightstand, and I swear the silicone inside has turned on by itself. Stupid phantom buzzing.

"I can't," I whisper into the quiet room. "Can I?"

Reaching over, I slide the drawer open and feel around blindly until my hand wraps around the only cock I've had in a very long time.

Looking at it with a mixture of contempt because it isn't Jack and hunger because it's *something*, I shrug and burrow under the blanket.

"Fuck it," I say as I push the button and close my eyes.

* * *

The bonfire crackles in the field behind the barn, sending sparks spiraling into the air like tiny fireflies.

It's a "casual night" for filming, which means the contestants had been told to dress casually and pretend they knew how to roast marshmallows. There are hay bales, throw blankets, and lanterns hung from fence posts, and a full camera crew lurks just out of the frame.

I stand near the edge of it all, clutching a mug of hot cider like it might save me from my bad thoughts.

Those of which are currently parading around in tight jeans and perfectly curled hair, trying to get Jack's attention while he leans up against a fence post and looks like *that*.

He's wearing faded jeans, dusty boots, and a flannel shirt that I might plot to steal later.

One of the contestants leans in, laughing and brushing invisible lint off his arm. I bite my tongue so hard I taste copper.

He doesn't pull away. But he does glance past her. At me. And it isn't a casual glance. It's a loaded one.

The kind that says "I see you. Get me out of here. I feel like I can't breathe."

Love nudges my leg, sensing my complete inner collapse. I kneel to pet her and whisper, "He's going to kill me with that face."

She licks my hand as if she agrees.

"Hey," Poppy says, appearing at my side with her own cider. "You okay?"

"Define okay," I reply.

"You're watching Jack like he's on a dessert cart, and you're on a juice cleanse."

I groan. "Do I look that obvious?"

"Yes. But in a cute, slow-burn-rom-com way." She shrugs. "You can make it work."

"He's doing it on purpose," I complain.

"He absolutely is," Poppy agrees.

I glance back over, which is a *mistake* because now he's laughing at something one woman says, but his eyes are still locked on *me*. Like he doesn't care who's standing next to him. Like he only cares about me.

Poppy grins. "Oh yeah. He's one step away from body-checking someone into the fire pit to get to you."

I harumph.

"Why don't you just go over there?"

"Because I'm trying to be chill," I say.

"You're about one eyebrow raise away from setting the barn ablaze. There is nothing chill about you right now. Absolutely nothing."

I sigh and take another sip. The cider isn't helping. It's not even distracting me.

The fire glows brighter as one contestant passes Jack a

marshmallow roasting stick. He takes it, twirls it in his fingers, and winks at me.

I nearly drop my mug. "Oh, for the love of God," I mutter.

"You know," Poppy said, "you *could* just jump his bones and put both of you out of your misery."

I shake my head.

Poppy gazes at Jack and says, "You know, God gave us men. But then he gave us Jack Jessop as an apology."

I snort and shake my head. She's not wrong.

"No one has to know. You guys can have a little hate fuck action. You know that would probably be so hot."

I snort laugh but it's not funny. Hate fucking Jack does sound so hot. Especially after he walked around in a towel last night.

I shoot her a look and tease. "If one of them touches him again, I will throw hands."

"I would *pay* to see that," Poppy snorts.

Love barks.

"I think she would too," Poppy says as she reaches down and pets her.

I take a deep breath, adjust my ponytail, and step forward, only for Jack to excuse himself from them and meet me halfway.

Like he knows. Like he's been waiting for me to make the move.

He stops in front of me, marshmallow stick still in hand.

"Hey," he says, voice low.

"Hey." I shrug.

"You've been avoiding me."

"I've been working," I say as I look everywhere but at him.

"You've been watching."

I swallow. "So have you."

He smirks, leaning just a little closer. "You look good tonight."

"Only tonight?"

"Don't start with me, Wilder."

I look up at him and notice the firelight casting shadows across his stupidly perfect jawline.

"Where's Beau tonight?" he asks as he narrows his eyes.

We stand there, suspended in the firelight and tension, neither one of us quite ready to break it.

"Flirting with Jenna, and she's flirting back," I admit with a grin.

He says nothing but just stares at me, and the corner of his lips quirk.

"You wanna kiss me, Jessop?" I ask, feeling bold.

"I want to," he admits.

"Then do it," I tell him, thinking about how I challenged him to this same kiss years ago and it went completely different afterwards. But now we're adults, and we've changed. I try not to think about our past and what happened all those years ago.

He takes the mug from my hands, sets it down on the nearest hay bale, and drags me by the hand away from the firepit, about twenty yards up the hill and down a path behind a smaller barn.

I don't move and can barely breathe.

My back hits the side of the barn, wood warm behind me, and Jack steps in close enough that I can smell the mix of cedar and leather and the faint hint of soap on his skin.

He plants both hands on either side of my head on the barn wall, blocking me in, his eyes on mine, and they're full of heat and longing.

He leans in and his nose traces a soft path up my neck before he cups my face, his fingers diving into my hair, his body pressing me up against the barn, our bodies flush. And damn how we fit together like puzzle pieces.

"Jack—"

I don't get another word out.

He kisses me.

No warning, no slow build. Just heat, hands on either side of my head and *him*. His mouth is demanding, desperate, like he's run out of patience and decided to ruin us both in the best possible way.

I gasp and moan against him, but that only seems to spur him on. His tongue tips into my mouth like he's been dying to do it for years, and honestly? It *feels* like he has. Like every kiss I've ever had before was just a warm-up for this kiss right here, right now.

My hands find his shirt, fisting it like it can anchor me when my knees are very much not cooperating. His body presses into mine, solid and hot and entirely too much and not enough.

When he finally breaks the kiss, we're both breathless. My lips tingle, and my brain is fried. I can still feel his lips on mine.

He rests his forehead against mine, voice rough and low. "What are you thinking right now?"

I don't know what I think anymore. My brain is a half-melted puddle.

I open my mouth to say something, but then...

"Jack?" a voice trills, too close. "Jack! I think I lost you!"

No. I groan.

Jack stiffens.

I blink up at him, stunned, and then I start shaking with quiet laughter. I can't even help it.

He groans and drops his head to my shoulder. "I want to walk straight into the woods and never come back."

I sigh, still breathless. "Better get back to your date, Jessop."

He pulls back just enough to meet my eyes and gives me that look that nearly undoes me all over again.

"Please don't make me," he pleads, voice low. "I'll kiss you again if you tell Jenna I got sick and had to leave."

My heart trips over itself. My entire body is still pressed to the barn like it's the only thing keeping me upright.

Somewhere behind us, the voice calls again, closer now. "Jaaack?"

He sighs and finally, finally steps back. His hands twitch like he wants to touch me again.

"This isn't over," he says, like a threat. Or a promise.

My lips still buzz from that kiss. My heart still races.

"Damn right it's not," I say, and mean every word.

I want to have hate sex with Jack Jessop. Or whatever kind of sex. I just want him. I need him.

Chapter 21
Jack

Don't Mind If I do by Ella Langley, Riley Green

Cami stands twenty feet away, looking like the damn poster girl for a hot cowgirl rancher. She's covered in dirt, sweat, and what I think is a smudge of dust across her cheek. Her braid's falling out, her boots are caked with mud, and she's laughing at something Ollie says as they tag-team another calf like they've been doing this together for years. Which, okay, they kind of have.

At the Wilder Ranch, the town would all pitch in. Growing up, our ranches did not co-mingle. My father forbid us to step foot on Wilder Ranch property after a big falling out at some point. And he sure as hell didn't ask the town for any help on his own ranch. He had wranglers for that. But the Wilder Ranch was always more about community and the town coming together to help out. And I always wished we'd had that at the Jessop Ranch. And now seeing it happen? That fills me with hope. Hope that we're turning this around and making this ranch the way it should be: a place that serves the community with good products and is helpful to our neighbors.

Cami and I have never worked together. Sure, we were secret friends as Cami and Ollie were with all of us. Not until everything changed. Not until Dad was gone. But it always had to be done in secret because our parents didn't like each other. Cami's grandparents were another story. They were very special people. When I was little, they were very kind to me and my siblings. I never forgot that.

The ranch feels different now. Better... lighter. Like we stopped holding our breath. It doesn't feel like we're constantly waiting for the next boot to drop. Tucker laughs more. Weston actually *shows up*. Jenna comes back to the ranch, even if it means dragging a damn reality show here. And me? I'm... hell, I'm kissing Cami Wilder against barn walls like I'm a teenager again and desperate for just one more minute with her. Because, well I am. I've wanted to kiss Cami again since we were teenagers. I've always wanted to redo that day that I broke her heart.

That kiss. Damn. It knocked something loose in me. Something big. She kissed like she wanted to crawl inside my chest and set up camp. And damn, I'd let her. Like she was daring me to stop her. And I didn't. I never could. I've had zero willpower when it comes to her.

And now I can't stop looking at her. Can't stop thinking about that kiss...

"Jack!"

The high-pitched voice jerks me back to reality. My date for tonight—Savannah? Hannah? Really need to start writing their names down—is trying to loop her arm through mine while I'm holding a branding iron. Great timing.

"Don't touch the metal," I say flatly.

She giggles and says in a flirty voice, "Ooooh, is it hot?"

I stare at her, and she winks. Pretty sure this is for the show, but I can't tell with them. They're smart as hell and doing their jobs and doing it well.

Across the field, Mack and Beau work the coffee trailer, serving up coffee and baked goods like it's the dang Kentucky Derby. Beau works alongside her, and they seem to be holding down the fort while Cami brands. We're short-handed since we've been cleaning out the wranglers and hiring new ones. We need all the help we can get.

Walker sidles up next to me, squinting at the horizon. "That Beau seems like a good guy."

I grunt and clip. "No, he is not."

He holds one calf for me and says, "You seem pretty bothered by him."

I glance over at him. "What makes you say that?"

He laughs. "Dude. You look like you want to murder him every time he's near Cami."

Before I can reply, Jenna stomps by, hair flying, clipboard flapping in the wind. She stops in front of all but one of the contestants, huddled under a tent like the sun is attacking them and the dirt scares them. The other one whose name I can't remember is actually out wrangling, and she looks like she *likes* it. *Damn.*

"You want screen time?" she asks the contestants under the tent. "Try *doing something*."

They blink at her like confused baby deer. One of them fans herself with a perfectly manicured hand. Her boots are blindingly white.

"You know," Walker says, sipping his coffee, "this is the best day we've had out here in a long time."

He's not wrong.

People showed up. Neighbors. Old friends. Even Sheriff Matthews brought his wife and a pie. Which is huge. Usually, my father's trouble brought Sheriff Matthews to the ranch. His coming out here for branding day is a show of support. And that means a lot. There's music playing from a truck bed, kids running around with stick horses, and someone's dog has stolen an entire pack of hot dogs off the grill.

Tucker and Weston walk over, both sweaty and grinning like idiots. Weston claps a hand on my shoulder.

"This was a good call," he says.

"We were just talking about that," I agree.

"The branding. The people. All of it," Tucker adds. "We needed this."

And we did. The ranch doesn't feel like a place of doom anymore. It feels like it's *ours*.

Out in the corral, Cami turns her head and catches me watching her. She doesn't smile.

She smirks.

That smug, cocky little tilt of her mouth makes me want to throw her over my shoulder and drag her into the nearest horse stall and kiss her again.

Even better, it makes me want to see those lips wrapped around my dick. Fuck. Now I've gotta hide a boner while I wield a hot branding iron.

I pull it together and, surprisingly, stay focused on what we're doing.

We end up side-by-side after lunch, working through a batch of calves like we've been doing it together our whole lives. We move in sync. Toss banter back and forth like it's second nature. And I love every minute of it. I like being the one to put that smile on her face.

"Watch it, Jessop," she says as I nearly trip over her foot. "Wouldn't want to get branded by mistake."

"You branding me now? I thought we were taking things slow." I cock my eyebrow at her.

She doesn't miss a beat. "Depends *where* I get to put my initials."

I almost drop the iron. The cameras are definitely rolling. I don't even care.

I can't stop glancing over at her. She looks beautiful. Wild. Sweaty and flushed and in her element. Ranch life has always been what lights her up. Her eyes are bright, her laughter easy, and she fits here. On this ranch with my brothers, my friends, this town. And *with me*.

I don't want the day to end. Not the branding. Not the flirting. Not this strange, perfect peace that's settled over the ranch like a warm comforting blanket. I glance over at her one more time and think, *Damn*.

* * *

My collar is too damn tight. I don't know who thought buttoning it all the way up was a good idea, so I'm going to blame Jenna. She gave me 'The Look' this morning. You know the one. The don't-you-dare-embarrass-the-family-on-camera look. It came right after she adjusted my shirt collar like I was five and muttered something about "presentable for television."

And now I'm on this date, if you can even call it that with Ruby. She's been talking nonstop for the last fifteen minutes about the benefits of oat milk instead of cow's milk. Then she went on and on about how she once modeled for a boot brand that didn't make her touch real dirt, and she was so grateful for that.

She keeps touching me. Light taps on the arm, fake laughs with a hand on my knee. I've been shifting away for the last ten minutes, and now I'm about a foot off the damn picnic bench. Meanwhile, my shirt's stuck to my back, my jaw's locked from fake smiling, and I'm fantasizing about cattle rustlers riding in to save me.

When she pulls out a compact mirror to reapply lip gloss while I'm trying to explain why we use a squeeze chute, I excuse myself to "check the gate."

Instead, I head to Kyle and pull him aside. "Kyle, you know Steamy Sips?" I nod to the empty and closed up trailer for the night.

He nods and smiles, "Yeah?"

"I will make sure you get free lattes and muffins for the rest of the show if you get Ruby home safely and tell her goodnight for me," I tell him. "Tell her I didn't feel well."

He looks like he's thinking about this for a second and glances at Jenna who is across the pasture, talking to a camera person. Then he looks back at me, "Yeah, sure. Okay..."

I turn and keep walking. And I don't stop. I walk out past the barn. Past the trailer. Past the crowd and the cameras and a few of the contestants doing yoga in their rhinestone jeans.

I walk until I find myself on Wilder Ranch, straight to the back pasture, far from the crowds and people. I finally breathe a sigh of relief as I plop down by mine and Cami's tree, the old cottonwood behind the north pasture. The one with our initials carved into it from the summer we were sixteen and stupid. J + C. I sit down in the dirt, arms draped over my knees, and stare at the carving.

I groan. "I hate this show."

"That bad, huh?"

I glance up and find Cami standing there, holding two sweating mason jars of sweet tea. She hands one to me.

"Thanks," I say, cracking it open. "How did you know I was out here?"

She shrugs, dropping down beside me like she belongs there. "You practically ditched your date mid-sentence."

I huff a laugh. "I thought her name was Ruby. Might've been Savannah. I panicked."

"You called her Shania at one point."

"Damn it."

Cami snorts and takes a sip. "To be fair, she called you Jake. That's a new one. I'll call you Jake from now on. At least she was funny about it and teased you back."

I scoff. "Do not call me Jake."

We sit there for a second, quiet except for the low hum of the ranch in the distance, drinking our tea.

"You looked good today," she says after a beat.

I raise a brow. "Covered in dirt and sweat? You don't think I needed a shower?" I ask smugly since she gave me shit the other day.

"No, I mean it. You looked... happy. Like you're finally where you're supposed to be."

I glance at her. "You looked pretty happy, yourself."

She grins. "I am."

God, I want to kiss her again.

"Hey, Cami?"

She turns to me.

I reach out and trace my thumb along her cheek. There's a smudge of dirt I pretend to wipe away, but really, I just want an excuse to touch her.

"I like kissing you."

Her eyes flick to mine, then my mouth, and back. "You're not terrible at it, I guess," she says, a little breathless.

"Not terrible?" I snort. "You seemed into it, Wilder."

She shrugs. "I've had worse."

"Should I try again?" I whisper roughly.

She leans in, close enough for me to smell the mix of sun and cinnamon on her. "You trying to win gold in the flirting, Jessop?"

I smile at her, slow and sure. "Just aiming for my personal best."

She rolls her eyes, but she's smiling too.

And under the old cottonwood tree with our initials carved in its bark and the sun dipping low behind her, I feel it again.

That thing she knocked loose in me with one kiss. The feeling of hope for more of this with us. And I decide that hope isn't enough. Not anymore. I lean even closer and trace the curves of her face, finally touching her the way I've always wanted to. Hope is not a strategy. I want *her*.

Hesitating for half a second about whether I should kiss her again or not, she answers the question for me by covering her mouth with her hand and yawning dramatically.

"I could fall asleep out here," she says, as she stretches out beside me, her legs somehow finding their way over mine like we're playing a full-contact version of Twister.

"Please don't," I mutter. "I'll have to carry you all the way back to Wilder Ranch house."

But I'd secretly love to carry her. I love having her in my arms.

"That sounds better than walking," she says primly, flicking a leaf off her shirt.

I roll my eyes and settle back against the tree, arms crossed behind my head, pretending like she doesn't just fit here like she's always belonged.

The leaves above us rustle in the breeze. It's quiet out here, too quiet. That kind of quiet that makes you start thinking things. Dangerous things. Things like *what would happen if I kissed her again? Would she let me? What would she say or do?*

"So," she says like she is easing into something. "Poppy and I were talking the other day about hate sex—"

"Pause. Hate sex?"

"Yes, you know, hate sex. Anyway—"

I shake my head. "What exactly do you mean by hate sex?"

She blinks at me. "Are you okay? Did you hit your head again? Do you not know what sex is?"

"I'm well aware of what sex is, Cami," I tell her dryly.

"Okay, well anyway." She stretches again, all sin and smugness. "We were talking about hate sex."

I choke on air. "What about it?"

"Hate. Sex." She enunciates each word like she's giving a spelling bee answer. "It's a concept. A vibe. A very intense, very combative form of therapy."

I blink. "Why were you talking about that with Poppy?"

"Because it's hot, Jessop. Keep up."

"I'm not sure what's more alarming—that you said that... or that I kinda want to argue with you just to test the theory."

She turns her head on my shoulder to look up at me, all fake innocence and sparkling mischief. "We were just debating if it's a thing. Poppy said no. I said absolutely. *Some* people bring you flowers. Others shove you against a wall and hate fuck you hard until you come."

I cough again. "And which category do we fall into, exactly?"

She smirks. "You? You're one argument away from me throwing you against that tree and questioning *all* my life decisions."

"Jesus, Cami."

"What? It's hypothetical."

"It is *not* hypothetical if you say it while actively laying on me."

Her brows lifted. "Are you blushing, Jessop?"

"I don't blush."

"Sure," she says, patting my chest. "Whatever helps you sleep at night, Jessop."

I suck in my breath at her touch and the way this conversation is going. It's making me sweaty again. What in the actual hell is coming out of her mouth right now?

She's smirking like the devil, talking about hate fucking like it's just another topic over coffee. Like we're chatting weather and feed prices. And I—God help me—I can't breathe.

Cami, the only woman who's ever made me feel like my heart's not just something taking up space in my chest, is lying here talking dirty to me. With a straight damn face.

And now she's all casual, like she didn't just light my entire nervous system on fire. My brain's short-circuiting. I'm sweating. My jeans are suddenly way too tight.

What am I even supposed to say to that? "Yeah, hate fucking sounds great, when do you want to pencil that in?" Jesus. Get it together, Jack.

She keeps going, and now she's teasing me about being speechless. And she's right. I've fought wars, branded wild cattle, stared down my father without blinking, and yet Cami smirking like she knows exactly what she does to me has got me tongue-tied.

This is dangerous. This is *so* dangerous.

Because if I let the words that are currently screaming through my bloodstream come out of my mouth, we're not coming back from that.

And part of me doesn't want to.

Because hate fucking? That's not what this is. That's not what I want. I don't want rough and angry. I want *her*. All of her. But she's throwing gas on a fire that's been burning between us for a decade, and I'm one wrong look away from losing every shred of control I've got left.

And damn it, she *knows* exactly what she's doing.

We fall into silence, and for once, it wasn't awkward. Not exactly. Just tense enough to be interesting.

I looked down at her, hair coming out of her braid again, lips pursed in that permanent *I'm planning mischief* grin. "You really fantasized about hate sex with me?"

She rolled onto her side, facing me, elbow propped up like she was getting comfortable. "I didn't say it was with *you*."

This makes me almost sit up straight. Who else is she thinking about this with? Oh, hell no.

"Oh, so you fantasized about hate sex with someone *else* while sitting at our tree with me? That's comforting."

She grinned. "I'm just saying, if someone's being an arrogant pain in the ass, sometimes the only logical next step is tearing their shirt off and shutting them up with your mouth."

I stare at her. My mouth opens and closes again, and I suck in a deep breath.

She stares right back. God, I want her. So fucking bad. But not here. Not like this. I don't hate anything about Cami. Far from the opposite. I'd love to have her. But not in a one-time way. She's my forever. She just doesn't know it yet. When we're on the same page, there won't be any hate in there.

She grins at me. "You couldn't handle me, Jessop."

"No, you couldn't handle me, Wilder."

"See? You're already halfway to hate fucking me. Admitting it is halfway to doing it."

"You're unhinged," I manage to say.

"Thanks," she says sweetly, resting her head back on my shoulder.

Her hand finds my stomach again. Not in a suggestive way, more like a cuddling kind of way. Still, I have to focus very hard on the leaves above us and *not* the fact that she's basically using me like a human heating pad while casually discussing hate fucking me like we're talking about taking a drive.

"I'm not saying we *should*," she says after a beat.

"But you're not saying we shouldn't."

"I'm just saying if the tension gets any thicker around here, one of us is going to combust, and it's probably going to be you."

"Why me?"

"Because you're already halfway to a meltdown every time I so much as blink in Beau's direction."

I glare at her.

"Exactly." She winks. "Plus, I take care of myself, so I don't combust."

Oh, holy hell. She's trying to kill me. She really is. And this is it. The moment I realize she's going to drive me to the edge. Now, I for sure won't get any sleep in my sleeping bag on the floor, picturing her down the hall in that huge bed making herself come. Jesus.

"Let's go," I say, groaning as I stood and pulled her up with me. "Before you say something else that makes *me* combust."

She brushes herself off, lips twitching. "You're not denying it."

"I'm pleading the fifth."

"You're pleading for self-control, and it's *adorable.*"

"You're a menace."

"And you love it."

"God help me," I mutter, as she saunters ahead of me, hips swaying like she knows exactly what kind of chaos she's leaving in her wake. She does, and I'm in so much trouble. I want her so badly. I've wanted her for years, and now that she's finally giving me a sliver of a chance and flirting with me, I have this stupid show in the way.

Chapter 22
Cami

Don't Mind If I do by Ella Langley, Riley Green

"So, I talked to Jack about hate sex."

Poppy blinks. "Like... *talked* talked? Or banged talked?"

"Talked. Joked about it." I roll my eyes and laugh. "He choked on air. It was adorable."

Poppy cackles from the corner of her shop, where we're currently sprawled out with root beer floats from the Drug Store and an open bag of pretzels between us. The scent of engine oil and cinnamon-sugar pretzels fill the room. Her auto shop is my favorite chaotic safe space.

"Wait, what exactly did you say?" she asks, leaning forward, eager to hear the details.

"I may have mentioned that I have been taking care of myself."

Her eyes widen. "And he didn't bang you right on the spot?"

"Nope, not at all," I shrug. "He went full deer-in-headlights.

I thought he was gonna short-circuit and sputter out like a weirdly hot tractor."

"He is a weirdly hot tractor," Poppy says, sipping her drink. "With emotional baggage in the trailer bed."

"Facts."

Just then, the front bell jingles, and Violet breezes in with a bakery bag in one hand and mischief in her eyes. "Okay, what did I miss?"

I grin as I hand her a root beer float. "I traumatized Jack with a conversation about hate sex."

"*Oh*, this I need details on."

She plops down beside us, handing out mini pumpkin donuts like the giving queen that she is, and gave me her full attention.

"So, I'm lying there, under our aspen tree—"

"*Your* tree? The one you guys played in as kids?" Poppy swoons, "How romantic."

"*The* tree, yes, and I casually mentioned to Jack that Poppy and I were talking about hate sex."

Violet nearly drops her donut. "Please tell me you hate banged at the end?"

"Obviously, no. But also... he looked *so* confused. Like he didn't know whether to be turned on or offended."

Poppy laughs so hard she snorts. "That man was turned on, trust me."

"And then," I continue, "I implied I'd wanted to hate-hook-up with *him,* and he just sort of... stared at me like I was a cyborg or something."

Violet leans back, hands clasped. "God, you two are exhausting. In a soulmates-who-don't-know-it-yet way."

I roll my eyes. "He practically *turned me down.* Like—he wasn't even interested in fucking me."

"Oh, Jack is very interested," Violet says, sipping her root beer like its wine. "He's had a lot thrown at him lately. He's emotionally constipated."

"Okay, but *same*," I mutter. "Like, join the club."

"I don't think he hates you at all, Cami," Violet says, eyes soft. "I think you're his whole plan, and he just doesn't know how to tell you."

Poppy nods. "You two are endgame. Can't you see it?"

I sigh and pick at my donut. "Yeah, but he's got all this pressure with the show, the ranch, his dad's mess... I think he's trying to wait for the 'right moment.'"

"Well, that's dumb," Poppy says. "There's never a right moment. There's just hot moments and missed chances."

"Well, he definitely had his chance," I say dryly. "Many chances. He's blown them all."

"Maybe let him blow something else." Violet leans in with a smirk. "So, what's your plan?"

I snort and shake my head at her innuendo. "Guess I'll go back to giving him hell. It's fun. And at least when I make him mad, he gets all tense and growly, which makes me so hot."

Poppy grinned. "Speaking of which, want to spy on his date at Harvest & Honey?"

My head snaps up. "He has a date? When?"

"Tonight," Violet says, as she glances at her watch. "It's one of those 'reconnect with the final contestants' things for the show. Supposed to be romantic and rustic. Jenna told me about it."

"Oh, let's go see how it's going," I say, trying to play it cool. "Let's watch Jack act like our very own Bridger Falls Cassanova."

"Wait, we're really doing this?" Poppy asks, laughing. "You're oddly calm about this." She stops laughing and glances at Violet, concern sweeping over her face.

"Okay, fine. I'm not calm. I'm absolutely feral. Happy? Let's go," I say as I grab my hoodie.

"Oh, we're doing this."

"I think she definitely wants Jack..." Violet mutters as she grabs her drink and follows us. "And she's the best out of all of them."

"Hold up! I have disguises!" Poppy says excitedly.

* * *

So, I'll admit we are three grown women dressed in all black, oversized sunglasses, and varying levels of hats through the hedges behind Bridger Falls' restaurant like discount Charlie's Angels.

I'm parked on a park bench, Violet has commandeered a to-go menu as a disguise and sits next to me, and Poppy pretends to tie her shoe for the third time while glancing around. The only problem is, she's wearing boots that don't tie. We are terrible spies. And I'm hungry. I'd never make it in a stakeout.

"This is the best idea we've ever had," Violet whispers.

"Disagree," I whisper back. "That night we almost got arrested for pie theft was the best idea we've ever had."

Violet grins. "At least we got pie out of that one. That night was delicious. I should have brought Mack. She would have so much fun with this. And she would have thought to bring food."

"Where is she?" I ask.

"With Maggie at the farm," Violet whispers back.

"Why are we whispering?" I ask.

"I have grease on my hoodie," Poppy mutters. "We are not meant for espionage. Everyone can tell who we are."

"There," I hiss, pointing toward the patio. "That's their table."

Jack sits across from Elena, who is gorgeous and poised.

He looks... fine. Handsome. Relaxed. His shirt is rolled to the elbows, one hand wrapped around a glass of water, the other resting on the back of his chair.

But his shoulders aren't as loose as usual. And every time she says something, he kind of smiles and looks past her, like he's trying *really* hard to be polite.

"He's not into her," Violet says.

"Nope," I agree. "Look at his eyes. They're not focused on her. Like he's thinking about his taxes."

And I really like Elena. She's really fun to talk to, and I get her sarcastic humor. It is still weird though to watch Jack on a date with someone else, even if I know that it's not technically real. My brain knows it, but my heart hates it.

Poppy snorts. "Or hate sex."

"Shut up," I hiss, laughing into my sleeve.

And then—

"Are you guys *seriously* spying right now?"

We whip around to find *Jenna,* arms crossed, one eyebrow raised so high it nearly disappeared into her hairline.

"I—uh—" I flail, caught mid-sentence. "We're... birdwatching."

"What kind of birds?" Jenna questions, hands on her hips.

"Um...black birds," I say quickly.

She gives me a dry look. "You're staring at my brother like he's an endangered species."

"Well," Poppy says, shrugging, "emotionally available cowboys *are* rare."

Jenna laughs and joins us. "You're all insane."

She peers over our shoulders. "Oof. He's not even pretending to flirt like I told him to."

I take in how good he looks, and how he looks uncomfortable but he's trying not to show it. He's a gentleman, and he doesn't want one of the contestants to have a bad time. He cares about all of them. That's obvious and mostly because Jack is a good guy deep down. Nobody can tell me different. They don't make 'em as good as Jack Jessop, that's for sure.

A feeling fills me that I can't place right away, and it feels like sadness, or longing when I realize I've never really had a sit-down meal with Jack intentionally in the years I've known him. Sure, I've sat down at the bar by him, but we haven't ever had time together like that. I have never seen him in candlelight. I want this. I want Jack to look at me over candlelight. It sounds simple and possibly silly, but that's what I want. All the moments with Jack. I am a strong and independent woman. But I want to feel safe with Jack, a man like him who would move heaven and earth to be by my side. That's what I want. I want all the small things with him.

"What?" I try to say with surprise. "He looks like he's having a great time."

"You know he saw you the second you walked up," Jenna says dryly.

"What?" I twirl my hair around my finger. "We're just hanging out in town. That's not a crime."

"Girl. He's been glancing this way every thirty seconds, like he's hoping you'll rescue him."

My heart skips a beat.

I mutter. "Why would I rescue him? He looks like he's just fine."

"No, he doesn't," Poppy and Violet said at the same time.

And then it happens.

Jack stands up to pull Elena's chair back as she gets up for something. Maybe the bathroom? Hopefully leaving? His eyes immediately scan the patio and land on me. He definitely sees me. Not in the "maybe" he saw me kind of way. In the *locked-eyes, slow-burn, you-are-so-busted* kind of way. His brow lifts.

I duck down on the bench like a total coward. "Abort mission," I hiss. "We've been compromised."

It's too late. I hear his boots coming toward me. I peek through the slats and feel dizzy.

There he stands, hands on his hips in all his denim, sun-kissed, slightly irritated glory.

"Well," he says, crossing his arms. "Subtle."

Violet stands up, brushing off her jeans. "We're just supporting local businesses. That's not a crime."

Poppy nods as she holds up a jar of pickles she picked up from the farmers' market going on down the street. "Huge fans of artisan pickles."

Jack looks at me and gives me a slow and sexy grin that makes my panties practically melt. "You dragged them to spy with you? And nice disguises," he adds.

"I didn't *drag*," I say, standing. "They came willingly."

"To spy on me?" he smirks, clearly enjoying trying to make me squirm.

"No. I was casually observing the enemy."

He tilts his head, his lips twitching. "And how's it going?"

I huff. "Mediocre date. She told me this week at the coffee trailer that breakfast food is unnecessary."

"You're friends with her. She told me." He blinks. "And you once cried over a pancake."

"Because I *wanted* one, Jack."

He steps closer. "So, why are you really here?"

I shrug. "I just had an important question to ask you."

I inwardly groan because that is a terrible excuse that I just threw out there. Now I have to make something up.

He raises his eyebrows. "What's the question?"

I say the first thing that comes to mind, digging myself in further. "If I killed someone would you tell on me?"

His body shakes with laughter, and then he looks serious. "Who'd you kill?"

I shrug. "Well no one. *Yet*. But if I did, what would you do?"

He looks at me and says, "That's what you came to ask me?"

I look at him and say with all the seriousness that I can muster, "Answer the question, Jessop."

He grins and leans in and says, "I wouldn't tell. But I'd use it against you all the time. I'd be like 'Are you going to come for a ride with me or do I need to make a call to Sheriff Matthews?'"

I shake my head, grinning. "Just as I suspected."

"I'm going back to my date," he says, shaking his head, trying not to laugh. "You three try not to get arrested. Again."

"Have fun on your date," I call to him cheerfully.

He looks back at me and winks. "Hate you later."

Freaking winks.

He walks away, glancing back at me, slow, smug, *knowing*.

"We did *not* get arrested," I mutter, annoyed with myself that I let him get under my skin. And I hate how relaxed he looks. "I hate Jack. He's the worst."

"No, you don't." Violet grins. "And we got off with a warning. No arrest."

"The day is still young. We could get arrested," Poppy offers.

But it's Jenna that catches my attention when she turns back to us from talking to her assistant. "I have an idea."

I groan. "No, Jenna."

She nods and smiles. "Just wait and see..."

* * *

I didn't come to the lodge to rage bake. Okay, not entirely.

The double oven at the Jessop Lodge *is* amazing. The kitchen has way more counter space than the kitchen at the Wilder Ranch, and I may or may not be hiding from Jack. I know when he's done for the day, he'll go back to Wilder Ranch, and hopefully he won't think to look for me here at the lodge. Plus, I've had one of those shitty embarrass yourself in front of Jack kind of evenings, and nothing soothes the soul like chocolate and butter.

So yeah. Maybe this is a little in my feelings kind of baking. But mostly it's... therapy. With extra chocolate chips.

I'm rolling out pans of cookie dough when the side door creaks open, and two familiar figures wander in like they just smelled dessert through the walls.

"Please tell me those are for public consumption," Weston says with pleading eyes.

"If by public, you mean you guys, then yes," I say, scooping out the dough and plopping it on the tray like it did me dirty.

Tucker whistles low and leans against the fridge. "Man, when Jack said this oven was getting used more lately, I didn't realize it was for... emotional damage control."

I hold up a dough-covered spoon. "Mock me, and you get nothing."

Weston grabs a stool and pulls it up to the island. "I'm not mocking. I'm *supporting*. There's a difference."

They watch me work like they're in the front row at a baking-themed contest.

"You want to test the first batch?" I ask.

Weston practically moans. "That's the best sentence I've heard all week."

Tucker nods solemnly. "Might propose."

The kitchen is warm, golden, and full of cookie-scented comfort. I laugh and slide the tray into the oven. I've always loved spending time with Tucker and Weston. Honestly, the grown-up versions of the Jessop boys aren't bad company, surprisingly sweet for grown men who survived growing up with their dad. They're like brothers to me, and I've really enjoyed spending time with them. I'm going to miss them when the show is over.

Tucker takes a bite of a test cookie and groans. "This tastes like comfort and childhood. Tessa used to make us cookies like this."

"Can confirm," Weston agrees. "If Jack doesn't marry you, I might."

I snort. "Wow. You know how to make a girl feel special."

"We're just saying," Tucker adds, "Jack's an idiot if he doesn't see what's right in front of him."

"I'm *literally* covered in flour and butter. Your brother is on a date and has no interest in me."

Weston smirks at Tucker. "Exactly his type."

Before I can respond, the back door creaks open again, and speak of the devil himself, in strolls Jack.

Hair mussed from the wind, sleeves still rolled up, that permanent what now? look on his face.

He stops in the doorway, eyebrows raised, looking surprised to see me. "What are you doing here?"

I don't even flinch. I just smile too sweetly and say, "How was your date?"

Tucker coughs into his cookie.

Weston stands up so fast he nearly knocks over his stool. "And that's our cue to head out."

"Yep," Tucker says, already backing toward the door with both hands up. "We're gonna... go check on cows. Or something."

"Bring a flashlight," I offer.

"Have fun," Weston calls, dragging his brother out by the collar, but not before Tucker reaches over and swipes two more cookies off the tray like it's a hostage negotiation.

"I'm emotionally eating!" Tucker shouts as the door swings shut behind them.

The kitchen door swings shut behind them.

Jack stays where he is for a beat, watching me like he can't quite figure out if he's mad or amused or something in between that I can't read.

"I came for the oven," I say flatly, scooping more dough with extra aggression. "Don't worry. I'm not going to, like, sabotage you finding your wife or whatever."

He walks slowly toward the counter. "Didn't say you would."

"Bet you thought it."

He leans against the island across from me. "You seem mad."

I smile. "Mad? Me? Noooo. Why would I be mad?"

"I don't know," he says. "Maybe because you stalked my date, got caught, and then came here to bake out your rage."

I go back to scooping out dough. "Anyway, don't worry about me. I'm not your problem."

He's quiet for a moment. And then he says, soft but sharp, "You said something the other night."

I stiffen. "I say a *lot* of things."

"You said I definitely wasn't going to hate fuck you."

I freeze. Suddenly it feels like it's a hundred degrees in here.

"You do say a lot of things," he continues, voice lower and closer now. "But I heard that. Real clear."

I turn slowly, still dusted in flour, holding a metal scoop like a weapon.

"Okay. And?"

He steps around the counter, getting even closer. I back into the floured counter instinctively.

Big mistake. He boxes me in with both hands, palms flat on the table behind me, trapping me. My heart kicks into overdrive.

"I wasn't rejecting you," he says, quietly.

"Oh?"

"I was *imagining it.*"

I swallow hard. He leans in, close enough to whisper in my ear. "And I need you to understand something real clear, Wilder..."

My voice shakes. "W...what?"

"When I fuck you? And it's *when.* Not *if.* It's not going to be because I hate you."

I stare at him, swallowing the lump in my throat, my brain glitching, forgetting to breathe.

"But if you keep showing up everywhere and driving me crazy? I'm liable to forget my good intentions and act on the bad ones."

My breath hitches. "What are the bad ones?"

He grins. "You don't want to know."

My knees nearly give out. *Because I do. I really, really do.*

And then he leans forward, his hand reaching across the counter as he picks up a cookie and takes a bite, looking me right in the eye as he does it.

I stare up at him, speechless.

"You gonna finish these cookies?" he asks, voice infuriatingly casual.

I blink. "What?"

"The cookies?"

"Oh. Yeah. Sure."

"I'm going to go home and try to score some hot water before you do. I might even take care of myself and think about you while I'm at it," he smirks, throwing back in my face how I gave him hell and told him I took care of myself and thought about him.

He smirks and walks out, leaving a trail of smoldering destruction in his wake.

I stare after him. And then I mutter, to no one in particular, "This man is going to make me lose my mind."

Chapter 23
Jack

Feels Like Home by Parmalee

I'm stacking hay when I hear boots stomping across the barn floor like a woman on a mission. I look up to find Jenna. And she doesn't look happy.

"Jack Jessop," she barks, hands on her hips, sunglasses still on despite the dim light. "We need to talk. Now."

I sigh, wiping sweat from my brow with the edge of my shirt. "Can it wait? I've got about twenty bales left before—"

"Nope." She marches in, eyes blazing. "This isn't about hay. This is about you trying to kill the entire damn show."

I stare at her. "Excuse me?"

She yanks off her sunglasses, revealing fury in a pair of green eyes that match my own. "Are you trying to ruin the show on purpose, or are you just being a monumental ass? Because either way, I need to know so I can figure out what to do next."

My jaw clenches. "You coming out here just to insult me, Jenna, or did you actually have a valid reason?"

"Oh, I have a reason." She steps closer, jabbing her finger in my chest. "You and Cami are circling each other like you want to rip each other's clothes off, and then in the next breath, you're snapping at her in front of the cameras like a jealous ex-boyfriend. You're confusing the hell out of viewers, scaring off the contestants, and making the producers consider scrapping the show altogether because it's not working."

I take a step back, trying to keep my temper in check. "I'm doing my best, Jenna."

"Yeah, well your best is going to get this thrown out and then we won't get paid," Jenna snaps. "You agreed to do it. You knew what this was. And you're supposed to be building a connection with the contestants, not pining over Cami."

"I'm not pining."

She laughs, but it's sharp and humorless. "Jack. You have insane chemistry with Cami. It's not just obvious. It's blinding. Every time she's around, you look like you're trying not to kiss her or murder her. Sometimes both. And she's not any better. You two are a walking romantic disaster."

I turn away, gripping the edge of a stall. My shoulders and chest are tight. I don't want to talk about this. Not with her. Not with anyone.

Jenna keeps going, obviously unable to read the room. "If you're going to destroy things, could you at least wait until after the damn show is done filming? Because right now, you're about to take the whole thing down with you."

I spin around. "This isn't just a show to me!"

She blinks. "What?"

"This is my life, Jenna." My voice rises, unsteady with the emotion burning through me. "It might be some flashy reality TV for the world, but for me? This is my home. My name. Our family's legacy. And yeah, it's messy. And yeah, Cami gets under my skin. But I'm not acting. I'm not pretending to care about a woman that I don't have genuine feelings for a show. I can't."

"Then why did you agree to do this if you were just going to fall apart every time Cami's around?"

"Because I thought I could handle it!"

The barn falls quiet. Dust motes float in the sunlight slanting through the high windows. I run a hand through my hair, breathing hard.

"I thought I could keep it together. That I could fake it just long enough to save the ranch, play along, do what was needed." I look over at her, eyes wild. "But every time I look at her, I can't breathe. I can't think."

Jenna folds her arms. "Then admit it. To her. Stop letting it eat you alive."

My chest heaves. My hands curl into fists at my sides.

She softens. "Jack, you're my brother first. Sure, this show is my career, but I love you. And I love Cami. I want you to be happy."

And then the words are out before I could stop them. "I love her."

Silence crashes down. I stare at Jenna, my heart racing like I just ran ten miles.

"I love her," I say it again, quieter this time, but no less fierce. "God, I love her so much it makes me sick. My whole life, it's been shit up until now. I've just been trying to hold the pieces together. And then she walks back into it like a damn dream, and I can't wake up. I don't want to wake up. I want her."

Jenna opens her mouth. Closes it. "Well. Shit."

I laugh bitterly, scrubbing a hand over my face. "Yeah. That about covers it."

"Does she know?"

"I can't tell her this. I can't risk hurting her," I say and then quieter, "What if I'm like Dad? What if I mess it up?"

Jenna steps closer, her voice softer now. "First of all, you are nothing like him. And second, you can't keep pretending like you're okay. It's leaking out in every scene. Every look. Every sharp word. She's not the only one you're hurting. You're hurting yourself."

I look away. "I don't know how to stop."

"You don't have to stop," Jenna says. "You just have to wait it out. Play the game. We've got a few weeks left of filming. You make it through that, and then you can tell her everything. Hell, shout it from the mountaintops if you want. But if you crash and burn before then, we lose it all. You, her, the show. The whole thing goes down in flames with you."

The weight of it all presses on my chest. The cameras. The legacy. Cami. Always Cami.

"I don't know if I deserve her," I murmur.

Jenna nods slowly. "I get that. We don't really deserve anything, do we? We just work our asses off and be thankful for what we are lucky enough to have."

I shrug, "I'm sorry. I don't mean to mess things up with the show. I know how hard you've worked on everything."

Jenna softens. "Okay, then just hold on. Just a little longer. Don't ruin your own ending."

I close my eyes, feeling the truth of it settle like a stone in my gut. I want Cami. I want forever with her. But if there's any chance at that, I have to survive the next few weeks without blowing it all to hell.

When I open my eyes, Jenna watches me with something that looks a lot like sympathy.

"You're not a bad guy, Jack," she says quietly. "You're just in love. And it's messy. And maybe it doesn't fit in a tidy reality TV package. But if you love her, really love her, then you find a way to make it work. After."

I nod. My voice is hoarse. "After."

She gives me one last look, then turns to leave. Just before stepping out into the sunlight, she pauses. "For what it's worth," she says over her shoulder, "I'm rooting for you two. ... try not to mess it up."

I give a huff of laughter. "No promises."

I lean against the stall door, the heat of the afternoon bearing down, the scent of hay thick in the air.

I love her. And for the first time since this whole thing started, I said it out loud. Just not to her. Maybe that is the beginning of everything. And Jenna is right. I just need to hold on until this is over.

* * *

I wake up gasping.

Sweat soaks the inside of the sleeping bag, my T-shirt clings to my chest like I ran ten miles in a thunderstorm. My heart is pounding, breath ragged. I lie there, staring at the cracked ceiling of my best friend's childhood bedroom, trying to remember what the hell I'd just been dreaming about.

But the images are already slipping through my fingers like dust. Just fear. Pressure. Shadows. My dad's voice maybe. Or mine, twisted into something colder. I can't be sure.

What I do know is this, I can't go back to sleep.

I kick off the sleeping bag, peel off my shirt off, and swing my legs over the side of the makeshift mattress like it hasn't been three hours since I crawled into this miserable nest of polyester. The old floor creaks under my weight as I move through the dark. I grab clean clothes from my bag and step into the hallway, and creep toward the bathroom, trying not to wake Cami.

The water takes a full minute to get hot. Long enough for me to stare at myself in the mirror, jaw tight, eyes shadowed, and wonder, how the hell did I end up back here? In the one place that I ran from and now I'm back trying to save.

And the answer has always been for her. For Cami.

When the steam finally rises around me, I step under the spray and let it wash away the sweat, the nightmare, and the ache in my chest I can't name.

By the time I step outside, the sky is still pitch black. Not even a hint of dawn yet. Crickets are still humming. A breeze tugs at the hem of my hoodie as I walked across the quiet ranch yard, headed for the barn like muscle memory.

I don't need the light to find my way. The barn door groans as I pull it open, but the horses don't stir. They sense it's me. Trust me. I move between stalls with practiced ease—grabbing a pitchfork, tossing hay, checking hooves, murmuring greetings under my breath.

The smell of fresh hay and saddle soap ground me in a way nothing else does. The rhythm of it, the clatter of grain in the buckets, the warm huff of breath from a chestnut gelding, the scrape of my boots on concrete. This is what makes sense. Not some reality show. Out here, things are simple.

And maybe that's what hit me so hard when I started staying at Wilder Ranch. It feels different. It's built differently. Cami's parents didn't live up to what her grandparents had as a legacy. It's not the same with them gone. But the roots of Wilder Ranch are still here, and right now they feel stronger than the Jessop Ranch roots.

Wilder Ranch has heart. You can feel it in the way Cami keeps fighting for it like it's stitched into her bones. This place was built on love. The Jessop Ranch was built on expectations. On image. Or whatever my dad thought was important at the time.

I lean against one of the stalls, running a hand through my still-damp hair, breathing deep.

The quiet feels good. Better than it has in days.

Until I see the soft light in the kitchen window turn on, I realize she hasn't seen me. Her back is to the window, long hair tumbling in soft waves down her shoulders, falling over the straps of a faded tank top. There's a sleepy sway to her movements as she reaches up for a mug and flicks on the coffee maker like it's muscle memory. Her routine.

I remain completely still, like any movement would shatter the moment.

She's beautiful. Not just because of the way she looks, which is dangerous this early in the morning, especially in those shorts, but because of the way she exists. Soft, fierce, completely unaware of the way she lights up the dark without even trying.

I shouldn't want her like this. Not when I'm still figuring out how to untangle myself from my father's shadow.

But God, I want her anyway. Not her ranch, just her. I care about Wilder Ranch. But I love *her*.

And maybe my sister was right. I am scared. Maybe I've been hiding behind good intentions and timing and all the crap that made me feel like I was doing the "right" thing. But I've been too chicken shit to do anything about it and say something. I'm afraid I'll mess it all up.

But nothing about standing out here in the dark, watching her start her day, feels like I could do this every day. I don't want to live without her.

She stretches her arms up, back arching, and I make a strangled sound so loud that my horse side-eyes me.

I should look away. I don't. Because even from out here, even in the shadows, I know what she is. She's everything to me.

I'm so damn tired. Tired of smiling for the cameras. Tired of being someone I'm not. Tired of pretending like I hadn't fallen headfirst, heart-deep in love with Cami.

All I can think about is the look on Jenna's face when I told her I loved Cami. It had come out like a roar. Explosive. Raw. And maybe I needed that moment to stop holding it all in. But now it echoes in my mind.

I love her. God, I love her. And she has no idea.

I can tell my sister. I can tell Ollie. Hell, I can scream it into the Wyoming wind. But somehow if I look Cami in the eye and say it, it feels like there's a chance she might not love me back the same. I need to be the man that she can be proud of and trust. I'm trying desperately to be that man for her.

I'm a damn coward. I hate that I can fight my way back to Bridger Falls from the lowest points of my life, rebuild a ranch from ashes, take blow after blow to my reputation, but when it comes to her? My throat closes up. My heart panics.

I'm afraid. Afraid she won't love me back. Afraid I'll ruin the one good, wild, honest thing I've ever had. Afraid she'll see my dad when she looks at me.

That last one sticks a little more than the others. I press my hand against my chest, trying to ease the weight of it.

Every day, I try to prove I'm not him. That I'm not the man who wrecked our family name, who lied and cheated and dragged the Jessop legacy through the mud. But sometimes I catch my own reflection and see the same shadows in my eyes. That shadows that fight. But deep down in my gut I know that we fight for different things. I fight for the people I love, and my father fought for his own gain.

Cami has every reason not to trust me. And still, she let me in. A little. Enough to crack me open.

And now here I am, aching for her.

Not just her body, though, hell, the want for her claws under my skin like wildfire, but her laugh and her stubbornness. The way she fights for what she loves. The way she challenges me to be better, every damn day and everyone around her.

She's the only thing that feels real to me right now. This show might save the ranch, but Cami? She saved *me*.

Just a few weeks left of filming and pretending I'm not already hers in every way that matters. Jenna said to wait. After the show, I can tell her everything. But that feels like forever. Like asking a drowning man to hold his breath just a little longer.

But I will. Because she's worth it. All the ache. The fear. The waiting.

I'll survive this, somehow. I'll fight my way through it, just like I have everything else. Because if there was one thing I know for certain in this whole damn mess, it was this:

Cami is the only future I want. And I'll wait as long as it takes to have it.

Chapter 24
Cami

If I was a Cowboy by Miranda Lambert

The barn smells like cedar shavings and leather, but to me it smells like home. It's quiet out here, the quiet that settles into your bones. The quiet I used to chase as a kid when everything inside the house felt too loud, too tense. Now I'm grown, and somehow it still feels the same. Like this place is the only part of the world that makes sense.

I should be in bed. It's late enough the moon's high and the stars are showing off, but I can't sleep.

So here I am, kneeling in front of the water spigot near the stalls, trying to fix a busted pipe that started leaking. Like I've got something to prove. To whom exactly, I don't know. Maybe my mom. The wrench in my hand is too big, or maybe I'm just too angry to make it work right. Either way, I'm losing the fight.

I'm tired of fighting. I don't mind earning the things that I get. But fighting for them is exhausting. Like respect. People like Granger and Jace who don't respect me, want to hurt me or steal from me. And they've been awfully quiet lately. I wonder what their next move will be, and that's another fight I'm tired of fighting. Always being on edge, waiting for the next punch to land. Then there's Jack. The one constant through all this who makes me feel safe. And for that I'm grateful. I'm still worried about the ranch. I wonder if I'll ever truly bring my dreams to life here. But I know that with Jack around, it's going to somehow be okay. I'm so confused by everything with him. I love him so much; I want him so badly. But does he truly want me? And what if we don't work out? I'll have to walk away from the ranch and him. And the last part I couldn't handle. I'd walk away from this entire ranch and all my dreams for him. But I know he'll never let me do that. He cares about me and my dreams. Something no one has done for me before.

"Come on," I mutter, twisting it the wrong way for the third time. "Rusty, pain-in-the-ass—"

"You talking to the pipe or yourself?"

I freeze.

Jack leans in the doorway, arms crossed, moonlight catching on the mess of his hair. He looks tired. Soft. Like he was in bed, and I woke him up somehow.

"What are you doing out here?" I gripe, mostly to cover the way my heart just launched into my throat.

"Could ask you the same thing."

"Fixing something," I mutter.

He steps closer, boots scuffing the dirt floor. "Looks like you could use a hand."

I glare up at him. "I'm fine."

"Uh-huh."

He squats beside me, quiet for a second. Then, without asking, he gently takes the wrench from my hand. Our fingers brush. My breath hitches.

"Jack—"

"Let me help," he says softly.

He adjusts the wrench, twists it once, twice, and the bolt gives way with a satisfying click.

I stare at him. "Show-off."

He smiles, but it fades when he sees my face. "You okay?"

I look away. "Fine."

"You're not."

"I don't need you to fix me, too."

He sets the wrench down carefully and leans back on his heels. "What happened?"

He knows. Somehow Jack just always knows. And that's part of why Jack has always had my heart. Even when he doesn't deserve it.

"I was just talking to Ollie today about my mom and how she never supports me. It got to me. It's dumb. I let her get in my head. How she thinks that I'm wasting my time and that this ranch isn't worth saving. And that I'm not built for this kind of life."

He nods slowly. "I used to believe that about myself. That I wasn't built for anything good."

I glance at him, surprised. "What do you mean?"

He exhales. "My dad was mean. Mean in ways that stuck to your skin. Anytime he caught me hanging out with you or Ollie, he'd lose it."

My stomach twists and drops. "Lose it how?"

He finally looks at me. And the look in his eyes is something I'll never forget.

"He'd beat the hell out of me, Wilder. Every time. Didn't matter if we were just riding horses near your pasture or fixing a fence. If I was near you, I got it twice as bad. You know how it was between my dad and your parents."

I cover my mouth with my hand, horror booming in my chest. "Jack... I didn't know." I reach out and clasp his hand. I want to go back and find that boy who was abused and hug him and hold him. I hate that anything like this happened to Jack. That's why he left. He left to save me. To protect me. God, I hate this. He had to reject me, he didn't have a choice. My chest feels so heavy.

"I never wanted you to know. But it was worth it."

I drop my hand. "How could it possibly have been worth it?"

He gives me a smile, soft and broken and beautiful. "Because when I was with you, I didn't feel like trash. Your grandparents... your grandpa taught me things. Told me I was smart. Worth something. Your grandma made me cookies and never looked at me like I didn't belong."

He stands and pulls me with him onto a bale of hay, and I swing my legs onto his lap, leaning in towards him. He runs his hands up and down my calves as if he's soothing himself by touching me.

He swallows hard and looks around. "This ranch felt like home when nowhere else did. I miss them. Probably not like you do seeing as they were your family, but... I do. In some ways, they were like family to me, too."

I feel the ache rise in my throat, thick and sharp. "I didn't realize that meant so much to you. I'm glad you had that. I miss them too. Every day."

He shifts a little closer, voice low. "They believed in you, Cami. And so do I. You can do amazing things with this place."

I blink up at him, heart hammering. "What do you mean?"

He doesn't hesitate. "You're going to turn it into your B&B. You're going to make this place shine again. And I want to help you however you need my help."

Something twists in my chest, and I wrinkle my brow, confused. "Like business partners?"

His face falls. Just a flicker. But I see it.

"Yeah," he says, voice rough. "Business partners."

And damn it, that hurts more than it should, seeing something like disappointment crossing his face.

He clears his throat. "I'm sorry about your mom. Maybe she'll come around. But if she doesn't, that'll be her loss."

I laugh, watery. "You always say the right thing. It's annoying."

"I could say something dumb to balance it out. Want me to insult you again?"

I snort. "You try it, and I'll dump a bucket of horse shit in your truck."

He grins, and something in me eases.

Enemies. Friends. Something more. Whatever this is, it's feeling like *everything*.

Why is it that letting Jack in feels like the scariest thing in the world?

Chapter 25
Jack

Chapters by Trenton Tanner

I spot her the second the hospital automatic doors slide open at Bridger Falls Memorial.

Teresa Kendrick, otherwise known as Cami and Ollie's mom. She looks nothing like her daughter, as Cami always looked more like her grandmother.

Teresa's hair is pulled back in a tight bun that looks uncomfortable. Her scrubs are wrinkled, and a frown is etched deep into her face like it's lived there for years. She looks exhausted, probably not just from the night shift she just pulled. Teresa has been an unhappy person for a while, and everyone in town knows it.

She slows when she sees me, folds her arms over her chest, and glares.

Figures I'd be the last person she'd want to run into at the end of her shift. But I'm not here for small talk.

I hold up the coffee. "Peace offering."

Her gaze darts to the paper cup in my hand, then back to my face. "What do you want? Is this some kind of trap?" she mutters, tugging her jacket tighter around her.

"Nope," I say calmly, shaking my head. "Just coffee. And conversation."

She hesitates. Looks over towards her car and then back at me. "You've got five minutes."

It's more than I expected that she'd give me.

She walks over slowly, like she's still not convinced I'm not here to do something. I hand her the coffee, and she takes it with a sigh, wrapping her hands around it like it might burn through the chill in the air, and whatever guard she has up.

We lean against the hood of my truck in the half-empty parking lot. The sun's just starting to rise. The air smells like cold pavement and coffee.

"I'm not here to start anything," I say. "I just want to talk."

She looks at me over the lid of her cup. "What do you want to talk about?"

I glance over at her, sizing her up. "Do you love your daughter?"

Her shoulders are stiff. "Of course I do," she snaps, as if I've insulted her.

"Then why don't you show it?" I counter, softly.

That one lands, and she flinches. She blinks and looks away. "She's... hard."

"Hard?" I echo, feeling pissed off, but holding it back. "Hard what? Hard to love?"

She flinches like I've slapped her. She doesn't answer, just looks down at her cup.

I press on, my voice low but steady. "She's not hard to love. Loving her is the *easiest* thing I've ever done. I don't even have to try. I just do. It's like breathing."

Teresa doesn't move. Doesn't speak. But she looks surprised.

"I wake up thinking about her. Wondering what she's doing that day. If she's eaten. I wonder why she's still trying to do everything on her own. If she knows how amazing she is. How loved she is. And yeah, she's stubborn. She's sharp. She doesn't make it easy to get in. But if she lets you in?" I shake my head, throat tight. "It's the best kind of love there is."

Teresa stares out across the parking lot like she can't meet my eyes anymore. "She's been angry with me for so long. Probably since she was a teenager."

"She was a kid," I say. "And kids don't get angry without a reason. They get hurt. They get abandoned. They get tired of fighting for scraps of affection."

"She didn't make it easy," she says, voice rough.

"She's a girl who lost everything. Her dad abandoned her over and over. She lost her grandparents, the ranch, the one place that felt safe, and she's still fighting to keep it all together. She didn't need you to make it easy. She just needed you to *be there*."

Teresa swallows. Her eyes are glassy now, rimmed red from more than just the night shift. "I don't know how to get there," she whispers.

"But the real question is, do you want to? Because that's what I'm here to find out today. You see, I love your daughter. I'm going to marry her someday. We're going to have a family. And whether or not you get to be a part of that family is dependent upon how you act moving forward."

She turns to look at me, her face full of surprise. "Of course I love her. I'm her mother."

"Just because you're a parent doesn't mean you love your kid. I need to know whether you're going to get your shit straight or not. Because I can't have you tearing her up. I won't have it. You're either in or you're out, Teresa. You gotta pick one."

"I'm in," she whispers. Then she looks at me like she's seeing me for the first time. "She must really love you."

"She trusts me," I say. "Because I've never made her feel like she was too much. And I never will."

A tear slips down her cheek. She doesn't wipe it away.

I look over at her. "She doesn't need you to be a perfect mom. Just be willing to try. You don't have to know what to say. Just show up. Let her be messy. Let her be mad. And love her anyway. You do it for Ollie. You need to do it for her."

Her lip trembles and she nods. "She's never told me she needed me," she says quietly.

"She won't," I say. "But that doesn't mean she doesn't."

We stand there in silence, the weight of it all hanging between us. The sun is higher now, casting gold across the hood of the truck.

I nod toward her car. "You should go home now and get some rest."

She nods slowly, steps back toward her vehicle. Then pauses.

"Jack," she says as she turns back around. "Thank you."

"For what?"

"For reminding me what I've been missing. I've missed her."

I pull Teresa in for a hug, and she pats my back and holds me. She needed this.

I watch her drive away, my chest full of hope and ache and something heavier. Missing my own mom.

Because Cami doesn't know it yet, but someone's finally fighting for her in a way she never dared ask for. And I'll keep doing it. Every damn day.

* * *

I know something's off the second Cami walks into the barn.

258

She's too quiet. No stomping or muttering under her breath about the show annoying her or Beau baking. Just her boots against the concrete and the soft sound of her breath catching in her throat.

I look up from where I'm brushing Pesto. The second I see her face, I straighten.

She's pale. Eyes wide. Like she's been hit with something heavy and didn't see it coming.

"Wilder?" I say gently, setting the brush down. "What happened?"

She doesn't answer right away. Just stares at me. Searching. As if I've turned into someone she doesn't recognize. Or maybe someone she's seeing clearly for the first time.

"My mom came by Steamy Sips today," she says, voice soft. Almost dazed. "Just now."

I wipe my hands on my jeans, my heart thudding. "Yeah?"

"She... she brought me dinner."

That makes me pause.

"She's never done that," Cami adds, blinking.

I swallow hard staying quiet.

"She said she was sorry." Her voice cracks. "She said she's not good at this, but she's going to try. And then she said... she talked to you."

Ah. There it is. I wondered if she'd tell her we talked. I nod once. "Yeah."

Her lips press into a line, and she looks at me, confused. "Why?"

I shrug, but it's not casual. Not even close. "Because I don't want you to hurt anymore."

Her breath hitches.

"And I know what it feels like to grow up thinking you have to earn love," I say, stepping closer. "And trying to be strong all the damn time. But you shouldn't have to fight that hard, Wilder."

Her eyes shine. She blinks fast, like she's mad at herself for crying. "You didn't have to do that."

"I know," I say softly. "But I wanted to."

Her chin trembles. "She said... you told her loving me is easy."

"I did."

"You said it's like breathing."

I nod again. "Because it is."

A tear slips down her cheek. She swipes at it quickly, like she's still trying to be tough. But her voice betrays her. "No one's ever fought for me like that."

I step in fully now, closing the space between us. I take her face in my hands, gentle but steady, like I'm holding something sacred. "I will," I say. "Every damn day. Whether or not you let me in, Wilder, I'm gonna keep showing up. I'm gonna love you when you're fiery and loud and when you're quiet and scared. I'm gonna love you when you don't think you deserve it and when you push me away and when you're trying so damn hard not to need anyone. I'm going to do it even harder."

She lets out a choked sound, half laugh, half sob, and then she kisses me. Hard. Desperate. Shaking. Like she's trying to memorize this moment. Like she's finally letting go of the weight she's been carrying for years.

I kiss her back with everything I have. Every word I haven't said. Every promise I've already made with my actions. Like sealing it all with this kiss.

When we break apart, she leans her forehead against mine. Her voice is barely a whisper. "Thank you."

I close my eyes and smile. "You're pretty damn easy to love, Wilder."

She breathes out a laugh. "Still going to give you hell, Jessop."

"Wouldn't expect anything less."

She doesn't argue. She just leans into me, finally soft. Finally safe.

And I hold her like I never plan on letting go. She can call me her business partner all she wants. I'm not her business partner. I'm her life partner. She just hasn't figured that out yet.

Chapter 26
Cami

But Daddy I Love Him by Taylor Swift

The house is too quiet. In the quiet, I rethink everything I've said and done in the past few weeks. Even though chaos surrounds me right now, my heart feels so full.

I think about the way I must have seared him by the way he looked at me after I said, "business partners," like I'd sucker punched him right in the gut. God, I still can't get the look on his face out of my mind.

Or the way I can still feel the heat of his hand on the small of my back when he passed behind me in the barn earlier. It was barely a brush but enough to make my pulse trip over itself. Jack's always had that power over me, and now it's only gotten stronger.

He's downstairs in the living room. Probably watching some late-night rodeo rerun.

I hate how aware I am of him. We keep dancing around our past like ghosts around a campfire. I hate that he's here, and he feels like home, danger, and longing all wrapped in one.

I pad down the stairs in my bare feet, the floorboards cool under my toes, and I pause when I see the faint flicker of firelight dancing in the living room.

He's sprawled on the couch like some kind of shirtless cowboy centerfold with one arm thrown over the backrest, long legs stretched out like he owns the place. His chest is bare, golden in the firelight, all broad and annoyingly perfect. His hair's a mess, like he's been dragging his hands through it, and don't even get me started on the jeans slung low on his hips. My heart? In full cardiac arrest.

He sees me, and something in his expression shifts. Softens. Like maybe he's been sitting there thinking. Or maybe, just maybe, he couldn't sleep either.

I lean against the doorway, pretending like I'm totally unaffected. "Burning the midnight oil, Jessop?"

He grins, slow and sleepy. "Can't sleep."

"Too many feelings?" I tease, stepping into the room like my pulse isn't tap dancing.

He lifts a brow, eyes warm. "Only when I'm under the same roof as a woman who drives me absolutely insane."

I smile. "Aw. That almost sounded romantic."

He grins. "Almost."

"Mission accomplished, then," I say as I plop down on the couch beside him, a few inches of safety cushion between us. The fire crackles. Shadows play across his face. And when I glance sideways, he's watching me.

"What are you doing, Jack?" I ask softly, more serious this time. I hold out for a sliver of hope that he'll drop his guard and tell me what's really on his mind.

He clears his throat. "I've been thinking about a lot of things. Mostly about you and me."

I glance over at him. His jaw is tight. He's chewing on the inside of his cheek like he's nervous. Vulnerable.

"My dad did a number on me, Cami. On all of us. But I'm trying to move past it all and become a man who isn't him."

I blink, surprised by how quiet his voice is. "Jack…"

He shakes his head. "There's so much you don't know. It's the stuff I've been carrying since I was a kid. Every time he hit me, every lie he made me tell, every time he made me feel like I wasn't good enough—that cut me deep. And I've spent most of my life afraid I'd turn out just like him."

I shift, giving him my full attention. My heart is in my throat. "You're nothing like him, Jack."

He gives a bitter smile. "You don't know that. I've got his blood. His name. That name comes with a warning label. And I think… I think that's why I've kept my distance from you. Because you deserve someone without all that baggage. Someone who doesn't wake up wondering if the darkness inside him is gonna win one day."

"Jack." I reach out, my fingers brushing his. "That's not who you are. You're not your father."

He meets my gaze, and for the first time, I see the fear behind them. The vulnerability behind the swagger. He plays the alpha cowboy card so well. But this is a new side of him. One that he hasn't let me see before.

"But what if I can't be who you need me to be?" he whispers.

I slide closer, my hand finding his. "I don't need you to be anything other than who you are, Jack. Remember that boy I used to build forts with as a kid? That's still you. You're still my person. No matter where you've been or who you think you are now, that boy is still in there. And deep down, he's still my best friend."

Silence stretches, thick and electric. Then he shifts closer, so our knees touch. I don't know who moves first. Maybe it's me. Maybe it's him. All I know is that one second, we're just talking, and the next—

I'm in his arms. And it feels so good it hurts.

He wraps me up like it's the most natural thing in the world. My face finds his neck, and he smells like cedar and smoke and the man I've tried to hate and failed so epically.

"You always this cuddly after dropping emotional bombs?" I ask, trying to lighten the mood even though my voice is shaking.

"Only with you," he murmurs.

I laugh softly against his chest. "God, you're annoying."

"Still cuddling me though."

"Shut up, Jessop." I shift, and that's when I realize *just* how tangled we are. His thigh is wedged between mine, his hand flat against my back, my shirt rucked up slightly where his fingers brush skin. My nipples are pebbled and I— God, I want him to touch me so badly. My heart pounds in places I didn't know it could. I wonder if he can feel it, too.

His breath hitches. "Wilder...I'm sorry I left like I did," he whispers, voice strained.

I look up. Our faces are inches apart.

And then I kiss him. I don't hold back; I just go for it, praying he'll kiss me back. It's not planned. It's not gentle. It's heat and need and too many years of not having him when I should have.

He groans into my mouth and threads his fingers through my hair, deepening the kiss instantly. His mouth is hot and demanding, but careful, like he's trying to cherish every second. When he shifts and pulls me fully onto his lap, I gasp against his lips. He takes the opportunity to trail kisses down my neck, nipping just above my collarbone, and I swear I see stars.

"I hate how good this is with you," I whisper.

"You fuckin' love it. I love how good this is," he counters, voice thick.

He's right. I do.

My hands trace his neck and his skin is warm, solid muscle, and when he shudders under my touch, it flips something primal in me.

His eyes lock on mine, asking for permission without saying a word.

I nod, and he takes my oversized pajama top off and leans back to admire his view. His fingers trace over my breasts, and he moans softly.

He looks like he's about to come undone when he sees I have no panties on and am bare for him.

It feels slow and hot and *real*. We take our time. Like we're unlearning every reason we've been apart. Like we're rewriting our whole story with our bodies. And it feels so good. My body trembles, his touch steadying me.

His mouth goes to my breasts, and he takes his time, biting and soothing each sting with a lick. My hands grip his hair as he tugs on my nipples, making me moan.

My hands move for his jeans, unzipping them and pulling them down, as I feel his rock-hard cock under me. Ready for me.

We might be a mess in so many ways and have so much to work out, but this right here is happening. This feels right.

He takes his time kissing my breasts, licking, sucking and touching each one like they're prizes he's won. I moan and lean back, my hair tickling my back. "Jack..."

His eyes reach mine and they're hungry with desire as he watches me, going back to kissing me and touching me, palming me, not saying anything, but being in this moment with me that both of us need.

"Is this finally happening?" I whisper.

"Do you want this?" he asks, as he grips my waist, and I feel his rock-hard cock under me.

"Yes," I say quickly. "I want you, Jack."

He's all I can think about. I would give anything to have him inside me right now.

He pulls me closer and kisses me, sliding his tongue into my mouth, swiping at my lip, savoring me. His hands slide down my ribs and he finds my pussy and drags a finger through it, "Jesus. Is this for me, Cami?" he asks hoarsely.

"Yes," I whimper at his touch and arch for him.

He kisses me and works my clit with his fingers, and I grind into him, feeling his hard cock under me, moving on top of him as he groans.

He grips my bottom and pulls me up and stands, walking over in front of the fireplace and lays me on the rug. I lie there topless, my hair spread out around me, gazing up at him.

This is a man I could do forever with. He's making me believe it.

But tonight, tonight we're going to do this. Something we've been dancing around for so long.

The way my body reacts to his touch is crazy. Sometimes, just the way he looks at me makes me instantly wet and want him. The power that Jack has always had over me is something I've struggled with because, no matter how hard I fight him, he's always had that power. And probably always will.

"I've wanted you for so long, Cami."

"Take me," I demand.

He smirks as his hands gently spread my thighs, and he licks straight up my center. "Mine," he murmurs. He continues to take his time, sucking, licking, using fingers, and I bite my lip and arch my back, holding it back because this feels...so...good.

"Come," he orders as he continues working my clit and using his fingers and my body continues to tense, and finally...I shudder and come harder than I ever have before. I've been so worked up over Jack, I knew it wouldn't take much.

I shatter. Into a million pieces, my body, shudders, my breath choppy and my chest shaking.

He stands and takes off his jeans, dropping them and tugging down his boxers, his cock springing free and holy shit.

He's hard, and I want him so bad, right now.

"I don't have a condom, but I've been checked since I've been with anyone, and it's been a while," he says softly.

"I'm on birth control, and I want you right now, Jack. I need you," I whimper.

He kneels, leaning to kiss me and trails down to my breasts again. "God, these are perfect."

He takes his cock in his hand and strokes it and pushes the tip into me, and I suck in a breath and moan.

He kisses up my neck and over to my lips as he moves until the rest of him is inside of me and we're together. Finally. And somehow, I can't explain it, but it feels so right. And he feels so good. So good.

I know this is one night and I can't let myself want more. But damn, I could make this man dinner for the rest of his life.

He starts slow and moves firm and fast, and I build and build until I'm holding it back and he whispers, "Come on my cock, baby."

I moan, and my whole body surges, my hands pulling him to me as he grunts and pulses and comes hard, his eyes on mine, and I swear it is the most intimate I've ever been with a person. I've had boyfriends, had my fair share of sex. But this? This wasn't that. This was something I've never had with anyone before.

He searches my eyes and the smirk returns, "Why did we fight for so long?"

I sigh, content, my body relaxed, "Because there's no one in the world I'd rather fight with than you."

He laughs and shakes his head.

"And if we get to do this to make up, well, then we could have more fights, I guess." I smirk.

He kisses me softly and says, "There's no one in the world for me other than you, Cami. Never has been, never will be."

After we get cleaned up, we lie tangled in a mess of limbs and breath and firelight.

He strokes a thumb along my hip. "You okay?"

"Better than okay."

We lay in silence for a while, listening to the crackle of the fire and the slow thud of our hearts, which find the same rhythm.

Then I say, "I don't know how to do this."

He doesn't answer right away. He kisses my temple, pulls me tighter. He knows what I mean.

"We'll figure it out. Together."

I want to believe that. I *do*. But the scared part of me still whispers that people leave. That love fades. That I don't know if my heart could survive another loss. I close my eyes and press my face to his chest, listening to his heartbeat.

For now, that's enough.

Chapter 27
Jack

Hurricane by Luke Combs

The morning after changes everything for me. I've waited so long for her, and truthfully, I'd have waited for forever. I've always known that she was it for me. Even when I was on a ship halfway around the world, I knew. When I worked on missions and wondered if I'd make it out, it was her I thought of when shit went down. It's always been her, always will be her.

She's wrapped around me like she belongs there, her bare legs tangled with mine under the worn, thin quilt, the vanilla scent of her shampoo filling me. The back porch creaks gently under us as the breeze lifts through the screens. Sunlight filters through the pine trees, golden and soft. My arm is under her head. My hand is on her hip. And somehow, I never want to move again. I can't stop thinking about where we go from here. I told her last night that we'd figure it out together.

I've been thinking about my dad, Granger, and Jace. Opposition of what we're trying to do with the ranch. About the ghosts I still haven't faced and the fact that if I'm going to build something real with this ranch, with Cami, then I can't keep running from the past. I have to face things and put the things in the past behind me.

I kiss the crown of her head, then take a deep breath. "I think I should go see him."

She shifts against me, groggy. "What?"

"My dad."

Cami goes still. "Really?"

I swallow hard. "Maybe if I go see him in prison, I'll finally stop feeling like he's going to come back and ruin everything again. Maybe I'll get some closure."

And I can try to find out who is messing with the ranches. Because I have a feeling he's behind it and there are even more snakes around in plain sight I haven't figured out yet. Granger isn't smart enough to be doing what he's doing alone.

She props her chin on my chest, studying me. Her eyes are still sleepy, but alert. "I'll go with you."

My gut clenches. "No."

She blinks. "No?"

I shift, propping myself up slightly. "I want to protect you from him. From that place. From what he can still do to me if he has access to you."

She lets out a low laugh. "Jack, I don't need protecting. If you want to be with me, be a team with me. I can handle it. We can handle it. We can handle anything together."

God, she means it. I can see it in her eyes—the fire, the steadiness, the fierce loyalty. It hits me all at once: she's not just my partner on paper. She's my anchor. She's my shelter from storms. And I am hers. We always have been, even when we had years apart. She still had my heart even when she didn't know it.

I look at her, my chest tight, my throat thick. I nod slowly. "Yeah. You can go with me, baby."

"Baby?" she teases.

I kiss her head and pull her to me again. "Yeah, baby."

We sit like that for a while. Talking quietly. She teases me about my morning breath. I tell her she drools when she sleeps. She doesn't deny it. And in that soft, early light, with nothing but our honesty between us, I almost feel like I can do anything. Like facing him won't break me.

After checking on the visiting hours, we take off and drive in silence most of the way, the sound of the tires on the highway filling up all the space between us. Cami's hand rests lightly on my thigh, a steady rhythm that keeps me grounded. I keep glancing over at her, half-waiting for her to change her mind, to tell me she doesn't want to do this. She doesn't.

She sits there, strong and solid, her other hand gripping her coffee like it's a weapon. Occasionally, she hums along to the country music I barely have turned up, but mostly we sit in it— the quiet, the nerves, the unspoken.

I remember the last time I saw my dad. It was about six months ago. He'd just been sentenced. I sat in that courtroom and listened to him blame everyone but himself: the judge, the neighbors, even us kids. He looked over at me and told me that I didn't have what it took to be a real man. He said I was weak.

I knew he was a piece of shit long before that day. That day, his consequences caught up to him. Consequences that are his and his alone.

The prison looms like a ghost of everything I hate. Gray walls. Guard towers. Cold air. The smell of iron and regret clings to the place like a second skin.

I look over at her. Cami doesn't flinch. She squeezes my hand as we go through security, like she can feel the storm raging inside of me. And the more anxious I get, the calmer she seems to get. Which feels right. Cami has always been mine.

And then we're there. In the visiting room. Sitting at the cold metal table. Waiting.

Jack Jessop, Sr. shuffles in like he owns the place, even in his gray and white jumpsuit. His blond hair is short and thinner with more gray in it, but his green eyes are just as sharp. And just as mean.

He looks at me and smirks. "Well, well. Look who finally grew a pair."

I stare at him, not responding. Cami's hand tightens in mine under the table.

"Didn't think you'd come, *boy*," he says with a mean edge to his voice as he enunciates the word boy. "Let alone bring a Kendrick." He practically spits out that last part, clearly unhappy that she's here.

Cami bristles but stays quiet. Her gaze is neutral, and her body is calm, which calms me down. But what I really want to do is reach across the metal table and punch him. But that's what he wants. He wants anger and strife. And today I'm here for me. Not to give him what he wants.

"I bought Wilder Ranch," I tell him. "I'm rebuilding it alongside Jessop Ranch. The right way."

"Well, well, well." He laughs. It's harsh and cruel. "The right way? Don't make me laugh. You don't know the first thing about running a ranch. You were never smart enough to run it like a businessman. Always trying to play cowboy like it was some fairytale."

I feel my jaw lock. My hand curls into a fist in my lap. Cami watches him and still gives nothing away with her facial expressions.

But it dawns on me that he didn't show an ounce of surprise

when I told him that I bought Wilder Ranch. He already knew. Which means someone told him.

He leans forward, eyes gleaming. "You think you're better than me? You're not. You'll screw it up, and you'll screw up Wilder, too. And when it happens, you'll lose everything even worse than I did."

Cami speaks then, her voice low but fierce. "He *is* better than you."

My dad's eyes narrow, and he bites out, "Careful, sweetheart."

"Or what?" she asks, her voice steel.

Anger surges through me. But I let him talk. Maybe he'll slip up and say something.

I want to punch him. For all the times I was a kid bracing for a slap or a punch that never came in public, but always later. And I grew to expect it.

He keeps going. "I see the way you're looking at her. Like she fixes you. Like you're worth something. You ain't worth shit, boy. And one day, she'll realize it too. She'll be long gone."

I lean forward, elbows on the table, the air between us thick with heat and history. My teeth grit so hard I feel it in my molars. "Enough."

My voice is low, steady but sharp enough to cut through concrete. I've let him talk too long. I've let him *exist* in this space too long. This meeting? It was never about hearing him out. It was about confirming what I already knew. That he hasn't changed. That he *won't* change.

I shift my gaze to Cami. She catches it immediately and gives me the smallest nod like bwe're synced up, like she already knew the second we sat down what this would be.

But she doesn't stand yet. Instead, she turns her full attention on my father. And the air changes.

The fire in her eyes is ice-cold. The kind of cold that burns.

Her voice, when she speaks, is calm. Controlled. But it's laced with so much power it makes my skin prickle.

"You know," she says, tilting her head like she's talking to a particularly dumb child, "for a man who's spent a lifetime burning things down, you sure do act like the ashes should still love you. Newsflash...they don't. Nobody thinks of you anymore. They're all better off without you."

My father's smug grin falters, just slightly. Not much, but enough. Enough to make my chest swell.

She leans in a little, arms crossed, unflinching. "Jack's the best man I've ever known. And it's not because of you, it's *in spite* of you. You'll never get to take credit for the man he is or pretend your poison didn't cost him more than most people could survive. He's standing on the scars that you gave him."

She keeps going. God, I love her so much.

"And if you ever think about using that voice towards him again, the one that drips with disappointment like *you* have any high ground, I swear to God, I will make sure you regret it. And I won't even have to raise my voice to do it."

My father tries to laugh. It comes out brittle, like it's caught in his throat.

Cami smiles. Not warm. Not kind. Just a warning with lipstick.

Then she looks to me, her expression softening the second her eyes meet mine. "Let's go."

I push back my chair, heart pounding—not from rage anymore, but something else entirely. Something closer to awe.

She turns and leans into him and says something I can't hear, but I see his face tense up, and he grips the table, his cuffs clattering.

She puts her hand in mine. We walk out without another word.

Outside, I slump against the seat in my truck, relieved that is over.

Cami watches me, arms crossed. "You okay?"

I shake my head. "No. I thought I'd feel better. I feel worse. Like he had access to you, and he poisoned us."

Her eyes soften and she lays her hand on mine. "I'm proud of you. You might not feel better, but you did it. And now you know. He didn't change, and he probably never will."

"I can't end up like him."

"Look at me. You are nothing like him. Not even close. He's not even human. He's an animal who deserves to be in the cage that he's in. Look at you. There is so much good in you. *So much good*," she says as she motions to the prison. "There's no good in him, anymore. The only good part of him is that he made your brothers, Jenna, and you."

"Maybe we should slow this down," I blurt, panicked. "Maybe that's safer. I can't have him break you. I can't let him take you from me. He knew I bought your ranch. How could he know that? What if he can still mess with us from prison?"

She blinks. Her face twists like I slapped her. Then she sits back. Cold. "You know what, Jack? You don't get to keep pushing me away and pulling me back in. I can't keep letting you do that. I don't have space in my life for another man who decides to come and go as he pleases."

"Cami—"

Oh, shit. Just what I was afraid of. Messing this up between us. Again.

She turns and faces forward. Not saying another word. "Take me home."

She stares out the window the entire ride home. Her silence is worse than yelling. Worse than anything.

When we get back to the Wilder Ranch, she doesn't come

inside, instead she gets in her truck and leaves without saying a word.

I wait. I call. Nothing.

Hours pass. The sun starts to dip low. I clean the barn. I feed the horses and Love. I pace until my legs ache.

I pace the yard, petting Love and wondering how the hell I'm going to fix this.

I call Violet.

"Hey, have you by chance seen Cami?" I ask, trying to be calm, but my heart is racing.

"Yeah," she says. "She's here. She asked to stay at the cabin. And Jack? Don't you dare come over here unless you're ready to fix this."

I drive straight there.

She's standing on the porch of the little guest cabin behind Violet's place, arms crossed, fury glowing just under the surface when she sees me pull up. But she doesn't look surprised.

"Cami. Come home," I plead.

She lifts her chin. "I don't have a home, Jack. Just one I share with a business partner and landlord."

The words cut deep. I deserve it.

I climb the steps, stopping just in front of her. "I didn't mean it. I was scared. That man, he breaks things. He's broken *me* for most of my life. And the thought of him doing the same to you, I can't take it."

Her eyes glisten. But she doesn't move. "You said you wanted to protect me," she says. "But all you do is push me away."

"Because I love you too damn much." My voice shakes as I tell her.

Her eyes get glassier, and she sucks in a shocked breath. Her body tenses as she stares at me.

"I love you so much it makes me stupid. Makes me say things

I don't mean because I just want to keep you safe. But it doesn't work. It just hurts you. And me. And I'm so sorry."

She steps forward, tears brimming. "Then stop keeping me at arm's length. Let me stand beside you and fight the fire with you. Not behind you."

I take her face in my hands, heart hammering. "I'm sorry. For all of it. For not being stronger. For not believing in us and leaving before. I won't do it again. Come home with me. Please. Baby, please come home."

She closes her eyes. And then she nods.

Relieved, I grab her and pull her in for a hug and kiss her lips softly. "I love you so much, Wilder."

She nods, tears in her eyes, "I love you, too."

I press my forehead to hers. "Let's go home and make up."

She shakes and laughs, "Okay."

"Cami? What did you say to him when we left the prison?"

She looks me in the eye and says, "I told him he'd never know his grandchildren."

The world tilts, and I swear, I forget how to breathe. Because in that one sentence, sharp as barbed wire and quiet as a prayer, she just handed me the truth of everything I've ever wanted.

Not just *her*. But *us*. A future and a family. And the truth is, there's nothing I want more.

Chapter 28
Cami

Broke Down In A Truck by Kameron Marlowe

If someone had told me six months ago that Jack Jessop would be waiting on my front porch with a cocky smile, I would've laughed in their face.

And yet... here he is. A real-life dream come true that I can't help but feel like I need to pinch myself about. He's barefoot, and his shirt slightly wrinkled. Hair still damp from a shower. And a damn dish towel over his shoulder like he owns the place. Well, he does, I laugh to myself. That doesn't bother me anymore. I just want to be where he is.

"Don't freak out," he says the second I step out of the truck, my body sore from a double shift between the coffee trailer and baking for tomorrow. "I cooked."

I blink at him. "You... cooked?"

His grin is lazy, wicked. "Used the oven and everything."

My laugh bubbles out before I can stop it, the exhaustion in my bones dissolve like sugar in tea. "Should I be scared?"

"Definitely. But I also made brownies, so it cancels it out if it turns out bad."

God help me, I love this man.

Inside, he's lit a few candles, which he has no idea the significance of. I was just thinking about how I'd never eaten dinner with him in candlelight. Now here we are. And the whole house smells like garlic and herbs and something warm I didn't have to make with my own two hands. I kick off my boots, and before I can make it to the kitchen, Jack wraps an arm around my waist and pulls me into his chest.

His mouth brushes against my hair. "I missed you today."

"You saw me this morning," I murmur into his shirt, breathing in the scent of him and feeling relief pulse through my body. Home. He smells and feels like home to me.

"I know." His voice is low, rough. "Didn't help."

It should be illegal for a man who used to be a Navy SEAL and can out-stare a bull to be this tender. But he is. With me.

Dinner is simple. Baked ziti, a slightly questionable side salad, and the fudgiest brownies I've ever eaten. We eat cross-legged on the couch, plates balanced on our laps, a romcom playing low in the background.

I lean into him, legs tucked up under me, his arm slung around my shoulder like it belongs there. Like *he* belongs here. Because he does.

His thumb traces lazy circles against my arm. "You get enough to eat?"

"I'm stuffed. Just let me lay here and rot." I sigh, deeply content in his arms.

His lips touch my temple. "Never letting you go, baby."

We don't say anything for a while. Just breathe. Just exist.

This is what I've been craving. The quiet. The calm. The soft click of a future falling into place. Even if there are still cameras filming and people everywhere. It has to eventually calm down.

Later, we end up at The Black Dog with Ollie and Poppy, Weston, and a few of the crew members who've finally started packing up their gear and shipping it out. Only two more days of filming left, and it shows in Jack. He's looser tonight. Lighter. Definitely more relaxed. We've both slept better than ever. Having him in my bed feels right.

He's still got that spark in his eyes when he sinks a solid in the corner pocket and raises his brows at me. "That's three in a row, Wilder."

I glare, half-drunk on root beer and the way he looks in that fitted black T-shirt. "You're cheating."

"Pretty sure I'm just better than you."

"You're *not*."

"Then come prove it."

I stalk over to him, grab the cue from his hand, and use the opportunity to slide my body against his, slow, deliberate, playful. He growls low in his throat, arms coming around me. His mouth brushes my ear.

"You're gonna pay for that later."

I glance up at him. "That's the idea."

The others groan behind us, but Jack just laughs, that low rumble in his chest that vibrates through me.

This is what I missed. This version of us. No cameras, no pressure, no pretending. Just me and him, flirting over pool tables and stealing kisses in the corner booth.

I shoot and sink nothing.

Jack leans in. "Still better."

He is the best.

* * *

Back home, we curl up again on the couch, his fingers tracing idle patterns on my hip while Love snores at our feet. The energy of the bar still thrums in my veins, but next to him, everything feels grounded.

He kisses my neck. Slow. Soft. Thoughtful.

"I can't wait for this to be over," he murmurs, and I know he doesn't mean us.

"I know."

"They're almost gone. Jenna said we'll finish filming the last scenes this weekend. Two more, and I'm done."

I twist to look at him. "How do you feel?"

He hesitates. "Relieved," he finally says. "Antsy. Like I've been holding my breath and I'm finally allowed to exhale. All this pretending for a paycheck. Just waiting for the check to clear so I can help you start that B&B. Help you build what you really want. What we want."

I brush my hand along his cheek. "You've already done more than enough, Jack."

"Not yet," he says, voice tight. "But I'm about to."

And I believe him. Because this man doesn't make promises he can't keep.

And with every soft kiss, every quiet dinner, every damn brownie, he's showing me exactly the kind of future he wants. And I want it, too. God, I want all of it.

Chapter 29
Jack

You Don't Want That Smoke by Bailey Zimmerman

I'm sweating through my second flannel, Elena keeps teasing me about being like a soap opera lead, and the production assistant keeps asking me to repeat the word "saddle" like it holds dramatic weight in a fake southern accent. I've repeatedly told him that we're in Wyoming and people don't talk like that here.

"Say it again, Jack," he calls from behind the camera. "But this time like you're holding back a secret."

I squint. "What kind of secret?"

"Like... a devastating one." Kyle says with dramatic effect.

I look dead into the camera and say, "Saddle."

Someone cackle laughs.

Jenna storms over, clapping her hands. "Okay, that's enough improv, folks. Jack, Elena, with me. Now."

We follow her to the barn office, where she has two chairs set up across from her like this is a courtroom and we're about to be sentenced. I sit down. Elena looks mildly amused, like she's expecting snacks and drama.

I have to say, out of all of the women, Elena is probably the best out of all of them. She doesn't even seem like she's trying that hard. It's like she's just here to have fun, and honestly she's the only one I don't want to run away from.

Jenna shuts the door. Then she pulls out two manila folders, sets them on the desk, and slides them across.

"What is this?" I ask.

"Your future. Your finale and fake happily-ever-after," she says, like she's hosting a game show and also losing her mind. "You two are going to be *the* couple at the end of the show."

I blink. "Excuse me? Isn't there supposed to be a vote or something?"

She taps the folders. "Non-disclosure agreements. Sign 'em. You'll fake a big romantic ending, ride off into the sunset, whatever the people want. We air it, ratings skyrocket, and you keep your actual love life under wraps."

I glance at Elena, expecting her to protest, but she flips open the folder and snags a pen. "You're okay with this?"

She gives me a sheepish smile. "Yeah. I've been expecting this."

Jenna stands. "I'll give you two a minute. But don't take too long. You both signed contracts, and this is pretty much non-negotiable."

When the door shuts, I turn to Elena. "You knew?"

"Kind of. I mean, I assumed it's scripted and fake." She folds her hands on the desk. "Look, Jack. I know you don't want this. I don't either. But... I do have a favor to ask."

I stare at her. "A favor?"

"You're gonna laugh," she says, sheepishly.

"Try me."

She leans in slightly. "I'm actually engaged."

I choke on nothing. "You're what?"

She nods. "Yup. His name's Logan. We've been together for six years. He's at home up in Montana, working at a ranch while I do this show. We're saving up to buy land out here and start a small ranch of our own. Hence why I'm doing the show in the first place."

"Holy crap." I had no idea. She played the part so well.

"I know. It sounds crazy. But this show paid me more than I make in a year. And it got me out here. I never expected to stay this long, but then... I saw Bridger Falls. I saw this ranch. I fell in love."

"With the ranch," I clarify.

"Very much not with you, cowboy," she says with a smirk. "You're great, but I've already got my cowboy, and we're building our own dream life."

I bark out a laugh. This is absolutely nuts.

"So," she continues, "what if we help each other? We sign the NDA. Fake it for the cameras. Smile pretty for the big finale. And when this is all over, we both walk away with what we actually want."

"Which is... ?"

"Logan needs a job. We get a foothold here in Bridger Falls. You get to be with the woman everyone knows you love," she adds with a knowing smirk.

I stare at her. "You want your fiancée to work here?"

She nods and chuckles. "He's strong, reliable, and hard working. The opposite of me. But he loves this life, and he's a damn good wrangler. We just want a shot at settling in here and building something of our own someday."

I scratch the back of my neck. "This is so weird."

"Tell me about it. I've fake dated you for three weeks. I once had to rub sunscreen on your neck while you talked about barbed wire."

"I was being educational."

"You were sunburned and rambling."

I grin. "Okay, fine. Give me Logan's number. I'll talk to him. If he's half as cool as you, he's hired."

Her face lights up. "Really?"

"Yeah. I mean, this is unorthodox as hell, but... I respect the hustle. And I admire you for keeping this going as long as you have."

She exhales hard. "Thank you. And... for the record, I'm rooting for you and Cami. Hard. Like, I wrote fan fiction in my head during filming."

"Now I'm scared." I sigh. I don't even know what that means.

"You should be," she grins. "Love is scary. But it's worth it."

We both laugh and shake hands. Well, I'll be damned. This has not gone like I thought it was going to go, but it's a relief that I know how this ridiculous show is going to play out and I can finally breathe, knowing that this isn't going to last much longer.

I pick up the NDA and read over it. It says that Elena and I are not to discuss the ending of the show with anyone other than Jenna and ourselves. If we do, we are subject to a million-dollar fine and forfeit our rights to any income around the show as well as punishable litigation.

Well, that's just great. I can't tell Cami any of this, and she's going to be pissed.

"Let's finish this thing," I say. "And when it's over... we can begin our lives."

She high fives me and says, "Deal, cowboy."

Chapter 30
Cami

Your Place by Ashley Cooke

Jack won't tell me where we're going.

"Don't plan on wearing anything," he says, voice wrapped in mischief as he kisses the top of my head and tosses a duffel bag into the truck.

I squint at him. "What do you have planned?"

He grins, that full, crooked grin that makes my stomach flip. "You will love it. Promise."

"That's not exactly reassuring." But I climb into the truck anyway. Because it's Jack. And when it comes to him, I'd follow him to the moon.

We drive north, away from Bridger Falls, past winding trails and creeks flowing like they have somewhere to be.

When Jack finally turns off onto a dirt road, I catch a glimpse of a cabin between the trees with smoke flowing from the chimney. And then I see it, a charming cabin nestled in a private clearing, twinkle lights strung between trees like fireflies caught in tiny little jars.

I blink. "Jack...This place is beautiful."

He shrugs, suddenly sheepish. "You work harder than anyone I know. You've been going nonstop, baking at the trailer, cleaning up the lodge, helping with branding. I figured you deserved a break. So, I got with Tucker, we found the place to rent, and we set this up."

I stare. The man brought me out here to camp at this cabin. I love it.

There's a firepit ready to light, a cozy little setup with thick blankets, pillows, and a cooler beside two Adirondack chairs. Inside the cabin, I can already see a queen-size bed, fairy lights, and a thermos of what smells suspiciously like hot cocoa.

I look at him. "You made a romantic hideaway in the middle of nowhere for me."

Jack lifts a shoulder like it's no big deal, but his ears flush red. "I did. Because I love you."

My heart stutters. He's said it before, sure. But something about him saying it here, surrounded by pine and stars and silence, makes it sink deeper. I step closer, hands on his chest. "I love you too."

And then I kiss him.

The rest of the afternoon feels like magic. Jack shows me how he's packed a picnic, steak sandwiches, potato salad, and apple pie in mason jars. He got them in town, but they look and smell amazing. We sit on a quilt and eat until the sun begins to set, washing it all down with beer and cocoa.

We talk about everything and nothing. About how the film crew is almost gone. About how Jenna is flying back to L.A. soon to work on production duties.

"How do you feel about it all ending?" I ask, picking at a fray in the blanket.

He's quiet for a beat. "Relieved. I'm not a reality TV guy, Cami. I hated every second I had to pretend I gave a damn about finding a wife. But I kept telling myself it'd be worth it. For us."

"It is," I say softly.

He nods. "Soon as possible, you're getting your B&B. And I'm getting a hell of a lot more time with you. No cameras. No pretending. Just... us."

He brushes a strand of hair from my face.

"I want to wake up with you every morning. Build something real. You and me. A life out here."

"We already are," I whisper.

We sit by the fire until stars crown the sky, the flames casting gold across Jack's face as he plays with my fingers. It's the kind of moment you don't want to blink and miss. The kind you bottle up and save for later.

Later, we curl up together. Jack stretches out on the bed, pulling me into his chest like it's the most natural thing in the world. My legs tangle with his. My head rests where his heartbeat thrums steady and sure.

He tilts my chin up. "You deserve everything."

He kisses me, slow and reverent, his hands gentle at my waist.

And in that soft, glowing cabin, surrounded by quiet woods and stars, I fall a little more in love with him. Because he deserves everything too.

In the morning, I wake up to birdsong and Jack making coffee. He looks over his shoulder, grinning when he sees me wrapped in a blanket, bare feet cold on the wood floor.

"Mornin', baby. I put the cinnamon in just like you do."

I grin at how sweet he is. "Mornin', Jack."

He hands me a mug. I sip, watching steam curl into the air.

"We don't have to leave until noon," he says.

"Good," I reply, curling into his side. "Because I'm not ready to go back yet."

We stay like that for a while, wrapped up in each other and everything we never thought we'd have. No cameras. No pressure. Just Jack and me, building something beautiful in the middle of nowhere.

And for the first time in a long time, I believe in forever with Jack. All we need is each other.

Chapter 31
Jack

The Good Ones by Gabby Barrett

By the time I pull into Cami's driveway, I'm bone tired and more than a little dazed from the chaos of the day. Love greets me at my truck and wiggles her whole body when she sees me with happiness. I love that dog.

She's standing in the kitchen, barefoot in jeans and a soft t-shirt that's falling off one shoulder like she has *no idea* how sexy she looks. Her cheeks are pink. Her hair's pulled up in a messy bun, little pieces curling around her ears. She's stirring something in a pot on the stove like it's just a normal night.

I could come home to this every night. Every single damn night.

"Hey, baby," I say, shutting the door behind me.

She turns and smiles. Not her usual cocky smirk. Not the I-just-mouthed-off-and-you-love-it grin.

It's soft. A little nervous. *Shy.*

"Hey," she says. "You hungry?"

"Always," I say slowly, stepping forward. "Is that... my favorite?"

She nods. "Biscuits. Fried chicken. Mashed potatoes with the good gravy. And... peach cobbler for dessert."

I blink. "Okay. What happened. Am I dying?"

She laughs, cheeks flushing deeper. "No."

"You burn something down?" I tease.

"No, but thank you for thinking that's my version of affection."

I step a little closer, trying to make sense of her. "Did you drink Poppy's moonshine again?"

She doesn't answer.

Instead, she walks right up to me, looking like she has hearts in her eyes, fire in her chest, and wraps her arms around my neck like it's the most natural thing in the world.

And then she kisses me.

Her hands tangle in my hair, her body pressed against mine, and I kiss her back because I've been dying to for months. Years. Always. I grip her waist and pull her closer, her mouth sweet and warm and finally mine.

When we break apart, she's breathless. I'm stunned. And in love with her in a way that feels so *right*, it almost hurts.

I kiss her again. Harder this time. My hands sliding into her hair, her body melting into mine. Everything I've held back pours out of me all at once, months of pining, years of wanting. She's all heat and softness and impossible magic.

She reaches over and turns off the stove, dropping a lid on top of a pan. Dinner forgotten, we stumble toward the couch. She tugs my shirt up over my head like she's wanted to for years and never let herself. I trail kisses down her neck, her shoulder, whispering her name like a prayer.

Because this moment is what I've fought for. Even when I felt like I was fighting for this on my own, I've been fighting.

She whispers mine right back. And I love hearing her say it.

There's nothing rushed about this. Nothing frantic. Just hands and mouths and hearts colliding like they've been waiting for this moment forever. I take my time with her, worshipping her like she deserves. She pulls me close like she's never letting go.

This time, it's slow. Unhurried. Almost like all the promises we made materialize in this moment.

Even feeling like we have all the time in the world, the bedroom still feels so damn far away, so I walk backwards to the living room. With one hand on her throat, gentle pressure on each side to keep her exactly where I want her, and the other pulling her with me by the belt loops of her jeans, I sink down on the couch, and she follows, straddling me, giving me all her weight.

When her core presses against my cock, I hiss as my hips lift from the couch without my permission, grinding into her. The contact draws a long, low moan from her as she lowers her head and sucks my bottom lip between hers, nipping with her teeth.

"Cami," I moan, squeezing her ass and dragging her core down my hard ridge.

Seconds meld into minutes, and I could stay wrapped up in this woman forever.

* * *

Later, tangled together beneath a throw blanket on the couch, her head on my chest, her fingers tracing lazy circles over my ribs, I feel it settle in my bones.

This is it.

This is home.

"You know," she murmurs, "I still think your gates are obnoxious."

I grin, pressing a kiss to her temple. "You're going to marry me one day, and those gates are going to be *our* obnoxious gates."

She chuckles. "You proposing already, Jessop?"

"Not yet," I say, pulling her tighter. "But I'm gonna."

And from how she tucks herself against me and sighs like I'm everything she's ever wanted, I know she believes me. And that's all I'll ever need.

* * *

The world outside is dark and quiet, the kind of quiet that only happens late at night in Bridger Falls, when the wind settles and the stars take their watch. But inside Cami's bedroom, it's warm. Peaceful.

She's curled into my chest beneath a pile of blankets, one bare leg hooked over mine, her hand resting just above my heart like she knows exactly how fast it beats for her. Her hair smells like vanilla and honey. Her breath is slow. Steady.

We haven't moved much since we came up here after we made love and finally made it through dinner, just shifted enough to tangle together, limbs and hearts knotted so tightly I'm not sure where I end and she begins.

I think she's drifting off when her voice breaks the quiet.

"The bank was rude to me. I think I want to find a new one."

I glance down, brushing a hand slowly up her back. Her voice is soft, but there's something sharp beneath it. Hurt. Shame.

She continues. "They've always been rude. I used to tell myself I was imagining it. But I wasn't. I think I want to find a new bank."

My stomach tightens. I shift just enough to see her face. She's staring at the ceiling now, her brow furrowed, eyes distant.

"What do you mean?" I ask gently. "What happened?"

She swallows. "It's not what they said. Not exactly. It's the way they talked to me. Like I wasn't worth their time. Like I was some clueless girl with no idea what she was doing. Like... like Wilder Ranch didn't mean anything. Just a number. A dying piece of land with a dumb little girl clinging to it."

I feel the anger rising, steady and hot. I know what that feels like. I've felt it before. It's the way people look at someone they've already decided isn't worth listening to. How our family has felt and how we've been working so hard to rebuild our name with the community.

"They acted like I was ridiculous for trying to save it," she says quietly. "Gave me deadlines they kept changing. Bullied me into signing paperwork. They kept telling me I'd need a miracle if I wanted to keep it. Talked me in circles. Sometimes I think that if I were a man, they never would have done that to me or treated me that way."

My jaw clenches. "Why didn't you tell me before now?"

She nods once. Doesn't look at me. "I was just embarrassed. I wanted to save the ranch. I didn't want to lose it."

"You did save your ranch." I brush my knuckles down her cheek. "That's why I wanted to fight with you. I saw how hard you were fighting."

Her eyes finally meet mine. "Thank you, Jack. You didn't have to do that."

The vulnerability in her voice guts me, and I whisper, "Of course, baby. I'd do anything for you."

"I always pretended like I could handle things. Like I was strong and capable and didn't need anyone. But I did. I needed you."

I lean in and press a kiss to her forehead. "You *are* strong. And capable. And so damn smart. And you're not alone."

She sniffs, blinking fast. "It felt like the town saw it too. Like people knew I was barely holding on. They were polite but... distant. Like they were waiting for me to fail."

I exhale slowly, keeping my voice low and steady. "People in this town don't always know what to do with someone who fights for what they love. But that doesn't mean they look down on you. That means they don't know how to measure your kind of strength."

She closes her eyes for a second, her forehead pressing to my chest.

"I didn't want you to save me at first," she whispers. "Because I didn't want you to see me as some damsel in distress."

I tilt her chin up gently. "I've seen you shovel horse crap in a blizzard while screaming at a raccoon to get out of your hay barn. You're the least damsel-y woman I know."

She laughs through her tears, and I smile, brushing them away with my thumb. "I'd forgotten about that," she says softly.

"I think that was the night I fell in love with you," I add, my voice quieter now. "We were just kids, but even then I knew."

She nods, her fingers curling tighter against my chest.

"I just want us to work," she murmurs.

"We will work. Every single day," I say, and I mean it with every part of me. "You're everything to me."

She exhales shakily and shifts closer, tucking herself tighter under my arm like she's finally letting herself rest.

"I wish I'd told you sooner," she says softly.

I kiss the top of her head. "You told me now. That's enough."

We lie there in the quiet, hearts beating in rhythm, wrapped up in warmth and truth and everything that's been waiting between us for years.

She's not hiding anymore.

And I swear, I'll never let anyone, especially not a damn bank make her feel small again.

That night when she's sleeping, I fire off a text to Weston and Tucker and tell them to meet me at the bank in the morning.

It's time we handle business around town and let people know that neither Wilder or Jessop Ranch is going anywhere. And we won't be putting up with anymore bullshit.

Chapter 32
Cami

Memory Lane by Old Dominion

I wake up to the smell of coffee and the feeling of being loved. A warmth fills me that I didn't realize I needed.

There's a soft clink on the nightstand, followed by the slow creak of the mattress. Then, warm hands slide around my waist, and Jack's mouth brushes my shoulder. "Wake up, baby," he murmurs, voice still thick from sleep.

I hum into the pillow, my body heavy with that delicious post-sex, post-emotional-vulnerability-last-night kind of bliss. "If this is a dream, I swear to God..."

"It's not. But I did bring coffee and your cinnamon scones."

My eyes snap open. "Say less."

I roll over and sit up, hair a total disaster, wearing nothing but Jack's worn and soft flannel. He's beside me on the bed, shirtless, looking at me like he's the damn patron saint of morning-after romance.

God, he's mine. It was exhausting pretending to hate him when I love him so much it hurts.

Faint light from the lamp spills across his bare chest, his hair is still messy from sleep, and he looks at me like I personally hung the stars.

"You're ridiculous," I whisper, taking the mug.

"You love me."

I do. I really, really do.

Before I can respond, he leans in and kisses me soft and slow, like we have all the time in the world. And when I kiss him back, something in my chest breaks open. It's terrifying. And electric. And a little bit magic. It feels like...I'm home. Like, everything makes sense with him here.

"Okay," I breathe when we finally pull apart. "You don't have to try so hard to get me to fall in love with you, Jack. I'm already there."

"Too late," he says, grinning. "I watched you do it in slow motion last night. Twice."

I grin. But he's not wrong. God, he's cocky. But he's also perfect. And mine.

"What are you thinking?" he asks as he reaches over and picks up his own mug that used to be my grandpa's.

"Just wondering how the show is going to go and what's going to happen," I admit. "You've been looking awfully cozy with Elena."

He sighs and looks at me. "Jenna had us sign NDAs. But I can tell you that if I had to give up everything for you, I would. But we just have to hold out a little longer."

"Very cryptic," I shrug and take a sip of my coffee. "Mmm, Jack. Did you put cinnamon in it?"

He smiles. "Learning from the best."

A little later, we're saddled up and riding out past the barn, coffee thermos and treats for the horses and Love in the saddlebags like habit. The air is cool and crisp, the quiet that only belongs to early mornings on the ranch. Our favorite time of day.

Jack looks stupidly good on a horse. Relaxed, confident, like the land is part of him. And the way he glances at me every few minutes like he still can't believe I'm here? Yeah. I'm toast.

I squint up at him as he shows off like some kind of Marlboro ad. "Flexin' on a horse like a romance novel cover?"

He throws a smirk over his shoulder. "Jealous?"

"Of your ego? Never. Of the horse? Maybe."

He laughs, and dammit, it's unfair how good he looks doing it. "Don't worry, you can take me for a ride later."

I laugh. "Deal. But don't let it go to your already-too-big head."

"You weren't complaining about the size of my dick earlier..."

"Jack!" I playfully laugh.

We ride for a while in comfortable silence, sipping coffee, pointing out calves and fence lines. Then we come over the ridge, and there it is.

Our tree.

The big, crooked oak in the middle of the pasture. Twisting, defiant, beautiful. Half hers. Half his. Just like always.

I slow my mare without thinking, my chest suddenly tight.

Jack pulls up beside me, watching me carefully.

"This tree," I murmur, "has always felt like ours."

His brows lift. "It is ours."

My fingers tighten the reins. "When we were kids, after everything... we'd meet here. Sit up in the branches like we owned the world. Like we were safe."

"You were always safe with me," he says softly.

I look over at him.

His voice is quiet. Sure. Full of things he doesn't always say. "You still are," he adds.

And just like that, I'm falling all over again.

I blink hard, staring at the tree. "I think part of me always thought that if we ever figured it out, it would be here. With this land. That tree. You."

He reaches across and takes my hand in his, right there across our saddles.

"I think everything in my life led me back here," he says. "To you."

Tears sting my eyes, stupid, inconvenient feelings, and I laugh to cover it up. "God, you're so cheesy."

He grins. "You love it."

"I really do." God help me, I love everything about him. His quiet steadiness. His stupid perfect smirk. His stubborn protectiveness. His deep, fierce love.

This is what it feels like to be chosen. To be safe and to be home.

We ride a little further, then loop back to the tree. Jack pulls a blanket from his saddlebag, because, of course, he brought one, and we sit beneath the branches like we used to, but we are older now. Wiser. A little more broken in. Just like that tree. It kept growing, and it was always here. Like it was waiting for us to get it together.

He pours the rest of the coffee into the mugs, hands mine over, and says, "So... when we combine the ranches, we're building our house here, right?"

My heart flips so hard I swear I feel it in my toes. For a moment, I just stare at him, the way the early light hits his face, soft and golden, like the universe is underlining this very second. And all I can think is, he means it. He really means it.

Not just a someday promise. Not a maybe. Not a when-it's-convenient. He's building me a home. Not just any home, *our* home. In the place where my dreams first took root. The place where his arms feel like the only shelter I'll ever need.

My breath catches. "You're serious?"

He nods and looks out over the field. "Where do you want your big farmhouse kitchen?"

I picture it. The kitchen. The wide porch. Bread baking while he chops wood. Holidays with friends. Mornings in bed. Dogs at our feet. A future so vivid I could almost reach out and touch it.

I look at Jack, this man who used to drive me absolutely insane, and now loves me like it's the easiest thing in the world.

And I realize, I'm not dreaming. I'm already home.

I glance up at the tree again, sunlight filtering through the leaves, casting shadows over the grass. "I don't mind where it is as long as you're in it with me."

He smiles as he stares out as if he's imagining it.

"Our house by our tree," I whisper.

"Yup," he says, nudging my boot with his. Casual. Like, he doesn't just say things that wedge themselves under my ribs and stay there.

I glance down at our boots, then back up. "Is this your new thing? Emotional whiplash with a side of flirt?"

He shrugs, grinning. "Hey, if it gets you to smile..."

And damn it, I do. I bite it back, but it's there.

"You're such a menace," I say, my voice a little too soft.

"Maybe," he says. "But I'm your menace."

I roll my eyes, but it's useless. I'm already smiling. Already feeling that stupid burn behind my eyes I pretend isn't there.

I shake my head, laughing just enough to keep it from turning into something else. "You're lucky I like you."

"Yeah," he says, quieter now. "I really, really am."

He watches me for a beat, then leans in and kisses me slow, reverent, like I'm something holy.

And I realize something deep in my bones. I'm not just

falling for Jack Jessop. I'm already his. And this? This is where I was always meant to land.

* * *

Later on that morning when I pull into the parking lot of Bridger Falls Community Bank, I almost reverse right back out. When Jack asked me to meet him in front of the bank, I wasn't sure what he was up to. Now, I'm really wondering what he's up to.

Because standing out front with cowboy boots planted, arms crossed, all intimidating and rugged as hell, are the three Jessop brothers.

Jack. Weston. Tucker. Just... waiting. My heart kicks into gear like a spooked colt.

I park and climb out of the truck slowly, eyes narrowing. "Okay," I say warily as I walk toward them, "what are you guys doing here?"

Jack's the first to move. He steps forward, that calm, steady look in his eyes that always makes me feel a little braver than I am. "We all need to handle some ranch business."

I glance between them, Jack, Weston, Tucker. All of them watching me and they're serious.

"We?" I ask slowly.

"All of us," Jack says.

My spine straightens before I even know what I'm doing.

I glance at Weston. He gives me a single nod, eyes steady. Tucker tilts his chin like hell yeah, you too.

I swallow. "What do you need me for?" I ask, and my voice cracks just a little.

Jack's voice is soft but certain. "You're a part of major ranch decisions now. You're one of us."

It hits me like a punch to the gut. The good kind, the one

that knocks the air out of your lungs and fills your chest with something bigger than fear. I look at them again. Really look. They're not humoring me. They're not doing this out of guilt or pity or some weird cowboy chivalry.

They mean it. *Holy shit.*

The girl who used to get talked down to at this very bank, the one who fought tooth and nail to hold on to her land, who everyone thought would lose it. And here I am, standing outside the same bank, shoulder to shoulder with three of the most powerful ranch owners in Bridger Falls.

And they're waiting for me. "I—" I clear my throat. "Okay."

Jack steps closer, taking my hand, pressing a kiss to my palm, before giving it a reassuring squeeze. "You belong here. Right next to me. Always."

And just like that, something inside me clicks into place. "I guess it's time we show this town what Wilder and Jessop Ranch can do together."

Weston grins. "Damn right."

Tucker smirks. "Let's go handle some business."

I square my shoulders and nod, still not sure what business we're handling. "Let's."

And for the first time ever, I walk into that building not alone.

I walk in like I've got an empire at my back.

Because I do.

* * *

The bank conference room is cold and sterile, like it's designed to make people feel small. I used to feel that way in here, small, and out of place. I used to have to wear a business suit to amp myself up with confidence. Now, I'm sitting here in jeans, a button-down shirt, and scuffed boots. I'm more confident than I've ever been.

Today I walked in with Jack on one side, Weston and Tucker flanking us like a damn cowboy SWAT team, and I take a seat at the long, polished table like I belong. My boots scuff the tile, and my back is straight, with my pulse thundering—but I don't let it show.

We sit and wait.

And when Sterling Atwood walks in, holding a sleek leather portfolio and a fake little customer-service smile, he freezes when his eyes jump from Weston to Jack to Tucker, and then to me.

Finally, he tenses. And for the first time, Atwood's gaze doesn't drop to my chest. He doesn't leer. He looks nervous.

Good.

"Gentlemen," he says with a stutter-step and then adds, "And Miss Kendrick."

I arch a brow.

Atwood clears his throat and takes a seat at the head of the table, clearly thrown off by the testosterone in the room, and the fact that I'm not alone.

Weston leans forward, resting his forearms on the table, voice calm and razor sharp.

"Let's not waste time. We're here because we know you've been talking to a few investors around Bridger Falls. Quiet little backroom chats about opening up a business venture on the edge of town. A boutique farm stay experience. Horse rides. Dinners under the stars. Guest cabins."

My stomach turns to stone. That's my plan.

Atwood starts to object, but Weston lifts a hand, casual and terrifying. "Don't insult us, Sterling. We *know*."

Jack and Tucker both fold their arms across their chests like synchronized cowboy bodyguards. The energy in the room shifts—like a thunderstorm just rolled in and decided to join us at the table.

I stare at Atwood, jaw clenched so tight it hurts. "You stole my business plan?"

He stammers, "Now, I would say there were some good ideas there, but Cami, you didn't have the—"

"Don't." My voice slices through the air.

Everyone goes quiet.

I feel rage bloom in my chest, hot, full, and old. "This is a small town. We're supposed to support each other. Lift each other up. But you? You've done nothing but dismiss me, belittle me, and now steal from me?"

His face reddens. He tries to gather his composure, but I'm not done.

"You're a thief, Atwood. And if you think I'm just gonna let this slide—" I lean forward, locking eyes with him, "—you picked the wrong woman to screw over."

He opens his mouth. I beat him to it. "I'll be looking into litigation. And today, right now, I want all of my money withdrawn. Every account. Every cent. I want all my accounts closed."

I feel Jack go still beside me. Then he nods in approval.

Weston lifts his chin. "Ours as well."

Tucker adds, "We'll find a new bank. One that doesn't get in bed with crooks."

Weston looks right at Atwood. "As of this moment, Wilder and Jessop Ranch have no ties to you or this institution. And we will be pursuing legal action against you for sharing confidential client business plans with other businesses."

Sterling looks like he's been sucker-punched. "Now wait, I —this can be resolved. We don't need to be rash—"

"No," Jack says quietly, deadly. "We do. You messed with one of us."

Tucker leans forward, glare sharp. "You messed with all of us."

There's a long beat of silence. The kind that makes grown men sweat.

Atwood shifts in his seat. "There's no need for threats."

Weston tilts his head. "We're not threatening. We're stating facts and consequences."

Jack leans forward slightly. "Did you have anything to do with Granger and Jace who were messing with Cami and her property?"

Atwood stiffens. "Absolutely not."

Judging by the surprised look on his face, I don't think he did. But I am glad that Jack thought to ask.

Then, Weston rests his hands on the table, calm and composed as ever. "And one more thing. I know you've been to visit our father."

Sterling freezes again.

"That's not our business," Weston continues, "but it is... interesting. That you're associating with a convicted felon. Of grand larceny, no less. Something the board of this bank will be made aware of. Immediately."

Sterling opens his mouth. Nothing comes out.

I sit back slowly, my heart thudding.

I should be shaking. I should be crying. But all I feel is clarity.

Because for the first time, I'm not fighting alone. I'm not clawing my way to respect. I have it.

And not just because of the men beside me, but because I finally believe I deserve it.

My chest pulls tight. I nod once, swallowing down the lump in my throat. This time, I don't cry in the bank parking lot. This time, I walk out with my head high.

Tucker breaks the silence with a low whistle. "Damn, Cami. I'm glad we have you on our team."

I snort. Jack grins, proud and flushed.

"But seriously," Tucker adds. "You were scary. Like... impressively scary."

Jack leans over, voice low. "We fight right. And for the right things."

And three cowboys walking right beside me.

* * *

My heart's still racing, and my adrenaline's still high. But underneath all of it is this strange, steady hum in my chest.

I didn't cry or crumble. I stood up for myself—for my ranch, for my name—and the men beside me didn't speak for me.

Nope. They stood with me.

Jack's hand brushes mine as we walk, and it's warm, solid, familiar. But the second we round the corner of the building— out of view of Weston and Tucker—he stops.

"Come here," he says, voice low and rough.

Before I can say anything, he pulls me toward him, arms wrapping around my waist, and kisses me.

Hard. Like he's been holding it in all morning. Like kissing me is the only way to say what he's feeling.

My fingers dig into the front of his shirt as he deepens it, one hand sliding up to cup the back of my neck, his thumb brushing just behind my ear. His body is all heat and tension, every line of him pressed against me like he can't get close enough.

When he finally pulls back, his forehead rests against mine, breath warm against my lips.

"Do you have any idea what you just did in there?" he whispers, voice wrecked in the best way. "You were fire, Wilder. You were... damn."

I groan, a little breathless. "I thought I was going to lose it on him."

"You held your own."

I search his eyes—green and steady and filled with something that makes my chest ache. "Was it too much?"

"Not at all." He kisses the corner of my mouth, slow and soft. "You fight with your whole heart. You make people want to be better."

I blink fast. "I didn't think anyone would ever say that to me. Not really."

"Well," he says, tilting my chin up, "get used to it. Because I'm gonna say it every damn day."

My heart flips. Fully, stupidly flips.

"You were so calm in there," I whisper. "So steady."

He smiles, brushing his thumb across my cheek. "Only because I knew you had it handled. I've never been so proud in my life."

"You're gonna make me cry, Jessop."

He kisses me again, gentler this time, like a promise. "Then let me distract you."

"Hmm." I grin against his lips. "What's the plan? Carry me off to the barn like some cowboy romance fantasy?"

"I could." His hand slides just a little lower. "But I'd rather take you home. Make you lunch. Kiss every freckle on your body. And tell you a hundred times over that you're the best damn thing that's ever happened to me."

I melt. Fully. Into him. Against him.

Because that's what Jack Jessop does.

He holds the fire and the softness. The loyalty and the heat. And he gives it all to me. All of him.

Chapter 33
Jack

One Man Band by Old Dominion

The sun sets behind the barn, casting golden light across the fields like the universe is trying to be romantic on purpose. Which is probably good because none of this feels real or romantic in the least. Elena stands beside me in a pastel floral dress that matches her lipstick. Her hair is curled, and her smile is camera-ready.

She's playing the part. The only problem is that I'm not. I'm struggling so badly with all of this.

I stare at the camera crew gathering by the gate, trying not to look like a man who's about to commit televised emotional fraud.

"You ready?" Elena asks, looping her arm through mine like we're prom dates instead of two people pretending we're about to fall in love.

I nod. "Sure."

She glances up at me. "That was... convincing."

I wince. "Sorry. I'm just tired."

I'm not. I'm panicked.

Because tomorrow's the big finale. The part where I'm supposed to stand in front of Bridger Falls and America and declare that I've found love. Only I have. It's just not with the woman next to me.

It's Cami, and it's always been Cami. And it will only ever be her.

And the thought of standing on camera and saying it's Elena makes my stomach turn inside out. Even pretending just feels so wrong. I know what I need to say. I just don't think I can say it.

Tucker sidles up next to me with a microphone clipped to his shirt and a hot dog in hand. "You look like you just watched someone run over your heart."

"Thanks," I mutter.

He takes a bite. "This is what you get for signing up for a dating show, man. You fly too close to the drama sun, you get burned."

"You okay?" Weston joins us, holding a clipboard Jenna shoved at him earlier, looking extremely done with all of it. "You look like you're either gonna pass out or propose to the wrong woman."

"I *am* about to propose to the wrong woman," I hiss.

Tucker coughs on his hot dog. "Wait. You're actually gonna do it?"

"I don't know! I'm not *proposing* proposing. It's like a... symbolic finale moment. But I don't think I can even do that."

Weston gives me a sympathetic look. "Because of Cami."

I nod.

They both fall silent.

Then Weston sighs. "Man, you really are in love with her."

"Of course I am."

Tucker whistles. "You're so screwed."

Gee, thanks, guys.

* * *

Later, when we're on a break and cameras aren't rolling, I'm in the barn when I hear Elena scream.

Not a terrified scream. A shrieky, joyful scream. Like someone just told her she won the lottery, and it comes with a year's supply of eyelash extensions.

I walk outside just in time to see her run across the pasture like she's in a rom-com. Straight into the arms of a tall, broad-shouldered guy in jeans and a button down who spins her in a full dramatic circle before kissing her full on the mouth.

Tucker walks up beside me, watching this scene in front of us unfold with disbelief. "Okay, uh... Jack?"

"That's Logan," I say, not taking my eyes off what's unfolding. "Her fiancé."

There's a beat of stunned silence. Tucker chokes. "Her what?!"

Weston appears as if he sensed a disturbance in the sibling force. "Did I just hear the word fiancé? Is someone getting punched?"

I hold up a hand and say dryly. "Nobody panic. I've known about this."

Weston blinks at me. "You knew and didn't tell us?"

"I couldn't. Jenna made me sign an NDA," I shrug.

"Pretty sure that little PDA right there violates her NDA," Weston shakes his head, chuckling.

"Who would we have told?" Tucker says dryly.

"I don't know why you're making this a big deal. Reality television is mostly fake. Don't you guys know this?" I say, folding my arms over my chest.

"I don't know, *Jack*," he says, dramatically waving. "Maybe give us a heads up that the finale is about to turn into The Notebook but with a surprise fiancé."

Weston stares at Logan, who's now twirling Elena like a Disney princess. "So... who is this guy? And why is he dressed like he's about to fix a tractor?"

"He's a wrangler, and he wants to work with us," I explain. "Grew up on a ranch in Montana. He and Elena want to settle down around here and buy some land."

Tucker's still blinking. "What now?"

"Yeah," I say. "We do need good wranglers."

Weston throws up a hand. "I leave for one hour and come back to everything a mess again. Jenna is going to kill you."

"We're hiring him," I say.

At that exact moment, Logan turns around, walks up, and extends a hand. "Hey! I'm Logan. I hear y'all might need some help with ranch work. I've got references and a full resume if you want to take a look."

Weston stares at the handshake and finally shakes his hand. He's still so confused. "This is so weird."

Tucker, however, leans over and mutters, "Okay, but... we really do need good wranglers."

Weston sighs. "This is your mess with Jenna."

"Nice to meet you," Tucker says. "Look at him. He looks like he'd fit in here."

I sigh, pinching the bridge of my nose. "So we're all clear. You guys are not to tell anyone, right?"

"Elena just brought her fiancé to the finale," Tucker says. "If that's not a mic drop, I don't know what is."

Logan grins. "My momma sent down a few pies for y'all, too."

"Oh, hell yes," Tucker says, instantly won over. "Welcome to the team, buddy."

And that's how we hired my fake fiancé's fiancé.

***

It's a circus out here.

Camera crews, PAs with clipboards, a catering table that's somehow already out of the good sandwiches, and everyone walking around like we're all pretending this is normal. This is the most awkward, tension-filled finale wrap-up in the history of reality TV.

Real actors would have a hard time making this believable. But we're real people, real ranchers who are not actors.

Jenna has her work cut out for her, that's for sure. She's doing that high-pitched, fake laugh she reserves for when she's fully spiraling. Weston and Tucker are by the horses with Logan, asking him about welding like they didn't spend earlier scrutinizing him and his intentions.

Logan's actually a solid guy. Which somehow makes this weirder.

I scan until I spot Cami near the back of one of the horse trailers, half-shielded by the shadow of the hauler and out of sight from the crew.

I make my way over, slow and steady, heart pounding like I'm walking into something fragile. She doesn't turn around when I get close. Just crosses her arms tighter and stares off toward the pasture like she's trying to breathe through the madness.

"Hey," I say quietly.

She jumps a little. Then relaxes when she sees me. "Thought you were Jenna."

I smirk. "Do I look like I'm about to demand someone do something?"

She huffs out a laugh, but it's tired. Worn down. Real.

I step closer. "How you doing?"

She shrugs, arms still crossed. "Honestly? Just ready for whatever."

There's a beat of silence. Wind tugging at her hair. Dust kicking up in the gravel.

I reach out and gently touch her waist, turning her toward me. She lets me. I look her straight in the eyes.

"You know it's you, Wilder," I say, voice low and certain. "Always been you. And always will be you. There will never be anyone else for me."

Her eyes flash with something, hope, maybe. Uncertainty. And I hate that uncertainty is there. I want her to have hope and love. She deserves that.

"This is almost over," I add. "We're almost out of this mess. And then we can finally just be us. No cameras. No pretending. Just... you and me."

She doesn't answer right away. Just looks up at me with that guarded softness that always makes me want to pull her closer.

And then slowly, carefully, she nods. "I'm trying to believe it's real," she whispers. "That it'll actually end. That we'll get to be normal."

I lean in and kiss her. Not hard. Not rushed. Just... honest and real.

Her hands slide up my chest and into my shirt like she's grounding herself. Like I'm the only thing holding her to the earth right now.

When we break apart, I rest my forehead against hers. "I've got you. No matter how weird this gets. No matter what."

She exhales. "We just need the finale to be over."

"Then it's done," I repeat. "And I'm yours."

She finally smiles, just a little. "You've always been mine, Jessop."

I kiss her again because I can. Because we're almost through the storm. And we're still standing.

*** *** ***

There's hay scattered across the makeshift stage inside the barn, fairy lights strung across the rafters like they can distract from the disaster about to happen. Everything smells like sawdust and fake happiness. The camera crew is whispering in frantic tones off to the side, and Jenna's pacing like she's one unflattering angle away from a nervous breakdown.

I'm standing under a big-ass wooden arch someone zip-tied roses to, wearing a clean flannel I hate and holding a ring box that feels like it weighs a hundred pounds.

Elena stands a few feet away in a flowy dress and heels that are completely impractical for the barn floor. She's smiling.

Because she knows. We both do. It's all for show. But that doesn't make it any easier.

I shift my weight and scan the crowd gathered in the barn: family, neighbors, tourists, and half the crew all pressed in on hay bales like it's opening night at the county fair.

And that's when I see her. Front row. Cami. She's sitting between Ollie and Logan, of all people, and my chest goes tight at the sight of her.

She's wearing a red dress. Not just red. *Red.* The kind of red that makes your brain short-circuit. Her long black hair is down, curled, wild in a way that makes me want to bury my hands in it and never let go. And that lipstick, God help me, is doing things to me that should be illegal on a family-friendly TV set.

She crosses her legs and smiles at something Ollie says, and it hits me like a punch to the ribs. I'm supposed to walk out there. Say Elena is my choice. Kiss her. Maybe even fake-propose. And the love of my life is sitting in the front row in a red dress, watching me do it.

My throat dries out. My heart's pounding too fast. I take a

step toward the center of the stage and almost stumble. Jenna appears beside me like a vision of stress and caffeine.

"Okay," she hisses, fake-smiling at the cameras. "Remember the lines. Choose Elena. Say something swoony. Then we do the fake proposal. Big kiss. Crowd goes wild. We roll credits. You get your money, I get my finale, and no one dies."

I nod numbly. "Right." My hands are shaking. The box in my pocket feels like it's burning a hole through my soul.

Elena walks up next to me, her smile soft. "You okay?"

I glance at her. "Not even a little."

She squeezes my hand quickly, under the radar. "We can get through this. One more scene."

I look back at Cami. She's looking at me now. And she knows. I can see it in her face. In the way her smile slips just a little. In the way her fingers tighten around the armrest.

She knows I'm about to choose someone else. And she has no idea it's all pretend. I take a step forward. The crowd quiets. The cameras zoom in. And I try to breathe. But I can't.

I look at Elena. Then I look at Cami. And everything in me says no.

I take another step. Then stop. I can't do this. I physically cannot say the words. My mouth opens. Closes. Opens again.

Elena shifts beside me.

Jenna hisses from offstage, "Say the damn line, Jack!"

I look out over the crowd again. At Cami. Beautiful. Brave. Mine.

I swallow, hard. Then I drop the script entirely. "This isn't real love," I say.

The crowd goes completely still.

"I'm supposed to say that I've found love. That I've made a choice. That I've fallen for someone over the course of this wild, chaotic show." I glance at Elena. "And I have. But not with you. I'm sorry."

Elena nods softly, stepping back.

There are gasps in the audience.

I take a shaky breath. "The truth is, the woman I love has always been here. Long before the cameras showed up. Long before the show. Long before I ever knew what the hell I was doing."

I step off the stage. Walk straight down the aisle.

People part like the Red Sea.

Cami looks up slowly, stunned.

"Jack..." she whispers.

I stop in front of her.

"You don't have to say anything," I tell her. "You don't have to do anything. But I need you to know this whole time, it's been you. Every second of it."

She blinks up at me, wide-eyed. "You're really doing this?"

"I already did."

She stares at me for a long, breathless moment. The barn is dead silent. The cameras are rolling.

Then she says, "I love you, Jack."

And she kisses me.

It's not careful. It's not neat.

It's messy and red-lipstick-stained and real.

The barn erupts into noise. Someone wolf-whistles. Jenna screams, "CUT!" like it's an exorcism. Logan leans over to Ollie and says, "Well, that took a turn."

I pull back and rest my forehead against hers. "I love you," I say.

"I love you too," she breathes.

Jenna marches over, flinging her clipboard down. "Okay. FINE. Great. We'll spin it. 'Local cowboy finds unexpected love in childhood rival.' We'll use soft lighting. Maybe a voiceover. I hate all of you."

Tucker claps me on the back. "That was better than TV, man. That was, like, *feelings*."

Weston smirks. "I'm telling you, if this ranch thing doesn't work out, you've got a future in soap operas."

Cami wraps her arm around my waist, eyes still locked on mine.

"Now, can we be done with all of this?" she asks.

I grin. "We're done."

She leans up, whispering in my ear, "Good. Because I'm taking you home."

And just like that, we walk out of the barn. Hand in hand. Together. No cameras or pretending. Just us.

Because in the end, that's what really matters. Not the show, not the ranches, it's her. I want the world to know that she's my everything. I don't care what anyone thinks. She's my heart.

Chapter 34
Cami

Springsteen by Eric Church

I wake to the warmth of Jack's hands on my waist and the press of his mouth against the back of my shoulder. Sunlight's barely stretching across the curtains, golden and soft. Outside, the ranch is still asleep.

But here, it's just us.

I shift slightly and feel his chest against my back, the heat of him sinking into me. His hand slides up under the hem of his shirt, the one I stole last night after he made me forget my own name.

"Morning," he murmurs, voice still rough and sleepy.

"Mmm," I hum, eyes still closed. "Is it?"

He laughs softly, then kisses the curve of my neck, his stubble scraping just right.

I roll to face him, and the look in his eyes nearly knocks the breath from my lungs. All sleepy heat and absolute *adoration*.

"I love you," he whispers, brushing his thumb across my bottom lip. "I never stopped."

I stare at him for a long beat. Then I pull him down and kiss him like I believe him, because I do. Because I feel it. Because I *know* it now.

And as the sun creeps higher outside the window, we forget everything else.

The only things that matter are lips, skin, tangled sheets, and whispered promises we mean this time.

* * *

I'm still floating on the sunrise high of Jack's hands and his whispered promises when the white SUV pulls into the driveway.

I freeze mid-coffee sip. "Uh, oh."

Jack, shirtless on the porch like a damn cowboy ad for sin, squints toward the gravel. "Expecting someone?"

"Nope," I say grimly. "That's my mother."

He straightened slightly but didn't flinch. "Want me to tell her you're busy?"

"Just... let's see what she wants. Behave," I warn with a smirk.

My mom has been oddly trying. While I am giving her a chance, a part of me is still waiting for the other shoe to drop.

"No promises," he mutters with a grin.

The car door opens and out steps Teresa Wilder, hair smooth, outfit crisp for Bridger Falls. Her expression is unreadable as she takes in the porch, the coffee mugs, Jack.

She walks toward us with slow, deliberate steps, like she's preparing for battle or a funeral. Or maybe both.

I steel myself, preparing for the other shoe to drop with her.

She's been on her best behavior lately but that doesn't mean we're over everything that has happened.

"Morning," she says, and her voice isn't sharp. It's... cautious. *Interesting*.

"Hey," I answer, unsure whether to go full sarcasm or play it safe. I land on cautiously neutral.

"Teresa," Jack says with a polite nod.

She glances at him, then, surprisingly gives him a small smile. "Jack. You look well."

"Thanks," he replies. "Ranch life agrees with me."

"That's good," she says, quieter.

There's a pause, and for once, it's not filled with passive-aggressive daggers.

"I heard about the show," she continues, glancing between the two of us. "The... finale. And everything that's happened since."

I tense, waiting for the lecture. But it doesn't come.

She looks at me fully now, eyes softening in a way that guts me. "You look happy, Cami."

I blink. "I... am."

Teresa nods once. "Good. That's all I've ever wanted. Even if I didn't always say it the right way."

I stare at her, stunned. Jack rests his hand lightly on my lower back, grounding me.

"You came all the way out here just to say that?" I ask.

She huffs a small laugh. "And to see it for myself."

There's a beat of silence.

Then Jack, God bless him, steps forward slightly. "I love your daughter. I know we have history. But I'm not going anywhere. And I'm going to spend the rest of my life making sure she knows she's happy."

Teresa studies him for a long, long moment.

Then, shockingly, she smiles. "I believe you."

She turns to me. "You've grown into something strong and fierce and bright. I see it now. I just wanted you to know... I'm proud of you. Both of you."

That's when my throat tightens.

Because that's something I never thought I'd hear from her. Maybe she's not perfect. Maybe she's not the warmest or easiest. But she's trying. And right now? That's everything.

I nod, blinking fast. "Thanks, Mom."

She gives one more small smile, then turns back toward the car. "I'll let you two get back to your morning. I hear there's a party tonight?"

"At The Black Dog," I say. "You coming?"

She pauses. "I might stop by."

Then she gets in the car and drives away, dust trailing behind her, leaving Jack and me on the porch in stunned silence.

He bumps my shoulder. "That went better than expected."

"She said she was proud of us."

He smiles. "She did."

I lean into him. "Yeah. She did."

And somehow, the whole world feels a little lighter.

* * *

By the time we get into town, it's *everywhere*. Everyone is discussing us and our ranches. We're way more exciting than the reality show that is finally packing up and leaving town.

Wilder and Jessop Ranch are *officially* the romantic scandal of Bridger Falls.

We stop at the feed store, and Earl grins at me like a kid on Christmas.

"Took y'all long enough!" he cackles. "I lost thirty bucks in the pool!"

"There was a *pool?!*" I say, teasing him because Earl is just the best old man there is.

Jack grins, "Of course there was."

"Everyone bet you two would implode by the second week of filming," Earl adds. "But dang if you didn't do the slow burn proud."

"Is this why Mrs. Thornton from the post office winked at me this morning?" I mutter.

Jack grins. "You're famous now."

"Correction," I hold up a hand, "we're famous now. God help us."

The whole damn town is packed into The Black Dog when we get there. Like standing-room-only, every-table-taken, people-out-on-the-patio kind of packed. We can barely find a parking spot. There are even tents outside and people are selling merch. I take a deep breath and sigh when I see t-shirts with our faces on them. "Okay, that's just weird," I lament.

Making our way inside, we're met with string lights glowing overhead, country music drifting from the jukebox, and the smells of barbecue, whiskey, and trouble heavy in the air.

Someone, probably Maggie, has strung a banner across the back wall that reads:

"LOVE WINS (AND COWBOYS LOSE BETS)" in bold red glitter letters.

Jack laughs when he sees it. "Subtle. I take it Maggie won."

I nudge him. "You're the one who made it all dramatic. Walking off stage. Confessing your love. Kissing me like the cameras weren't rolling."

"You kissed me back," he hedges.

"You kissed me *first.*"

"Pretty sure we're both guilty then," he says as he leans over to kiss me.

"Pretty sure you're lucky I didn't punch you in front of the whole town for almost fake-proposing to someone else."

He grins, grabbing my hand as we move through the crowd. "But you didn't."

"Barely."

People notice us. It's not subtle.

"Oh my God, it's them!" someone shrieks near the dartboard. "It's cowgirl Barbie and ranch Ken!"

"Hey, put that on a t-shirt!" someone yells across the bar. "I'd buy it!"

"That was *way* better than any finale I've seen on Netflix," says Mrs. Fernandez as she fans herself with a bingo card.

"Lost twenty bucks on them," grumbles Dale, nursing a beer at the bar. "Thought for sure he'd pick the influencer."

"Pay up, Dale!" Maggie calls from over by the bar. "I had 'slow-burn chaos love confession' on my bingo card."

I blink. "There was a *bingo card?*"

"There were also *brackets*," Tucker yells from across the room, holding up a laminated sheet of paper. "Brackets, Cami! I was eliminated in week one when Jack kissed the dog before he kissed anyone on camera."

Jack tips his hat to him. "Love *is* my favorite dog."

We weave our way through the crowd, people patting us on the back, handing us drinks, shouting congratulations, and thinly veiled gossip. My cheeks hurt from smiling, but for once, it didn't feel like too much.

It feels *right*.

We finally find a corner table near the back, tucked between the pool table and a decorative saddle mounted on the wall. Jack pulls me into the booth beside him, one arm draped behind my shoulders, his fingers lazily playing with the ends of my hair.

"Still feel like chaos?" he murmurs, lips brushing my ear.

"A little," I admit.

"You okay?"

I glance at him. This man. My man. The same boy who used to sneak me licorice from the gas station. The one who broke my heart when he walked away after high school. And the one who put it back together one sunrise ride, one confession, one kiss at a time.

I nod. "I'm better than okay."

A cheer goes up from the other side of the bar. Weston's trying to teach someone how to two-step while Maggie claps and encourages this. Good, Weston can be her next match-making project. Poppy and Ollie are dancing like lunatics on purpose in front of the old jukebox, and people are laughing. I glance over, and Jenna's sitting at the bar, drinking a martini and muttering to herself while Tucker tries to convince her this was actually good for her career.

Jack's still watching me. I can feel it without even looking. "You sure you're okay with all this attention?" he asks, voice low.

"Nope," I say. "But I'm okay as long as you're by my side."

He turns toward me slowly, that easy cowboy smile curling at the edges. "Say that again."

"I'm okay with you," I say softly. "And your stupid hat. And your early morning rides and the way you make everything feel bigger and steadier and, ugh. Don't look at me like that."

"Like what?"

"Like you're in love with me, and it's the best thing that ever happened to you."

He grins. "That's because I am and it is."

I lean in, resting my head on his shoulder. "Then you better dance with me later."

"I was *planning* on it," he says with a smirk that tells me he isn't talking about actual dancing.

I don't know how long we sat like that. People come by.

Talk. Laugh. Slide drinks down the table. Poppy shows up with a plate of nachos and no context. Someone gives Jack a baby goat sticker wearing a cowboy hat. He slaps it onto his phone case like it's a badge of honor. Somehow Walker's goats have made it into merch, and everyone is obsessed with goats now ever since he thought he was buying two and somehow ended up with two dozen.

Later, when the lights dim a little more and the music slows down, Jack tugs me to my feet and pulls me into the open space in front of the bar.

He wraps his arms around me. I slide mine around his neck.

"Wilder," he whispers, spinning us slowly. "You look like trouble in that dress. I can't wait to take it off of you later."

"Good," I whisper back. "You deserve some trouble."

We dance. Not perfectly. Not gracefully. But I wrap my arms around him and hold him tight.

The song's soft and slow, something about home and heartbeats, and Jack's fingers curl around my waist like he's memorizing the shape of forever.

"This is real, right?" I ask because sometimes it still feels like it could all slip away.

He kisses my temple. "It's real. It's messy. It's *us*."

"You gonna build me a porch swing?"

"Already halfway done."

"You gonna kiss me under our tree again?"

"Every damn day."

And when I lean in and kiss him under the fairy lights, surrounded by the loud, nosy, ridiculous town that raised us, it's not about performance or drama or proving anything anymore.

It's just love. Loud. Wild. Rooted. Ours.

Chapter 35
Cami

What Kinda Man by Parker McCollum

It was my idea to have a big dinner at the Wilder House. Now that the show is over, it's great to just relax and enjoy ourselves without cameras around. By the time the roast is in the oven and the cornbread in the cast iron is ready, I've already dropped my wooden spoon, burned my forearm on the stove, and threatened Tucker with a rolling pin when he stole a bite of mashed potatoes.

But the house is loud, full of laughter, and great food smells that I am grateful for every second.

Which means: *things are going well.*

The kitchen is chaos in the way that makes me feel weirdly alive. Every burner's going. Dishes are stacked on the counter. Poppy's chopping salad with way too much dramatic flair, and Jack's trying to sneak a biscuit off the tray before they're done.

"What is it with these thieving Jessop brothers?" I grumble but can't help but grin.

"Don't even think about it, Jessop," I say, tapping his hand with the back of a wooden spoon.

He grins, all cocky and unrepentant. "They smell so good, baby."

"You'll live." But then I see the look on his face and say, "Okay, just one."

He steals a kiss from my cheek and takes one, disappearing into the dining room with a smug little whistle. God help me if our kids give me that same look. They'll get away with murder.

I take a deep breath and look around.

This isn't a holiday. It's not a party. But somehow it feels like *more* than that. It's the first time both families Wilder and Jessop are sitting under the same roof. No cameras. No chaos. Just us. And I cooked for them. Dishes full of love.

The back door swings open, and my mom walks in, holding a pie tin and looking like she had to psych herself up for twenty minutes in the car before knocking.

I brace myself, mentally and emotionally, but instead of a lecture or a critique about the state of my kitchen, she gives me a warm-ish smile.

"I brought coconut meringue," she says. "From scratch."

I blink. "You made a pie?"

"I do cook, Cami."

I smile at her and say, "It looks good, Mom."

She exhales like she's trying and looks relieved.

I don't know what to say, so I just take the pie and put it on the counter.

"You're feeding everyone tonight?" she asks, surveying the kitchen.

"Yep."

"You always cook like this?"

"Only when I'm trying to impress the entire town *and* make sure no one dies from under-seasoned mashed potatoes."

To my surprise, she smiles. And then she does the last thing I expect and pulls me in for a hug. "I love seeing you happy, Cami." And by the look on her face, she means it.

I smile, "Thanks, Mom."

She reaches out and adjusts a dish towel on the oven handle. "Now, let's feed everyone. Put me to work. You've built something good here, Cami. This place is warm. Real. And from what I hear around town, it's not just this kitchen you've got plans for."

I turn slowly, heart pounding. "You've heard about the B&B idea?"

"Maggie," she says with a sigh. "She's got all the details on everything."

I wait for the eye roll. The warning. The sarcastic comment.

But instead, she rests her hand lightly on the back of a chair and says, "I think your grandpa would've loved it. You turning Wilder Ranch into something new—*without* losing what made it ours."

My throat tightens. "Really?"

She nods. "He always wanted people to feel welcome here. You're making sure they still do."

She pats me on the back and heads off into the dining room to chat with everyone. And just like that, I could cry into the green beans.

Before I can even process that emotional bomb, Mack barrels in from outside, covered in dog hair and grinning like a maniac. "Tucker let me drive his truck!"

"Be careful!" I shout.

Tucker yells from the porch, "She barely hit anything!"

Jack slips into the kitchen beside me, wraps his arms around my waist, and murmurs in my ear, "This is what you wanted, right?"

I lean into him, dizzy with it. "Yeah. It is."

By the time dinner's served, it's full-on controlled chaos. The long farmhouse table is overflowing with food. Everyone's laughing too loud. Weston is trying to "gracefully" flirt with Maura, a single teacher who is new to town, and Logan's showing Ollie pictures of goats in sweaters on his phone like they've known each other forever.

Elena is helping me in the kitchen, and we've surprisingly become friends. She's great, and she and Logan fit in with everyone well. It sure is weird when people see them at the ranch, but all the locals have welcomed them in, and they fit in great. It doesn't hurt that they have Maggie's stamp of approval, and she let everyone know it.

Mom sits beside Maggie, and they're whispering with suspicious levels of intensity.

Poppy nudges me. "Your mom just smiled at Jack and didn't look like she wanted to kill him."

"Yeah," I whisper. "She does that now."

Jack catches my eye from across the table, raises his glass, and gives me the softest, most heart-melting smile I've ever seen.

And in that moment, I realize something: This is my home. My future. My *family*.

And he's *mine*.

* * *

Jack's been busy.

Not like he's pulling away. Not like *before*. But he's... quiet. Elusive. Gone before I wake up, vague about what he's working on, barely sitting still long enough for a full conversation.

He kisses me quick. He smiles when he looks at me. But there's a part of him that's been tucked away the past few days, and the longer it goes on, the louder my brain gets.

Tonight, though, he told me to: *Come to the Jessop Ranch around seven. Just trust me.*

Which, historically, means either he's building me something... or he's about to emotionally body-slam me with some other surprise that will make me want to take off all his clothes and climb him like a tree.

I pull up the long gravel drive just as the sky's starting to burn orange and gold over the mountains, ready to figure out what he's up to when I see the gate. I hit the brakes so hard the truck lurches.

Because the old sign, the monstrosity that was over the top and loomed over this ranch forever, bold blocky letters spelling out "Jessop Ranch" like a branding iron across the sky is *gone*.

In its place is something new. And beautiful. A wooden sign, simple and hand-carved, stained in warm cedar and mounted between two beams. And across the front, burned into the wood in clean, elegant lettering: **Wilder Ranch.**

My breath leaves my body. I don't move.

Jack stands beneath the sign, hands in his back pockets.

My boots hit the gravel before I know what I'm doing.

He doesn't say anything right away. Just watches me walk toward him like he's nervous to hear my reaction.

"What... what is this?" I manage. "Did they put it up at the wrong ranch?"

"This is your name," he says softly. "Your legacy. And now... it's ours. The Jessop Ranch is no more, and now they're both just Wilder Ranch."

My heart does a full somersault. "Jack," I whisper, staring up at the sign again. "You changed the name of your ranch?"

He nods, a little breathless. "It's ours."

The sunset glows behind him. His hair is tousled, his sleeves rolled, and he's got that look in his eyes, the one that used to make me nervous. That makes me feel *safe* now.

He steps forward, pulling something from behind the fence post. It's another sign. A matching one.

"For the other gate," he says. "We'll hang it tomorrow."

I press my fingers to my mouth. "You... you made matching signs."

"We're merging everything," he says. "Your land. My land. The cattle operations. The dairy setup. All of it. It's Wilder. To honor your grandparents. And to build something that *feels* like all of us."

Tears spring to my eyes so fast it shocks me.

"We're expanding," he continues, voice catching. "Meat store's been busier than ever. We're gonna open the B&B by next fall with the restaurant, farm to table, Bridger Falls-style. Weston's already working on the building plans. Tucker's got Maggie's whole chili operation in his pocket and is going to do some fundraising. And Jenna says she can rebrand all of it by next week. We're going big, Cami. Together. All of us."

I blink hard, swallowing the lump in my throat. "Why would you give up your ranch's name?"

He steps closer, hand brushing mine. "Because I'm so in love with you," he says quietly. "And I want a future with you. This land. This town. This... *life*. It's all better with you."

I laugh through the tears and shove him, just a little. "You're amazing."

"I know. You love me," he grins.

I look up at him, smiling through everything pouring out of me. "I *do*."

He takes my hand fully now. "There's a future here," he says. "Not just for us. For Weston. For Tucker. Jenna too, if she sticks around. And for every kid who wants to grow up on land like this and make something good."

I blink again. "And Weston, Tucker, and Jenna are good with all of this?"

"More than good with it. They came up with the idea. Apparently, your grandparents weren't just special to me. They were special people to them, too."

That's when I fully lose it. Like, ugly tears. No warning.

Jack just pulls me in and holds me tight, forehead resting against mine.

"I know what this place meant to you," he whispers. "What it *still* means. And I want to build a life where that never fades."

I bury my face in his shirt and breathe him in. Hay and cedar and future.

After a while, we sit on the fence rail under the new sign, my head resting on his shoulder, fingers tangled together.

He presses a kiss to my temple and whispers, "We're home, Wilder."

And for the first time in a long time, it truly feels like home to me.

Chapter 36
Jack

Ends of the Earth by Ty Myers

Sheriff Matthews pulls up in that dented county cruiser like it's been to war. Dust kicks up around his tires, and the second he climbs out and fixes his hat, I know something's up. He's here in a professional capacity.

"Jack," he calls. "Cami around?"

I glance toward the barn where she's saying something to Love and holding a half-empty feed bag. Her hair's a mess, cheeks flushed, and she's somehow the most beautiful damn chaos I've ever seen.

"She's around," I say. "What's this about?"

Matthews sighs and adjusts his belt like he's about to step into a minefield. "Better if I talk to you both."

"Hey, Sheriff," Cami says as she walks up. "What's going on?"

Matthews clears his throat, avoiding eye contact. "Got a complaint this morning. From Granger."

Cami crosses her arms. "Tell him to file it under 'not my problem.'"

Matthews coughs. "He claims you pepper sprayed him."

Her eyes go wide. "Excuse me? This was weeks ago, and he came at me with a knife in my barn. Now I know I should have reported it, but why is this just now being reported?"

"Once the video went viral, he came forward to claim that you pepper sprayed him. But I suspect because he's facing losing his ranch. He's desperate."

The image of Granger anywhere near her has my jaw tightening.

Cami scoffs. "I didn't pepper spray him."

Matthews winces. "Cami..."

"I didn't! Technically." She lifts her chin. "I used bear spray."

Matthews just stares.

Cami throws her arms up. "He was trying to break the windows out of my trailer! What was I supposed to do, make him a coffee?"

I bite back a laugh and rub a hand over my mouth.

"It was a *controlled* spritz," she mutters. "More of a warning mist."

Matthews doesn't even try to hide the smile. "He's trying to press charges. Says you 'violently attacked' him."

"Oh, please," Cami says. "He tripped over his own boots and screamed like a baby when he ran. I never physically touched him. If anyone's pressing charges, it should be me. He spray painted my trailer."

Matthews pulls out his phone and scrolls. "I wasn't gonna make a big deal out of it. But then... this happened."

He turns the screen toward us, and Cami leans in.

It's a video on social media that Poppy posted, caught from the trail cam Cami had set up. Cami storming out of her trailer like a queen with a canister raised and ready. Granger looks like he's screaming at her and waving a bat like a lunatic. And then a direct hit from the bear spray. The sound's cut, but Taylor Swift's *Karma* plays over it like a battle anthem.

I cover my mouth to stifle a laugh, but Cami's already groaning. "Oh my *god*, Poppy. When did she post this?"

Matthews nods. "The video went viral. Someone even added sparkles and a slow-mo shot."

"Karma is the guy on the screen," I quote softly, unable to help myself.

Cami shoots me a glare. "Don't you start."

Matthews flips the phone back. "The video's... everywhere. Maggie called a town safety board meeting."

Cami blinks. "A what?"

"It's basically a get-him-out-of-town intervention. She's catering in pie."

I laugh. "Of course she did."

Matthews scratches the back of his neck. "Look, legally speaking, it's a gray area. He was trespassing. You defended your place of business. It's just... the optics."

Cami throws her hands up. "The optics are *incredible*. Honestly, I should be in a commercial. Bear spray sales are going to skyrocket."

"Like a feral Disney princess," I mutter.

"Exactly!"

Matthews shakes his head. "Anyway, he's being fined. Harassment, property damage. The video helped more than hurt, honestly. But I had to follow up."

Cami smirks. "So he gets hit with fines, a viral humiliation, and Maggie's public disapproval?"

"His ranch is going up for sale," Matthews adds. "Word is, it's been struggling. This just pushed it over the edge."

I glance at Cami, expecting triumph.

But instead, her smile falters for just a second. Just long enough for me to catch it.

"He deserves it," she says, quieter now. "But it still sucks. That land was good once."

Matthews nods like he understands and turns to leave. "Just try not to spray anyone else this week, alright?"

"No promises," Cami calls, grinning again.

He waves without turning around.

When the sheriff's cruiser disappears down the road, Cami lets out a breath like she's been holding it for days. She turns to me, eyes wide but dry, tough as ever even when the wind's knocked out of her.

"Okay," she mutters. "That was not what I expected."

I raise a brow. "You think?"

She shakes her head, half-frustrated, half-exhausted. "He came at me with a knife that time, Jack."

The way she says *that time* like it's just time out of many that she was messed with. And I hate that I wasn't there to protect her. The memory hits me hard and hot. The rage I felt then comes back in a snap, curling tight in my chest. I can still see her standing there—fists clenched, chin high, not backing down. But she shouldn't have had to be brave that day or any other day. She shouldn't have had to face any of that.

"I should've done more," I say quietly. "I should've kept him away from you the second he tried to step foot on your land."

Cami looks at me, eyes softening. "This isn't on you."

"It is," I say, voice low. "He doesn't get to keep showing up in your life like this. Doesn't get to mess with your peace. Not anymore."

She doesn't say anything right away, just leans into me, shoulder against my chest, forehead almost brushing my jaw. It's not dramatic. Not even obvious. But it guts me a little how natural it feels.

I wrap an arm around her, pull her in tight. Her body softens like maybe, just maybe, she knows I mean it when I say I've got her. That I always will.

Knowing Granger's out there trying to twist this story, painting her like she's the threat? It makes my blood simmer. The guy's a coward. And worse, he's dangerous. The fact that he's still trying, still reaching for any scrap of power over her, it makes me wonder how far he'd go. What kind of man he really is when no one's watching.

I press a kiss to the top of her head without even thinking. "He's not stepping foot on this property again. I'll make damn sure of it."

She exhales again, slower this time. "I know."

And I think maybe she's finally starting to understand this. It's about time.

"I love it when you get so protective and all broody alpha cowboy, Jack," she says as she gives me a sexy look.

I pull her into my arms, and wrap my arms around her, "Oh, yeah?"

"Wait until you see my new dress I got to wear to Walker's party..."

"I can't wait," I murmur. I can already see us dancing under the moonlight and not letting her out of my arms.

Chapter 37
Cami

Wishful Drinking by Ingrid Andress, Sam Hunt

There's something about a night in Bridger Falls under the stars that feels like magic. Maybe it's the lake, warm and still under the fading sun, a cool breeze coming off the lake. Maybe it's the way the fireflies drift like glitter through the pine trees. Or maybe it's the fact that Violet and Walker threw the kind of party you only see in movies, complete with fairy lights, a dock stage, famous musicians from their new label, Red Records, and food so good it makes me want to cry.

I'm barefoot on the grass, already one cocktail in, wearing a borrowed red dress from Jenna that slips over my body like it was made for me. It's got one strap over my right shoulder, leaving my left shoulder bare. It has a slit up the thigh, and I feel sexy as hell in this dress. I'm going to ask her if I can keep it. When I showed up, Violet swore it would "bring him to his knees."

She meant Jack. But he's been across the lawn all night, leaning against a post with a bottle of beer like a cowboy in a cologne ad, doing that broody thing he does, watching me like he wants to worship me and take me home.

And I don't know which option I want more.

Walker and Violet's lake house glows with life. Music spills from the stage, currently a group of Red Records artists doing a bluesy cover of *Jolene*. The smell of hickory-smoked sliders and peach-glazed wings wafts from the catering tables, courtesy of Harvest & Honey, and people are dancing in the grass, slipping out of their shoes, hollering along to the lyrics.

"Cami, come taste this cornbread," Maggie yells, practically dragging me toward the food.

She's in a boho dress covered in sunflowers, her cheeks sparkling with glitter she applied herself. There's a daisy tucked behind her ear, and her hands are full, one holding a bourbon cocktail, the other a tiny plate loaded with a butter-drizzled triangle of cornbread.

I take the bite she offers. It's still warm, buttery, laced with honey and some kind of secret herb I can't place.

"Holy hell," I groan, covering my mouth. "So good."

"I know," she says smugly, sipping her drink. "If I wasn't already married to this town, I'd marry this cornbread."

Beside us, Mack is double-fisting mini cupcakes and deviled eggs like she's at an eating competition. "I don't know what's in these, but I'm getting seconds."

Maggie has been making sure everyone eats, while handing out tiny bottles of rosé from a cooler labeled **Maggie's Magic Juice**. I've already had two. I'm not sure what exactly is in them, but they're good. Could be dangerous, but who cares. We're having fun tonight.

On the lawn, Poppy and Ollie sway together, slow-dancing to the next song, which is something dreamy and gravelly sung live by one of the artists. The stage lights shimmer off the lake behind her, and she looks like she stepped out of a dream, barefoot and golden-haired and singing her soul out.

Poppy's arms are looped around Ollie's neck, and he's got that look on his face, the one that says *I would fight a bear for this woman*. His hand drifts low on her back, and her mouth curves like she feels it. Their foreheads brush, eyes locked.

"God, they're gross," Mack says around a mouthful of cake. "Are you sure they're just friends?"

"They're perfect," I whisper.

"Yeah, they're still claiming they're just friends," Maggie says and gives me a look like she's not buying it, either. Poppy and Ollie look very close dancing.

And then I feel it, like a tug on the back of my spine. I turn and find Jack.

Still leaning. Still watching. Still wrecking me with one goddamn look.

He's in jeans and a black button-down, sleeves rolled to the elbow, forearms flexing just enough to make me forget what I was doing. His hair's mussed from the breeze, and the shadows from the fairy lights kiss his cheekbones in a way that feels personal.

"Go talk to him," Maggie hisses.

I swallow. "I'm not—"

"He's been staring at you like he wants to ruin that dress."

I spin to glare at her. "Would you stop reading my mind?"

"I'd rather read his."

She winks and shoves a bourbon lemonade into my hand. "Liquid courage, baby."

I take a sip. It's too strong. It's perfect.

Across the yard, Weston is tossing bean bags at a cornhole board with a country singer from Red Records who might've won a Grammy. Tucker's perched on a cooler nearby, flirting with a backup singer wearing boots and a barely-there dress. Walker and Violet slow dance near the dock, her in his arms like something out of a romantic movie.

The music softens again, turns smokier.

And suddenly, Jack's there. Like he stepped out of the shadows and directly into my bloodstream.

He doesn't say anything at first, just takes the drink from my hand and sets it on a nearby table. His fingers brush mine. Sparks.

Then, with that deep, velvet voice, he says, "Dance with me."

"What if I don't want to?"

"Do it anyway. The last time you danced with me was Homecoming. You were seventeen, and you spilled Coke on my boots."

"You kissed me behind the bleachers."

"And I haven't wanted to kiss anyone else since."

That shuts me up. I've thought about that night and that kiss more times than I will ever admit to anyone.

He holds out a hand. I take it.

The wooden stage creaks under our weight as he leads me to the edge, where fairy lights glint off the lake like a mirror full of stars. The music plays on, slow and sexy and meant for trouble. Jack pulls me close, one hand sliding around my waist, the other gripping my hand like he won't let go even if the world ends.

"Did you do this on purpose?" he murmurs.

"What?"

"This dress. That look in your eye."

"You think this is for you?" I tease as I smile at him, not able to hold it back.

He leans in. "I *hope* it is."

I hate how much I melt. Hate how my knees feel like they might go out if he says one more thing in that voice.

"I'm still going to give you hell," I say, trying to be brave.

"I know," he murmurs, pulling me closer.

"I still think you're impossible."

"I know that too," he grins.

His hand moves down, skimming the open back of my dress, fingertips grazing bare skin. "And I still want you every second of every day."

My breath catches.

We sway to the music, the rest of the world disappearing. It's just him and me and the heat between us, undeniable, dangerous, stupid.

His breath hits my cheek, then my jaw, then lower. My heart pounds.

"Jack," I whisper.

"Yeah?"

"If you kiss me again..."

"I won't stop this time," he finishes.

His eyes are heavy on mine, like gravity and sin and all the things I swore I'd never let myself want again.

He leans in, then he turns back to me. "Where were we?"

I raise a brow. "You were about to make a terrible decision."

He leans in again, slower this time. "Then let's at least make it together."

And when his lips meet mine, everything else fades. The stars. The music. The chaos of Bridger Falls behind us.

All I know is the way he kisses me, slow and deep and with every ounce of tension we've been holding back. His hands grip my waist like he can't help it. Like I'm not something he's choosing, but something he needs.

It's not sweet. It's not polite. It's desperate. And real. And *everything*.

When we finally break apart, breathless, his forehead rests against mine.

"You're dangerous," I whisper.

"So are you."

Then, softly: "You were always the one, Cami."

And for once, I don't argue.

Not when the stars are overhead, the lake laps at the dock beneath us, and the whole town is losing their minds behind us.

Maybe we're a little reckless. But damn, it feels like fate.

We stay like that, pressed together in the soft sway of music and lake wind, the rest of the town a blur behind us. Jack doesn't speak, and neither do I, not when silence says more than we know how to. It's the kind of quiet where a person can fall in love and not even realize they've done it until it's already too late.

Eventually, someone shouts, "Get off the damn stage, you're making us all feel bad for being single!"

It's Tucker. Of course it's Tucker.

"Eat a cupcake and cry about it," I call back, not even glancing away from Jack.

He smirks. "How does it feel to be in love with me, Wilder?"

"I think it feels pretty good." My heart lurches. God, he's dangerous like this—smiling at me like I hung the moon, like I've never broken his heart and he's never broken mine. And for a second, I think he might kiss me again.

But the music picks up, a faster beat now. We move back toward the lawn, hand in hand, though neither of us says a word about it.

Violet appears out of nowhere, breathless and radiant. Her hair's up in a loose twist, glitter on her collarbone, a champagne flute in one hand and Walker's flannel tied around her waist. "You two looked like a *music video*."

"I'm not sure that's a compliment," I murmur.

"Oh, it is," she says. "The kind where everyone ends up making out on the tailgate."

Jack coughs. "I'll let you two talk," he says, but his fingers trail down my arm before he walks away—just enough touch to make me crazy all over again.

Violet watches him go, then turns back to me. "Girl."

"I know."

"No, *girl*."

"I *know*," I groan, fanning myself.

"Do you? Because that man just looked at you like you're his reason for existing."

"I've seen him look at bacon the same way."

"Not with that much heat."

We both dissolve into giggles, champagne sloshing, as Weston walks past with two margaritas and a cowboy hat he definitely did not show up wearing.

"Where did you get that hat?" Violet asks.

He doesn't even slow down. "Don't ask questions you don't want the answers to."

Maggie, now halfway into a red feather boa she absolutely wasn't wearing before, climbs up on the dock with a plastic microphone and shouts, "Karaoke in ten minutes! Come prepared to sing!"

"She's drunk on life," Violet whispers.

"More like drunk on Maggie juice," I say.

"Same thing, really."

Poppy and Ollie walk by, flushed and glowing. She's got her shoes in one hand, and he's got his jacket slung over her shoulders.

"You okay?" she asks me, tilting her head.

I nod. "Yeah. I think I'm—yeah."

She gives me a look. That *I know you better than anyone and you're definitely lying but I'm not gonna call you on it yet* kind of look.

Then: "You're in it deep, huh?"

I shrug. "I always was."

Ollie ruffles my hair as they pass. "Don't overthink it. You deserve a little good."

And God, wouldn't it be nice to believe that?

I drift toward the edge of the party, toes curling in the grass. The lights shimmer in the lake's reflection. A couple little kids are petting a few baby goats, shrieking with laughter. Someone's set up a s'mores table, and Weston is roasting marshmallows for two very starstruck girls who can't stop staring at him like he invented cowboy boots.

Elena and Logan are dancing, and I wave to them, and they wave back.

"Some good things came out of the show. Love that Logan and Elena are moving here."

He nods, "Yeah, it'll be nice to have them."

The music dips again, another slow track echoing across the water.

"Want to dance, Wilder?"

I spin, heart stuttering.

Jack's back.

And this time, he doesn't wait for me to answer. He just pulls me in again, slower, closer, his body pressed to mine like he belongs there.

"We already danced," I whisper.

"This is a second chance dance."

"Thought you didn't believe in those."

"I didn't," he says. "But I do now."

My heart slams against my ribs. And I'm about to say something—something dangerous, something *real*, when Beau and Jenna walk by again, still holding hands.

Jack mutters, "Jesus."

Then adds, "You know what this means, right?"

"What?"

"You and me aren't the most scandalous thing happening anymore."

I laugh, soft and startled. "We never were."

He tilts his head. "Maybe not. But we were always the real thing."

And suddenly the air shifts. The mood changes. He's not teasing anymore.

"Cami," he says, voice barely above a whisper. "You don't have to pretend you're not feeling this."

I look up at him. "It's not about that. It's about all the ways this could go wrong."

His hands tighten on my waist. "Then let it go wrong. Let it be messy. But don't walk away from it."

Emotion swells in my throat.

The firelight dances over his face, catching in the flecks of green in his eyes, and I think, *this is how it happens*. This is how girls fall in love with cowboys. In the middle of a party, with music playing and the scent of summer on the breeze, and the boy you've always loved holding you like he'd burn down the world to keep you safe.

I don't know how long we stand there like that, maybe a minute, maybe a lifetime.

Eventually, Maggie shouts, "Jack and Cami, you're up next for karaoke!"

We both groan.

"I am not singing," I say.

"Oh, you *are*," she calls back, waving the mic in one hand and her drink in the other. "And if you don't, I'm gonna get Weston to sing 'Pink Pony Club' again, and we *all* remember what happened last time."

Jack sighs, tugging me toward the stage. "Come on, Wilder. Let's show 'em what we've got."

I dig my heels in. "Absolutely not. I draw the line at public humiliation."

But I'm laughing. And I let him drag me anyway.

Because that's the thing about Jack Jessop.

He feels like home.

Chapter 38
Jack

Marry Me by Thomas Rhett

Two months later...when you know, you know.

The morning sun stretches over the hills like honey, warm and slow. It's branding season, which means long days, short tempers, and the kind of sweat that clings to your spine long after the sun goes down. But today, I'm not thinking about cattle or fence lines. Not when I've got Cami in the saddle next to me, wind in her hair, sunlight catching on that smile that belongs to me.

She doesn't know yet. That I've got the ring in my pocket. That we're not just riding to check the perimeter like I told her. That I've been building up to this moment for decades.

She looks over and grins. "Race you to the ridge?"

"You trying to lose again, Wilder?"

She kicks her horse and takes off, laughing. Damn if I don't love that woman like a storm loves the sky.

We gallop across the back pasture, wind tearing past us, hooves thundering. The ride that thunders through your chest. And then we crest the hill and they're there.

The wild mustangs.

A few dozen of them, wild and breathtaking, grazing near the stream that cuts through the eastern edge. Cami slows beside me, mouth parted in wonder.

"Jack," she whispers. "They're breathtaking."

"Yeah. Thought you'd want to see them."

She swings down from the saddle, boots sinking into the grass. I follow, heart kicking up hard now. The horses don't spook, just lift their heads and watch us, cautious but calm. A foal steps between its mother's legs, ears twitching.

Cami doesn't speak, not at first. Just watches them like she's trying to memorize the moment.

I slide my hand into hers. "The state brought them up a few days ago. Been hanging out near the back fence. Figured... maybe it was a sign."

She tilts her head, curious. "A sign of what?"

I tug her a little closer to the big oak tree that anchors the ridge. Our tree. The one we used to meet under when we were kids. The one she carved our initials into at fifteen. The one I kissed her under the first time I ever told her I wanted her.

She turns when I stop walking, eyes catching on mine.

And I drop to one knee.

Her hands fly to her mouth. "Jack."

I pull the box from my pocket. My hands shake with nervousness as I pop it open. My voice is steady, somehow. "I love you. I've loved you since we were dumb kids hiding out in this tree, and I'm gonna love you when we're old and gray for the rest of our lives. I want to build a life with you. There's no one else I want to give me hell every day and make every day beautiful."

I take a breath. "Marry me, Cami. Let me love you for the rest of my life."

She doesn't answer with words. Just drops to her knees and kisses me like she's been holding it back for years. When she finally pulls away, she whispers, "Yes. Yes. God, *yes.*"

When I look at her, I see everything. I see our future together walking down an aisle, her holding our babies, and us riding horses with our grandkids someday. I see it, and I know it's right. This is it for me. It's her, and it's always been her.

I scoop her up as I stand and throw her over my shoulder, carrying her towards the blanket I had the forethought to bring with me.

Laying her down, I lower to my knees and pull her boots off her feet and toss them over my shoulder.

"Watch it, cowboy. Those Tecovas didn't come cheap."

"I'll buy you a new pair," I grunt.

"Such a caveman," Cami says with a hearty laugh.

I unbutton her jeans and slide them over her hips and down her legs, adding them to the pile with her boots. Prowling up her body, I don't stop until I hover over her, pressing my lips to hers.

Her fingers sink into my hair, and she squeals when I wrap my fist around the lace separating me from her pussy and tear it from her body.

"Jack!"

"I'll buy you ten more pairs," I say, winking down at her.

"What is it everyone says abanout marriage? What's yours is mine and what's mine is mine?" She titters out a laugh as I growl at her trash talk.

"Baby, what you don't understand is everything I have has always been yours."

"Damn it, Jessop. I'm trying to intimidate you and you're being all sweet."

The Next Morning

The sun isn't even fully up when I hear the familiar crunch of truck tires in the drive. I'm in the kitchen, frying bacon and trying not to grin like an idiot. Cami's still upstairs, wrapped in my flannel shirt and probably stealing all the covers.

Weston and Tucker knock softly and then walk in like they own the place.

"Hope you're cooking for three," Tucker says, already reaching for a mug.

"Four," I correct. "Cami's up there somewhere."

Weston tosses a manila folder on the table. "We've got news."

I flip off the burner. "What kind of news?"

"Granger news," Weston says, sliding into a chair.

I grunt. "Not interested."

"You will be." He opens the folder. Inside are documents, printed emails, and a property map. Tucker grins like it's Christmas.

"We got him," Weston says.

I raise an eyebrow.

"Turns out, destroying fences, raiding people's properties while threatening them, and dumping trash on someone else's land comes with fines. Big ones. We documented everything. Weston filed complaints. He got everyone involved. He's on the hook. And with the way his finances are..."

"He's cooked," Tucker adds. "The ranch is going under."

"So we're letting him rot?" I ask.

Weston shakes his head. "No. We're buying it."

I blink. "Excuse me?"

He slides over the breakdown. "We double our grazing range. We add land access for the town, trails, events, maybe even a little campground if someone gets the itch to run it. We clean up that dump of a property and make it part of Wilder Ranch."

"You serious?"

"Dead. We made him an offer. He took it."

I let out a low whistle. "That... that'll burn."

Weston smiles. "Let it."

The sound of soft footsteps on the stairs cuts through the quiet, and we all turn as Cami walks into the kitchen, her hair a mess. She's got sweatpants and a t-shirt with my flannel still wrapped around her like it was made for her.

"Mornin'," she says, rubbing sleep from her eyes.

Tucker grins like a damn fool. "Well, *that* shirt looks familiar."

Cami shoots me a sleepy smirk and pours herself some coffee.

Weston's eyes land on her hand. "Hold up. Is that what I think it is?"

Cami freezes, halfway to her seat.

Tucker leans over for a better look. "Holy hell, it is! That's a ring."

I chuckle as Cami turns beet red. "We were gonna tell y'all tonight."

"You *got engaged* and thought you could hide it from us?" Weston shakes his head, pretending to be offended.

Tucker claps his hands together. "About damn time! Took you long enough, Jack."

Cami rolls her eyes, but she's glowing. "Y'all are ridiculous."

"You love us," Weston says, grabbing a biscuit. "And we love you. Congratulations, Cami. You make him better."

I meet his eyes, and there's something unspoken in the moment. Gratitude. Pride. Family.

"We were just talking about the future of the ranch," I say.

Weston nods. "We're adding space now. Room to grow. Room for wild horses and weddings and whatever else you two dream up."

Cami leans into me as she sips her coffee. "It already feels like home."

And damn if that isn't the best thing I've ever heard.

We sit there around the table, passing biscuits, trading stories, talking about barns and what the new pasture should be called. It's messy and loud and full of love.

And it feels like the start of forever.

Epilogue

Wild As Her by Corey Kent

The sun climbs over the eastern ridge, painting the Wilder Ranch in soft gold, and the morning air carries the scent of wild sage, fresh dirt, and something sweet, my cookies, and breads on the racks outside the micro bakery stand.

Kids' laughter floats up from the meadow where Jack's setting up archery targets with Weston, both of them wearing t-shirts with **Wilder Ranch Nature Camp** in bold green letters on them.

We're wrapping up the first week of our summer-long nature camp, and I already know this is going to be one of those things people talk about for years.

The show aired several weeks ago, and it really put Bridger Falls on the map. We've been flooded with tourists who want to catch a glimpse of Jack and me and our ranch. We can barely keep up with orders, we're booked solid for horse training, and we've already got reservations into next summer and our B&B isn't even open yet.

Jenna and the producers did a great job on the show. The executives loved the twist in the ending. We did interviews in New York City with Good Morning America and The Today Show. Jack hated it but we did it for the ranches. Well, I guess just the ranch now. Everything's combined and flowing great. It's been so much fun, and it feels good. Much to the producers' dismay, we turned down a second season as did Weston and Tucker. We had our fifteen minutes of fame, and now we're set to just live life. Happy and content.

Every week when a new episode would air, Maggie set up a projector and everyone joined in for a watch party. Jack and I went, but it was painfully, hilariously hard to watch ourselves on television. We both agreed that we're terrible at it. But we had fun. Mack and her friends set up a concession stand and made an event out of it. One thing's for sure, it definitely brought the town together and the Jessop name doesn't feel like a foul word in anyone's mouth anymore. Nobody can forget Jack Sr and the things he's done, but he's a thing of the past and everyone is talking about new things now.

Every morning starts with a line of dusty trucks and SUVs weaving up the road. Every evening ends with s'mores, sunburns, and stories around the fire pit. Parents come early just to sit in the grass and listen to their kids talk about feeding goats or learning about soil health or riding a horse for the first time. It's pure magic. We've even talked about somehow including the parents more because they seem to want to be a part of this, too.

And it's saving us.

The camp tuition goes straight into finishing the B&B, our dream project turned real-life construction site just beyond the main barn. The bones are done, the porches are being painted and stained. Inside, the rooms and bathrooms are all getting a complete remodel, and if we keep up this pace, we'll be ready by fall. Just in time for flannel season, leaf-peeping tourists, and my dream of serving cinnamon rolls at sunrise in our great room.

Honestly? It's working.

The garden is bursting this year. Heirloom tomatoes bigger than the size of fists. Rows of basil and lavender and carrots so sweet they taste like candy.

And then there's Steamy Sips. It's busier than ever and I have a few employees running it full time.

Our roadside produce stand and now *bread* stand, is officially busier than ever. Jack joked that I've become some kind of frontier food influencer after someone from Denver drove three hours just to get one of my jalapeño cheddar sourdough loaves and take a photo with it.

The meat and dairy store at the old Jessop Ranch, now new Wilder Ranch, is thriving as well, and they can barely keep up. Weston added online orders, and we've hired a few dozen more workers.

But the best part?

We've partnered with local dairies and ranchers, and now people drive in from three counties over to get produce, meat, cheese, and bread, all grown and baked right here.

Sometimes I walk through the aisles, and watch people point at my sourdough like it's something worth making a trip for. It knocks the air out of me.

There's a chalkboard sign by the door that says **Welcome to Wilder Ranch** in swoopy, hand-lettered paint. Underneath, Jack added, in tiny letters: **Home of the best damn bread in Wyoming.**

Tucker's thinking about going back on the circuit, at least for a few months. Says he's got the itch and needs to chase some adrenaline before settling back down. But he's still around enough to teach rope tricks to the campers and tell tall tales during story hour like he's got his own live podcast.

Weston finally moved down from Montana for good. He pretends like it was a practical choice—closer to family, the ranch expansion, all that. But I know better. He's running from something, and he's been broody and moody. I'll get to the bottom of that sooner or later.

And me?

I've never felt more like myself. Not since I was a kid running barefoot through the fields behind Wilder Ranch, pretending I was queen of my own tiny country.

Now I get to build it.

Kids run past me, heading toward the riding arena, all chatter and freckles and summer joy. I wave them on, then tuck my basket of fresh cookies under my arm and walk toward the hill to restock the microbakery.

Jack is leaning against a post, arms crossed, a smudge of dirt on his jaw and a grin that's pure trouble.

"Wilder," he says. "You come bearing treats?"

"Always," I say, handing him a still-warm basket of cookies. "Your reward for being Wyoming's most patient camp counselor."

"I knew marrying you would come with perks."

He pulls me close, right there in the middle of camp chaos, and kisses my temple like we're in our own quiet universe.

We stand there for a moment, watching the mustangs grazing beyond the fence line.

"I still can't believe this is ours," I whisper.

"It was always going to be," he says. "You just had to be patient."

I glance at him. "What are you guys cooking up next?"

He grins. "Fall guests, cinnamon rolls, trail rides through the leaves. Maybe even a glamping tent or two if Weston gets his way."

"And the wedding?"

Jack kisses the corner of my mouth. "Whenever you want. I'd marry you right now in the middle of the goat pen."

"Tempting."

A camper runs up to us, breathless. "Miss Cami! There's a goat loose again!"

I laugh. "On it."

As I jog off in the direction of the goat pen, Jack calls after me, "Don't forget the campfire tonight!"

"Wouldn't miss it."

That night, the meadow glows with fairy lights strung from tree to tree, and a crackling fire draws kids and parents and volunteers like moths. Everyone's bundled in sweatshirts, sticky from roasted marshmallows, smelling like smoke and sugar.

Weston passes out mugs of cider while Tucker leads a cowboy singalong that's mostly off-key but charming as hell. Someone breaks out a guitar. Maggie twirls in her boots, glittery as ever, dragging Mack into an impromptu dance near the fire pit. Jenna rolls her eyes, but she's smiling.

Jack finds me on a log with a flannel blanket draped over my shoulders, the stars bright above us and the fire flickering low.

He sits behind me, wraps his arms around my waist, and rests his chin on my shoulder. "Hey baby," he murmurs. "Someday we're going to have our own kids running around here."

I smile and lean into him. "I can't wait."

We sit like that for a while, warm and quiet and content.

Then he says, "What do you think about starting with elopement this fall? Just us and the mountains. And maybe a big ol' party after the new year."

I twist to look at him. "You serious?"

"Dead. I don't need anything fancy. I just need you."

I kiss him, soft and slow. "Let's do it."

Someone hands us s'mores. Fireflies dance around the trees. A kid falls asleep next to his mom in a camp chair. It all feels so good, it hurts.

Later, after the fire dies down and the stars stretch wide above the ranch, Jack and I walk back to the house barefoot through the dewy grass, hand in hand.

The porch light glows, warm and steady. The farmhouse smells like coffee grounds and lilacs. My sourdough is cooling down on the counter for tomorrow's deliveries.

Jack pulls me into the porch swing and tucks me against his side. The crickets sing. The moon hangs low. The ranch is quiet now, but alive in a way I've never felt anywhere else.

"This is everything," I whisper.

Jack kisses the top of my head. "And it's just the beginning."

And he's right.

Come fall, the B&B will open. We'll welcome our first guests and tell stories under this same wide sky.

Come winter, the campfire will become a fireplace, the garden will sleep under snow, and we'll still be here building a life, day by day.

The future's not just a plan anymore.

It's Wilder Ranch. It's home. And it's ours.

About the Author

Erin Branscom is a creator of happily-ever-after's, crafting spicy, Hallmark-like romances that make readers fall head over heels for charming small towns. When she's not writing heartwarming stories, Erin can be found anywhere there are dogs, with a cup of coffee in hand, or lost in a good book. As a passionate Scorpio, she brings intensity and heart to everything she does. Dive into her world and discover love, warmth, and a touch of spice in every story.

Acknowledgments

To my family. I love you all and you are my reason for working hard every day. I'm so thankful for all of you and your support. Thank you to Nicole, Beth, and Deb for making Cami and Jack's story come alive.
To all my readers, thank you for always showing up for me and being excited for my books!

Want more of Cami and Jack?

Check out this bonus scene for Wild As Her when you sign up for Erin's newsletter!

Scan the QR code to get your bonus scene:

Love Autumn books and want more?

Let me introduce you to Freedom Valley, New Hampshire. I wrote a series that takes place at a quaint New England small town Inn. The first book will take you to a Stars Hollow like town with all of the Gilmore Girls vibes, cozy feels, fall festivals, pumpkin spice lattes, and more! You can read the whole series right now on Kindle Unlimited, ebook, paperback, as well as audio. Here's the first chapter...

Chapter 1: Falling Inn Love

Beth
No, there's no one.

I wasn't sure where I'd end up today, but this sure as hell wasn't it.

"Great. Just freaking great," I mutter as steam pours out from under the hood of my ten-year-old green Subaru. My car smells awful, like something burning or melting.

I pull off to the side of the road and park, a sitting duck in my no-longer-trustworthy SUV,

hoping I'm not going to be turned into roadkill by a big semi coming down the highway.

I reach across the seat and pull my phone over to me by the charging cord. Thankfully, it's fully charged.

"Where the hell am I?" I cringe as I open a navigation app.

Freedom Valley, New Hampshire.

I cup my face with my hands. My chest tightens as I begin to cry. I'm running out of money and time, and it's starting to get dark out. Hot tears streak my cheeks. I just want to go home, but

I don't have a home anymore; I haven't for the past six years. Nowadays, home is

this nomadic lifestyle I've chosen for myself.

I hear a light tapping on the window and look up to see a tall, dark-haired man with the most gorgeous light green eyes peering down at me.

Great. Now this is the part where I get murdered on a highway all alone.

I roll the window down a little and the man leans in, looking concerned. "Are you okay?"

"Yeah, I'll be fine. I just pulled over for a rest," I say, forcing a smile and wiping my eyes, quickly trying to look away and not stare too long. His hair topples over his forehead as he inches closer. He has a full, dark beard that makes me weak in the knees. Are beards out? Because if they are, they should definitely be back in. This guy makes it work. I've never seen a more gorgeous man, and this beard makes him dark, scary, and handsome all at the same time.

"Are you sure? I think something is wrong with your car. If I had to guess, I'd say it's the radiator. Do you want me to take a look?" He cringes as he turns his head away from the awful, acrid smell of the smoke continuing to barrel out of the hood.

It occurs to me that I could possibly be his next intended victim on this lonely New Hampshire two-lane highway, where no one would ever hear me scream. He doesn't look like a murderer, but I'm basically an expert in Dateline and forensics and murder shows on Netflix, so here we are. Where it all probably ends.

He holds up his hands and says with a smile, "I'm Evan."

"Hi," I say quietly.

"Hi," he replies softly, his eyes taking in my face with curiosity. "Can I help you? I can't just leave you here. My mom would kill me."

Great. A family of murderers. Hey, I've seen that movie Wrong Turn.

"Okay, but can I stay in the car?" I ask. I'm nervous. I am all alone out here and I don't know this guy.

"Yep, just pop the hood," he says, then walks to his old retro truck parked in front of me with its hazards blinking.

I take him in. He's even nice-looking from the back, as well. Maybe even more so. Why am I admiring this stranger's backside? This isn't good.

He's tall, wearing form-fitting jeans and brown boots. He's not wearing the flannel. It's wearing him. Damn. He's a walking lumberjack snack. He pulls a pair of gloves from his truck and strolls back to my car, using his gloves to lift the hot hood that seems to have finally stopped steaming.

From the safety of my car, I hear him messing around with some things before he shuts the hood and taps on my window. I roll it down again, still unsure of this guy.

"It's your radiator, so I wouldn't drive it anymore. It needs to be towed into town to Sam's to get looked at. I can give you a ride to wherever you're going," he says as he tucks his gloves into his back pocket.

I nod, my chest tightening up again. "Okay, but I don't know where to go. I was staying in my car and dry camping," I admit, looking out the window. I realize I shouldn't have told him I have nowhere to go, but what other options do I have?

A car zips past us, making me jump. When I glance back at him, I notice he's still staring at me, looking a little bit in shock.

"Staying in your car? Is that safe?" he asks, his eyes narrowing like he wants to give me a dad lecture.

"I have nowhere to go or stay now," I say motioning to my car. "This was my plan."

He strokes his chin, looking frustrated. "Grab whatever you need for tonight and I'll take you to the inn up the road. I know the owner. You can stay there until you figure out your car."

"Why would you do that?" I ask nervously, crossing my arms, starting to shiver.

"Because if my mom and sister knew that I left you out here on the side of the road and didn't help you, they'd be really angry. And trust me, you do not want to see those two angry or disappointed. It's the worst. Come on, get your stuff, we don't have all night. I'll give you a lift and call the tow for you. It'll be fine."

I finally just blurt it out. "Are you a murderer? How do I know you won't kill me and bury me in the woods somewhere out here?"

He sizes me for a minute then bursts out laughing. "You're funny. Come on, get your things. You'll be fine. I only murder on the weekends."

"It's Friday. It is the weekend."

"Fine, I only murder on holidays," he deadpans with a smile, rolling his eyes and turning to look down the road.

"If you murder me, I will come back as a ghost and haunt you for the rest of your life."

"Fair enough," he says as he shrugs his shoulders, looking like he's trying to hide another smile.

I take a deep breath and gather up my phone, charger, and purse.

"Is that all you'll need for a few nights? It might be a few days before Sam can fix this."

I get out and open the trunk, pulling out my overnight bag. Before I can sling it over my shoulder, Evan gently takes it from me and steps back.

"Anything else?" he asks.

I lift my laptop backpack out of the car, then lock up and walk toward Evan's truck. He tucks my bag into the back and opens the passenger door for me. He has this nice, warm, small-town vibe, and it works for him. I still hope he's not a murderer, though, because what a

waste of a good-looking guy that would be.

"I like your truck," I say, glancing around at it. It has an old, worn but colorful blanket on the bench, probably to conceal decades of wear and tear.

"Thanks. It was my grandfather's and then my father's. It makes me feel close to them when I drive it."

Wow, that is heartwarming. I couldn't imagine having anything of my mothers, let alone my grandmother's.

"Where are you coming from?" he asks as he pulls back onto the road.

I debate over how much is too much to tell him, but I've already jumped in his truck with him, so what's the point of holding back now? He seems like a nice guy, and he's definitely attractive. I watch his profile as he drives, his green eyes striking against his dark beard and his big hands... Okay, focus, Beth. Geez.

"Boston," I say, glancing out the window as the scenery changes to beautiful fall foliage along the road to the inn.

He's playing eighties music—which I love—on the radio. He turns it down to ask, "So, what brings you to Freedom Valley?"

"I'm a writer and I travel around for work. I was looking for a place to stay for a few weeks to finish a project and see New England in the fall. What about you? What do you do?"

"You're looking for work?" he replies, ignoring my question.

He's misunderstood what I do for a living, but to be honest, the writing has not been going well lately. I've been doing various admin jobs and some bartending between writing projects, and I could use the extra cash again now, so I nod.

"I think the inn might be looking to hire a front desk manager. Would you be interested if it's still available?"

"Yes."

He turns onto a winding road that leads up to a big white inn with a beautiful white sign that reads The Golden Gable Inn in gold script. There's a large main building with a lot of small cottages around it. Hunter green shutters grace the front, making it feel more like a home than a hotel. The large front porch stretches across the front of the main house and has white rocking chairs and potted mums of various fall colors bunched around the chairs and pumpkins stacked

on both sides of the doors. It is one of the most comforting places I've ever seen. It feels like coming home. To a real home. I thought places like this only existed in Hallmark movies.

My heart pulls as I remember my small front porch in Texas that I decorated similarly with a fall wreath, pumpkins, and mums every year. Autumn has always been my favorite season and my heart feels sad to think I no longer have a home to decorate.

I start to panic because there's no way I can afford to stay here for a night, let alone a few nights, and I definitely don't want to owe this guy any favors. I'm still not sure why he's helping me. I want to trust people, but history has taught me not to trust anyone, including random strangers who are eager to help. There's a good reason I keep to myself and don't talk to very many people while traveling. I've come across a few creeps.

"Evan, I don't think I can afford this. I'm sorr—"

"Relax. I know the owners. I'm sure they'll be more than happy to set you up for a few days." He smiles at me reassuringly.

Evan parks and grabs my bag from the back. As we walk up the steps, I run my hand over the railing and glance around at the fall leaves, breathing in the autumn air. It's getting dark and I'm relieved to not be stuck on the highway anymore.

"It's a pretty special place," he says as we walk through the entrance. "Been in the same family for three generations now. You'll love it here."

We head up to the desk and I set my backpack down. I freeze when Evan walks behind the desk and begins typing on the keyboard.

"What are you doing?" I ask, confused.

He smiles sheepishly at me. "Told you I knew the owner."

"Evan, honey, is that you?" a voice calls from the back as a short, round woman with a cropped, white-blonde bob and bright green eyes approaches.

She kisses Evan on the cheek before turning to me and smiling warmly. "Who do we have here? Checking in? I'm Margie, welcome to The Golden Gable Inn."

I turn to Evan, unsure what to say. It dawns on me that she might be his mother. Their eyes match, but other than that, they don't look alike.

Finally, I say, "Hi, I'm Beth Markwell. I'm not sure what I'm doing just yet..."

Evan, still typing, says, "She'll be checking in for the weekend."

"You work here?" I ask in disbelief, looking at him while this woman curiously watches me.

"Yes, my family owns the inn," he says. "Okay, I've got a queen bed available on the first floor. Will that work?" he asks, his green eyes peering at me, his gaze lingering on my mouth as he bites his bottom lip.

Holy shit. This man melts me like butter in a pan just from looking at him. I know I just met him, but I feel this connection with him. I don't think I've ever felt instant electricity with someone like this, but I can feel it radiating off him, too. It isn't just me.

"I don't know how I can pay you," I reply nervously. I wish the world would swallow me up, I'm so embarrassed.

The woman tilts her head and asks, "Where are you from, honey?"

Okay, I'm from the south where people are typically overly friendly—you know, the whole southern hospitality thing. But so far, everyone is even nicer here. I'm hesitant to talk about myself, but something feels different here. I slowly feel my guard letting down, and if I'm being honest, it actually feels good.

"Originally Austin, Texas. I travel a lot now; I'm a writer. I was hoping to stay in the area for a while, if I can find a place to stay and find part-time work."

She looks at Evan and murmurs, "No show on our interview today." Then she turns to me. "Well, we could use some help around here for a while. Would you be available to lend a hand? Front desk help, maybe in the dining room, too, if we need it?"

I hesitate for a moment then realize I have no other options. "Sure," I finally say. Thankfully, the murderer vibes aren't here.

Evan slides a key on a vintage-white, worn motel keychain with the inn's logo in gold script and a form across the desk for me to sign.

I sign it and slide it back, palming the key. Evan then picks up my bag and heads down the hall.

"I'm glad I found you and that you're safe," he says as I catch up to him. "I can't imagine my sister breaking down like that and not having anywhere safe to go. Is there anyone you can call?" he asks.

My shoulders sag. I miss having a person to call.

"No, there's no one," I say quietly.

Freedom Valley Series
Falling Inn Love
Baked Inn Love
All Inn Thyme
Love Inn Books
Forever Inn Love
Snowed Inn

Bridger Falls
Forever To Me
Wild As Her
Always You
High Road

Non-Fiction
Writers Inspiring Writers with Jennifer Probst

Wisteria Cove
The Pumpkin Spice Spell
Mistletoe & Magic
Hexes & Honeysuckle

Cozy Creek Collection
Fall Too Well

You can find all of Erin's books on her website:
Erinbranscom.com

Always You

Want more of Bridger Falls?
Scan the QR code to read Poppy and Ollie's story:

www.ingramcontent.com/pod-product-compliance
Lightning Source LLC
Chambersburg PA
CBHW011315310726
48973CB00011B/2932